GIVE

A Novel

BY ERICA C. WITSELL

Virginia

Published in the United States by BQB Publishing
(an imprint of Boutique of Quality Books Publishing, Inc.)
www.bqbpublishing.com

Printed in the United States of America

ISBN 978-1-945448-34-8 (p)
ISBN 978-1-945448-35-5 (e)

Library of Congress Control Number: 2019936660

Book design by Robin Krauss, www.bookformatters.com
Cover design by Rebecca Lown, www.rebeccalowndesign.com

First editor: Michelle Booth
Second editor: Caleb Guard

Praise for Erica Witsell and Give

"*Give* is a striking, often unflinching, depiction of a doomed marriage and its enduring consequences. Erica Witsell is a very talented writer and her debut should garner a wide and appreciative audience."

> – Ron Rash, author of the 2009 PEN/Faulkner Finalist and New York Times bestselling novel *Serena*, in addition to four other prizewinning novels

"A very unusual family saga written with unusual intelligence and compassion. Erica Witsell has a gift for depicting complex relationships."

> - Phyllis Rose, author of *Parallel Lives*, *The Year of Reading Proust*, and *The Shelf*

"This is a gripping narrative about family, identity, and loyalty. The themes are both uniquely modern and timeless. I fell in love with the characters as they struggled to understand themselves and reconcile with one another. Beautifully written!"

> – Kate Rademacher, author of *Following the Red Bird*

"This is an engrossing novel about family and forgiveness. Tracing the lives of five characters over the span of thirty years, Erica C. Witsell shows us that family is about choice as much as it is about blood and that sacrifice and selfishness both play a role in how we parent and love."

> – Sarah Viren, author of *Mine*

"What will you give for your family—love, forgiveness, second chances? Everything you are? What if they don't give back? *Give* shines a light across the best and worst of us all, asking what will you give? At times subtle and at times cutting to the quick, *Give* digs deep into the heart and soul of a family as connected as it is torn apart. *Give* pulls no punches, delivering an honest look into the lengths we will go for family. What we will give and what we won't."

— Amy Willoughby-Burle, author of *The Lemonade Year*

"*Give's* imagery is spot-on, excellent dialogue, . . . and a sly sense of humor. Very poignant! This novel won't let go of me."

— Jenny Anna Linde-Rhine, columnist at *Zinnig*

"A family drama with depth and complexity; it was hard to put this book down."

— Jennifer Arellano

"*Give* grabs your attention on the first page and holds it through-out as it weaves the complicated web of one family."

— Kristen Schlaefer

"Put it down and you'll be thinking about it until you pick it back up again. Which will be as soon as possible."

— Lindsey Grossman, blogger at www.lindseyliving.com

For my children,
Clayton, Dee Dee, and Sylvia

Things fall apart; the centre cannot hold;
Mere anarchy is loosed upon the world,
The blood-dimmed tide is loosed, and everywhere
The ceremony of innocence is drowned

W.B. Yeats

PART ONE

1974-1979

CHAPTER 1

Laurel

The two couples huddled together on the beach, their shoulders hunched against the wind as colorless waves chased each other onto the sand. They had just arrived; inside the small motel a block away, their weekend bags lay unopened on their beds.

Ten minutes ago, Laurel had rapped at her friend's door.

"Alice, you guys in there? Want to walk down to the beach with us?"

In fact, Alice hardly counted as a friend. Laurel knew her only from the biology lab on campus, where both worked as assistants, cleaning test tubes and preparing slides. But Laurel had needed her for this weekend. She had told her husband, Len, that this weekend getaway was Alice's idea, had convinced him to come along only by arguing how rude it would be of them to refuse.

Len had thought only of the practicalities: the expense, the babysitter, the weekend he would miss with his beloved daughter. He didn't understand how much Laurel needed this: two precious days to feel like herself again, without her two-year-old daughter clinging to her legs or nattering on at her from the moment she awoke.

And now they were here, at last, the sky above them another sea of gray, the afternoon sun a hazy brightness behind the clouds. Laurel peeked at Alice's husband; she had never met Michael before today. He was tall and small-waisted, with sand-colored hair and gray eyes the color of the sea. He caught her looking and gave her a good-natured smile.

"Brrr," he said, putting his arm around Alice and pulling her against his side. "Whose idea was this, anyway?"

Laurel's eyes shot to Alice's face, worried she would give her away. But it didn't matter now. They were here, the off-season rate for their room paid for in advance on the one credit card they kept for emergencies. That morning, while Len had read books with Jessie on the couch, Laurel had thrown her graying, milk-stained bra into the hamper and excavated a black and lacy thing from the bottom of her underwear drawer. Now she could feel the underwire pushing uncomfortably against her breasts, and she resisted the urge to reach back and unfasten the clasp. Instead, she gave Michael a small, open-mouthed smile.

"Oh, come on. It's not *that* cold." Sucking in her breath, she broke away from Len's side and bent down to pull off her shoes.

"Laurel, please," Len said, rolling his eyes. "Don't be silly. It's freezing."

Laurel caught Michael's eye. "You want to come?"

"Are you nuts?"

"Laurel," Len said. "Don't. It's way too cold."

He held out his arm then, for her to come back to him, and for a moment she was tempted. It would be so easy to slip back into the warmth of his side, to let herself be quieted. But it was not quiet that she wanted. She raised her eyes to the gray slate of the ocean and undid the button on her jeans. Beneath her clothes, the monotony of her life clung to her like a film on her skin.

"That baby's going to strip your youth right off you," her mother, Pearl, had said dryly, two and a half years ago, when Laurel had first told her she was pregnant. "You mark my words."

But her mother had been wrong. Having a baby hadn't stripped youth from her. It had simply buried it in a viscous layer that Laurel could not scrape away, no matter what she did. No, she hadn't come here to stand mutely in the wind, safely tucked away beneath her husband's arm. She had come to scour herself clean, to peel away the gauzy membrane that the last two years of motherhood had swathed her in. *That* was why she had cajoled and pleaded for this weekend at the beach without her daughter. She didn't plan to waste a minute.

She pulled her arms from her jacket and dropped it in the sand.

"Laurel," Len said sharply. "We're in public."

She wouldn't look at her husband; he couldn't stop her. She looked at Michael instead and saw that he was watching her, his mouth pulled up on one side in amusement, showing a row of even teeth.

Laurel gestured widely at the empty beach. "Len, there's no one here."

Len nodded curtly at Alice and Michael. "They're here."

"That's right," Michael said, running his fingers through his dirty blonde hair. "What about us? Are we nobody?"

Laurel grinned; a flush of warmth went through her. She wriggled out of her jeans, the wind raising goosebumps on her bare skin. Miraculously, she had managed to shave her legs just this morning, hunched over in the shower while Jessie stood at the edge of the tub, pulling back the curtain and reaching for the pink plastic razor in Laurel's hand.

"Dessie do!"

"No," Laurel had said sharply. "You'll cut yourself."

But in the end, it had been Laurel who had cut herself, moving the razor too quickly over her knee, leaning awkwardly to keep away from Jessie's grasping hands.

"Damn it, Jessie," she had muttered. "See what you made me do."

Her daughter had watched as the blood rose on her mother's skin.

"Uh-oh, Momma. Boo boo. Boo boo wight dare." She pointed in alarm at Laurel's knee.

Laurel had rolled her eyes. "Yeah, boo boo right there. Well, what do you expect? I can't even shave my freaking legs in peace."

Now, the newly shaved skin almost hurt, the way the follicles raised up, trying futilely to warm her. But Laurel could still feel Michael's eyes on her—felt, too, the little flare that had gone on inside of her. For a moment, she forgot the cold. Her skin tingled, alive. She glanced at her husband. Len stood with his broad shoulders turned away from her, long arms loose at his sides. The wind whipped a curl of black hair into his eyes, and he pushed it away impatiently. *Why won't you look at me?* she wanted to shout at him. But her husband's mouth was set in a grim little line and he would not meet her eye.

Laurel let out a wild little laugh. "Here I go!"

She pulled her shirt over her head and tossed it in the sand beside her discarded jeans, then ran quickly toward the water. With each step, she felt her bottom jiggle. She had not lost all the extra pounds of her pregnancy, and it was with an effort that she fought the impulse to reach back and prod the flesh there, testing its firmness.

When at last Laurel reached the water, she was relieved. The water would cover her. But Laurel had not reckoned on how low the tide was. The water barely reached her knees, the skin on her legs stinging with the salt and cold. She ran a few more steps, but it was awkward running in the shallow water, the way she had to splay her legs out to the side with every step. She didn't look back, but still she felt them watching her.

A few steps more and finally the water reached above her knees. This morning's razor cut stung sharply and she looked down. Her legs were hidden now beneath the churning water, but she imagined that the cut was bleeding again, imagined the blood seeping out of her into the vast ocean. She tried to summon the thrill she had felt while she'd stripped on the beach, the heat of Michael's eyes, but both were gone. She hugged her upper body and scanned the ocean for another swimmer. Surely there must be at least a surfer in a wetsuit, some other human form to make her feel less alone. But there was no one.

Laurel took a deep breath and threw herself forward into the water. A wave crested over her, the water so cold it made her temples ache. She thrashed wildly for a second, forgetting how shallow it was. But then her hands grazed the bottom, and she pushed herself back to standing, gasping with the cold.

She ran back to the beach immediately, the useless bra struggling to contain her bouncing breasts, heavy strands of hair flopping against her face. She was not thinking, now, of how she looked to the others, whom she could see standing together on the beach. Michael and Alice stood pressed together; Laurel noticed how perfectly Michael's slender hip fit into the curve of Alice's waist.

By the time she reached them, she had begun to shiver uncontrollably.

Michael grinned at her. "You call that a swim?"

She did not answer. Her teeth began to chatter. Len scooped her shirt from the sand and held it out for her.

She shook her head. "I'm soaked."

"Put it on," he said, reaching for her jeans.

The jeans wouldn't go on easily; her numb fingers fumbled with the waistband. Michael and Alice looked away, then took a few steps down the beach.

"Where are they going?" Laurel said, her teeth clattering over every word.

"Just get dressed," Len said.

That evening, the four of them had dinner at a small Italian restaurant near the motel. Condensation streamed down the windows, blurring its neon sign.

"Cozy little place," Michael said, looking around. Each table had a classic red and white checkered tablecloth, a burgundy candle wedged into an empty wine bottle. He smiled at Laurel pleasantly.

Michael ordered a bottle of red wine, and Laurel's mood lifted as she drank. She was warm at last; she felt her skin glow. She finished her glass during the appetizer and smiled gratefully when the waiter refilled it, glad that Len would not see her reach for the bottle.

Her food arrived, the pasta still steaming beneath its dollop of dark red sauce. Laurel could not help closing her eyes and leaning over it, just to feel the moist warmth against her face. Once she would have taken this for granted—this simple, overpriced meal. Now she knew better. Now she knew what it was worth, this meal that she had not prepared with a toddler hanging on her leg, this meal that she would eat without once having to get up for *more this* or *more that*, to mop up a spill, or retrieve a sippy cup thrown purposefully to the floor.

When she opened her eyes, she saw that Michael was watching her. She smiled at him and drew in her breath deeply so that her chest pushed out against her shirt.

"Bon appétit," she said. "Or rather . . . *Buon appetito!*" She raised her wine glass to her lips. Inside her, something fluttered and awoke.

When the meal was over and Alice rose to excuse herself to the ladies' room, Laurel pushed back her chair.

"I'll go, too."

Neither of the women spoke while they were in their stalls, but afterwards Laurel sought out Alice's eyes in the mirror above the sink.

"You having fun?"

"Sure."

"I like Michael. He seems . . . nice."

Alice nodded but said nothing; she was touching up her face. She pressed her lips to a paper towel, leaving a perfect red kiss on the fold. Then she balled up the towel deliberately and held it in her fist. She nodded at the wastebasket on Laurel's other side.

"Excuse me," she said.

Instinctively Laurel stepped aside, but something in Alice's tone had jarred her.

"Is something wrong?" she asked.

Alice threw away the crumpled paper towel and turned to meet her eye.

"You told him this weekend was our idea, didn't you?"

"Who?"

"Your husband."

Laurel shrugged noncommittally, and Alice stared at her with wide, mascaraed eyes.

"Laurel, that's not true," she said fiercely, the color rising in her pale face.

"Oh, come on, Alice. What difference does it make? He would never have come otherwise. And we're having fun, right?"

Alice shook her head. "I don't get it."

"Look, Len's like that. He would never have agreed to this weekend if it had been just the two of us. And I can't tell you how much I needed—"

"So you used us?"

"Of course not. I wanted you to come."

Alice frowned.

"Look, I'm sorry if—"

Alice shook her head.

"It's fine. It doesn't matter." She bared her teeth in the mirror, checking for lipstick.

"Come on," Laurel said, reaching for the door. "You look great. And the boys will think we've fallen in."

She forced a smile, but Alice brushed past her without meeting her eye. Laurel made a little face at Alice's back as she followed her down the tiny hallway to the dining room. She knew from work that Alice could be meticulous about details, but she had never seen her like this, so stone-faced and grim. Alice was younger than Laurel by a few years; she had taken the job at the lab while an undergraduate at Humboldt State and had stayed on after both her graduation and her wedding, grateful to have a job at the same university where her husband had begun his master's.

Laurel, in comparison, was a newcomer. She had been seven months pregnant with Jessie when she had followed Len to Arcata, a small college town on the coast of northern California. Len had just earned his PhD in theoretical mathematics at Berkeley, and Humboldt State had offered him a teaching position. With only seven weeks until her due date, it was a ludicrous time for Laurel to look for work of her own. But by her daughter's four-month birthday, Laurel had been desperate for a job—*any* job—just so she would get to leave the damn house alone for a few hours.

The timing had not been good. It was January of 1973, the economy on the brink of recession. No one had been interested in hiring a new mother with an English degree. In the end, it had been Len who had used his connections at the university to get her the job at the lab, and although Laurel despised nothing more than being patronized, she had swallowed her pride and leapt at it.

On the first day, Laurel's stomach had churned with nerves. She had not set foot in a science lab since the ninth grade, when her lab partner had used their Bunsen burner to scribble curse words on their table, then set them alight when the teacher wasn't looking. But Alice had taken Laurel under her wing. You didn't need to know a thing about biology, Alice had assured her, as long as you cleaned the test tubes properly and left no fingerprints on the cover slips.

At the lab, Alice had always been pleasant and attentive, listening with sympathetic noises as Laurel vented to her about the drudgeries of motherhood. Now she wondered if Alice had only liked listening to her because it made her feel so good about her own life. Newly wed and childless, Alice didn't need an off-season weekend at the beach to spend time with her gorgeous husband. And she wasn't paying out the nose for a babysitter, either.

At the thought of the sitter at home with their daughter, Laurel felt a rush of irritation at her mother. Pearl lived alone in Los Angeles in a rented apartment; Laurel had seen no reason her mother couldn't have moved to Arcata, too, to help her after Jessie was born. But Pearl had declined without apology. Her apartment was rent-controlled, she'd said. She couldn't afford to give it up.

"Nobody helped me when your father left," she'd said. "And I managed."

"Mom, I was five by then."

Pearl snorted. "You think it gets easier?"

When she and Alice got back to their table, Laurel plopped down in the seat beside Michael before Alice could sit down. She reached across the table for her glass and tossed the wine back. Almost instantly she could feel the alcohol buoying her, a flush of recklessness just beneath her skin.

"Sit there, Alice," she said, gesturing to the empty seat beside Len with a smile. "I see Len all the time. I want to get to know your husband."

Alice stared at her, and for a moment Laurel wondered if she would make a scene. But just then their waiter came to check on them, and rather than stand there looking a fool, Alice slipped into Laurel's empty seat.

"Can I get you anything else?" the waiter said. "Dessert?"

Laurel held up the empty wine bottle like a beacon.

"Another of these, please."

"Laurel—" Len began, then looked to Michael and Alice. "Do you two want more?"

"Not for me, thanks," Michael said, leaning back in his chair.

"Alice?"

"No."

"Laurel, I don't think we need—"

"Oh, none of you are any fun. Just another glass then, I suppose."

CHAPTER 2

Len

When her wine came, Laurel sat leaning forward over the table. She was angled in her chair toward Michael, one elbow propped on the checkered tablecloth, the other arm hidden in her lap. She held her wine glass loosely by the stem, her upper arm pressed against one breast, hoisting it upward. Her shirt was scooped low in front, revealing the deep chasm of her cleavage. Len's face flushed and he looked away.

"So," he said, scooting his chair back a few inches and catching Michael's eye. "What, um, what do you do exactly, Michael? What's your field, I mean? Your profession?"

Out of the corner of his eye, he saw Laurel make a face and he grimaced; even he could hear how awkward he sounded. He had never been good at this. Even when he was young, the easy chatter of the other children had intimidated him; they seemed to speak a lingo he had never mastered. But how dare Laurel mock him now? If it had not been for her insistence on this ridiculous trip, he would be at home putting Jessie to bed, instead of stumbling through this awful small talk.

He looked back at Michael, suddenly annoyed by the other man's happy-go-lucky ease, his insouciant good humor. What did Len care what he did for a living? Still, he leaned in a little, readying himself to smile and nod. But Michael was not looking at him; he seemed not to have registered Len's bumbling question after all. Instead, his eyes darted around the room, his eyebrows raised slightly, as if in surprise or appraisal.

"Earth to Michael," Alice said sharply. "Len just asked you a question."

Len blushed. "It doesn't—"

"I'm sorry," Michael said, bringing his attention back to the table with an effort. "What did you say?"

"Oh, for heaven's sake," Alice said. She threw her napkin onto the table and glanced at Laurel, who still clutched her half-full glass of wine in one hand. "Are we ready to go?"

Len nodded gratefully and beckoned the waiter for the check.

"But, Len," Laurel said, her voice girlish. "I'm not quite finished." She drew the words out, enunciating carefully.

Len glanced at her sharply. "I think you've had enough."

Laurel rolled her eyes at him, then deliberately tossed back the rest of her wine. She set her glass on the table with elaborate care.

"There," she said, cutting her eyes at Michael. "Now I'm finished."

The four of them made their way back to the motel, their chins tucked inside their collars against the wind. In the lobby, Michael unzipped his jacket and gestured toward the bar.

"Len? Laurel? Anyone for a nightcap?"

Len glanced at Laurel and she nodded slightly.

"Maybe just one," Len said.

But when Michael moved to let Laurel go ahead, she threw back her head and laughed.

"Oh, *I'm* not going." She looked at Len. "*I've* had enough?"

"Laurel, if you're not going to—"

"Oh, for Christ's sake, Len. Just have another drink."

Alice stood watching them, her face unreadable.

"I'm going to bed," she said flatly. "You three figure it out."

"Alice!" Michael called after her. "Come on. One drink."

"I'm tired, Michael," she said, not looking back.

"She's tired," Laurel repeated quietly. "You should let her go."

"Michael, look," Len said. "I don't want to be a party pooper, but if the girls—"

"*Girls?*" Laurel said, arching her eyebrows.

"I mean, if Alice and Laurel don't want to, maybe we should—"

"Len, it's *fine*. Just have a drink already. I'll be in the room."

She shot Michael a look that Len could not read and turned away.

Len shook his head. "Jesus," he muttered.

Len and Michael leaned against the bar while the bartender got their beers. They said nothing, but Len felt that it was a companionable silence, tinged with a shared relief to be free of their wives for a while. He regretted his flash of annoyance earlier; Michael seemed a decent enough fellow.

In the silence, Len felt the floor begin to vibrate. He looked down to see that Michael's heel was pulsing rapidly, the movement causing his whole leg to shake. Len smiled to himself. He remembered when his own leg had used to vibrate like that, at school while he worked his math problems, or at the dinner table. It had driven his older sister Margie crazy.

"Sit *still*, Lenny," she would say. "I can't digest with all that jiggling."

He could still hear her voice as she said it, the grown-up tone she used to scold him whenever their father was there to hear. It was a tone that said that their father needn't worry, that she would fill in for their mother now. *God, how I hated that tone*, Len thought, smiling to himself at the memory.

Michael glanced at him. "What's funny?" he said.

"Oh, nothing. Just . . . your leg reminded me of something."

Michael clamped down on his thigh with one hand and shook his head.

"Sorry. It does that when I'm nervous."

Len nodded. "What's there to be nervous about?"

Michael took a long sip from his beer. "Well, it's not like in the movies, is it?"

"What isn't?"

Michael narrowed his eyes at him. "You saw that movie, *Bob and Carol, Ted and Alice*?"

Len shook his head. "I don't think so."

"You'd remember it. I . . . I thought maybe that was where you people got the idea."

"What idea?"

"Oh, I don't know. What *do* you call it?"

Len looked up sharply and saw that Michael was grinning at him.

"I'm not really used to this kind of thing," Michael went on. He swirled the pale liquid in his glass before taking another sip. "Arcata's never been Berkeley, you know. I mean, of course we heard about stuff like this, but I seriously never thought I would ever be in a position to . . ." He paused, then went on hurriedly. "I'm not saying I'm not game, though. I mean—your wife. She's something."

Len drew his eyebrows together. "Laurel? Yes. I suppose she is."

Michael raised his glass to his lips and drank quickly, his Adam's apple bobbing with each swallow.

"I'm not sure Alice caught on, though," Michael said at last, setting the empty glass on the bar. "Don't be surprised if she's, um, *surprised*." He let out a little burst of a laugh. "What was your room number again?"

"116."

Michael stood up. "212."

"What?"

"I guess I won't need your key." Michael opened his wallet and tossed a bill on the counter.

Instinctively, Len reached for his own pocket.

"No, let me—"

But by the time he'd gotten his wallet out, Michael had gone. Len watched his back as he walked away. He felt dumbfounded, speechless. He wanted to call after him, to confess that he was lost, that he had not followed what Michael had said. But Len did not like—had never liked—to admit when he was in the dark. He had learned long ago that if he just kept quiet, kept thinking and puzzling, the answer would come to him. In college and then in graduate school, the technique had earned him the reputation for being both taciturn and brilliant. But Len secretly knew that he was not brilliant, not like they thought. He was only patient.

Len took a deep swallow of his beer and tried to remember exactly what Michael had said. In an instant, the pieces came together. How could he have not understood before? He stood up so quickly that his barstool tottered.

"Goddamn it, Laurel," he muttered.

The bartender glanced at him. "You need something?"

Len shook his head as he steadied the stool. He left his half-empty beer glass on the counter and hurried out of the bar. He did not know what he would say when he caught up to Michael, but that was what he meant to do. Catch him, tell him that no, he had misunderstood. There had been no plan to . . . *wife-swap*? Is that the term that Michael could not recall? He did not blame him—it was a vile term.

No, that had never been the plan. Laurel just . . . Suddenly, Len paused in the hallway that led to their room. Laurel just *what*? Felt up her friend's husband under the table? He saw it clearly now: Laurel's flushed face and absent hand, Michael's obvious distraction when Len had asked him about his job.

"Goddamn it, Laurel," he said again. He continued walking in the direction of their room, but his steps slowed. *Had* Michael misunderstood? He thought of Laurel on the beach, pulling off her clothes. He had taken it for exhibitionism; certainly that was nothing new. He had grown used to his wife's stunts, her need for all eyes to be on her. He had been embarrassed for her. But what if

Michael was right? Had this whole weekend been a pretense? Was it all unfolding exactly as she'd planned?

Len turned the corner of the hallway. Their room was three doors down, and Michael was not in sight. A "Do Not Disturb" sign hung on the door. It was this detail that pushed Len over the edge into fury. He wanted to ram down the door and shake her. This time she had gone too far.

But Len had not taken two steps toward their room when he stopped himself. Would he knock at his own door, then? Knock and wait for it to be answered like a petulant child? *I didn't understand* . . . He would be made a fool in front of Michael—a fool and a cuckold. He fingered the room key in his pocket. He didn't *have* to knock. But the thought of barging in, to see Laurel, surely already half-naked in the bed, and Michael's startled face—that would be worse. Len had never liked to make a scene.

A few feet from the door, he turned around and strode back down the empty hallway. In the lobby, he hesitated, then went back inside the bar. The bartender looked up in surprise.

"Oh, sorry, man. I cleared your beer. But let me—" He reached for another glass.

"It's fine," Len said. "Don't bother."

He turned again and left the bar, hesitating in the lobby once again. *Room 212*, Michael had said. *She might be surprised.* He thought of Alice, with her petite waist and small breasts, and felt a stirring of desire. He looked toward the stairs. Why not? But Len could not see himself rapping at Alice's door any more than he could bear to knock at his own. Laurel had made her bed, he thought bitterly, and she would lie in it. He would not make his own.

Impulsively, he pulled his room key from his pocket and tossed it on the front desk, then pushed through the glass door onto the street. Outside, the wind scoured his face, but once he was inside the car, stillness descended. The hands of the clock on the dashboard glowed faintly in the dark, and Len was shocked at how early it still was. It was barely after ten; if he hurried, he'd be home by one. He started the engine and backed the station wagon onto the street.

Len held the wheel with two hands to stop them from shaking, but his mind would not relent. It rubbed itself raw on all the humiliating details of the evening, like a tongue on a chipped tooth. The licentious horror of it propelled him through the small town, but once he reached Highway One, the long, serpentine road home loomed before him. The car slowed, his foot uneasy on the gas. He laid the chilled fingers of one hand against his cheek; his face still burned with shame.

He saw again Laurel's flushed face at dinner, her absent hand, and a flash of fury shot through him. He leaned his foot onto the accelerator, felt the engine strain as the car lurched into the next curve. Now he imagined Laurel, bleary-eyed and hungover, waking to find that he had not returned. What would she do? He let out a short, bitter laugh. Take a bus, beg Alice and Michael for a ride home—it was no concern of his.

And he? What was *he* going to do? What would he tell the babysitter when he arrived home in the middle of the night without his wife? What would he tell Jessie? He thought of his daughter, with her chubby knees and sly grin, the sweet warmth of sleep that clung to her bare limbs in the morning when she woke. No, to her he wouldn't have to explain a thing. "Mommy's not here," he would say, and then he would take her to the kitchen to make pancakes as if it were any other Sunday morning.

In all the week, it was his favorite time. He loved his daughter's stubby, flour-covered fingers, the delight with which she stirred the milk and eggs into the batter.

"You just get the fun parts," Laurel had accused him once, watching them together. "You don't know how infuriating she can be."

This wasn't true; he *did* know. His daughter's stubbornness often sparked his own temper, and more than once he had drawn back his hand to spank her as he remembered his father spanking him. But Laurel was right, too: Jessie didn't get under his skin the way she did her mother's. Jessie's two-year-old tantrums could throw Laurel into answering fits of rage. She resented the child's relentless demands: "I want duice! Read a book! Dessie up!"

"Do I look like a slave to you?" Laurel would hurl back at the toddler, and when that happened, Jessie's startled eyes and wrinkled forehead were almost more than Len could bear.

"I'll get her juice," he would say. "Why don't you take a break?"

But his attempts to intervene only stoked Laurel's rage.

"I don't need a break! I need our daughter to learn some goddamn manners."

Laurel seemed almost to thrill in her angry outbursts at the child, as if the collapse of her patience and the scale of her anger were flags she waved to Len: *See how much I have to endure?* Later, she would apologize—but only to Len, never to Jessie—and inevitably her remorse would cast her into the ready wallow of self-pity.

"I'm just not cut out for this, Len," she would weep. "God, I'm a bad mother."

Len had first met Laurel at Berkeley, when he was in the final stretch of his PhD program and she was a senior co-ed. Laurel was voluptuous and dark-eyed, full-lipped in a way he had found sexy then. She wore flowing pants that flared at the bottoms, her dark brown hair loose to her waist. For weeks, he had barely surfaced from the abstract math of his dissertation; Laurel's free spirit had been a breath of fresh air.

Back then, the ease with which Laurel cried had endeared her to him. Tears did not come easily to him, but he was, at heart, a sentimental man. On one of their first dates, they had seen a reshowing of *To Kill a Mockingbird* at the campus theater. He had heard Laurel begin to sob quietly beside him as soon as the jury entered the courtroom. He had taken her hand, then, and had felt the tightness in his own throat relent. Later, they had snuck onto the roof of Laurel's dorm and watched the moon rise over the bay. Despite his protests, Laurel had gone to her knees before him. Gathering her hair in his hands, Len had felt some reserve in him loosen and give way.

They had not been careful; Laurel was pregnant by Christmas. She had cried as she told him, but, holding her against his chest, her head tucked beneath his chin, his own tranquility had surprised him. He had always assumed that he would marry, someday, just as he had always known—ever since he'd been old enough to understand such things—that he would get a doctorate in math. His PhD in hand, it seemed only fitting that a wife and baby would come next. And he had worked so hard for the degree. If the family came more readily, he had seen no reason to rail against his fate.

Len stopped at a gas station for coffee in Leggett, then picked up 101. Here the highway no longer hugged the coast, and the driving was easier. He drank the lukewarm coffee as he drove and let his mind go slack at last.

It was just after one in the morning when he pulled into their narrow drive. Inside, he resisted the urge to reach for the lamp, but by the pale light seeping in from the porch, he saw that the usual chaos of the living room had been ordered. Jessie's books were stacked neatly on the coffee table, her toys collected in a bin. He went first to Jessie's bedroom at the end of the hall, where she slept, as usual, with her bottom raised in the air and her favorite stuffed animal, a yellow duck named Quack, wedged in the crook of her elbow. He kissed her lightly and pulled her purple blanket over her, a rush of tenderness rising in his throat.

The babysitter was asleep in the master bedroom, where Laurel had insisted she make herself at home. Len tiptoed by her to get to the bathroom, where he rooted for an extra toothbrush beneath the sink. As he left, he paused for a moment by the bed. The young woman's face was flushed with sleep, her auburn hair loose on the pillow. Quickly, he looked away, but not before a shadow of the same tenderness he had felt for his own sleeping daughter swept over him. Then his mind darted back to Laurel, and he turned away, grimacing.

He eased the bedroom door shut, then tiptoed back down the hall and through the living room to the kitchen, where he brushed his teeth at the sink. A pale orange film clung to the white porcelain. Len found a can of Ajax under the sink and scrubbed at it with a scouring pad. Only after the kitchen sink was clean did he pull a blanket from the closet and stretch out on the couch, the stacks of Jessie's books on the coffee table beside him like a battlement against the coming day.

CHAPTER 3

Len

Len was still asleep when Sarah stepped out of the bedroom in the morning. She was wearing light blue pajamas, her hair mussed from sleep. She gave a little cry of surprise when she saw him.

"Dr. Walters!" she said. "I didn't know you were here."

Len pushed himself up on the couch. "Please, call me Leonard—Len."

"But—"

"There was a change of plans. I didn't want to wake you to let you know. Laurel—Laurel will be back soon."

Sarah crossed her arms against her chest. "Oh. Well, hold on a minute. Jessie is awake, I think."

She took a step back down the hall toward the nursery, but Len stopped her.

"Please. I want to see her." He pushed himself up to standing, ran his fingers through his hair and rubbed his eyes.

Sarah nodded. "I'll just get dressed then." She turned back into the bedroom and closed the door behind her.

In the nursery, Jessie was standing at the railing of her crib. She was playing with a toy that he had found at a yard sale. The straps were broken, but he had strung some wires through it and attached it to her crib. There was a little rubber button that rang a bell, and a little wheel, striped red and white like a peppermint drop, which became pink when you spun it. Jessie was spinning it now, with purpose, talking to herself under her breath, and the sight of her filled Len with so much love he felt his chest might burst.

He stood silently at the door for a moment, watching her, but she sensed his presence and looked over.

"Da-da! Wook, Da-da. Pink!" She spun the wheel again, watching in amazement as the red and white stripes spun into a blur of pink.

Len laughed. "Would you look at that," he said.

He realized with unexpected relief that Jessie was not at all surprised to see him. He had tried to explain—could it only have been yesterday?—that he and Mommy would be going away for a little while, but that they would come back in two days. "Two days," he had said, holding up his fingers.

"Two," Jessie had parroted, but she couldn't understand yet, could she? Her whole life so far was lived in the present, the past quickly forgotten but for little snapshot memories of her favorite things—the jays at the park, for instance, or the library. The future was unimaginable.

"Dessie too," she had said, and at first he had thought she meant could she come, too, and his heart had given a little leap, as if, with Jessie on his side, he might convince Laurel that their daughter ought to be allowed to come along. But then he had seen her struggling to arrange her hand so that two chubby fingers were raised.

"Dessie two," she said again, and at last he had understood.

Now Len went to stand by the crib. He reached through the bars to swipe his finger across another of the toy's gizmos, a spinning cylinder with blue barbershop-style stripes.

"Da-da make boo," Jessie observed. 'Dessie make boo?'"

Len laughed. "You say, 'Can *I* make blue?'"

Jessie spun the cylinder, batting at it with the palm of her hand, ignoring the correction.

"Okay, Jessie," Len said at last. "I've got to pee. Let's go."

He carried her into the bathroom with him, then put her down so that he could urinate. His piss stank of coffee and Jessie scrunched up her eyes.

"Da-da pee yucky."

He flushed quickly. "Sorry. Do you want to try to sit on the potty?"

She nodded, and Len stooped down to take off her sodden diaper.

"Okay," he said, scooping her up by the underarms and sitting her on the little potty. She was up in an instant.

"No pee."

"That's okay. Thanks for trying."

At the sink, Len helped Jessie to wash her hands and then splashed cool water on his face. It ran down his unshaven chin and neck, soaking the collar of the button-down he had put on for dinner the night before.

"Come on, Jess," he said, taking his daughter's hand. "Let's go get dressed."

In the nursery, he found her a new diaper and some clothes. He wanted to change, too, but his bedroom door was closed when they passed it in the hall, and he wasn't sure if Sarah was still inside. But when they emerged in the living room, there she was, standing by the door, a small, blue duffel bag by her feet. She had changed into jeans and a green sweater, her hair pulled back in a ponytail. She smiled when she saw Jessie.

"Good morning, sleepy head."

Jessie ran to her and she dropped to her knees to hug the little girl.

Then she stood and turned to Len.

"Well, I guess I'll go, since you're here now," she said uncertainly.

She reached for the doorknob slowly, and at once Len understood.

"Wait. I'm so sorry. We'll pay you for the whole time, of course." He patted his back pockets for his wallet, but it was not there. "Just a minute, please."

He found his wallet and keys between the stacks of books on the coffee table. "Oh, and thanks for tidying up. How much is it?"

"Well, Laurel said one hundred," Sarah said apologetically. "But that was supposed to be until this afternoon."

Len swallowed hard against the surge of bitterness that rose in his throat. One hundred dollars! How could he have agreed to such a thing?

"Just one more sec," he said, then disappeared down the hall to his office. It was hardly more than a closet, really. A bonus room, the realtor had called it euphemistically when she'd shown them around the house.

His desk drawer opened with a squeal, and he pulled out the envelope that held their cash for the week. One hundred dollars— what a waste. He counted out the bills, then returned to the living room and handed them to her. She pushed them into her bag without looking at them.

"Thank you. Bye, Jessie. Be good." She knelt to hug his daughter again, and Jessie threw her arms around her neck.

"No Sarah go!"

Gently, Sarah disentangled herself. "Your daddy's here now. And I'll be back to play with you tomorrow."

Jessie started to cry, then, and Sarah looked at Len helplessly as she pulled the little girl toward her and stroked her back.

"Do you like pancakes?" Len asked impulsively. "Jessie and I like to make pancakes on Sundays, don't we, Jessie? Unless you have somewhere else to be."

Sarah shook her head. "Pancakes sound great."

Sarah sat at the kitchen table, sipping coffee, while Jessie helped Len make the batter, and then she held Jessie in her lap and helped her do a wooden puzzle while Len made the pancakes at the stove.

There was no syrup in the cabinets or in the refrigerator. Len clenched his teeth in annoyance, sure he had written it on the list the last time Laurel went shopping. He pulled a jar of strawberry jam from the refrigerator door and put it on the table, muttering apologies.

"I like pancakes with jam," Sarah said. "Don't you, Jessie?"

"Yes! Pee butter and dam."

"Oh no, sweetheart," Len said. "We don't put peanut butter on pancakes."

"Actually, that's how they eat them in Wyoming," Sarah said.

So Len got out the peanut butter, too, and watched as Sarah made Jessie a pancake sandwich. He was surprised, and a little envious, at the easy familiarity between them. This woman was a stranger to him, yet clearly she mattered to his daughter. He did some quick math and realized with a start that Sarah had been babysitting for them for over a year now, although he had seen her only a handful of times.

"So," he said, ladling batter onto the skillet. "You're from Wyoming?"

"No," she said. She leaned forward to wipe jam from Jessie's cheek with a napkin. "I just drove through it once. We saw a sign for a free church breakfast, so we stopped."

Len smiled. "Where then?"

"Nowhere, really. We moved a lot."

"Military?"

Sarah nodded. "My dad's in the army."

Len passed her a plate of pancakes. "So how did you end up here?"

"I'm not sure," she said noncommittally. She moved one pancake off the stack and spread it with a thin glaze of jam. When she took a bite at last, Len found himself watching the subtle motion of her jaw as she chewed. He looked away.

"Sorry," he began, "I didn't mean to pry."

"Oh, you weren't. It wasn't a monumental decision or anything. My dad was stationed at a base in Redding when I was in high school. He was talking about retiring, and I thought they might stay there. Humboldt State seemed like the right distance away. By then, I felt like I'd already been all over the world. I didn't feel the need to go far."

Len nodded. "So you're in school." He wasn't surprised. With her blue jeans and her ponytail, her slender frame and the splash of freckles across her nose, she looked like she could be a student in one of his classes.

"Graduate school, yes."

He started. "You seem so young."

She shrugged. "I think Laurel and I are the same age, actually. Isn't she twenty-five?"

"Yes, I think so." He faltered. "Yes, that's right."

He was flustered now and couldn't think what else to say. He busied himself with the spatula and skillet.

"I also liked the trees."

"Sorry?"

"You asked me why here. I think some of it was because of the trees—the redwoods. The summer I was sixteen it was incredibly hot in Redding, and one Saturday my dad told my mom and me to go and get in the car, that we were going to Arcata. He said it would be twenty degrees cooler here, but I didn't believe him. He was right, though. We went to that little park with the redwoods. You know the one? Up on the hill? Those trees . . . They made quite an impression on me." She laughed softly, as if mocking herself.

Len glanced over at her and met her eye. She shrugged. "At eighteen, it seemed as good a reason as any other."

Len smiled. "The trees," he repeated. "That's . . . nice."

Sarah shrugged again. "It's a pretty stupid reason, I guess."

"No, I mean it. So many people are here for reasons . . . Well, reasons that aren't as nice as that."

Another silence fell between them, but this one was easier.

"So, what are you studying in graduate school?" Len asked, bringing the last of the pancakes to the table.

"Anthropology."

"Margaret Mead?"

Sarah smiled. "Among others."

"I thought you were tired of traveling the world."

She shrugged. "There are people here, too."

"I'm sorry?"

"Anthropology is the study of humanity. Of cultures. We've got those here, too."

"Oh. Right."

"What about you two?" Sarah asked. "You three, I mean. What brought you to Arcata?"

Len colored inexplicably. He wondered whom she had forgotten to include—Laurel or Jessie. He had offered no explanation for Laurel's absence and was grateful to Sarah that she had not asked. He gestured vaguely with the spatula.

"Oh, you know. The university. Young professors—we pretty much have to go wherever we can find a job."

"But Laurel . . . She's from around here, isn't she? I thought she said—"

"Oh, no. Well, not really. Laurel's mother was raised in Mendocino. Not the coast. Inland. Bay . . . Bay something. Laurel was born there, but she grew up in LA. She just likes to pretend that she's a local."

Sarah laughed good-naturedly at this. "Well," she said, standing up and pulling Jessie from her high chair. "I don't think people who really *are* from here would consider Mendocino local. Too close to San Francisco, and that's a whole 'nother planet." She shifted Jessie on her hip. "Come on, Jessie. Let's go wash your hands so you don't get everything sticky, okay?"

When Sarah returned to the kitchen, his daughter wasn't with her. She didn't sit down again. Len looked at her plate; the two remaining pancakes in the stack were untouched.

"You didn't—" he began.

"Jessie's happy looking at a book in the living room, so I'd better take off now. Thank you for breakfast."

"Of course. Thank you for helping me avoid a tantrum."

She smiled. "No problem. How was that restaurant, by the way?"

Len's heart jumped. "What?"

"I recommended a restaurant in Fort Bragg to your wife. I just wondered—"

Len looked away. "Yes," he said abruptly. "It was fine. It was good."

Sarah glanced at him, her expression unreadable. "Well," she said. "Thanks again."

Len gestured toward her plate. "You sure you don't want—"

But Sarah just shook her head. "I'm good, thanks. Tell Laurel I said good-bye. I'll see her Monday. Tomorrow."

Len heard the click of the front door as it closed behind her. With Jessie quiet in the other room and Sarah gone, the house felt suddenly empty, and Len's exhaustion caught up to him at last. He sat down, rested his head on the kitchen table, and closed his eyes.

"Da-da?" Jessie said, appearing in the doorway. "Da-da sleeping?"

Len sighed. "I'm just resting my eyes."

"Dessie 'side!" she said. "Dessie park!"

Len shuddered and shook his head. He could still feel yesterday's chill on his skin, the cold wind that had battered them on the beach. He glanced at the window, expecting the usual square of gray, ready to make up an excuse. But the sky beyond the glass was surprisingly blue.

"Okay, Dessie," Len said resignedly. "Let me clean up this mess and we'll go."

He washed the dishes quickly, then retrieved the peanut butter from the cupboard. There was no bread, so he did as Sarah had and used the leftover pancakes to make two sandwiches, which he wrapped in foil. He found an apple in the fridge that he cut into slender slices, then poured juice into a sippy cup for Jessie. As he packed their picnic, he felt his spirits rise. He would spend a beautiful Sunday with his daughter. He would not allow himself to think of Laurel.

Later, Len and Jessie had their picnic on the bench by the park, and then spent several minutes throwing bits of their pancake sandwiches to the jays that hopped around them in the grass. Afterwards, Len pushed Jessie in the swing, and then caught her again and again at the bottom of the slide.

When it was time to go, Len's head felt groggy with weariness. Jessie had grown cranky, too.

"No home!" she wailed, clinging to the rung of the slide's ladder. "Dessie park!"

Eventually, Len had to unwrap her fingers himself, then buckle her into the stroller as she screamed. His head pounded with her cries and with his own mounting fatigue. Back at home, she continued to cry while he changed her diaper.

"No nap!" she screamed, knowing what was coming.

"I tell you what," he bargained. "What if you sleep with Daddy in the big bed?"

She quieted but looked at him skeptically. "Da-da nap?"

"You got it," he said.

They read a book sitting up against the headboard, but when he set the book on the bedside table and lowered himself down on the pillow, Jessie did not complain. She settled in next to him, so that the top of her head was pressed against his underarm. He curled his arm around her and was asleep within seconds.

CHAPTER 4

Len

"Well, isn't this just great?" Laurel's voice was shrill with annoyance.

Len glanced at the clock groggily. It was not quite two-thirty; beside him, Jessie still slept.

"Shhh!" he said. He nodded down at Jessie.

"Len, you know how I feel about this. I don't want her sleeping in here with you. It makes it so much harder. She'll never want to nap in her own bed if you—"

"Will you *shhhh*?" Len whispered harshly. "She's sleeping."

"Do you think I can't see that?"

Carefully, he extracted his arm from around his daughter and eased himself from the bed. He took Laurel by the upper arm and steered her from the room, closing the door quietly behind them.

"I can't believe it, Len. I must have told you a hundred times. She *has* to nap in her own bed. Otherwise, she'll never—"

"Are you kidding me?" Len interrupted her, his voice cold.

"No. Every time you let her nap with you, the next time she puts up more of a fuss."

"Are you *kidding* me?" Len could barely contain his rage.

"What? What are you so pissed off about? I'm the one who'll have to—"

"Laurel, you are unbelievable. You march in here after what happened last night, after what you did, and have the nerve to bitch at me about where Jessie naps? You have got to be kidding me."

"After what *I* did? What about what *you* did? You just left me there. I'm your *wife*."

"Oh really? Forgive me if sometimes it's hard to tell."

"What are you talking about?"

"Jesus, Laurel, what do you think I'm talking about?"

"What's the big deal, Len? So I wanted to have some fun. And it turns out you got the long end of the stick, anyway."

"What is *that* supposed to mean?"

Laurel laughed derisively. "You figure it out."

"Damn it, Laurel," Len slammed the side of his fist against the wall. "You went too far."

"Len!" Laurel cried out. They both watched as the single framed print they had on the wall jiggled off its nail and crashed to the floor.

A second later, Jessie began to cry. "Da-da!" she called.

"Great," said Laurel. "That's all we need right now."

"I've got her," Len said.

"Don't expect me to clean that up," Laurel called after him.

Len paused at the doorway to the bedroom and turned to face her. "Just for the record, Laurel, I did not get the 'long end of the stick.' I did not go to Alice's room. I came home. *That's all*."

He did not pause to watch this register on Laurel's face. He turned away, opened the door, and went to his daughter.

That night, and for the rest of the week, Len slept on the couch. On Friday, Laurel appeared in the doorway of the living room. She leaned against the frame, pulling her light robe around her and retying it at her waist.

"How long are you going to keep this up, Len?"

Len glanced at her, then let his eyes fall back to the article he was reading. "I don't know."

"I miss you."

Len snorted, but he did not look up.

"Look, I'm sorry, okay? I didn't think you'd get so bent out of shape about it."

He met her eyes at last. "Laurel, I don't think you thought at all."

Laurel looked away. "Maybe not."

Neither of them spoke for a moment. "Please, Len. I said I'm sorry. Can't we put this behind us?"

Len shook his head. "I don't know, Laurel. I don't think this is working anymore."

"Len, it was one night. And I said I was sorry."

"It's not just that, Laurel— although maybe that clinched it." He paused, his eyes scanning the room as if looking for something. Finally, they met Laurel's. "We're not happy together, Laurel."

"I'm happy."

"No, you're not. You complain all the time. You cry."

"But I could be. We can make it better. I can—"

Len sighed. "I don't think I can be."

"What? You don't think you can be *what*?"

"Happy." He said it with such sad finality that Laurel's chin began to tremble.

"Oh, Len. I'm sorry."

"I know. And I forgive you, I suppose. But I don't think I want to live like this."

"You can't mean that. What about Jessie?"

"You think I haven't thought of that? That's all I've thought about. All week she's all I've thought about."

"Just Jessie," Laurel said, and the bitterness in her voice was unmistakable. Then, with an effort, she changed her tone. "So how can you leave?"

"I'll stay close. I've worked it out. It doesn't have to change much, for her. I can still come over in the evenings, feed her, put her to bed . . . Just like I do now."

"But Len—"

"Well why not?" he interrupted her. "She'll hardly know the

difference. I almost never see her in the mornings anyway. It'll be almost exactly the—"

"Leonard."

"Laurel, I just can't do—"

"Len, I'm pregnant."

Len felt the room begin to spin. Then a face materialized: Michael's, flushed with anticipation, his eyes bright. Len swallowed deliberately. "With Michael's."

Laurel laughed shrilly. "Jesus, Len. That was a week ago."

Len took a slow breath, let his eyelids close. It couldn't be. He felt the weight of his head fall back against the rough canvas of the couch. Last Saturday, as he drove home alone in the dark, he felt as if he had stumbled into a lewd movie which would, eventually, come to a distasteful but welcome end. The feeling had persisted most of the week. Every morning as he walked to his office at the university, he could feel himself waiting for the plot to resolve. But on Thursday evening, when he had opened the front door and found Jessie in tears on a carpet littered with Cheerios, and Laurel stony-eyed at the kitchen table, a vodka and tonic already in hand, something had shifted in him. A thought seemed to materialize in his mind, the words clicking together like the terms of an equation: *I can leave.*

Now, the bad-movie feeling returned in a rush. Without opening his eyes, he imagined striding into the nursery, lifting Jessie from her crib, hoisting her onto his shoulder, and leaving the house. He felt the impulse to do it in his whole body, a need as real as hunger.

With an effort, he opened his eyes. He didn't look at Laurel.

"Are you sure?"

"Yes."

"Did you know last weekend, when you—"

Laurel cut him off. "Of course not."

"How pregnant?"

"Nine weeks."

"Jesus, Laurel! How could you not have known?"

"Don't you yell at me," Laurel said bitterly. "How was I supposed to know?"

"Oh, I don't know," Len said sarcastically. "Because you hadn't had a period in what . . . nine weeks?"

Laurel glared at him. "You think I have time to count? I barely have time to—"

"Oh, spare me. It's pretty convenient, isn't it? If I don't know, I can keep drinking. I can fuck my friend's husband—"

"Len, that's not fair."

"Isn't it?"

"No, it isn't. My periods haven't been regular—I was nursing, remember? Okay, sure, maybe in retrospect I should have wondered, but I just didn't think . . ." She trailed off, and silence fell between them.

"Plus, it's not like there have been a plethora of occasions when I could have gotten pregnant."

Len heard the note of accusation in her voice and let out his breath audibly. It was almost a laugh, but bitter and hard.

"And you're . . . you're sure it's mine?"

"Jesus, Len. Is that what you think of me?"

Len scoffed. "I don't know. After last weekend I'm not sure what I think."

Laurel began to cry then, and Len looked away.

"I said I was sorry, Len. Please."

He said nothing.

"Len, we're going to have another baby."

He met her eyes at last. "Laurel. Are we sure we want to—"

Laurel's body stiffened. Her shoulders went back, and she put one hand across her belly defensively. "Len. I'm nine weeks. The baby—"

"I know," Len said quickly. "You're right."

Len drew in a deep breath and let it out in a short burst, like an athlete preparing himself for a sprint.

"Well then. I guess we're going to have a baby."

And with that, he felt his resignation settle over him like a new skin. The bad-movie feeling was gone, and so, incredibly, was his urge to escape, to pick up the one thing he loved purely in this world and be gone. How this had become his life, he didn't know, but it was his, undeniably. Another thought ordered itself in his mind like math: *We are not meant to be happy.* And there was some satisfaction in it, to have figured out this small, pure nugget of truth at last.

He looked up at Laurel, and she gave him an uncertain smile.

He patted the couch beside him, and she crossed the room in quick little steps and sat down heavily at his side. With an effort, he put his arm around her shoulders, and she leaned her head awkwardly against his chest.

"Well, I guess Jessie will have to learn to sleep in a big-girl bed." The thought of his daughter was like a light turned on inside of him. A brother or sister for Jessie—she would be delighted, he thought. Len felt his mood begin to lift. Somehow, he had arrived here. He would just have to make the most of it. He gave Laurel's shoulder a little squeeze.

"It'll be okay, Laurel," he said.

He felt her let her breath out, as if she'd been holding it.

She looked at him with doe eyes. "Really?"

He couldn't hold her gaze. "Yeah," he said. "I think so."

In the morning, Len was eating cereal when Laurel came in. She was braless beneath her robe and her heavy breasts sagged loosely beneath the fabric. Her eyes were swollen and the skin on one side of her face was creased where it had been pressed into the pillow. He felt a little bubble of despair rise up in him, but he swallowed it down and summoned his resolve. He smiled at her.

"Good morning."

"Morning."

He took a last bite of cereal and rose from the table.

"Can I get you something?"

"Oh, so now it's 'Can I get you something?' You ignore me all week . . . I should have said I was pregnant sooner."

Len gritted his teeth. "Laurel."

"What?"

"I thought we were going to try to make it . . . to be better."

"Did we say that?"

"No, I guess we didn't. But can we?"

Laurel sighed. "Yes."

"Good." There was a pause. "So, can I get you something? Tea? Cereal?"

"Tea, I guess." She sank heavily into a chair. "Thank you."

She thanked him again when he gave it to her, and again when he placed a piece of toast in front of her, already spread with butter and jam.

"You're eating for two now."

They were polite with each other all morning. It felt like a charade, but it was a pleasant one, at least. Len felt his spirits lift.

He gathered up his briefcase and his packed lunch, then paused at the door.

"Give Jessie a hug for me."

"I will."

He had almost closed the door behind him when a thought occurred to him. He turned back.

"You won't drink, now, will you? For the baby?"

She looked at him dryly, then shook her head. "Of course not."

They stayed on their best behavior. For the remaining seven months of Laurel's pregnancy, Len did his best to dote. He made Laurel breakfast each morning before he left for work. More protein, the OB had said. So Len cooked eggs: fried, scrambled, boiled, poached. The house smelled perpetually of bacon.

In the evenings after dinner, he played with Jessie, gave her a bath, put her to bed first in her usual crib, and then, as Laurel's pregnancy progressed, on a twin mattress that he pushed up against the wall in her room. Afterwards, there were the dinner dishes to wash and the toys to tidy up. Laurel watched him from her place on the couch, a science-fiction novel held slackly against the bulge of her growing stomach.

"Oh, Len," she sometimes said. "Just leave them."

But he shook his head.

When the house was reasonably tidy, he went to the small office to grade papers or prepare his lectures. Only when he could no longer keep his eyes open did he put down his pen. In the bedroom, Laurel would almost always be asleep. He would stretch out carefully beside her; it seemed he was asleep almost before he closed his eyes.

The morning came quickly. He rose, with an effort, at the first alarm. Laurel complained if he hit the snooze; she couldn't go back to sleep instantly like he did. He showered and dressed quickly, made coffee, pulled the eggs from the fridge.

The months passed quickly. Each day was hazy under a patina of exhaustion. Only when he was with Jessie did the film seem to dissolve. He seldom thought of the baby that would soon be with them, for when he did, he felt uneasy. His love for Jessie was like a cool lake. Deep and clear, he could plunge into it and feel himself renewed, redeemed. It seemed impossible to him that he would love this new baby with the same raw intensity.

And yet even as he avoided thinking of it, still the baby's coming lent a bittersweetness to his time with his daughter. He could not take her to the park without thinking that their times there, just the two of them, were numbered. He could not hold her against his chest without being aware of the monumental change that was to come.

CHAPTER 5

Eight Months Later

Len

"Len. The baby." Laurel nudged her elbow into his side.

He couldn't rouse himself from sleep.

"Len! The baby!" Laurel said again. Her voice was piqued with annoyance, and, not quite waking, Len heard the tone but not the words.

"Is she really?" he murmured agreeably, to placate her.

"Len, for crying out loud, wake up. The baby's crying. She'll wake Jessie." The elbow jabbed into his side.

At last, Len was awake. "Sorry," he muttered as he swung his legs off the bed, then shuffled down the hallway to the nursery. The baby—Emma, they had named her—was crying in earnest now, her face red and her eyes scrunched closed. The sound she made was more animal than human; more than once, Len had mistaken her cry for a cat fight out in the yard.

Incredibly, Jessie never seemed to be disturbed. He glanced at his older daughter, fast asleep on her mattress, with her yellow duck tucked in the crook of her elbow and her bottom in the air. He picked up the wailing baby.

"Shhh," he whispered. In his arms, Emma's cries quieted somewhat, but that almost made it worse. Len hated what came next. Quickly, he lay her down on the changing table to unpin her wet diaper. For a fraction of a second, her cries ceased. Her little mouth worked, searching for the nipple. When it was not to be found, when instead the cool air hit her damp bottom—oh, her rage! How he hated it, to feel all that helpless fury directed at him. Every night it was the same ordeal: he had to torture her, enrage her, when every impulse in him demanded he appease her.

"Why can't you just nurse her first?" he suggested to Laurel. He wouldn't mind getting up again to change her diaper. He felt he would do anything to avoid her desperate cries. But Laurel liked to nurse in bed, lying on her side. She didn't want the baby's wet diaper soiling the sheets. He had suggested a towel, but Laurel had scoffed at the idea. Any way you cut it, it would just be more laundry. "How would *you* like to nurse a wet, stinky baby?" she had said.

He had shrugged in response, defeated.

Plus, Laurel had added more kindly, she liked how she and Emma fell asleep together. She wouldn't want to have to disturb her, afterwards, to change her diaper.

Len had become practiced at squelching his own bitterness, but the thought had come anyway. *Disturb the baby, or you?* Still, he had held his tongue.

Now, he jutted out his chin in concentration as he quickly folded the dry diaper and pinned it into place. Then he slid his large hand under his daughter's torso and lifted her to his shoulder. She cried frantically until he settled her against Laurel's side. Laurel helped Emma find her nipple, and, then, oh, the sweet bliss of it. He always had to stand there, just for a moment, watching her suckle.

How beautiful she was. His second daughter seemed vulnerable to him in a way that Jessie never had. His memory of Jessie from the night he had driven home alone had stayed with him—the perfect innocence of her. Her sleeping form had held the essence of peace exactly when his whole world had felt tainted and in turmoil.

With Emma, the feeling was not dissimilar. His youngest daughter had come into being at the nadir of his marriage, and yet she had come untouched by all its ugliness. But while Jessie seemed to exude resilience, as if her little toddler self was protected by some force field he could not see but could only sense, his newborn daughter seemed innocently helpless, dangerously vulnerable. He reached out his hand now, to stroke the back of her tiny head, the pink skin of her skull still visible through the fine hair. Laurel, sensing his movement, opened her eyes and looked at him questioningly.

"What is it?" she asked.

And because he was so impossibly tired, and because he did not have the right words for all that he felt, and because, even if he could find them, he knew he would not risk handing them over to Laurel's derision, he said only, "Nothing. I just like watching her nurse." He moved his hand purposefully from Emma's head to Laurel's shoulder, just for a moment, and then he returned to his spot in bed, the sheets already cool against his skin.

CHAPTER 6

Laurel

In the morning, Laurel was nursing on the couch in the living room when Len appeared. He smiled at them both.

"Emma's up? I didn't hear her."

"I know." She couldn't help the bitterness that seeped into her voice, and he paused on his way to the kitchen.

"I would have gotten her if—"

"It's fine." She stroked the baby's cheek with the back of her index finger, feeling her resentment rise. He would have gotten Emma *if* he'd heard her—that was what he meant. But he never did hear her. Every time she had to roust him; it was like waking the dead. And wasn't she just as tired?

She leaned her head back against the couch and closed her eyes. She could hear Len in the kitchen, running water and making coffee, and she even envied him that quotidian task: that he could just saunter on in there, no baby on his hip or at his breast, and make himself whatever the hell he pleased.

She opened her eyes when the sounds ceased, and there he was in the doorway, a mug in each hand.

He glanced at the clock that hung above the bookcase. "Do you want me to make you some breakfast?"

She could tell that he was rushing. "No, it's fine."

He set one of the mugs on the end table beside her, but somehow the gesture only made her feel more irritable, as if that little bit of gallantry could make up for the next two hours, when she would be alone with their children, with all of Jessie's morning demands and the baby to attend to.

"Have a good day," he said, putting his lips against Emma's silky hair. He planted another quick kiss on the top of Laurel's head.

She nodded, knowing that if she spoke, whatever she said would be laced with sarcasm. When the front door closed behind him, tears came inexplicably to her eyes. Just once she would like to know what it felt like to leave the house like him, to slip out the door while the baby was nursing peacefully and Jessie still slept. No wonder he loved them so much. She knew she should be gratified by Len's devotion to their children, but she didn't feel gratified. She felt affronted, challenged, as if his love were the gold standard against which her own would never measure up.

And no wonder. He wasn't saturated with them like she was. He left in the morning, closing the door behind him on a quiet house. He saw the girls only for a couple of hours before bedtime, when it was all sweetness: bath time and footy pajamas, books and good-night hugs. He didn't understand how they wore her down so that she fantasized about two things only. One was walking out the door unencumbered, without a baby on her hip or a tugging hand in hers, without a diaper bag or stroller, a sippy cup or snack. The other was the drink she would allow herself to make when it was finally five o'clock.

The second fantasy she never spoke of; she saw the way Len glanced at her hand as he came in the door, checking for a glass. The first, though, she hadn't been able to keep to herself.

"You get to do it *every* day," she had said to Len once. "And you don't even appreciate what a luxury it is."

He'd regarded her seriously, surprised by her vehemence. But, she *did* get to leave the house unencumbered, didn't she? Len had asked. She had her little job at the lab. Was that how he had put it? Her "little job"? If not, she could practically read the thought in his brain: *At least Laurel has her little job*. And it was true, it was not much: a few hours every morning during the week, her meager wage barely covering what they paid Sarah to watch the girls. Oh, but it was worth it. As soon as Sarah put down her bag, always in the same spot by the front door, Laurel would rush to the bedroom to get ready.

What a relief it was to pull off her shapeless T-shirt and floppy nursing bra. She loved getting dressed for work, while Sarah played with Jessie in the other room. The anticipation of walking out the door, with only her handbag over her shoulder: that was the best part, really. The work itself was tedious and fiddly, worse now that she and Alice had fallen out. Before, only their conversations had made the work bearable, the time pass quickly. Now, they worked in stony silence.

Laurel had tried to speak of it once. "I'm sorry about how it worked out," she had said. "It wasn't supposed to happen like that."

But Alice had only glared at her, so that Laurel still wasn't sure if it bothered Alice more that Laurel had slept with Michael, or that Len had walked out on the whole affair, leaving Alice out entirely. Laurel knew that they all blamed her—Len and Alice, probably Michael, too, although she had neither seen nor spoken to him after that weekend.

Laurel leaned her head against the back of the couch and sighed. She reached for the coffee Len had left her, but it was lukewarm now and bitter. She drank it anyway, thirst flaring up in her. It was a vivid thirst: she could almost feel the fluid seeping from her shriveled cells and rushing to the breast where her daughter suckled it away. She wanted not coffee, but water: a huge cool glass of it. She wished there were someone there to bring it to her. And that wish, absurd as she knew it to be, only made her feel lonelier. She wiped fiercely at her eyes, wondering that she had any liquid left in her for tears.

Alice hated her. Her mother had forsaken her. Len, she felt

sure, no longer loved her as he once had. She couldn't bear to think of her Berkeley friends, whom she imagined not with their own husbands and babies, which surely some of them must have by now, but as the single women they had been when she had known them.

She looked up at the clock; only ten minutes had passed since Len had left. The day seemed to stretch before her endlessly. There was still an hour and a half to get through before Sarah came at nine. Then the hours at the lab, with the cover slips fragile as blown sugar between her fingers, and Alice always waiting, she was sure, for her to break one.

At least it would be quiet. At least there were no little hands tugging at her clothes, no cries or whines or whimpers. But, God, it was boring; she couldn't help watching the clock. And then, when her time was up, she always had to hurry home. Sarah needed to leave by one-thirty; she had a class at two, she said.

Inevitably the baby would start crying as soon as Laurel walked in the door.

"She knows you're back," Sarah would say, smiling, as if Laurel might be glad of this. And perhaps she was, in a way. Emma always wanted to nurse as soon as Laurel arrived, even when Sarah insisted she had just been fed. And even though Laurel was always starving by then herself, still it was nice to sink down onto the couch with her baby, to catch Jessie's eye and pat the space beside her. Jessie would climb up next to her and watch, playing with the baby's tiny toes as she nursed, talking and talking in an endless stream of two-word sentences: "Momma home. Baby hungry. Mama milk. Baby toes . . ."

It was only afterwards, when Sarah had gone and the baby was asleep, that Laurel would unravel. She just wanted to eat her lunch in silence. Was that too much to ask? But Jessie never left her alone. She wanted to crawl into Laurel's lap. She wanted a bite of her sandwich. She wanted her *own* sandwich. She wanted juice.

She wanted a book. She wanted. She wanted. She wanted. Until, at last, Laurel would lose her temper.

"*Goddamn* it. I don't care what you want. Just leave me alone for a minute, would you?"

And once she had lost her patience, it was impossible to regain it. Every little thing—a spilled drink or a tripped-over toy—was a new irritant. And as her general annoyance mounted, so did her resentment, so that by the time Len came home in the evening, she was drowning in it.

"How was your day?" he would ask, his voice tired, and even his weariness irritated her. What did he have to be so tired about?

Today, Laurel thought now, summoning her resolve and gently shifting the baby in her arms. *Today will be different.* She wiped her eyes with her free hand, wishing for a tissue. Looking down, she saw that Emma had stopped nursing and lay quietly, watching her. Laurel listened for Jessie but heard nothing.

"Come on, then, Emma," she whispered. "Let's make a picnic. For later. We'll go to the park."

She carried Emma into the kitchen and set the baby gingerly in a bouncy seat on the floor. She backed away slowly, expecting her to protest. But Emma made no sound. Laurel found a napkin and blew her nose, then stood at the sink and drank three glasses of water, not bothering to turn the faucet off between them. Her stomach felt bloated, but almost immediately she felt her energy return and her mind clear. She glanced at Emma, kicking contentedly in the bouncy seat, then got out bread, peanut butter, and jam. She was spreading peanut butter on the second sandwich when she heard Jessie crying from the other room.

"Just a second!" she yelled. Quickly, she plunged the peanut-buttery knife into the jam jar. *If I could just finish one single thing,* she thought.

But the crying continued, louder. She could hear Jessie sobbing her name. "Mama!"

Laurel rested the knife against the half-finished sandwich and started for the bedroom.

She opened the door to find Jessie, still sobbing, in the middle of the room.

"Mama!"

"Jesus, it stinks in here." Laurel said. "What is it? What's wrong? I was trying . . ."

"Dessie wet," Jessie said tearfully, and immediately Laurel saw that it was true. The back of her nightgown clung to her legs.

"Jessie! Where's your diaper?"

Jessie pulled up her sodden nightgown to reveal the diaper beneath. "All wet," she said, sadly.

"Jesus." Laurel looked towards Jessie's bed. The bedding would be wet, too. "This is just great."

Breathing through her mouth, she unpinned Jessie's soaked diaper and pulled the wet nightgown over her head.

"Jessie, you're a big girl now. You have to pee on the potty."

Jessie shook her head. "Dessie yittle."

"No, you're big now."

"No. Dessie yittle!" She grabbed at Laurel's leg, but her mother shook her off."

"Let go of me. You stink."

Laurel began to pull the sheets from the bed. This would mean another trip to the laundry, and just when was she supposed to fit that in? She was bundling up the sheets as best she could, trying to avoid the wet parts, when she heard cries coming from the kitchen.

"Goddammit," she muttered.

She left the wet sheets in a heap on bedroom floor. In the kitchen, Emma was arching her back in the bouncy seat, twisting against the strap that held her in. Her face was red with rage.

"Baby sad," Jessie observed. She had followed Laurel from the bedroom and now stood beside her, naked, looking on.

"You think?" Laurel said. Jessie nodded solemnly.

Laurel reached down to unbuckle the baby, then slid her hands under Emma's armpits to lift her from the seat.

"Baby poop!" Jessie said urgently, just as Laurel brought the infant to her chest.

"Ugh!" For Jessie was right: the small of Emma's back was covered in poop where it had seeped up out of the top of her diaper. At once, Laurel registered the warmth against her arm.

"Jesus." She held Emma away from her body and glanced down at the bouncy seat. There was a small imprint of feces, almost heart shaped, in the seat. She watched Jessie notice it, too.

"Do not touch!" she ordered.

Quickly she got Emma by the underarms again, and holding the baby out in front of her, she retraced her steps to the girls' bedroom and lay her down on the changing table.

"Baby stink?" Jessie asked, and Laurel nodded wryly.

"Yes. The baby stinks, too."

She wiped up Emma as best she could, but clearly a bath was in order, for both of them.

"Come on, Jessie. You and your sister are going to take a bath."

The tub in the master bathroom was not the cleanest. Laurel did her best to rinse it out while holding Emma with one arm.

"Let me just get Emma situated before you get in," she told Jessie. She ran a few inches of warm water, then lowered the infant into it.

"Okay, Jessie. Can you get in now?"

Jessie climbed over the edge of the tub where Laurel pointed. But as soon as her feet were submerged in the warm water, she began to pee, the stream of urine yellowing the water between her legs.

"Jessie! What are you doing? You're *peeing*!"

She snatched the baby out of the water. "You just peed in the bathtub. With your sister right there. Get out. Just get out!"

Jessie started, looked down between her legs, and then stared at Laurel incredulously.

"I said, GET OUT."

At that, the baby started to cry; goose pimples were dimpling her pale skin.

"Now look what you've done," Laurel said.

Laurel drained the bathtub and ran the water again. Jessie sat in it, sniffling, while Laurel bathed the baby.

She left Jessie in the tub while she took Emma back to the bedroom to diaper and dress her. When she had seen to the baby, she lay her down in the crib. Emma started to cry at once.

"How can you be hungry? You just ate."

But the baby only howled at her, red with indignation.

"You're just going to have to wait a minute," Laurel said. She turned away from Emma and went back for Jessie, who, with more room to play now, was swirling the washcloth through the water.

"Okay, Jessie. Time to get out."

"No."

"GET. OUT. OF. THE. TUB."

Without waiting for a response, Laurel reached in, grabbed Jessie under her arms, and lifted her from the bath.

"No!" Jessie screamed.

"Yes," Laurel said through gritted teeth. She carried the toddler back into the nursery, where she diapered and dressed her without speaking. All the while, the baby cried. Laurel felt her milk let down; two damp circles formed on the front of her shirt. Where did it all come from, she wondered. She felt sucked dry, and yet there it was, still surging out of her, as if her infant daughter had more control over her body than she did.

When Jessie was finally dressed, Laurel picked up the baby and collapsed into the rocker. Once she began to nurse, Emma fell asleep almost immediately, although her mouth continued to suck gently in her sleep.

"See," she muttered to the sleeping infant. "You didn't even want it. You just wanted to suck. I'm just a giant pacifier to you."

Jessie giggled uncertainly. "Baby tired," she observed.

Laurel leaned her head against the back of the rocker and closed her eyes.

"Mama tired," she said.

Soon enough, she felt Jessie's small hands against her leg. She kept her eyes closed.

"Mama? Dessie eat?"

When Laurel finally looked at the clock, she was shocked to see that it was barely eight thirty. The morning had seemed to last for hours. She had, at last, risen from the rocker to get Jessie's breakfast. While Jessie ate, she crept into the girls' room and shoved all the laundry—the wet sheets and sodden nightgown, Emma's feces-stained onesie—into a large garbage bag, which she placed on the stoop outside the front door. She had meant, then, to eat something herself, but when she returned to the kitchen, her eyes fell on the soiled bouncy seat. Making a face, she wiped up what she could with paper towels and then spent several frustrating minutes trying to figure out how to remove the cloth cover from the frame.

She had just added that to the bag of dirty laundry on the stoop when she saw Sarah approaching the house.

"Good morning," Sarah called cheerfully.

Laurel grimaced. She felt weak with hunger, close to tears. There was no time to shower. She washed her face quickly, brushed her teeth, ran a brush through her hair.

Getting dressed, she tried to summon the same surge of elation she normally felt: in a moment, she would be free. But then she thought of the monotony of the hours ahead of her, and Alice's hateful eyes, and despair overwhelmed her.

She didn't go into the kitchen to say goodbye to Jessie. If Jessie clung to her or cried, as she sometimes did when Laurel left, she felt she could not bear it.

"Have a good day," Sarah called to her.

Fat chance, Laurel thought, but clenched her teeth against the words. Sarah was always so . . . so . . . *calm*. The children never seemed to rattle her.

"Don't you ever lose your patience?" Laurel had asked her once. Sarah had considered the question, then shrugged.

"Not much, I guess."

This morning, Laurel just couldn't stomach it. She slunk out the door without saying good-bye.

Three blocks away, Laurel was sure she could still smell the rank odor that had been with her all morning. Probably it had fixed itself in her nostrils, she thought. But a minute later, she glanced down at herself doubtfully. And there, on her arm, just above the elbow, was the telltale brown smudge.

"Goddammit." Her purse lay on the passenger seat, and with her free hand she dug around in it blindly. She found only a used tissue. At the red light, she spit on it and scrubbed, her eyes filling with tears.

CHAPTER 7

Laurel

They didn't go on the picnic that afternoon. Laurel returned home at one-thirty to find Jessie at the kitchen table, eating the peanut butter sandwich Laurel had left, unfinished, on the counter that morning. Sarah sat beside her, giving Emma a bottle. Laurel felt a surge of irritation. Maybe Sarah was like Mary Poppins, practically perfect in every way, never losing her patience or raising her voice. But nursing was Laurel's job. It was the one thing she felt she couldn't mess up, the one time she was free of the nagging sense that motherhood was a role she just wasn't cut out for.

Sarah looked up apologetically. "She wouldn't settle," she said. "And I couldn't stand to hear her cry. But she just started. Do you want to . . . ?"

Laurel shook her head with a sigh. "It's fine. Where's the other sandwich?" Her words sounded barbed, even to herself, and Sarah looked up quickly.

"In the fridge. I wrapped it up."

"We were going to take a picnic."

"Oh! I didn't know. I saw the sandwiches, but—"

"No, I didn't say anything. I . . . The morning was too crazy."

"Picnic?" Jessie said.

Laurel sank heavily into a kitchen chair. "Not today. I'm too tired."

"Park?"

"No."

Jessie's face fell; Laurel could see her daughter's color rising.

"See? She's gearing up for a fit. The minute I get home . . ."

Sarah looked at them both sympathetically. "It's okay, Dessie. I can take you to the park tomorrow when I come. Okay?"

She said it to be conciliatory, Laurel thought, to head off her daughter's tantrum, and surely more for Laurel's sake than for her own. But oh, how it grated on her. Sarah always got to be the nice one, taking them to the park or the library, fixing Jessie's lunch, while she . . . She just got nagged at and shat on.

"You called her 'Dessie,'" Laurel observed coolly.

Sarah laughed. "Oh, well. That's what she calls herself. I guess I picked it up. But I don't have to if . . ." She paused, uncertain.

"It's fine. Her dad calls her that, too."

Sarah smiled. "Yeah? Well, it's cute."

As soon as Sarah left, Laurel regretted having let the bottle-feeding go. Her breasts were painfully full, like two aching rocks beneath her shirt. Emma slept on and on where Sarah had left her in the bassinet. Laurel put Jessie down for a nap in her bedroom, then steeled herself against her screams.

"No nap! No Dessie seep!"

Laurel stretched out on the couch in the living room and picked up a book, but it was impossible to concentrate.

Just stop, she willed her daughter. *Just be quiet.*

And then, suddenly, she was. Laurel sighed, closing her eyes in relief. The kitchen table needed clearing, she thought. And surely it would be okay if she took the laundry down, quickly, while the girls were asleep? But she couldn't muster the energy to do any of it. She lay there with the book on her stomach, her breasts aching, breathing deeply as if her lungs craved, not oxygen, but silence.

Jessie woke first, banging at the nursery door. "Mama!"

Laurel, waking suddenly, felt disoriented and groggy. She hadn't meant to fall asleep. She swung her legs off the couch, sitting up. The sudden pull of gravity on her breasts made her cry out. Gingerly, she probed them with the tips of her fingers. They felt as hard as kneecaps, the skin stretched taut.

Jessie, as always, was tearful after her nap. She wouldn't play by herself, but clung to Laurel's leg, whining.

Laurel tried to read to her, but after one book she couldn't stand the pressure in her breasts. Every time Jessie tried to cuddle up to her, pain shot through her chest. Desperate, she woke up Emma, who looked around with startled eyes. When Laurel brought the baby to her breast, the pent-up milk shot out at her. Her breast was so swollen that Emma struggled to latch on. But at last she managed, and soon the pressure began to ease. Laurel's other breast was leaking freely now, soaking her shirt. After a few minutes, Laurel slid her finger into Emma's mouth, breaking her hold on her nipple. The baby protested with an angry little cry. Quickly, Laurel shifted her to the other side.

Afterwards, there were the diapers to change, and the kitchen to clean up. Laurel watched the clock, the minutes creeping forward. *We should have gone to the park*, Laurel thought, chiding herself.

At last it was four o'clock. With a sigh of relief, Laurel turned on the television.

"Grover!" Jessie said gleefully, plopping herself down on the rug. Laurel sang along with the theme song, suddenly cheerful. She would have an hour now without Jessie asking her for one single thing.

But within minutes Emma began to fuss. Laurel looked around for the bouncy seat in which to put the baby, then remembered how she had dismantled it that morning. She tried to lay Emma down on a dish towel on the floor, but Emma howled as if she were being tortured.

"Oh, come on," Laurel said, exasperated. At last she fetched the sling from the closet, fastened it around her neck, and positioned the baby inside. She opened the refrigerator awkwardly, standing sideways so that the door would not hit Emma in the sling, then stood staring at the nearly empty shelves inside. Laurel let out a groan; she suddenly remembered that she had promised she would go to the store today.

But how could she, now? To tear Jessie away from *Sesame Street* would mean another tantrum, another fight. Laurel didn't have the heart for it. She found half a box of spaghetti in the cabinet. There was no sauce, but they had butter, didn't they? In the bottom of the freezer was a bag of frozen peas, icy with freezer burn. When she was pregnant, Len had insisted that each meal have a protein, but now, it hardly mattered. *He can fry himself an egg if he wants protein*, Laurel thought. She was sick to death of eggs.

Inside the sling, Emma wriggled and whimpered unhappily. *Just one more minute*, Laurel told her silently. She glanced at the clock, then filled a glass with ice and unstoppered the vodka. There was only half an inch of tonic in the bottom of the bottle; she emptied it into her drink.

Emma was red-faced and sweaty when Laurel pulled her out of the sling at last and settled her at her breast. As the baby latched onto her sore nipple, Laurel raised the glass to her lips.

"What's all this?" Len said when he opened the door. He held the bag of dirty laundry in his hand. Laurel had forgotten it on the stoop.

"Hello to you, too," she said dryly. Then, "Jessie wet the bed. And Emma pooped all up her back and all over the bouncy seat. And me."

Len smiled.

"It wasn't funny."

Laurel saw Len look to the kitchen counter and followed his gaze. There was the empty canister of frozen orange juice, its ruffled white band lying beside it in a puddle of melted concentrate.

"I made juice," Laurel said. "There's no milk."

Len glanced at Laurel's glass, then at the empty tonic water bottle peeking its incriminating head out of the garbage.

"No tonic, you mean." He took the sponge from the sink and began to scrub at the mess.

"I was going to clean it up. But I had to put Emma down for a nap. She wouldn't settle."

Len said nothing.

"I didn't make it to the store. But there's some spaghetti—"

"We'll need milk for the morning."

"We can drink juice."

"On cereal? I'll go to the store after dinner."

"And leave me with these kids again? No, *I'll* go. I was going to. I was just waiting for you to get home."

Len looked again at Laurel's glass. He put the sponge down deliberately. "You shouldn't be driving."

Laurel scoffed. "I'm fine. I've just had two." But in truth she felt giddy-headed, and when she stood up her chair scraped the floor a little too loudly.

"You've got to stop this, Laurel. You're drinking too much."

Laurel laughed shrilly. "Oh, that's just fine for you to say. Do you know the kind of day I've had? You sashay in the door with your recriminations—"

"What recriminations? I didn't say any—"

"What's this laundry? The kitchen's a mess. You didn't go to the grocery store. You're drinking too much." Laurel's voice was sour with mimicry. "You have no idea what it's like. All day I've been pooped and peed on, fussed at, whined at . . . And then you get on my case about having a drink or two? You have no idea—"

"Mama!" Jessie called from the living room. "Grover bye-bye?"

Laurel glanced at the clock. Oh, God, was it over already? She felt her chin begin to quiver and looked quickly away; she knew how Len hated it when she cried. But the tears came anyway, and what a relief they were. She gave herself over to them, sinking heavily into the chair and lowering her face into her arms.

She heard Len's steps on the orange linoleum, felt him standing over her, silent. At last, she felt his hand on her back, the gentle pressure of his palm and each long finger. She felt the weight of his hand pushing down on her heavily, as if to ground her. She shifted on the table and let out a deep breath, half sob, half sigh. And then she didn't move, but concentrated on the imprint of his hand on her back, as if her neurons could push their way out of her skin and wrap their frilled tendrils around each finger like a plant clinging to its trellis.

But in another moment Len took his hand away, and Laurel felt the warmth of it dissipate almost at once, leaving a hand-shaped imprint of chill against her skin.

"I'm going to take the girls to the store. Give you a chance to pull yourself together. Will Emma be okay? Has she nursed at all recently?"

Laurel, not raising her head from her arms, nodded slightly.

Laurel heard him shut the kitchen door behind him. She heard him speaking with Jessie in the next room, heard their voices fade as they went to the nursery to get Emma. Laurel listened to her faint cries as Len changed her diaper. In a minute their voices were back in the living room. Laurel could make out the sound of Jessie's two-word chirp and the deep tones of Len's answer. The front door creaked open and then closed, the latch clicking into place. And then—silence.

Laurel knew she should luxuriate in it. That was what Len had intended, wasn't it? These were his tiny, measured gifts to her. First, the momentary pressure of his hand. Then, this. Forty-five minutes, an hour perhaps, of silence. Of solitude. But this silence didn't feel luxurious. It felt sad, recriminatory. She remembered the heavy click of the door, and how abruptly it had cut off their voices. It was like they had abandoned her. And the thought—even though she knew how melodramatic it sounded, knew, ultimately, how untrue it was—made her begin to cry again. Oh, she would never be a part of their cheerful little crew. She was . . . She was just different.

With a sob she rose from the table. She saw that Len had returned the vodka to its place on top of the kitchen cabinets, out of Jessie's reach. Laurel climbed up on the counter and got it down, then mixed in some of the watery orange juice. She took a deep sip, not tasting the alcohol now but feeling it seeping through her. She felt her heart lift a little, her cells hum.

She drank again, then, with an effort, made herself put the glass down on the counter. She had to do something, she thought. She couldn't let them come home and find her just as Len had left her, glass in hand.

She went into the living room and looked around for the garbage bag of soiled laundry. She could run it down to the laundry now; it would be easy, without the kids. But she didn't see it there, nor was it on the stoop.

Len must have taken it with him, she realized, her heart sinking. Of course he would take it. He always had to prove just how easy it was.

She went back to the kitchen to get her drink, and then began to tidy up the living room, tossing toys into the plastic bin they kept at the end of the couch. When that was done, she returned to the kitchen. They'd still need to eat, wouldn't they? She put two pans of water on the stove, one for the peas, a larger one for spaghetti. The table was damp where she had been crying. She wiped it down and set out the butter, the green canister of Parmesan, and two forks. When would they be home? Was it too early to turn on the water? She felt that time was crawling again; it was impossible to judge how long they had been gone.

Restless, she went into the girls' bedroom. The rubber sheet on Jessie's mattress glistened in the overhead light. She fetched sheets and made the bed, then arranged Jessie's stuffed animals on top of it, imagining her daughter's delight to find them all sitting together like that, as if for a party. The bed looked cozy, and suddenly Laurel's weariness returned. She set her empty glass on the bookshelf and stretched out on her daughter's bed.

She woke to their voices in the kitchen. She went in and found Jessie on her booster seat, her face covered in spaghetti sauce.

"Mama!" she said, and Laurel felt her heart give a lurch.

Len looked up from his plate.

"Want some spaghetti?"

"I was going to make it . . ." Laurel began. "Where's the baby?"

Len nodded to the floor. "Right there."

He had spread out a blanket in the corner, and Emma lay on top of it, kicking and content.

Laurel hesitated, feeling superfluous, like she had interrupted them somehow. How happy they all seemed.

"Come on," Len said good-naturedly, pulling back a chair with one hand. "Sit down. I'll get you a plate. We were just missing you."

But afterwards, once the girls were both asleep, his mood sobered. He came into the bedroom where Laurel lay stretched out on the quilt, reading. She lowered the book.

"Thanks for shopping tonight."

He nodded, then sat down next to her. She felt the mattress tip beneath his weight. She moved her legs so he would have more room.

"What is it?"

"Laurel, I can't go on like this."

Her heart missed a beat. "What do you mean?"

"I mean, I can't keep coming home and finding you like this."

"Like what?" she said, indignant. "I told you, it was a rough day."

"But it's not just today. It's practically every day. Either you're half-drunk or you're in tears. Or both. I think—" Len hesitated.

"What? Go ahead. Say it."

"I think you're depressed."

Laurel let out a little snort of laughter. "Really?"

"Yes. You just mope around all the time."

"It's not moping! I just feel so . . . so . . . *overwhelmed* all the time. You don't understand what it's like."

"So you tell me. So, why don't you . . . Why don't we find someone? Someone you could talk to?"

"You mean like a shrink?" She let out another dry laugh. "I don't need a shrink."

"Someone, then. Don't you have any friends you could talk to?"

Laurel thought of Alice then, how they used to talk and talk, the hours in the lab skipping by. Len was right. It *had* made a difference.

"Len, it's not a math problem. You can't just solve it."

She saw his expression shift, saw the concern change into something else, something harder.

"Well, you have to do something. If not for yourself, for the family. It's intolerable."

Laurel wanted to cry again then, at the coolness of his tone, the hardness in him. She tried to summon the tears, so he would know how cruel he was being, but for once they wouldn't come. She said nothing, staring at the wall.

"Look," he said, at last. "Isn't there anyone you could talk to? Maybe have some fun with?"

At that, Laurel snorted. "You think I have time for fun?"

"We could make time."

"When? You're gone all day."

"There's the weekend. I'll take care of the girls. What about—" Here, Len hesitated, and Laurel knew he was thinking of Alice, too. "What about your cousin? What's her name again? She doesn't live far, does she?"

Laurel sighed. "Rosie?"

"Yeah, Rosie." He said her name with just the slightest note of triumph.

Laurel rolled her eyes. "We have nothing in common."

"She has kids."

"Yes. But they're older."

"So? Surely, she'd be happy to—"

"What?" Laurel interrupted. "Just call her out of the blue?" She raised her fingers to her ear, a mock phone. "'Hi Rosie. This is Laurel. My husband thinks I'm depressed, that I need to talk to someone, have some fun. And since I don't have any friends, I thought I'd just call—'"

"Laurel," Len said sternly. "I'm telling you, it's a problem. I'm just trying to find a solution."

She sighed. "But how could I—?"

"Just call her. She's your cousin." He stood up from the bed so suddenly the mattress bounced beneath her.

"Where are you going?" she called after him.

"To get your address book."

"But it's late."

"It's eight-thirty."

When he returned, he had her worn address book in hand, already opened to the page with Rosie's number. He carried the phone in the other hand, his long fingers holding the receiver in place, the phone cord trailing behind him, as if marking his way out of a labyrinth.

"Here," he said, handing Laurel the mouthpiece but keeping the base of the phone on his lap. He dialed the number quickly, leaving his index finger in each hole as it unwound, hurrying it along. She didn't protest. She listened to the distant ring, heard the clatter of the receiver as someone fumbled it. And then Rosie answered.

"Hi, Rosie. This is your cousin, Laurel," she said. Len grinned at her. She rolled her eyes at him and shooed him away with her hand.

CHAPTER 8

Laurel

Later, but before everything fell apart, Laurel thought she had Len to thank for that call, and thus for everything that followed it. Rosie had been surprised to hear from her, of course, but she had masked it well, for which Laurel had felt a surge of gratitude. But when, as the conversation wound down, Laurel had to say— had to, she felt, because otherwise Len would not let her be—that it would be great to get together soon, to really catch up, Rosie sounded doubtful.

"I don't have much free time," she said. "With the kids and all."

"Oh, I know," Laurel began, feeling the first wisps of relief. She could already imagine her report to Len. Yes, she had suggested something, but Rosie just didn't have the time.

"Unless—"

Laurel sighed. "Unless what?"

"Well, unless you'd like to come with us on Saturday. With Ryan and me, I mean. Ryan's a senior this year and he needs all those hours, you know? So on Saturdays he volunteers at the food bank in Eureka. And I have to drive him over there anyway, so I just decided, well, why not help out, too, you know? I mean, I'm there already."

Laurel's head spun. Every sentence out of Rosie's mouth was like a question Laurel was supposed to know the answer to. *No, I don't know,* she wanted to scream. But she took a deep breath and steadied herself.

"I'm sorry. What do you do there?"

"Oh, different things. Sort food, mostly. You know, for people who need it."

"But . . . why?"

"Well, because they're poor, I guess."

"No, I mean—"

"Oh! You mean, why is he volunteering there? It's not just him. There's a bunch of teenagers, actually. They all need hours to graduate."

"Hours?"

"You know, community service hours."

"Oh."

"So, what I was saying was that you could come along if you wanted. The work's pretty easy, you know. And we could work next to each other and, well, catch up. Like you said."

Laurel sighed again. Just what she needed—more mindless work. *But it would appease Len,* she thought. She smiled grimly, imagining telling him that she was going to volunteer at a food bank. That was just the sort of thing he would love.

"Yeah, okay," she said to Rosie. "I'll go. I mean, I'd love to."

They had almost been late that first Saturday. Rosie had gushed too long over the girls when she'd picked Laurel up, and she kept at it once they were finally on their way.

"Oh, that little baby smell," Rosie said, backing her car carefully out of Laurel's driveway. "Don't you just *love* that smell?" She caught her son's eye in the rearview mirror. "Ryan, honey, aren't your second cousins just adorable?"

From the backseat, Rosie's son made a vague, guttural noise that might have been assent, and Rosie rolled her eyes at Laurel cheerfully.

"See what you're in for? Oh, but the stage you're at now. Jessie's three, isn't she? That's such a fun age, don't you think? When their little personalities really start to show?"

What was there to say to any of this? Rosie had clearly forgotten there might be anything less than delightful about breastfeeding and diapers. Laurel nodded vaguely and slumped in her seat, annoyed by the disappointment that swept over her, for she had actually found herself looking forward to this morning. She had even thought grudgingly that maybe Len was right. Maybe it *would* feel good to talk to someone who had been through it all before. But now she saw how it would be: sunny, chipper Rosie finding the best in everything. Laurel gazed out of the window as they drove, only half-listening as Rosie prattled on.

It was a relief when they arrived at the food bank. As soon as they were inside, Ryan disappeared into a gaggle of teenagers. Laurel looked around uncertainly. About two dozen people were standing in the lobby of a large warehouse, all clustered in little groups of three and four. Before Laurel could even begin to get her bearings, she felt Rosie take her arm.

"Ryan has made it very clear that I'm not to have anything to do with him and his friends," she said, smiling broadly as if to say that she took no offense. She steered Laurel past all the people and across the warehouse to where several long tables had been set up in rows.

"So I take the farthest table I can."

Rosie and Laurel stood side by side at the table with a half a dozen other volunteers, sorting food into what the volunteer coordinator had called "weekend packs." Into each bag went six items: a box of spaghetti, a can of sauce, a fruit cup, an envelope of powdered milk, and two snacks. The work was mindless, but easy, and the boxes of donated food on the tables emptied quickly as they filled the packs. When that happened, one of the volunteers was supposed to replace the empty box with a new one from a nearby pallet.

Laurel liked to do this; it seemed to her slightly less tedious than the endless filling of the packs. So when the fruit cups began to run low, she dumped the remaining ones onto the table, set the empty box on the floor, and went to get a full one, only to find that the pallet was empty, too.

Picking up the empty box, she walked over to the dumpster, where a man with thick, tattooed forearms was breaking down the empty boxes and tossing them into a large, gray dumpster. From the authoritative way he wielded the box cutter, and the fact that she had seen him roll the dumpster away to empty it, Laurel assumed that he was an employee of the food bank.

"Do you know where there's any more fruit?" she asked, holding out the empty box.

He took it from her and in one deft motion sliced the tape along the bottom.

"What?"

"We're almost out of fruit cups, and the pallet's empty," she explained, gesturing. "Where can we get more?"

He chuckled slightly. "Sorry, but I'm just the guy who breaks down the boxes. Ask . . ." He looked around, then gestured with an incline of his head toward a small office at one side of the warehouse. "Ask in there."

"Oh! You're not—"

He grinned at her. "No. Just a volunteer like you. More or less."

"Oh," she said again, coloring a little at her mistake. "Well, thanks anyway."

She was heading for the office he had pointed out when she noticed a forklift lowering a new pallet of fruit. The tattooed man got there before her and sliced through the plastic wrap that held the boxes in place. Then he bent to lift one off for her.

"Where do you want this, then, darling?" he asked, and, blushing again, she pointed to their table, where the volunteers stood idly, half-full plastic bags in hand, waiting for the fruit cups.

As he slid the new box onto the table and cut it open, Laurel took her place beside Rosie. Her cousin glanced at her.

"What'd he say?" Rosie asked. "I saw you talking."

"That he doesn't work here," Laurel said. "But they got us more fruit." She lifted her chin in the direction of the restocked pallet.

"Doesn't work here?" Rosie said, surprised. "He's here all the time."

Laurel reached for a box of spaghetti and shrugged.

"Maybe he just happens to be here when you're here."

"Wonder why he *is* here," Rosie said.

"What do you mean?"

"DUI, probably. That's what it usually is."

Laurel looked up. "How do you know?"

"Oh, I hear them talking. At the break. How many hours they have to do and all that."

A volunteer like you. More or less.

"So all these people," she said, "they're not all actually volunteers?"

"Oh, no. A lot of them are working off community service hours. They're not always the most savory people. That's why I don't like to just drop Ryan off, you know?"

At the break, the volunteers crowded into a small room at the back of the warehouse. There was mediocre coffee and a cardboard box full of the same kinds of snacks they had just been sorting into the weekend packs.

Laurel got coffee and a bag of mini muffins and sank gratefully into a chair beside Rosie, but in another minute her cousin was back on her feet.

"Better go to the ladies' room," she said. "Want to come?"

Laurel shook her head, glad for the reprieve from Rosie's chatter. She leaned back in her chair and sipped her lukewarm coffee, letting her eyes wander over the other volunteers. When her gaze fell on the box man, she paused, wondering about him. Then he turned and his eyes met hers. She looked away at once, but not before she thought she saw him wink. Or had he? She finished her coffee and mini muffins self-consciously, sensing that now *she* was being watched. She could feel his eyes on her, and she felt herself grow warm under his imagined gaze. She didn't look back, although she wanted to, because she felt that she could not bear it if she were wrong. It was too good a feeling, being watched like that. She didn't want to ruin it.

Now, Laurel worked harder to be the one to take the boxes to the dumpster, sometimes emptying them onto the table when they were still partially full. No one seemed to mind; it kept the table stocked, so the work went smoothly and the boxes of weekend packs grew.

Each time she handed the man an empty box, he grinned at her, and she could feel a familiar heat go through her, so that by the time she returned to her table, she felt her body glowing. She never looked back, but she imagined his eyes were on her as she walked away, and she swung her hips a little, just in case.

The hour after the break passed quickly, and Laurel was surprised when the volunteer coordinator emerged from the little office and told them to wrap things up. She looked down the table and saw that one of the other volunteers was emptying their few remaining snacks into the box at the adjacent table.

"Here!" Laurel said quickly, reaching for the empty box. "I'll take that for you."

She brought the box over to the dumpster and smiled when the man took it from her hands.

"I'm Kent," he said, grinning back at her. "Haven't seen you here before."

"Laurel. This is my first time."

"Got hours?"

She let out a little nervous laugh. "No. Um, I came with my cousin."

"Oh, I see. The goodness of your heart and all that." He chuckled dryly.

Laurel shrugged. "I guess."

"All right then. Well, maybe I'll see you again."

He tossed the flattened cardboard into the dumpster and held out his hand for her to shake. When she took it, she could feel the ridged calluses on his palm and fingers.

"Maybe," she said.

He held her hand just a moment too long, but long enough that she felt, again, that flush of heat go through her. When he let it go at last, he ran his index finger along her palm, so that she took in her breath a little too quickly and looked up at him in surprise. He grinned at her.

"I hope so."

It was just a harmless flirtation, she told herself. And it felt so good! She had almost forgotten what it was like to be flirted with, to be seen. She was glowing and almost gleeful for the rest of the day, so that even Len noticed.

"See," he gloated. "I told you it would do you good to get out. Are you going to go back?"

Yes. She called Rosie on Tuesday and asked if she could join her again. The next Saturday was the same as the first, except that each time she handed over the empty boxes, Kent's large hands would brush against hers. He took to getting the new boxes for her, too, and when he slid them onto their table, he stood so close that she could feel the heat of him through her clothes.

She started wearing lipstick and low-cut shirts that she covered with little jackets when she left the house on Saturdays. She always stood on the side of the table where she could watch him as he worked. Kent was a big man, broad-shouldered and powerful, and the veins under his tattoos bulged when he lifted the heavy boxes. When he touched her, it was so obviously on purpose that Laurel's mouth went dry and desire leaked out of her.

She was doing nothing wrong, she told herself. It was all so harmless, a junior high flirtation, propelled along by stolen glances and the accidental-on purpose brush of hands.

And then, one day a month later, Rosie told her that Ryan had completed his hours.

"I think I'm going to take a break for a while myself," she apologized. "Not that I don't think it's worthwhile or anything. I'm sure I'll be back soon enough, since Debbie'll be in high school next year, too."

For one heart-stopping moment, Laurel thought that it was over. No longer would she have those hours that sustained her, those few precious hours of the week when she actually felt alive. But then relief swept over her; *she* didn't have to stop.

When she told Len, he nodded heartily. "That's a great idea. It certainly does you good."

And so that Saturday she drove herself to Eureka and found her place at the usual table.

Kent noticed immediately.

"Where's your cuz?" he asked the first time she brought him an empty box. He held his hand over hers, so that she couldn't let go.

"Her son finished his hours."

Kent gazed down at her for a long moment.

"So you're on your own, then?" he said at last.

She gulped for air. "Yes."

At the break, Laurel was waiting in line for coffee when she felt his hand on her back.

"Come with me," he said, his voice low. "I want to show you something."

She followed him out of the break room and across the empty warehouse, then through a door and down a narrow hallway.

"Where are we going?" she asked. She felt a prickle of anxiety. *Less than savory*, Rosie had said.

"Shh," he said. "You'll see."

They had reached a narrow staircase, and he didn't glance back as he started to descend. She bristled a little at this, that he was so confident that she would follow him, but her feet did not hesitate on the stairs.

There was another small hallway at the bottom. Kent paused in front of the second door, his large hand on the door knob. He looked at Laurel at last.

"Do you want to go in here?"

Laurel's heart was beating fast. "Why? What's in there?"

"Not much. Brooms and mops, mostly."

He looked at her significantly. "And us, if you want."

Laurel felt the blood rush to her face. It suddenly seemed impossible that it wouldn't have come to this, eventually. All those stolen touches and laden glances: they were all leading here. And if she refused, that would be the end of it, and she would be a blue-baller and a tease.

Her mouth was so dry she couldn't speak.

"Well?"

She nodded, and Kent grinned and eased the door open.

Afterwards, she followed him quietly up the stairs. When they got back to the warehouse, the break was already ending, and it was easy to weave her way through all the workers, back to her spot at the table, without anyone noticing her. At the end of the shift, Kent winked at her.

"See you next week?"

The next Saturday, she pretended to go outside during the break, then slipped back in and down the hallway while the other volunteers milled around the coffee and snacks. She was wet by the time she reached the bottom of the stairs. Kent was waiting for her in the broom closet. He opened the door for her without a word.

CHAPTER 9

Laurel

It went on for months. The hour and a half she spent sorting food before the break was an eternity. Twice the volunteer at the end of the table who tied off the packs reprimanded her for forgetting the can of sauce or the powdered milk. Laurel rarely caught Kent looking at her now—"I've got to keep up appearances, darling," he had told her—but she knew that when it was time for the break, he would be waiting for her downstairs, fumbling with her skirt as soon as she stepped inside. She stopped wearing underwear on Saturdays.

Somehow, she got through the days between. She nursed the baby and changed her diapers. She read Jessie books without focusing on the words, so that when her daughter asked her questions—"Why Mommy?" or "Who's that?"—she had to struggle to understand. She found that her affair didn't distance her from Len. It had awakened her. She lay sleepless until he had finished in his office and come to bed, her secret humming inside her, leaving her quivering with a desire that could not wait until Saturday.

At six months, they started Emma on solid foods. Her poops changed from innocuous yellow smears to lumpy, awful things. The nursery reeked. Laurel held her breath when she entered, but couldn't be bothered to take out the diaper pail. Sarah would do it when she came. At the lab, the hours passed more quickly. Laurel often caught herself smiling as her mind wandered; she hardly noticed Alice now.

It was Halloween, and then Thanksgiving. She wasted weeks

dreading the Christmas season, sure that the food bank would close, only to learn that the charity stepped up their efforts at Christmas-time. She told Len she wanted to volunteer on Wednesday evenings for a while, too, to help with the holiday food drive.

"Do you want us to come with you one time?" he asked gamely. "It's so great what you're doing, Laurel. It would be good for Jessie to see, to know that not everyone is as fort—"

"No!" she said, her heart in her throat. "Jessie's too young to understand. And . . . they don't allow children."

She turned away from Len's hurt look. "It's because of liability," she mumbled. "Too much equipment and heavy boxes."

On Christmas morning, Len gave her a framed picture of their daughters. She gave him a sweater. Together, they watched Jessie play with her new toys. In her head, Laurel counted the days until Saturday.

Then, in the middle of January, Kent surprised her by approaching her at her table before the shift had even begun.

"I need to talk," he said.

She shrugged. "Okay."

"Okay," he said. "Later."

She nodded, but she was surprised. They never did talk, or hardly. Their whole affair consisted of quickies in the dark closet, of moans and gasps and hurried caresses.

It was no different that day, except that, afterwards, instead of opening the door for her as usual, Kent reached for the chain of the light bulb that hung overhead.

"I won't be around for a couple of months," he said.

"Oh no? Why?" Laurel tried to sound nonchalant, unbothered, but her stomach clenched.

"I'm going out of town."

"On vacation?" she asked, picturing him with just whom, exactly? He didn't wear a ring, but there might be someone. She had never asked.

"Business."

Already, it was their longest conversation. She cleared her throat, adjusted her skirt.

"What do you do?" She felt a stirring of . . . was it relief? Maybe she could stop it all now, no harm done.

"Roofing, mostly. There's a job up in Oregon I couldn't turn down."

She nodded. "Well, I'll see you, I guess. You'll be back?"

He nodded, then surprised her by taking her hand. "I've never asked, but . . . Could I . . . Would it be okay if I called you?"

She took a step back, and her shoulder blades touched the wall behind her. Kent caught a broom as it fell. He grinned at her.

"Shhh."

She said nothing for a minute, and perhaps he sensed the hesitancy in her.

"Well?" he said, just as he had that first time, before it had all started. He settled the broom against the wall, then took her hand again and ran his index finger lightly over her palm. It had been months since he had done that; they were so far beyond that now. But it had its effect.

"Can't I just call you?" she asked.

"You could, but I don't know the number. Not sure where I'll be staying yet."

She nodded reluctantly. "Okay. You can call."

Quickly, he produced a pen and a little scrap of paper from his shirt pocket. He'd been planning this, she realized, feeling both flattered and predictable.

She put the paper up against the wall and scribbled her number. But when he held out his hand for it, she held it out of his reach.

"But only on weekdays," she said. "And only in the afternoons. And never after five."

He kissed her deeply then, switching off the light. "Got it."

The weeks dragged on. Emma was ten months old now, already

pulling herself up to stand at the coffee table, where she would bounce on her chubby knees, beaming with pride.

"Momma, look! Look what Emma can do!" Jessie would say. And when the baby dropped back to all fours to cruise around, Jessie would drop down, too.

"Look, Momma! Two babies!"

At times like those, Laurel's heart felt so full of love for them that her throat clenched with guilt. Why weren't they enough for her? They *could* be enough, surely. Couldn't they? She would resolve to tell Kent when he called: it was over.

But those moments did not last, nor did the memory of them sustain her. By the middle of the afternoon, when Jessie had begun to whine and Emma had made one mess after another, pulling dirt by the handfuls out of their one houseplant or dumping all of Jessie's tinker toys onto the floor, Laurel knew. She would not give Kent up. While she fished Jessie's favorite stuffed animal out of the toilet or pushed the books back onto the bookshelf, she was listening for his call.

The call, when it finally came, was not so very different from their encounters in the broom closet.

"What are you wearing?" he would ask, and even if she was in a stained T-shirt and her worst underwear, she would make up something sexy. She had never had phone sex before. It was thrilling, to stand at the kitchen sink with the phone clenched under her ear and her hand pushed between her legs, while Bert and Ernie argued on the television set in the living room.

Sometimes, though, Laurel would feel so buried with the frustrations of her day that she would try to describe them to him first, just to blow off steam. He would listen to her rave, but the things he said afterwards—"Sounds like hell" or "Jesus, I couldn't stand it"—only made it worse. Surely, he meant to sound compassionate, she thought. But she didn't feel comforted; she felt even more alone, as if she were the sole inhabitant of some horrible planet on which he wouldn't dream of setting foot.

And then, one Tuesday morning, after Len had left for work but before Sarah came, the phone rang, and it was him.

"I know you told me only to call in the afternoons," he said, no hello or anything. "But I'm back."

Her heart flip-flopped in her chest. She began to count on her fingers. "Wednesday, Thursday, Friday, Saturday. Jesus, four days."

"I don't want to wait that long," he said. "What are you wearing?"

"I can't right now, Kent. The sitter's coming."

He laughed. "Not now. But later? And not the phone again."

She giggled nervously. "What do you mean? A motel or something? I wouldn't know what to tell Len . . ."

"What about—" he hesitated. "Could I come there?"

"But the girls."

"Couldn't the sitter take them out for a while?"

"She only comes in the morning, when I go to work. She has classes in the afternoon."

"Oh." There was a pause. When he spoke again, his voice had changed, hardened. "Well, I'll see you, I guess."

Laurel caught his tone and felt rebuffed. An inexplicable panic rose in her. How could she stand it all, without him? But—it was absurd, wasn't it, to let him come here? Unless . . .

"Wait, Kent. Maybe . . . Maybe it could work. The girls nap. We'd have to be quick."

"Well, we're good at quick, aren't we?" Kent said, the warmth back in his voice.

CHAPTER 10

Sarah

When Sarah pulled into the Walters' driveway behind Laurel's hatchback, Jessie was sitting on the stoop with an elderly woman in floral print, a mason jar of daffodils between them. The little girl ran to Sarah, throwing her arms around Sarah's legs.

"Well, *you're* clearly not a stranger," the woman said, rising.

"Did you find her mom?" Sarah asked, patting Jessie on the head.

Fifteen minutes ago, Sarah's phone had rung as she sat at her kitchen table, studying for a statistics test she had the next day. The woman on the line had said she'd seen a little girl on her own, dangerously close to the road, picking daffodils at the curb. She had rung the doorbell at Jessie's house, but no one had answered.

"But how did you get *my* number?" Sarah had asked, confused.

Apparently, Jessie had said her mother might be in the kitchen. The woman had followed the little girl inside, but they hadn't found Laurel. Instead, the woman had seen Sarah's number taped to the wall by the kitchen phone.

"Thank you so much for coming," she said now, wringing her hands as she stepped off the stoop. "I'm very sorry to have bothered you, but I didn't know what else to do."

"Did you check the bedroom?" Sarah asked. "That's her car, so she must be here somewhere."

"Oh, no," the woman said. "I didn't want to intrude. Like I said, I saw your number. You don't mind taking over from here, do you? I mean, I would stay, but . . ."

"Of course not. I'm sure everything's fine."

The woman patted Jessie on the head once, and then hurried to her car. Sarah turned to Jessie.

"Where's your mom, Dessie?" she asked, as cheerfully as she could.

Jessie shrugged and pointed to the daffodils.

"Flowers for Mommy!" She hoisted up her skirt and tugged at the diaper underneath. "Sarah take it off?"

"Jessie, were you supposed to be sleeping?" Sarah asked. She had thought Jessie was done with diapers now, but maybe Laurel still used them at naptime.

Jessie nodded solemnly. "I waked up."

Sarah knelt and unpinned the diaper, while Jessie watched her carefully.

"No pee," she said.

"You're right. Good job. Do you need to use the potty?"

Jessie shook her head.

"Well, you can't run around with no underwear on, so let's go get you some." She stood up and took Jessie's hand. "Where's Emma?" she said suddenly.

"Sleeping. Shhh!" Jessie put her finger to her lips.

Hand in hand, they went through the front door, then tiptoed down the hallway to the girls' bedroom. Inside, Emma was awake, standing up in her crib. When she saw Sarah, she began to bounce happily. Quickly, Sarah found Jessie some underwear in the chest of drawers and helped her put them on. Then she picked up the baby.

"Now, let's go find your mom."

Sarah had just stepped out into the hallway, Emma on her hip, when the door to Laurel's bedroom opened.

"See," she was about to say, "she was just napping." But then the door swung all the way open and a man appeared, naked except for his boxers.

For a split second, Sarah thought it might be Dr. Walters; she had not seen the girls' father for some time, and her memory of him was hazy. But then she registered the look of shock on his face, and the way Jessie had suddenly moved behind her legs, as she did whenever they met strangers. Her stomach plunged and she took a step backwards, almost knocking Jessie down.

Who intrudes in his underwear? He was smiling at her now, his teeth yellow and uneven between chapped lips. She collected herself immediately.

"If you're looking for Laurel, she's in there," he said, gesturing with his head. "She's asleep."

Sarah could feel him looking her over. She moved the baby against her chest, to shield herself.

"Well," she said coolly. "I think she needs to wake up now. Jessie was out on the street."

The man glanced down at Jessie, but Sarah had the sickening feeling he was looking not at the child, but at her own bare legs. Finally, his eyes returned to hers.

"Laurel," he called, not moving. "Laurel, wake up. We've got a situation here."

For an instant, there was silence, and then Sarah heard movement inside the bedroom.

"What is it?" Laurel called suddenly, her voice panicked. "Is it Len?" In seconds she was at the doorway, pulling a robe around her.

"Oh, Sarah! Thank God it's just you." She sank against the door frame. "I thought maybe Len had come b—"

"Mommy!" Jessie called, stepping out from behind Sarah. She ran toward her mother and threw her arms around Laurel's legs, just as she had done with Sarah a few minutes before. But Laurel's robe was not secure, and Sarah saw a flash of pale flesh underneath.

"Jessie, be careful," Laurel said sharply, tying the robe more tightly around her waist. Then she met Sarah's eyes, looking guilty and defiant all at once.

"Sarah," she began, "it's not how it looks . . ." Suddenly her eyes narrowed. "What are you doing here?"

Sarah shifted Emma to her hip. "A woman called me. She was driving by and saw Jessie near the street."

"Jessie! You know you're not supposed to go—"

"Mommy, flowers! Flowers in a jar."

Laurel arched her eyebrows at Sarah. "What?"

"Jessie was picking you daffodils beside the road. The woman who stopped . . . I think she got her a jar to put them in."

"She was inside our house?" Laurel looked at Sarah accusingly.

"She was looking for *you*." Sarah said, disgusted. "Jessie thought you might be on the phone."

At that, the man gave a little guffaw, and Laurel cut her eyes at him, coloring.

"But why did she call *you*?"

"She said she saw my number by the phone."

In the silence that followed, Sarah was struck by how absurd it all was: all five of them crammed in the narrow hallway, she with this baby who wasn't even hers, while the baby's mother stood there, half-naked, and this creep of a man leered on. What was *wrong* with Laurel? Why didn't she tell him to go put on some clothes? Why didn't she reach out for her daughter? Why wasn't she falling over herself with Oh-my-Gods and apologies?

Oh, it was none of Sarah's business! She was just the babysitter. She almost stepped forward, then, to hold out Emma for Laurel to take, but something stopped her. She didn't trust this man. She didn't trust Laurel, either, she realized suddenly, and as soon as the thought caught hold, she knew instantly that she never had. A foul taste formed in her mouth, and she had to fight the urge to spit.

"Look," she said, shifting Emma in her arms again. "I'm going to go change Emma's diaper. And then I'm going to take the girls to the park for a while, so you can—" She hesitated. "Put yourselves together."

Relief flooded Laurel's face. "Oh, would you? Thank you! I can pay you . . ."

Sarah shook her head, then held her hand out for Jessie. "Come on, Dessie," she said. "Let's go use the potty and then we'll go to the park."

"Come on, Dessie. You can make it. Your house is right up there," Sarah said. Emma had fallen asleep in the stroller as they walked home from the park, and Jessie was rapidly losing steam. Sarah was pushing the stroller with one hand and pulling the little girl along with the other, when one of the stroller's wheels veered off the sidewalk. Sarah let go of Jessie's hand for a moment to straighten it.

Out of the corner of eye, she saw Jessie begin to dash away; instinctively, her hand shot out and clutched at the back of the little girl's shirt.

"Sarah, let go," Jessie protested, trying to twist out of her grasp. "I see Daddy!"

Sarah looked up. The late afternoon sun was in her eyes, but she made out the silhouette of a man hurrying toward them.

"Jessie!" he called. "Emma!"

Sarah let go of Jessie's shirt, and Jessie catapulted into her father's arms. "Daddy!"

Her father's long arms engulfed her, and he kissed the top of her head. Then he looked up at Sarah.

"You don't usually watch them in the afternoons, do you?" His voice was puzzled but even, and Sarah knew instantly that Laurel had told him nothing. She looked away quickly.

"No, not usually."

Dr. Walters scooped Jessie up and settled her onto his shoulders. She gave a little shriek, half fear, half delight, and grabbed wildly at his head. Gently, he reached up and repositioned her hands.

"You can't cover my eyes, silly girl," he said. Then he looked back at Sarah quizzically. "Did something happen today?"

What had Laurel said? Clearly she had told him where they

were; he had been coming to meet them. But what else? What kind of excuse had she possibly made? Sarah hesitated. She felt an urge to tell the girls' father everything. He deserved to know, didn't he? Sarah had fumed all afternoon about Laurel's reaction when she had learned that her three-year-old daughter had left the house and wandered down the street, all while she was in bed with her . . . her *what*? Her lover? Sarah had always loathed that word; it sounded so lewd, somehow. She thought of the man in the hallway, with his self-satisfied eyes and gaudy tattoos, his soft, pale belly and sunburnt nose. She regretted now how polite she'd been. She wanted to go back and scream at Laurel: "You're a *mother*. You don't get to do this."

Surely, if Dr. Walters knew, he would be disgusted—outraged. And how she longed to see it—to see her own revulsion, her own fury, mirrored in someone else, so she would not feel so alone with it. All afternoon at the park she had pretended with the girls that everything was normal, when she had been dying to rave to someone—to anyone—about how awful it had been. There had been another family at the park, a young woman with a little girl about Jessie's age and a baby dangling from a baby carrier against her chest. The mother had smiled at Sarah and asked about her kids.

"Oh, they're not mine," Sarah had said, as she always did. "I'm just the nanny."

Something shifted in the woman's expression.

"Oh. I'm sorry. I just assumed they were yours."

"It happens all the time."

"Do you bring them here often? I haven't seen you." Probably she had been looking for a playmate for the little girl, Sarah thought, or another mom to talk to. Maybe she was wondering if Sarah might do, after all.

"Not in the afternoon, usually. But today—" For a moment, Sarah had imagined telling this woman everything. She could almost picture her face as she listened, the aghast expression that would mask a salacious interest, the boredom of the playground for once held at bay.

"Today," Sarah began again. "Today is actually my last day." She had lowered her voice, so that Jessie would not overhear.

What a relief it had been to say it out loud, so that she could stop turning it over and over in her mind. Because what was there to decide after all? She couldn't work for Laurel anymore.

Now, Sarah looked up at Dr. Walters, weighing her words. He was watching her closely; she had been silent too long.

"What *happened* today?" he asked again, and there was an urgency in his words that made her heart go out to him.

She took a deep breath. She would tell him only what it was her place to tell. So she told him about the lady's phone call, and what she had said. She told him that after they had found Laurel, she had offered to take the kids to the park, and Laurel had agreed.

"And we had fun, didn't we, Dessie?" she said finally, reaching up to where the little girl perched on her father's shoulders and giving her foot an affectionate jiggle. Sarah's heart ached to think that these were the last moments she would spend with the girls. Tomorrow Jessie would ask for her, and Laurel or Dr. Walters would explain that Sarah wouldn't be taking care of her anymore. And just like that, Sarah would disappear, first from the child's life, and then, inevitably, from her memories, until the time they had spent together would shrink into an unremembered interval of her childhood.

"But where *was* Laurel?" Dr. Walter's insisted, his voice strained. "Why didn't she know that Jessie was outside, for God's sake? Was she dr—" He cut himself off.

Sarah said nothing. She pushed the stroller with both hands now, following Dr. Walters down the sidewalk, back to their house. Sarah did not want to go inside. She didn't want to see Laurel, didn't want to hear her shrill voice or be a party to whatever deception she was playing out.

"Dr. Walters," she began.

"Please, it's Len."

"Please tell Laurel . . . I won't be able to take care of the girls anymore."

"What?" Len stopped abruptly and turned to face her. "What *happened*?"

"Please. I just can't. I'm sorry it's so sudden."

"But *why*? What happened? It's because of today, isn't it? Something happened. Surely there's an explanation. Just let me talk to Laurel—"

Sarah shook her head. "No, Dr. Walters. I just can't."

"But—" Sarah watched how carefully he reached up for Jessie and swung her to the ground. She bent down and gave the girl a hug.

"I won't see you for a while, okay?" she said. "Be good. And when your little sister wakes up, will you tell her I said good-bye, too?"

She watched Dr. Walters' expression change; he didn't say anything else to persuade her. Instead he reached his hand behind him and pulled his wallet from his pocket.

"How much do we owe you, then?" His words were not cold, but distracted. His eyes darted toward the front door of their house, and Sarah felt how desperate he must be to get inside, to get to the bottom of things.

"You don't owe me anything. Laurel paid me this morning."

"But for this afternoon? Surely she didn't—"

"Nothing, seriously. I wanted to."

He sighed so wearily then that, again, her heart went out to him. But it wasn't her business, now less than ever. She tousled Jessie's hair one last time, got in her car, and drove away.

CHAPTER 11

Len

That night, as Len read the girls their good-night books, he was still seething with irritation. How could Laurel have allowed it? Surely most mothers would not have slept through all of that. Her daughter leaving the house, and then some stranger bringing her back again? What if she had crossed the street? What if someone had taken her? How could Laurel have taken a nap with two kids in the house and the front door left open? What if there had been an intruder?

"I'm sorry," Laurel had said, again and again. "I was just so tired. I can't believe I didn't wake up either."

But Len would not, could not believe it. "You were drinking, weren't you? You were passed out."

"No."

"Laurel, you were shit-faced when I got home this evening."

"I'd had one drink. You'd want one, too, after all that. It was awful."

"Oh, sure. It was awful. But then you send them to the park with the babysitter? Come on, Laurel."

"I was shaken. I didn't trust myself. And I didn't send them— Sarah offered."

It had gone on and on like that, Len irate, Laurel in tears, until at last he could stand no more of it and had gone into the living room to watch the end of *Sesame Street* with the girls. Afterwards, they had ordered pizza, and Len had tried to act as if nothing were the matter, for his daughters' sakes. He gave them their baths and found their pajamas, then sat on the edge of Jessie's bed with Emma on his lap and Jessie beside him.

"Daddy," Jessie said accusingly when they were halfway through the second book. "You read that part already. Emma, stop it."

For Emma, as always, was trying to turn the page. Jessie tried to push her sister's chubby hands away. "Daddy, make her stop. We're not done."

"She doesn't understand, Jess. She's just a baby. She likes turning the pages. She thinks, 'Book, oh goodie, pages to turn.'"

Jessie giggled a little at that, but she kept her hand on the page, holding it open. "Just finish it, Daddy."

He started to read again, but after a moment, Jessie interrupted. "Is Sarah coming tomorrow?"

Len's stomach fell. What had Jessie overheard? How much had she understood? He shook his head sadly, bracing himself for his daughter's disappointment.

"No, sweetheart. She's not going to be able to come . . . for a while." It was a lie; he suspected that Jessie would know it was a lie. But he couldn't help himself. How could he say, *No, she's never coming back?*

Jessie said nothing for several moments, and Len let Emma turn the pages.

"Don't worry, Jess," he said, at last. "We'll find a new babysitter . . ."

But Jessie cut him off. "That man was scary."

Len's heart stopped. *Had* there been an intruder? What else had Laurel slept through?

"What man?" he asked, trying to keep his voice calm.

"The scary man."

Len's stomach plummeted. Automatically, he put his arm around Jessie, pulling her against him.

"What scary man, Jess?" he said. "Who are you talking about?"

"The scary man in Mommy's room."

"There was a man in Mommy's room?" As soon as the words were out, they ceased to be a question. There was a man in Mommy's room.

Jessie nodded.

"Did Mommy see the man, too?" he asked needlessly. Laurel had not slept through an intruder. She had invited him. To their house. While Len was at work, and their daughters napped. Heat coursed through him. His skin burned, and the hand that still held the book began to shake.

Jessie was nodding, answering his question. "Sarah seed him. Mommy seed him. I seed him. Emma seed him." Jessie, looking down at the book, noticed his trembling hand.

"Daddy, are you scared?" she asked. "Is that man coming back?"

Len steadied his hand. "No, I'm not scared, Jessie." He drew in a deep breath. "And no, that man is not going to come back."

There was a brief silence. Then Jessie wriggled out from under his arm and pried the book out of Emma's hands. One by one, she flipped the pages back to where they'd been and settled against his side.

"Daddy read the book now?" she said.

Len read on, not registering a single word. He laid Emma in her crib and kissed both his daughters good night. Only as he reached for the cord to turn off their light did he notice that his hand was trembling again. He had told Jessie that he was not scared, and he had believed it to be true: his hands shook not from fear but from anger. And yet, he *was* scared. There had been a man in Mommy's room, his daughter had told him, and in that instant, he had understood. All these months that he had breathed easier, thinking Laurel was happy. Oh, what a fool he had been! He had been convinced it was the volunteering that had made a differ-ence. Week after week, he had watched Laurel's spirits rise, and never once had he begrudged her the Saturday mornings she spent away from home.

To every problem, there is a solution: this had always been

his mantra. But not now. Not here. He had tried to fix this before, and look where it had brought him. His future had become a vast, blank void, and it terrified him.

And that man . . . Oh God. Len's stomach turned to think of him, for he *would* come back, wouldn't he? For a moment, the world seemed to spin wildly outside of his control. Laurel would do what she wanted; she always had. And at that thought, the heat of his fury rose in him. It propelled him out of his daughters' room, the door clicking closed quietly behind him, down the hall, and into the kitchen, where Laurel sat at the kitchen table, a book open before her, a glass of wine in hand.

"This is over," Len said, his heart pounding.

"Oh!" Laurel said. She looked up at him and clutched at her glass, as if that was what he meant. Her drink, her drinking: over. The gesture disgusted him. But for his daughters in the other room, on the precipice of sleep, he would have taken the glass out of her hand and hurled it at the floor. Instead, he said again, "This is over," and at "this," he traced a little arc with his chin, a gesture that took in the whole of their dingy kitchen but meant all of it: the house, their family, their lives together.

"Oh, Len," Laurel began, understanding dawning. "I promise you . . . it won't happen again."

Len made a low growl of disgust in the back of his throat.

"Jessie told me about 'the man,' Laurel. 'The scary man in Mommy's room' is what she said."

Laurel's eyes widened. "Oh," she said again. And then she started to cry.

"For God's sake, Laurel. Spare me." Len gave a little shudder, and then he left the kitchen and stormed out the front door.

As soon as Len reached the sidewalk, he began to run. His heart still pounded in his chest, but as he ran the awful pressure of it eased. Sweat rose on his skin and cooled immediately in the brisk air. The furious heat that had coursed through him prickled in his pores, then dissipated into the April night. Len ran down three empty blocks and passed the park, its rusted structures standing like lonely skeletons in the pale moonlight. Only when he had run out of his neighborhood did his steps slow to a walk. And as he walked, an unexpected exhilaration filled the space inside him that his rage and his fear had made. It was *over*. He would never have to deal with Laurel again, not with her drinking, nor her selfishness. Not with her incorrigible laziness nor her saccharine tears. It was over, at last. He was free.

As he walked, Len's feet tapped out the steady rhythm of the words on the sidewalk: *It's over. It's over. It's over.* Len emptied his mind of everything but those words, but by the time he had walked two blocks to their persistent refrain, he had begun to understand that, like everything else he had said that evening, they were not true. He had told Jessie he was not scared, when he was terrified. He had assured her that the scary man would not come back, when Len knew that he would. And he could walk clear across town to the beat of *It's over*, each step an echo of his proclamation, but they would never, *could* never be true. The sky, which had seemed so immense above him as he ran away from his house, now pressed down on him. Len let out his breath, turned on his heel, and walked slowly home.

Except for the soft creak of the door as he eased it opened, the house was silent when he slipped inside. He did not pause as he strode down the narrow hallway. In his daughters' room, he swept one arm over the rug, clearing away the clutter of stuffed animals and toys. Then he lay down on his back in the space he had made on the floor. When he reached out his arms, one hand touched the base of Jessie's bed, the other found a leg of Emma's crib. He curled his fingers around it. Len lay like that for a long time, arms outstretched, and at last he fell asleep.

CHAPTER 12

Len

"Hello?"

"Margie. It's me—" Len began at once, forgetting that she would not hear him.

"You have a collect call from Len Walters," the operator interrupted him. "Will you accept the charges?"

"What? Yes. Of course."

"Please hold the line." There was a click as the operator hung up.

"Lenny? Are you there? What's happened?"

"Hello, Margie."

"Lenny, what is it? Is it one of the girls?"

"No. No," he said quickly, to reassure her. "They're both fine."

"Then why are you calling collect? I mean, I don't mind but . . ."

Len understood her agitation; he had called her collect only twice before, each time from the same hospital pay phone after the birth of Jessie, then Emma. Margie lived in St. Louis with her husband. She and Len had not seen each other since soon after Jessie was born, when she had insisted on flying out to California to help with the newborn. But Margie and Laurel had not gotten along, and neither had suggested that Margie come again after Emma's birth.

"I'm not at home, Margie. I'm at work. But I'll pay you back. I just needed to talk to someone. I . . . I needed to talk to you."

"Lenny, what's wrong? What's happened?"

Quickly, Len told his sister about Laurel's affair and the chain of events that had brought it to light.

Margie was silent for a long moment. Then she let out a sigh. "So—now what?"

Len exhaled deeply. He had counted on that—on his sister's boundless practicality. She would know what to do.

"Margie, what can I do? I feel so paralyzed." The sky outside his tiny office window was a deep, distant blue, radiant with the possibilities of spring. But how false it was! Soon enough the blue sky would be shrouded in summer's fog. And then there would be months and months of gray.

Len slumped in his chair, the receiver tight against his ear. He couldn't shake the caged feeling that he had had since the night he ran from home, when the dark sky had seemed too close, pushing him back into the sickening sphere of his life.

"Lenny, do you hear yourself?" his sister said, exasperated. "There is only one thing to do. You leave. Oh, *that woman*."

Len laughed despite himself. "You've never liked her."

"No, I haven't. But I was happy to put my feelings aside if she was a good wife to you and a good mother to those girls. But she's been neither."

"But, Margie," Len said. "How can I leave? I can't leave Jessie and Emma. Not with her, not by themselves. I can't."

"No, you certainly can't." She paused. "Or rather, you could, of course. But you shouldn't. And you won't."

"See?" Len said. "So what do I do? She says she'll end her . . . her affair. That it won't happen again. I believed her once. I can't now."

"This isn't the first time." It was not a question, but Len answered it anyway.

"No. It was different last time, but . . . no."

"Lenny, there's only one thing to do."

"I have to stay, don't I?" Len sighed. "For the girls."

"No. You most certainly do not have to stay. Leave, by all

means. Divorce that wretched excuse of a woman. But take the girls with you."

"Margie, how could I? I can't raise those girls by myself."

"You're raising them now."

"But not like that. Not alone."

"Do you honestly think that Laurel would do a better job?"

Len gave a little grunt of disgust. "No."

It was what had kept him there these last three days, sleeping on the rug in his daughters' room, sneaking out in the morning before they woke but returning each evening to feed and bathe them and put them to bed. He couldn't trust them to Laurel's care, certainly not in the evening, when Laurel was sure to be drinking.

"No, I don't think she would," he said. "That's why . . . That's why I haven't left."

"So, raise them yourself, Lenny. You'd do a good job. You know you would."

The tenderness in Margie's voice brought tears to his eyes, and it was a moment before his throat unclenched enough that he could speak.

"But," he said. "I'm not a mother." His voice sounded strangled; he almost put the phone down for a minute, so that he could cry, just to release the terrible tightness in his throat.

"Neither was I." The words were spoken in her usual matter-of-fact tone, but the weight of them! Len couldn't speak. He nodded, unseen. Margie had been only thirteen when their mother died of ovarian cancer. Old enough, their father had thought, to be the woman of the house. She had been the one to raise Len, the one who had checked his homework every night and taught him to mind his manners, while their father sat in his customary silence, hunched over the food that Margie had prepared, or studying the newspaper grimly, his glasses perched on the end of his nose.

"Do you mean to tell me," Margie said now, "that if Laurel was killed in an accident, you wouldn't keep the girls because you couldn't raise them alone?" His sister's voice was stern, indignant.

How many times had she begun her lectures this way? "Do you mean to tell me that you can solve the algebra problems in my textbook, but you can't write a decent paragraph?" "Do you mean to tell me that you had time to spend all afternoon at the lake, but didn't manage to take out the garbage?"

"Oh, Margie," he managed at last. "That's ridiculous. Of course I would."

"Well. There you go."

"It's not the same."

"Is it not?"

"No."

"So, you could raise the girls alone if Laurel somehow ceased to exist, but not now. You'd rather chain yourself to a hideous wife—there, I said it—or give up your daughters, rather than raise them on your own."

Len was silent for a moment. He looked out at the bright sky, and for the first time in days, his spirits rose a little. He had been trapped, but Margie had cracked the door. She had found a way out. "Maybe you're right," he said, hesitating, not trusting it.

"I *am* right," Margie said, and the smug certainty of her tone made Len laugh aloud. Oh, how he had hated those words, that tone, when he was young.

"It's not like you'd have to do it alone, you know," Margie pointed out. "Don't you have a babysitter who helps with the girls?"

"She quit. But yes, we did. Laurel's cousin is helping out this week, until we can—"

"Oh, well. She's not the only babysitter in the world. And I could come and help for a while, if you needed me to. Until you worked out the kinks."

"Oh, Margie. Thank you." Len stood up abruptly from his desk. For a moment, his heart soared. Margie was right. He could do it.

But a second later the impossibility of it rose up like a gale, slamming the door of his cage shut again. He sank back onto the seat.

"Oh, Margie." Len said again, but this time in despair. "How could it work—really? She'll fight me for them; I know she will. And what judge is going to give a father custody? I can hear it now: 'Children need to be with their mother.' To set my mind on it, and then lose? I couldn't bear it."

"But what about everything you've told me? The drinking? The affair . . . While the children were *there*, for goodness sake. Poor little Jessie wandering outside all alone. Surely a judge wouldn't—"

"Oh, you don't know Laurel, Margie. She'll put on a good show. 'Oh, poor me. Please, Your Honor, don't let him take my children.'"

Margie was silent for a minute. *She knows I'm right*, Len thought miserably.

"But what about Jessie leaving the house?" Margie insisted. "And Laurel not even knowing. Surely—"

"I doubt it. It happens, doesn't it? Parents lose track of their children. Don't you remember how I slipped out and went to try to buy ice cream by myself that time? I couldn't have been much older than Jessie is now."

"But I knew you were gone! I was sick with worry."

"I know. Margie, I'm not accusing you. You were a great—you did a great job taking care of me, and you know it. I'm just saying it happens, doesn't it? It wouldn't necessarily make a judge think she's unfit. And Emma is so little. She's still nursing. Laurel will use that, you can put money on it."

"She's thirteen months old, Len. She still nurses?"

"Not often. Sometimes."

"Well, I'd say it's high time to wean her then."

They were both silent for a moment, and Len's heart fell.

"I'm sorry," he said. "This must be costing you a fortune."

Margie ignored him. "There has to be a way."

"But how?"

"What if . . . ? Okay, so maybe you're right. Maybe if you fought her for it, you would lose. I can't fathom it, but I suppose it's possible. But what if it isn't a fight? What if you just asked Laurel for custody?"

"Ha," Len said dryly. "Even if she didn't want the girls, she'd keep them just to spite me."

"Are you sure? She's never . . . Well, she never really warmed much to motherhood, did she? How much does *she* really want to raise those girls on her own?"

Len hesitated. "I don't know."

"Lenny, I think it could work. Don't turn it into a battle. Just offer her something else. Something she wants more than those precious girls, God help her."

"But what? What could I possibly offer her?"

"You own that house, don't you?"

"Yes. Well, we owe on it still. But yes."

"The money Dad left you? You put it into the house?"

"Yes."

"Good. So you've got equity in it. Give her the house. Do you have savings?" She didn't wait for a response. "Give her that, too."

"And then what, Margie? Raise the girls with no place to live and no money?"

"Oh, come on, Lenny. Stop being dramatic. Do you want those girls or not? You have your job. That's more than a lot of single parents have. Find an apartment. Find a babysitter. And voilà."

She made it sound so simple. So easy. And Len couldn't object, for Margie never had. He had been barely four when their mother died; his sister had shouldered the responsibility for his care as if she had been born to it. She hadn't gone to her senior prom because he had come down with the measles. He had insisted he was fine, but his forehead had burned beneath her cool hand. "It's just a silly dance," she had said. "And you're my brother." As if that settled it.

"Well," Margie was saying now. "What do you think?"

Len sighed, but he could feel his mood lifting. It just might work.

"I think you're right, Margie," he said. "As always." The words were swollen with his unspoken gratitude. "Thank you, Margie," he added softly, aware, as ever, of the smallness of the words compared to the enormity of his sister's sacrifice, the vastness of her love for him.

"You're welcome," Margie said. "Now—we should really get off this phone. And I meant what I said—I'll talk to Daniel about giving you a hand, just until you get on your feet. Good-bye now, Lenny."

When Len hung up the phone at last, his ear burned where he had held the receiver against it. His tiny office was stuffy; the small window didn't open. Suddenly, the little room couldn't hold it all—the plans, the possibility. Len was suddenly desperate to be outside in the cool, spring sunshine. Quickly, he left the room, leaving the door open behind him.

The wind on his face, when he had made his way through the maze of offices and classrooms and stepped outside at last, was so cool and light that he felt his spirits soar, buoyed by Margie's confidence in her plan and set alight by the glorious breeze.

His step was light as he walked along the campus sidewalk. Even in the mathematics complex, the poetry of the spring morning was undeniable. Students lounged on blankets in the grassy quad, threw Frisbees, smiled.

Would it really be okay? Len wondered. *Was it possible?* He remembered the fleeting euphoria he had felt the last time he had decided to leave his marriage. It seemed a lifetime ago now.

It *was* a lifetime ago, he realized: Emma's lifetime. Laurel had derailed his plans then with the announcement of her pregnancy. The memory of it sobered him, slowing his steps and unsettling his stomach. Laurel wasn't stupid; she would find a way to do it again.

But then Len thought of baby Emma, of her bright, round face and serious eyes. He had been right to stay before, he thought. If he had left then, Emma might have been lost to him. But she was not lost, and somehow this thought gave him confidence. In geometry, two points made a line, but three—that was a plane, a whole shelf of possibility, extending infinitely in every direction.

It *was* possible, he thought with certainty now. He could do it. He could leave, and keep his daughters. They would be a family.

Please, he thought, raising his eyes to the startlingly blue sky. *Please, let it be possible. Please let us be a family.*

CHAPTER 13

Len

Len felt like hollering. He felt like sending Margie a dozen roses—two dozen. For she had been right. Wasn't she always right? His attorney had just called him at work: Laurel had accepted the terms of the divorce agreement. She was insisting on some minor modifications, his attorney had said. But the custody. She had agreed to the custody. She would not pay child support; he would not pay alimony. She would get the house, mostly paid for, and all the money in their savings account. And he—he would be free. He felt an unexpected bubble of gratitude rise in his chest. She was giving him the girls. *Oh, thank you, Laurel*, he thought. *Thank you.*

It took Len only one day to make the arrangements. The receptionist at the student housing office had frowned at him.

"These apartments . . . Professors don't . . . They're for graduate students."

But Len had not relented. The posting he had seen on the bulletin board didn't say 'graduate students,' he insisted. It said, 'members of the university community.' And wasn't he a member?

Shrugging, she had handed him the application.

"They're not that nice, you know."

She had been right. They weren't that nice at all. The carpet was dirty, the walls stained. The few pieces of furniture that came with the apartment were utilitarian and ugly, and the smell of old cigarette smoke hung in the air. Len stood in the doorway, the single key dangling from his fingers, and felt his spirits deflate.

But the girls wouldn't care, he told himself. So why should he? He spent all day on Saturday cleaning. He rented a carpet cleaner from the hardware store and shampooed every room. He scrubbed the tiny bathroom and the walls, and wiped down the cheap furniture with polish, so that the unmistakable lemony scent of it filled the rooms.

When he was finished, he drove to the Kmart in Eureka and pushed a cart methodically down the rows. He had not squabbled with Laurel over who would get which towel, which pot. In the lingering profusion of gratitude, he had told her she could keep it all. He had taken only his own things, and the girls'.

Now, he was struck by all that he would need. He chose things sparingly: a bathmat, three towels, baby shampoo. In the kitchen aisle, the cornucopia of cooking supplies overwhelmed him. Studying the prices, he picked out a frying pan, two pots, a cheap set of silverware, and some plastic dishes.

Despite his care, the items piled up. As he waited at the register, he saw another shopper move behind him in line, and then, seeing his cart, choose a different register. The total, when the salesgirl rang it all up, made his heart fall. But he pulled his MasterCard from his wallet and handed it over. There was nothing for it. They needed a home.

Back at the apartment, his spirits lightened. It was satisfying to take his bags of purchases from room to room, putting everything in its place. The neat order of it pleased him. When he was done, he took the boxes of his own things that he had taken from the house—Laurel's house, now—and unpacked them, too.

Only when everything was put away did he take out his wallet and pull from inside it a carefully folded piece of paper. When he had gathered his belongings at the house, he had copied down Sarah's number from the paper that was still stuck on the wall beside the phone.

He had not called her yet. Each time he thought of it, he had put it off. He was embarrassed, he knew, at all that she had seen. He was embarrassed by Laurel, he realized, and he understood immediately that it was not a new feeling: he had been embarrassed by Laurel for years. *But she's not my wife now*, he thought with relief. *This has nothing to do with her.*

Still, the feeling persisted, and he had not made the call. What must Sarah think of him? He told himself that setting up the apartment was the most important thing, although he knew it wasn't. They could survive without a towel or a frying pan. But there had to be someone to pick up the girls in the afternoon when their daycare closed; Len was teaching two evening classes that quarter.

She's not the only babysitter in the world, Margie had said, and of course she was right. But the girls knew Sarah; they were attached to her. And there had been so much upheaval. Tomorrow, Margie would arrive, and on Monday evening, he would bring the girls here. They would leave their mother and their home. He wanted to try, at least, to give them one thing that was familiar to them. He could picture Jessie's face lighting up, if he could just tell her that Sarah would be back.

The thought of it made him pick up the phone at last and carefully dial the number, waiting impatiently as the dial unwound after each digit.

Just as he had expected, Sarah refused at first. No, she really didn't think she should. She had meant her resignation to be final. But Len persisted.

"Please," he begged. "So much is changing for them. They're about to lose so much. They need—"

"That's not my fault, is it?" she said quickly, cutting him off.

Len's face burned. It was not his fault either, he thought, and yet he couldn't shake the feeling that he, too, was to blame.

"No," he said quietly. "You're right. I know it has nothing to do with you. I just thought . . . I just wanted . . . It's fine. I just had to ask."

He was about to hang up the phone when Sarah said, "Wait."

Len waited. There was silence on the line for a moment.

"Are you still there, Dr. Walters?"

"I'm here. And it's Len."

"I'll do it."

"Really?" he asked.

"Yes. They're good girls. I miss them. And if Laurel is really out of the picture, I guess it'll be okay. You seem like a good dad."

Relief washed over him. Then gratitude. "Thank you so much," he gushed. "Thank you."

"I'm not doing it for you, you know," Sarah said. "I need the job. But you're right, the girls could use a little stability."

"Oh, Lenny. Oh dear." Margie said when she arrived, standing in the doorway just as he had done and taking in the apartment.

Len sighed. "I did the best I could."

But all his efforts were nothing compared to Margie's. All week, she scoured yard sales and thrift stores, and by Saturday the kitchen was stocked. She packed up the plastic dishes and the cheap pots that he had bought and asked Len for the receipt.

"I'm taking these back," she said. "Really, Lenny, you can always find kitchen supplies second hand. And good ones."

The girls' room, too, was transformed. A framed picture of a puppy hung on the wall; the changing table had been thoroughly scrubbed and covered with a soft cloth. She had also put herself in charge of unpacking their things. She studied each piece of clothing, and then added it to one of three neat piles on the rug: to keep, to sew, to cut up for rags.

"Really, Lenny," she said. "The state of their clothes." He blushed and laid some bills on the table.

"Could you get them what they need?"

But that afternoon, the little pile of money was still there, and the girls' dresser was full of neat stacks of shirts and pants and dresses.

He smiled at her in gratitude. "Really, Margie," he said, echoing her. "You should have used—"

She cut him off. "I can certainly buy my nieces some clothes, Lenny. And don't worry, I didn't spend much. There's a nice little thrift store I found." She wrote the name down in neat letters and stuck it to the fridge with a magnet. "For next time, when I'm not here."

The best part, though, was how the girls loved her.

"You seed me when I was a baby?" Jessie asked, her eyes wide. "Like Emma?"

"Yes, I *saw* you. You were even smaller than Emma is now," Margie told her. "A little tiny baby."

"And Emma? You seed baby Emma, too?"

"*Saw*, Jessie, not *seed*. No, no. Emma wasn't even born yet. There was just you."

Jessie frowned at that, disbelieving, and Len smiled. Already Jessie could not remember a time when her little sister did not exist.

Len did not know how Margie did it all. By the end of the week, the kitchen cupboards were full, the freezer packed with Tupperware containers of frozen meals.

"Just remember to transfer them to a baking dish when you heat them up," Margie said, opening the freezer door to show him the neat stacks. "I did think about buying you one of those microwave ovens, you know. If anyone needs one, it's you. But I don't trust them. I heard somewhere recently that the Russians banned them—did you know that? And with these girls in the kitchen all the time—well, I just didn't think it wise."

In the afternoons, when Len returned from work, the girls were both in dresses, Jessie's longer hair in two neat brown braids tied with bows, Emma with a barrette on the top of her head.

The first time Len saw them like that, he laughed deeply. "Oh, Margie," he said. "They look so . . ." And he laughed again, "Ho, ho, ho."

"Daddy," Jessie said. "Laugh like that again. You sound like Santa!"

But Margie looked sheepish. "So . . . ?"

"So?" Len said.

"You said, 'They look so . . .' So what?"

Len reached down and swung Emma to his hip. "So beautiful," he said, grinning. "You girls look so beautiful."

Jessie looked down at her dress. "I don't like dresses."

"Oh, Jessie," Margie said. "You look nice."

"But I don't *like* dresses."

"Well, when Aunt Margie's gone, I guess you won't have to wear them," Margie said.

"You're leaving?"

"Yes, sweetheart. I have to go back to my home. But I will miss you very much."

"Are you leaving now?"

"No, sweetie. Tomorrow."

"When is tomorrow?"

"Well, you'll go to sleep tonight, and when you wake up, that will be tomorrow."

Len watched Jessie's face fall. "But who will take care of us?"

"Oh, sweetheart," Margie said, pulling her into her arms. "Your daddy will take good care of you. And . . ." she hesitated, looking at Len. He had not told them yet about Sarah.

"And Sarah," he said now. "Sarah will help take care of you, too."

"Sarah!" Jessie said. "Yay!" And she did a little dance around Margie.

That night, while Len graded quizzes, Margie sat in a straight-backed chair, sewing the last of the girls' clothes.

"Margie," Len said, at last. "I don't know how to thank you. You've done so much."

"Oh, pooh," Margie said. "It was my pleasure. They're such sweet girls, Lenny."

There was a tightness in her voice, and Len looked up at her and then away. She had never liked him to see her cry.

They were silent for a moment. How unfair life can be, Len thought. Margie had spent her youth being a parent; she had sacrificed so much. But when she had married Daniel and wanted children of her own—well, they hadn't come. It wasn't fair, he thought again, that someone like Laurel had children so effortlessly, while Margie, who was so good at motherhood, could not.

"You would be a wonderful mother," he said at last.

She smiled, but he could see the tears rimming her eyes.

"I mean, you *were* a great mother."

She shook her head. "I was never your mother, Lenny. I just tried to keep doing what Mom would have done."

Len did not remember their mother, not really. He had images in his head, but he knew they were inspired by old photographs he had seen of her, not true memories of his mother herself. It had always saddened him before, that he couldn't remember, but it comforted him now. If he did not remember his mother, or her death, then surely his girls would not remember the turmoil of this time, either. He would be a good parent to them, as Margie had been to him; that is what would stay with them. *That* is what they would remember.

"Well, you were all the mother I had," he said at last. "And I loved you like one."

Margie glanced over at him, and her cheeks were wet. "I did, too." She leaned forward to bite off a piece of thread. "I do."

Len looked away. He and Margie never talked like this. When he was a boy, she had told him "I love you" every night as she turned out his light. The words were spoken in her usual matter-of-fact way, and he had always answered in kind: "I love you, too." But that was ages ago; it had been over a decade since they had spoken of their feelings for each other with real emotion.

Len remembered easily the last time. On the morning that he was to graduate from high school, Margie had surprised him by bursting into tears as she fixed his tie.

"What is it?" he had asked, alarmed.

But she had shaken her head. "Nothing. I'm being silly. But— I'm just so proud of you."

Len had put his arms around her and pulled her to his chest. She was so small, he could rest his chin on her hair. He felt its softness against his freshly shaven skin.

"Thank you, Margie," he said, his throat tight. "And I don't just mean because you said that. That you're proud of me. Although that, too. I meant . . ."

Margie had giggled against his chest as he stumbled over the words.

"I know what you meant," she had said.

Now, as he looked at her, his heart swelled.

"It's not too late, is it?" he asked, emboldened by the moment that had just passed between them.

Margie glanced at her watch. "It's almost ten."

"I meant, for you to have children."

She sighed. "I'm too old now."

He did the math quickly in his head. She was only thirty-eight. "You're not old."

"Oh, I know. But for having kids, I am."

"But there's still a chance . . ."

She put the needle away and folded Jessie's dress into a neat little square in her lap. "It's okay, Lenny," she said. "I've come to peace with it. I'm happy with my life. I have Daniel. And I have you. And now I have those beautiful girls, too."

Suddenly she smiled. She took up the dress again and unfolded it, holding it up before her.

"Jessie's never going to wear this, is she?" she said, grinning, sheepish again.

Len chuckled. "Probably not."
"Oh well."

CHAPTER 14

Len

The next day was Sunday. Len and the girls drove Aunt Margie to the airport in the morning, and in the afternoon Sarah came to the apartment as arranged, so that Len could show her around and give her a key. She would start the next day. She and Len had already agreed on her schedule. Every day, she would pick up the girls from their daycare at two-thirty. That was when the school day ended and the after-care began. The girls could have stayed there until five, if Len paid the extra fee, but it would be such a long day for them, he thought. He preferred to pay Sarah. On Mondays, Wednesdays, and Fridays, he would be home by five-thirty. But on Tuesdays and Thursdays, he taught a class until nine, so Sarah would have to feed the girls and put them to bed.

As soon as the doorbell rang that afternoon, Jessie ran to greet Sarah, first hugging her legs and then taking her hand.

"Want to see our room, Sarah?" she asked, pulling her inside.

"Of course."

Len hung back, Emma on his hip. The easy familiarity between Sarah and Jessie made him feel self-conscious, superfluous. He did not follow them as Jessie gave her tour, but waited in the living room, seeing the drabness of the place anew.

When the two returned from the bedroom, Sarah was smiling. "I'm impressed. You've done a lot with the place."

Len shrugged. "My sister was just here. It was mostly her."

"Ah," Sarah said. "A woman's touch. I wondered, honestly. It's no small feat to make these places habitable."

"Do you . . . ?"

"Yeah, I have one, too. On the other side of campus, though."

Len nodded. "Well, the price is right. Do you live alone?"

Len watched as something in Sarah's face hardened. He instantly regretted his question. "I just meant, it helps if you can split the rent . . ." He faltered. "It's none of my business. Sorry."

Sarah reached down and lifted Jessie's braids. "Did your sister do these, too?" she asked cheerfully, and Len wondered if he had imagined the shift in her expression.

"Yes. She just went home this morning."

"Where's home?"

"St. Louis."

"Wow. That was nice of her. To come, I mean."

"Yes." He thought of saying more. His good-bye with Margie this morning had felt especially poignant after their conversation the night before. Even now, seeing the little touches she had made around the house, his heart filled with a raw tenderness for her. He felt the urge to speak of it with someone. He could imagine Sarah hearing him out, giving him the same patient attention that he had seen her give his girls. Still, he stopped himself. It was Sunday; already he was taking up too much of her time.

"Yes, it was very nice of her," he said. And then, "I can show you where things are now, if you want."

She nodded, then looked down at Jessie. "I get to put you to bed this week, Jess."

Jessie looked up at her with wide eyes. "Really?"

"Yes. Can you show me? Where are your pajamas?"

Len followed them back into the bedroom, Emma wriggling on his hip, his heart strangely full.

For a week and a half after Margie left, it wasn't so bad. There was food in the kitchen, and clean clothes still neatly folded in the drawers. Every morning, Len carefully pulled one of the meals she had prepared from the tower of Tupperware in the freezer and set it on the counter. And every evening, he inverted it into a baking dish as she had instructed him and warmed it in the oven.

But by Tuesday of the following week, the meals were gone and the laundry hamper full.

"Do you have a cookbook I can borrow?" Len asked one of the secretaries in the mathematics department, and the next day *The Joy of Cooking* appeared on his desk, with a little note: *Good luck!*

He scanned a few of the recipes and made a list. That evening he scrambled eggs for the girls for their dinner and then hurried them out to the car.

"But Daddy," Jessie protested. "It's bath time."

"We just need to get a few groceries," he explained. "Then we'll do bath time."

In the store, he set Emma in the seat in the front of the cart and made Jessie walk.

"But I'm tired," she whined. "I wanna ride, too. Emma gets to ride."

"Emma can't walk," he snapped.

"Yes, she can."

"Not like you. Now stay close."

But Jessie did not stay close. The piles of stacked produce were sirens for a three-year-old, their call irresistible. A tomato toppled to the floor.

"Jessie," he said sharply. "I told you to stay close." Quickly, he picked up the bruised tomato and replaced it on the stack. Then he scooped Jessie up by her underarms and swung her into the cart among the groceries.

"There," he said. "You wanted to ride. So ride."

"But there's no room," Jessie said, beginning to cry. Exasperated, he moved a box of cereal and a bag of apples, clearing a little spot for her.

"There. Now don't squish anything."

"But Emma has a seat," she wailed. He ignored her.

Jessie cried down three aisles. By the fourth, he couldn't take it.

"Stop your caterwauling," he told her. "Or I'll give you something to cry about."

He sounded just like Laurel, he thought, and felt an unexpected flash of sympathy for her. Len had always silently reproved Laurel for how quickly she lost patience with the girls, so that the shimmer of empathy he felt for her now was tinged with guilt. His loosened his collar.

In line, an elderly woman looked at him sympathetically. "Mother out of town?" she guessed.

He shook his head tersely.

"How about a lollipop?" she asked, pulling one from the display by the register and handing it to Jessie. "Will that make things better?"

By the time they got home, Jessie's hands and face were blue and sticky, the lollipop stick lost somewhere on the floor of the car.

"Don't touch anything," he told her, leaving her in the living room. He set Emma on the floor in front of a pile of toys.

He raced back to the car for the groceries—just the frozen ones. The others he could unload once the girls were asleep.

A minute later, he was back. Jessie started when she heard the door, looking up guiltily. She held *Go, Dog, Go* in her sticky hands.

"Jessie, I told you . . ."

"But Emma was gonna rip the pages!" she said. "I'm sorry." Tears welled up in her eyes.

Instinctively, Len looked for Emma. She wasn't there by the toys where he had left her. She had pulled up to standing at the small bookshelf and was pulling the books off, one by one.

"Oh, Emma."

He dropped the bags of groceries to the floor and scooped Emma up.

"It's okay, Jessie. Just put the book down. Let's go take a bath. And try not to touch anything else."

He undressed Emma as she stood, holding herself up at the edge of the tub and bouncing on her chubby legs. But when he unpinned her diaper, a large turd rolled out and onto the floor.

"Oh, Jesus," he said. "Emma, why didn't you tell me you'd pooped?"

"Oh, Daddy," Jessie said, amused. "She can't talk."

At last the turd was flushed, the floor spot-cleaned, and Emma's bottom wiped. He lifted her into the tub with her sister and sank down onto the toilet seat, watching them play.

"Okay, girls," he said at last. "Let's get washed." He hated to rush them, but it was after eight already. He hurried them into their pajamas, brushed their hair and teeth, and read them a few short books.

"One more book, Daddy. *Please*," Jessie began.

But he could see how tired she was. "Not tonight," he told her. "It's late."

Only when the girls were in their beds at last did he remember the groceries he had left on the living room floor.

"Damn it," he muttered, picking up the bag and taking it to the kitchen. The meat was soft but still mostly frozen—surely it would be okay. The tub of ice cream squished in his hand when he picked it up, melted ice cream leaking out from under the lid. He swore again under his breath and put it in the freezer, then went quickly to the car for the other groceries.

When he came back inside, he could hear Emma crying, and under the cries, Jessie's voice calling to him.

He put the bags in the kitchen and went to them.

"What is it?" he asked.

"Emma's crying," Jessie said. "And it's too loud. I can't sleep."

"Well, she'll go to sleep soon," he said impatiently. He wanted to get back to the kitchen and unload the groceries, and he still had a lecture to prepare for the morning. At the thought, exhaustion rose up in him like a wave. He longed for bed.

"Try to go to sleep now, Jessie, okay?"

"Okay," Jessie said, lying back on her pillow and cupping both ears with her hands. "I'll try."

There was a note of resignation in her voice, a sad weariness to her compliance. It made him pause.

"When Sarah puts Emma down for a nap, does she cry?" he asked.

"No."

"Why not?"

"She holds her. And she sings." His daughter looked up at him hopefully.

Len sighed. Emma was standing at the bars of her crib, her face red.

"You're tired, too, aren't you?" he said, picking her up and sitting down with her in the rocker. She leaned her head against his chest; he felt the heat of it through his shirt.

They were all quiet for a moment. He pushed the rocker with his feet.

"Are you going to sing too, Daddy?" Jessie asked quietly.

"Oh, I don't think so," he began. But why not?

"Row, row, row your boat . . ." he began.

Jessie giggled. "Oh, Daddy."

But she was quiet after that, and Emma lay motionless against his chest. He finished the song, keeping his voice low. Were they asleep? He heard Jessie stir in the bed, the rustle of her cover. He needed another song. Only one came to mind. It was not a lullaby, but he began it anyway, singing softly.

"I've been working on the railroad, all the live long day. I've been working on the railroad, just to pass the time away . . ."

In the quiet that blanketed the room when the song ended, he could hear the whistle of Jessie's breath. Emma was heavy against his chest, pinning him down. He leaned his head back against the rocker for a moment and closed his eyes. It would be so nice to fall asleep here, he thought. But there was still so much to do.

Reluctantly, he rose, holding Emma against his chest with both arms and then carefully lowering her into her crib. She stirred as her skin touched the cool sheet, and he held his breath. But she didn't wake. He closed the door gently behind him.

When the alarm sounded on Friday morning—thirty minutes earlier than usual—Len felt his exhaustion like a weight, pinning him to the bed. He staggered to the kitchen to make coffee, then began to prepare a dinner for that evening. The *Joy of Cooking* insisted on flopping closed, so he found a box of spaghetti and laid it lengthwise across the pages to prop it open. He followed the recipe carefully, first browning the chicken breasts in a pan and then adding two tablespoons of paprika.

He was just covering the dish with foil when he heard Jessie calling to him. His heart quickened with the triumph of it, and he smiled to himself as he slid the dish into the fridge. There! He had made dinner. He would write a note to Sarah, asking her to put it in the oven at five, so it would be ready when he arrived. His body buzzed with the accomplishment and the caffeine, but he could feel the edges of his weariness like a hazy frame around his brain. All day it would shrink closer and closer in, so that by early afternoon there would be just that terrible fog, no matter how many times he shook his head to clear it, or how many cups of coffee he drank. But for now it was held at bay, and he was grateful.

He wiped his hands on the kitchen towel. "I'm coming," he called to Jessie.

That evening when Len opened the door the smell of the chicken cooking filled the apartment.

"Daddy!" Jessie greeted him. "I'm hungry. What's for dinner?"

"Chicken Paprika," Len said triumphantly, hugging her. "Just you wait. It will be delicious." He looked at Sarah. "Everything go okay?"

Sarah nodded. "She's been begging for a snack, but I put it off. Whatever you made smells delicious. I didn't want her to spoil her appetite."

Len beamed. He imagined that he heard a new note of respect in Sarah's voice.

"Thank you," he said, grinning.

After Sarah left, Len opened the oven. The chicken did look delicious, reddish brown and bubbly. He boiled some frozen peas and together he and Jessie set the table.

"Is Emma going to eat this, too?" Jessie asked. "She only has five teeth."

"Oh, we'll mash it up for her." He put some of the peas and a small piece of chicken into a little bowl and mashed at it with a fork. Margie had suggested he buy a blender, but he hadn't; they had been getting by okay like this.

Len prepared a plate for Jessie and poured milk into her favorite cup. Then he lifted Emma into her high chair.

"Incoming," he said, making the spoon whir through the air like an airplane. As soon as Emma opened her mouth, he pushed the spoon inside. Immediately, Emma began to cry, her face turning pink as tears welled up in her eyes.

"What?" Len protested, his feelings hurt. "It can't be that bad. Jessie, go on. Eat."

Jessie took a small bite of her chicken and leaped to her feet.

"Ouch, Daddy! It hurts! It hurts!"

"Oh, for Christ's sake," Len said. The chicken looked perfect; he was proud of how perfect it looked. "Don't be ridiculous. Look." He grabbed a piece of chicken from Jessie's plate and popped it in his mouth. Immediately, he spat it into his hand.

"What the . . . ?" He looked at Jessie, who was guzzling her milk. "You're right, Jessie. It hurts."

In her high chair, Emma was howling and drooling, her slobber streaked with red. Len held her sippy cup to her lips and then went quickly to the cabinet, pulling out the little canister of red spice he had used that morning. In his exhausted fog, he had assumed that it was paprika, but now, even before he read the label, he knew what it would say. Cayenne pepper.

"Goddamn it," he said, hurling it into the sink. "I'm just so tired."

"Goddamn what?" Jessie said, looking at him over her cup. Her face was full of concern.

"Nothing. Nothing. And don't you use that word." He put his fingers to his temples. "Emma, would you please just *shush*? I can't even hear myself think."

Emma was howling loudly, her cup thrown to the floor.

"I know what we'll do." Quickly, Len pulled the ice cream from the freezer and opened the top. He could see the crystals around the edges of the carton where it had melted and refrozen the night they'd gone to the store. He grabbed a clean spoon from the drawer and scooped some ice cream onto it. Then he pushed it into Emma's mouth. Gradually, her sobs ceased. Len breathed deeply.

"Thank God."

"Daddy, I want ice cream, too," Jessie said.

"No, Jessie. No ice cream before dinner."

"But Emma got ice cream. It's not fair." Jessie glared at him with the injustice of it.

"I needed to get her to stop crying," Len protested. "The chicken hurt her mouth."

"The chicken hurt my mouth, too."

"I'll tell you what, Jessie. Eat your peas while I make some macaroni. And then we'll have ice cream."

"Two scoops?"

"Okay. Two scoops."

"It's a deal." She held out her little hand toward him, and he shook it.

"It's a deal," he repeated.

That night, Len felt defeated. Twice, he picked up the phone to call Margie, just to have someone to tell it all to. But he could already hear how whiny he would sound, and the tone of Margie's response: sympathetic, yes, but oh-so-matter-of-fact.

"Do you mean to tell me . . ." she would say. He couldn't bear it.

In the kitchen, the colander he'd used to drain the macaroni was still in the sink. With a sigh, he dumped the whole pan of chicken into it and turned on the faucet, watching as the stream of water washed the sauce away. Then he pulled off a piece of meat and put it in his mouth. It still tasted overwhelmingly of cayenne, but it was no longer painful. He got out Margie's Tupperware and lined them up on the counter, then divided the chicken between them. There, he thought wearily. Lunch for a week. But there was none of the morning's triumph in it. He sealed each container and placed them in the fridge, then quickly cleaned the kitchen, showered, and fell into bed.

He dreamed that Jessie was in a boat on a river, crying as the current caught hold of it, carrying it away. He stood on the shore, watching her, unable to move. In the dream, panic rose in him, so that it was almost a relief when he woke with a start and realized that the cries were real.

"Jessie," he called. "I'm coming."

But it was not Jessie after all, but Emma, who stood at the edge of her crib with the end of each little pajama-clad foot poking out between the bars. Len reached for her as his eyes sought out the shape of Jessie in her bed, his heart light with the relief of seeing her sleeping safely there.

He tried the rocker, as usual, but Emma would not settle. She kept sliding off his chest and wriggling to the floor. At last Len set her down, then got up and closed the door. He stretched out on the orange and brown carpet and pulled Emma against him.

"I've been working on the railroad . . ."

In the morning, he woke to find Jessie standing over him, a delightedly puzzled look on her face.

"Daddy! Can I sleep on the floor, too?"

"Where's Emma?" he asked, the panic of his dream washing over him again. "Where's your sister?"

"Daddy, she's right there."

Len looked where she pointed, and there Emma was, lying half on him like she had fallen there, with her cheek and chest against his belly and her knees tucked up under her on the carpet.

"Thank God."

Len's back ached and his bladder was uncomfortably full. Gently, he shifted out from under her, lowering her head to rest against the floor. Amazingly, she stayed asleep.

Len smiled at Jessie and raised his finger to his lips, and together they snuck out of the bedroom.

That evening, before bed, Len took Emma's blanket from her crib. Then he lay down on the carpet again, spreading it over his legs. He pulled Emma over so that she sat beside him.

"Daddy," Jessie looked at him in surprise. "Are you gonna sleep on the floor again? What about books?"

"We'll read books in a minute," he said. "Just wait. I want to show Emma something."

He pushed the blanket down so that it bunched around his ankles. Then he wrapped his arms around himself and shivered.

"Brrr! I'm cold," he said. "So, I reach down, grab the blanket, and pull it over me."

Jessie watched his pantomime with wide eyes. When he had pulled the blanket up to his chin and lowered himself back to the floor, she spoke up.

"I want to do it. Can I do it?"

She sat down on the other side of him and pretended to shiver, then pulled the blanket up around her.

"See, Daddy. I can do it."

Len sighed; Emma had crawled under the crib. "Yes, I see you can. But you're not the one waking up in the middle of the night because you're cold."

Jessie was quiet for a moment, still snuggled under the blanket.

"Maybe she's not cold, Daddy," she said at last. "Maybe she misses Mommy. Sometimes I miss Mommy and I cry."

Len looked at his daughter. "You do?"

"Yes." Jessie stared at him intently.

"Well," Len said finally, "you'll see her soon. And I'm here."

Jessie nodded. "I know. But sometimes I still feel the cry."

Len frowned. "I don't hear you crying, Jessie."

"I hold it in."

"Oh, Jessie. You don't have to do that. You can cry. It's okay."

"When Emma cries, you look so sad."

"Do I?"

Jessie nodded.

"I'm not sad because she's crying, Jessie. Sometimes, I'm . . . I'm just tired, is all. I probably just look tired."

"You look sad."

Len smiled. "Well, I'm not sad, okay? And it's fine if you cry. We all need to cry sometimes."

"Even you?"

"Yes."

"Daddy?"

"Yes?"

"Do you hold in the cry, ever?"

He looked at Jessie's serious face. "I guess I do, sometimes."

"So we're just the same, Daddy."

"Yes. But I'm a grown-up. Sometimes grown-ups have to hold in their cries."

"Why?"

"I don't know. Because we have responsibilities. We have to go to work. And take care of our kids. But you're a little girl. You don't have to hold it in."

"I know." But Len could tell by her face that she was not convinced.

"Look, Jessie. Next time I feel like crying, I won't hold it in, okay? And you do the same."

"Even if we're in the grocery store?"

"Even then." He grinned. "I don't know what people will think, though, when they see me crying in the grocery store."

Jessie smiled. "Maybe a lady will give you a lollipop, too, Daddy." She paused. "Can we read books here tonight, Daddy? I like it on the floor. It's cozy."

CHAPTER 15

Len

Summer came, and with it, the fog. The days hardly grew warmer, but the light lasted longer, and people's spirits rose. For Len, everything felt easier. There was one fewer class to teach, and all were during the day. The evenings were so long now that often after dinner he got out the stroller and they went for a walk. There was no playground near the campus, but it didn't matter. There was a long stretch of grass in front of the main library where the girls could play. Emma was walking in earnest now, and the closely cut lawn was perfect; she never cried when she fell.

Sometimes, Len would try to lie down in the grass while they played, gazing up through the misty air, or letting his eyes close, just for a moment. But Jessie would not stand for that.

"Come chase me," she would call to him. Or, "Fly eagle!" She would come and pull off his shoes and struggle to lift his feet to her belly.

"Come on, Daddy. Help. Your feet are too heavy."

Still lying on his back, he would fit his feet against her waist and, reaching for her hands to steady her, he would push her up into the air. "Fly eagle!" he would say, gently rocking her back and forth.

Emma liked to fly eagle, too, but he always kept hold of her hands. With Jessie, he could let go after a while and she would spread her arms wide.

"Look at me, Emma! I'm flying!"

They were flying eagle one Wednesday evening, Jessie suspended above him against the gray sky, when she suddenly dropped her arms and clutched at his hands.

"Daddy, get me down! I see Sarah!"

When Len had brought Jessie to the ground and pushed himself up to sitting, he saw her, too. Sarah was walking across the grass toward them, smiling and waving at the girls. They ran to her, Emma teetering a little on her chubby legs.

Sarah reached down and scooped Emma up before she fell, while Jessie did a little skip of delight in front of her.

"I was flying eagle, Sarah!"

"I saw that," Sarah said, grinning at her. "And I said to myself, 'What a beautiful family.' And then I realized, 'I know that family.'"

"And it was us?"

"It was you." She smiled broadly at Len and gently set Emma down. "They're getting so big, aren't they?"

Len nodded. Sarah had been watching the girls in the afternoon for almost four months now, and yet still Len could not stop the flutter of nerves he felt in her presence. He did not wholly understand it. For a while, he had thought it was simply the knowledge of all that she had seen, and that the unsettled feeling was just the remnants of his shame. But as the weeks passed, his disquiet had persisted.

Sarah was just so, so . . . so *what*? So *perfect*, was the word that came to mind. And she was, really; she was the perfect nanny. He looked forward to coming home every afternoon. The apartment was always tidy, although he had told her more than once not to worry about the mess, that he wasn't paying her to clean.

"Oh, I'm not worried," she had answered. "But the girls should learn to pick up after themselves."

For the first few days, he had scooped up Emma as soon as he came home and headed to the changing table. He did it out of habit; Laurel had never changed Emma's diaper if she expected him home. "I change enough diapers," she would say. "It's your turn."

But now Emma was always dry in the afternoons, and just that little thing—what a relief it was! Because now he didn't have to interrupt her if she was playing happily; even better, the evening didn't begin with tears.

"You can't believe how wonderful—" he had started to gush to Sarah once, but she had given him a look that silenced him, and he had understood. If the baby's diaper was wet, of course she would change it. There was nothing remarkable in that.

But Sarah *was* remarkable nonetheless, even though he soon learned that she grew uncomfortable if he said it. There was a fresh efficiency to her. She didn't bustle, like Margie did, or at least he never saw her. But the girls, when he opened the door each afternoon, were as neat as the apartment, their faces and clothes clean. He didn't know how she did it. On the weekends, when it was just him, the apartment would be in shambles by evening, the floor littered with books and toys. The girls' bath at the end of those days was a satisfaction—to scrub the grime from their faces and the dirt from their feet. On weekdays, when they had been with Sarah, they hardly seemed to need a bath at all.

Sarah made it seem so easy. Len felt blundering in comparison. He had wondered once or twice if Jessie had told Sarah about the disastrous chicken; his face burned just thinking of it.

But—he was doing, okay, wasn't he? He made sure the girls ate their breakfast. He got them dressed and brushed their teeth before they left the house each morning. And if he didn't fix their hair as Margie had, at least he pinned it back with a barrette, to keep it out of their faces.

He looked at Jessie now and saw that her barrette had come loose. It dangled from a strand of hair at the side of her face.

"Come here, Jessie," he said, patting his lap. "Let me fix your barrette for you."

But she just tugged it out and held it in her little fist, still beaming with the excitement of seeing Sarah here.

"No thank you," she said, tossing it at him. Then she took off running down the grass. "I don't need a barrette!"

Len didn't want to scold her. And she was right: she didn't need it. As she ran, the wind pushed her long hair back, so that it seemed to float on either side of her. Jessie turned and raced back toward them, her face so full of concentration and triumph that he and Sarah both laughed.

"You have beautiful girls," Sarah said. "Both of them." She tousled Emma's hair.

Len smiled. He felt his pride in his daughters well up in him so that he was brimming with it. He looked away, suddenly shy that Sarah would see it, that she, like Laurel, might find something laughable in it, something trite. But when he snuck a look at her face, she was watching Emma, smiling, and he let out his breath and held his arms open wide for Jessie, laughing as she barreled into him. His beautiful girls.

Something shifted between Len and Sarah after that evening in the quad. There was a new ease in their interactions, a lightheartedness that hadn't been there before. Len felt his shame lifting, and with it, the disquiet he had always felt in her presence. He found himself looking forward to seeing her when he got home. She would always ask politely about his day. If he shared a little, just to get it off his chest, she listened to him with the same attentive patience that she gave the girls. She talked to him more now, too, telling him about her afternoon with the girls as she gathered her things, while Jessie listened as rapt as he to hear how she would tell it. She spoke with fondness of his daughters, laughing at the funny things they had done or said, and it was a pleasure for him, not to be so alone in his delight in them.

One Friday, on impulse, he tried to get Sarah to linger a bit, offering her a glass of wine.

"Oh, I don't think so," she said, glancing at her watch. But he sensed that her refusal wasn't wholehearted, and he quickly got out two glasses and poured the wine.

"Consider it a shift drink," he said, handing one to her.

But it didn't go well. Len had not considered how jittery with anticipation Jessie would be; she and Emma spent Saturday mornings with their mother. He pulled out coloring books and crayons, trying to get her engaged in something, so that he could sip his wine and talk to Sarah. But Jessie kept pointing at the clock.

"When do we go to Mommy's house?"

"Not until tomorrow, sweetheart."

"When's tomorrow?"

"Well, you'll go to bed. And when you wake up, it will be tomorrow."

"Is it bedtime yet?"

"Not yet."

"When is bedtime?"

"Well, first we have to have dinner. Then take a bath. Brush our teeth. Why don't you color a little so I can talk to Sarah for a bit?"

Jessie frowned. "Isn't it time for dinner?"

Len looked at the clock. She was right; it was dinnertime. He sighed. Was it too much to ask for? Ten minutes—five—to have a glass of wine with another grown-up?

Sarah shifted in her seat. She took a final sip of wine and set her glass, still half full, on the table. She stood up, smiling at him with half her mouth, as if in sympathy, as if she had guessed how much he wanted this.

"I think it's time for me to go," she said. She knelt and gave Jessie a quick hug. "So you three can have your dinner."

The next morning after breakfast, he took the girls to Laurel's. Len always drove them to the house. He didn't want Laurel to come to his apartment. Despite its Spartan ugliness, Len felt a growing fondness for the place; it had become a haven to him. He didn't want to hear the cutting remarks Laurel would undoubtedly make if she saw it. He didn't want her taint on it.

Home again without his daughters, Len felt a little guilty about how much he enjoyed his Saturday mornings alone. He would pour himself another cup of coffee and read the paper while he drank it, savoring every sip. When he was finished, he would spend a little while cleaning, relishing the pleasure of completing a task uninterrupted, the quiet of the house. Afterwards, he would go for a run, or work for a while, or perhaps go to the grocery store, just for the ease of doing it without the girls in tow. He relished the lunch he made for himself at noon, how simple it was to feed only himself, how relaxing to sit at the table and eat without once having to get up, the order of the kitchen barely disturbed.

The Saturday visits didn't last long; Laurel always wanted him to pick up the girls before nap time.

"I don't have a crib anymore," she had said, with a note of accusation that Len ignored. "Where would Emma sleep?"

Len suspected that it wasn't just that, but he didn't say anything. If Laurel felt guilty for the afternoon when Jessie had wandered away—well, she should. And he was always happy to have the girls home for Saturday naps. They slept heavily, as if the visits there took it out of them. And it meant that Saturday afternoons had a sweetness to them, with all of Sunday together stretching out before them. And even though Len luxuriated in every quiet moment of their absence, when he saw his daughters again, that familiar joy filled him, and the loss of tranquility seemed a small, small price to pay for such happiness.

CHAPTER 16

Len

The summer light deepened; the evenings were not so long. If they walked to campus after dinner, it was twilight already when they got home. One evening, after putting the girls to bed, Len was sitting on the tiny porch when he heard the phone ring. He ignored it at first, watching the last of the summer fog rolling into the yard. The ringing stopped, then seconds later began again, persistent. Len roused himself and went inside to answer it.

It was Laurel. Did he have a minute? she asked. She had news.

Len leaned against the wall and closed his eyes.

"Well?"

"I just thought you should know. I'm putting the house on the market."

Len opened his eyes. "Why?"

"I'm moving."

"Oh," he said, feeling his annoyance rise. Of course she was moving if she was selling the house. "To where?" he asked, keeping his voice even.

"Ashland."

The name sounded familiar, but he couldn't place it. "Where's that?"

"It's small. Near Jacksonville."

"Florida?"

He heard the shrill peal of Laurel's laughter. "Not Florida. Oregon."

"Oregon! But what . . . what about the girls?"

For a moment, there was silence on the line. "I'm not the custodial parent, Len," she said at last.

"Yes, but . . . But that doesn't mean . . . I never thought you wouldn't want to see them."

"Len, it's Oregon, not China. It's just over the state line. I can still visit. They can visit."

"But it'll make it harder, won't it?"

Again, the peal of laughter. "Divorce does that, doesn't it?" She sounded almost gleeful, as if at last she had found a way to peg this all on him. She would consider herself free to move wherever she wanted, no matter what that meant for the girls. And in her mind, he would carry the blame, for it was he who had wanted the divorce, he who had asked for custody.

"So you'll keep seeing them on Saturdays?" he asked. "But where? I'm not going to take them all the way to—"

"Well, that's why I wanted to talk to you," Laurel interrupted him. "I'm going to have to skip a couple of weeks, I think. Just while I move. Get settled in."

Len's heart fell. A couple of weeks. To Jessie it might as well be a year. Already she didn't understand what "the weekend" meant, asking every evening when they would go to Mommy's house, how many days, how many times she would have to go to bed and wake up again before Saturday came.

"Laurel," he said at last. "Think about Jessie. This will be very hard on her."

"I can't imagine it will be any harder than suddenly not living with her mother."

Len said nothing. Again, silence descended on the line.

"Well," he said at last. "I guess you've made up your mind."

"Len, I had to," she said quickly. "I mean, it wasn't my idea. But . . . Kent is moving. He's signing on with a builder there. It's a good opportunity for him."

"Kent." It was the first time Laurel had spoken his name to

him; Len's stomach turned over to hear it. "And you're going with him. With Kent."

"Yes." Her voice turned petulant. "Why shouldn't I get to be happy, Len? You have the girls. I have nothing."

He sighed. "Laurel, you *gave* me custody. I didn't force you."

He could hear her crying.

"Well," he said at last. "I hope it works out for you. I hope you're . . . happy."

"You do?"

"Yes," he responded automatically, but once he had said it, he knew he had spoken sincerely. He wished Laurel no ill, but he doubted she would ever be rid of the discontent that hounded her. He had spent years trying to make her happy, but he was free of that now, and the relief of it made him beneficent.

"Yes," he said again. "I really do hope you'll be happy." He paused, unsure of what more to say. "Good luck," he said at last.

"Oh, Len." Laurel gave a little half-sob into the phone, and immediately Len regretted his words. He braced himself for another outpouring of self-pity. But after a moment of strained silence, Laurel cleared her throat. "Will you tell Jessie . . . Will you tell the girls for me?"

It was amazing how fast his repugnance came back. "Are you not going to say goodbye?"

"Oh, I can't. We're leaving on Friday."

"But before you leave?"

"Oh, Len. I just can't. There's so much to do. And don't you think it will be easier this way? Jessie has no sense of time, anyway. She'll hardly know I'm a little farther away, that she'll have to wait a little longer."

There were any numbers of things Len could say to this. Easier for Laurel, not easier for him. Certainly not easier for Jessie. He could have told Laurel how Jessie tried her three-year-old best to count the days until Saturday. But he bit his tongue; Laurel would do what she wanted. She always had.

Len did not think he could stomach Jessie's disappointment about Laurel's moving and the temporary cessation of her weekend visits with her mother. Whenever he imagined telling her, he could picture too clearly how her serious little face would fall, her forehead wrinkling as she struggled to understand. It left him feeling wretched, and so he put it off.

But on Thursday morning, he knew he could wait no longer. And so he armed himself against Jessie's misery as well as he could. As they ate their cereal together at the kitchen table, he set down his coffee carefully and said, "How would you girls like to go to the zoo on Saturday?"

Jessie whooped and Emma, not understanding, dropped her spoon on the floor and clapped her hands. Len sighed with relief. He took another sip of coffee and stole a glance at his older daughter. Jessie was regarding him seriously.

"Did you say Saturday, Daddy?" she said. "Saturday is . . . What about Mommy?"

"Mommy is . . . Mommy can't see you this Saturday, sweetheart."

He watched as Jessie's face fell; he saw the effort with which she fought back her tears and held his arms out for her. She buried her face in his chest, not making a sound.

"It's okay, Dessie," he said. "You don't have to hold in the cry."

He felt her body begin to shake against him, but still she made no sound. Holding her gently, he told her that Laurel was moving to another house, that she needed time to get settled in.

"Where is the new house?" Jessie asked him, her face still hidden against him. He could feel the wetness of her tears where they had seeped through the fabric of his shirt. "Is it far?" she said.

"Not too far," he said carefully. "You'll still get to see her."

"But far?"

He sighed. "Don't worry, Dessie. You'll see her soon, I promise.

And . . . we'll go to the zoo together, okay? We'll see otters, monkeys, maybe bjrafs . . ." He purposely pronounced it like she did, trying to get a rise out of her, but Jessie remained motionless in his arms, her face hidden.

"Maybe you can ride a camel?" He hesitated. The zoo in Eureka was small. They might not even have camels, he thought with despair. "If they have any," he added, not bearing the thought of having to disappoint her again.

"But we can get ice cream. They'll definitely have ice cream." He cast about for something, anything to mitigate her despair. "Maybe we could invite Sarah to come with us?"

Jessie stirred against his chest, pulling back her wet face to peer up at him. "Really?"

He smiled with relief. "Of course. We'll ask her this afternoon."

"And she'll come?"

He sighed. "I don't know, Jessie. But we'll ask, okay?"

"Can we ask her now?" Jessie asked.

"No, sweetheart. She might still be sleeping. We'll ask her this afternoon when she comes."

Jessie had been satisfied with that, but as soon as he got to his office, Len dialed Sarah's number. He knew that Jessie would almost certainly ask Sarah herself as soon as Sarah picked them up from daycare, and, without him, Sarah would have no way of understanding the seriousness with which Jessie made the invitation, nor the deluge of tears that might follow if she refused.

"No, sillypants," he could almost hear Sarah responding. "That's something for you to do with your dad." Or worse, "Don't you see your mom on Saturdays?"

Len waited anxiously as the phone rang. When Sarah picked up at last, her 'Hello?' a little breathless, Len was surprised by his relief.

"Oh, you're there," he said. "Thank God."

Sarah was immediately worried. "What is it? Did something happen?"

"Oh, no," he said at first. "It's nothing. Well, actually, it *is* something," he stammered. Quickly, he explained about Laurel, and how there would be no visit this Saturday, maybe none for a while, even, and how he had tried to circumvent Jessie's despair by suggesting a trip to the zoo.

"But it wasn't working," he said apologetically, "until I said we could invite you, too."

Sarah let out her breath. "Wow."

"I'm sorry, Sarah. I know this puts you in a strange position. But I just felt I needed to explain, before you heard it from Jessie herself."

"I understand. But Dr. Walters—how could you?" He heard her give a sharp, exasperated little sigh, but she didn't speak again.

"How could I?" he said at last.

"Oh, don't be dense. This is exactly why I didn't want this job. I *told* you. I didn't want to have anything to do with Laurel. This is not my business. And now *I'm* the one who has to disappoint that sweet little girl."

"I know—I know. You're right. I'm sorry. Of course you don't need to come with us. It's just that . . . I just couldn't stand to see Jessie so upset. But, you're right, of course. I shouldn't have brought you into it."

"No, you shouldn't have," Sarah's tone was sharp, and Len was surprised by how wounded he felt by it.

"You're right, Sarah," he said again. "And I am sorry. I just called to . . . I just wanted to explain the situation. So you'd know."

"Well, thank you." Her tone was brusque. "I'll see you this evening."

When Len hung up the phone, he felt deflated and regretful, like a child who had been scolded. Sarah was right; it hadn't been fair of him to bring her into this. It wasn't her job to protect Jessie from disappointment, nor should it be her lot to bear the guilt if she couldn't. He had passed the buck. He had set her up.

Oh, God, what she must think of him! Twice, he picked up

the phone to apologize again, but each time he hung up before he finished dialing the number. He passed the afternoon in a state of dread, anticipating Sarah's cool anger and Jessie's anguish.

But when he opened the door to the apartment that evening, Jessie greeted him giddy with excitement.

"She said okay, Daddy! She said okay! Sarah's gonna come!"

Len looked up to see Sarah standing in the doorway to the kitchen, Emma in her arms. She smiled at him ruefully.

"Really?" he asked.

"Yeah," she said. "I couldn't bear to disappoint her either." Then she narrowed her eyes at him. "But don't you *dare* pull something like this again."

Len's heart quickened. He looked away, feeling scolded again. "Yes, ma'am."

He heard Sarah's sudden laughter and dared to look up again. "What's so funny?"

"You don't have to look so chastised."

He grinned. "I can't help it. You're so . . ."

"I'm so what?"

"So . . . fierce."

She laughed again. "Am I?"

Jessie was watching them. "What does fierce mean, Daddy?"

Len leaned down and hugged her. "Fierce, you know. Like a lion." He raised both hands, curled his fingers, and gave a roar.

Jessie looked at Sarah, puzzled. "Sarah's not fierce."

"I wouldn't be so sure," he said, winking at his daughter, his heart suddenly soaring.

"You're not fierce, are you?" Jessie said, turning to Sarah seriously. "You're nice. Like a . . . like a rabbit."

"Thanks, Jessie," Sarah said. "Your father's just . . ." She trailed off, her grin fading.

"I'm just joking, Jess," Len said quickly, finishing Sarah's sentence before she could. Because he knew suddenly what she had been thinking: "Your father's just flirting."

Sarah was right—again. He had been flirting, or something like it. In an instant, Len understood. It was like one of those rare summer days in Arcata when the sun burns through the mist and the sky is so deeply blue that it is almost impossible to picture the fog that has shrouded everything only moments before. The sun is a refulgent orb in a brilliant sky, and everything sparkles and is clear.

Len watched Sarah gather up her things, and it was as if he saw her clearly for the first time. Whereas before he had seen only her calm efficiency, now he saw each movement as one of grace. He took in her slim waist and slender limbs, the firm curve of her breasts beneath her shirt. How had he not noticed how beautiful she was? When she passed Emma to him, his fingers brushed the bare skin on her arm. It was warm and smooth and, as they said goodbye, he had to suppress the impulse to reach out and touch her arm again, just to feel how soft she was.

CHAPTER 17

Len

It was awkward, standing in line at the zoo's entrance the next morning. Sarah stood a little apart from them, not speaking, with her bag slung over one shoulder. Len didn't know what to say.

"You could put that in the stroller, if you want," he said at last, just to say something. "Then you wouldn't have to carry it."

"I'm fine." Sarah glanced at the stroller. It was the flimsy umbrella kind, and Emma was inside; there was nowhere to put a bag.

"You could hang it here," he said, tapping the hooked handles.

"Really, I'm fine," she said. "It's not heavy."

They both watched Jessie, then, who was hopping from foot to foot impatiently. "When are we going to get *in*?"

Inside the stroller, Emma began to squirm unhappily, and both Len and Sarah bent down to her at the same time, their heads almost colliding.

"Sorry," Sarah said, straightening.

Len undid the stroller strap and lifted Emma out and onto his hip.

"Today, Sarah, you're off the clock. You don't have to lift a finger." Len laughed nervously and heat rose to his face. He sounded so grand—like a lord deigning to give his servant the day off.

Suddenly, the line moved, and Jessie rushed into the empty space that opened before them. "Come *on*, Daddy," she said.

But with Emma on his hip, Len had only one hand for the stroller. When he tried to push it forward, it tottered on two wheels. He looked at Sarah helplessly; she stood watching him with her hands on her hips, her eyes glinting.

"Yes?"

"Um, would you mind . . . ?"

"Lifting a finger?" she finished, and then they both laughed, Len laughing and blushing both, but his heart was soaring again, at the way she didn't shy from meeting his eye, and the delicious timbre of her laughter.

"Daddy, stop laughing and come *on*," Jessie said.

After that, the awkwardness was gone. Inside the zoo, there was nothing to do but keep up with Jessie, who rushed excitedly from one exhibit to the next, searching hard for whatever animal was inside before saying, "Let's see another animal!" and dashing off again. Len carried Emma, so that he could hold her up to see, and Sarah pushed the stroller. She had put her bag, at last, into the seat.

Len had thought Emma would be too young to appreciate the zoo, but he had been wrong. Each time she saw an animal, she squealed with delight, and watching her reaction, it was impossible not to smile, too. And so the day passed, the girls grinning about the animals, and Len and Sarah grinning about the girls, so that by lunchtime Len's cheeks felt sore from smiling.

They found a shady spot on a bench near the river otters, and Len brought out the peanut butter sandwiches and apples that he had packed.

"Sandwich?" he said, offering one to Sarah, but she had brought her own. It was wrapped in aluminum foil, and as she unwrapped it, Len eyed it longingly. The bread looked crusty and wholesome; he could see the frilly edges of lettuce between the slices, a bit of something red—tomato, perhaps, or pepper.

"Would you like some?" Sarah said, holding the sandwich out to him, her eyes gleaming; she was laughing at him again.

Len grinned. "No, thanks. I'm good with this." He raised the peanut butter sandwich at her. "Do you want a bite?"

Sarah made a face. "No, thank you. I can't stand peanut butter."

"Don't like peanut butter? Jess, can you believe it? Sarah doesn't like peanut butter."

Jessie looked at Sarah with concern. "But it's good."

"Well, I don't think so."

"I don't think we would survive without peanut butter," Len said. He handed a piece of sandwich to Emma.

Sarah ate only two-thirds of her sandwich. Then she wrapped it loosely in the foil again and handed it to Len.

"Here you go, Dr. Walters," she said. "I saw you eyeing it."

He blushed. "I wasn't."

"You were. And it's okay. I'm not going to eat it all anyway."

Len took the remains of the sandwich guiltily, but he couldn't resist. It was turkey, with a smoky cheese he didn't recognize, and tomato. He finished it in three bites and immediately regretted that it was gone.

After lunch, Len changed Emma's diaper, and Sarah checked the schedule; if they hurried, they could just make it to the sea lion show. They walked quickly to the small amphitheater, but when Len bent to retrieve Emma, he saw that she was already asleep. So they sat at the end of the first row, with the stroller parked beside them on the pavement. Jessie had slid onto the bleachers first, so Sarah had no choice but to sit next to Len.

The show began, but Len could not keep his eyes on the stage. He kept glancing down at Sarah's bare arm beside him. It was smooth, almost hairless, her skin the color of tea with cream. It was impossible to stop his gaze. Just beyond the arc of her biceps was the line of her green halter top, not low exactly, but low enough that he could see the golden slope of her chest, the soft ridges of her collarbones. Len's mouth went dry; with an effort he tore his eyes away.

"You there! In the green top. Come on up and give us a hand."

Len started, feeling caught out; blood rushed to his face. But the announcer was looking not at him but at Sarah, smiling his show-business smile and beckoning her to the front of the crowd.

Beside him, Sarah laughed as everyone in the audience turned to look at her.

"No," she mouthed toward the stage, shaking her head.

Len nudged her with his elbow. "Go ahead. Go on up there."

But the next moment it was clear that her reluctance was all part of the show. The announcer had counted on it.

"Give her a little encouragement, Archie," he said. The trainer made a gesture with his hand, and the sea lion leaned to one side and moved his flipper, as if beckoning her, too. The crowd laughed, and so did Sarah. Jessie bounced in her seat excitedly.

"Go on, Sarah! Go! Archie wants you to!"

Smiling, Sarah climbed off the bleacher and went to stand by the sea lion, where the trainer said something to her quietly and the announcer told the audience to get their cameras ready.

At a signal from the trainer, Archie stretched out his sleek neck and held his whiskered snout against Sarah's cheek. All over the stands, cameras flashed. Sarah didn't flinch, but when the kiss was over, she wiped her cheek with the back of her hand. The trainer tossed Archie a fish.

"Gives new meaning to morning breath, doesn't it?" the announcer joked, and everyone laughed.

When Sarah came back to her seat, Jessie was green with envy.

"I want the sea lion to kiss me," she said. "What did it feel like?"

"Wet," Sarah said. "And fishy."

Len grinned. He had no camera, but it didn't matter. He would never forget this day.

There was, in fact, a camel ride, much to Len's relief. They did that next, while Emma still slept.

"But she'll miss it," Jessie said, looking at her sleeping sister with concern. "Let's wake her up."

"Oh no you don't," Len said, intercepting her. "She's too little to ride the camel. It's just for big girls."

So Jessie rode the camel without her sister, but with three other children. Since she was the smallest, she got to be in front. Her short legs stuck out almost horizontally on either side of the camel's back. She let her body sway exaggeratedly from side to side as the camel lumbered around the ring. When she passed where he and Sarah stood watching, she beamed down at them.

Len heard Sarah make a noise beside him, an almost inaudible hum of appreciation. He glanced down at her and saw her smiling, and something quickened in him. Without thinking, he reached out and took her hand. He held it for just a moment, surprised by how light and cool it was. A moment later, she gently took it back from him, but he was not sorry he had done it. She smiled at him kindly as she did it, and he smiled back sheepishly, feeling that he had taken something from her that she had not offered. But, for once, he did not blush.

CHAPTER 18

Len

How different it felt after that day. Len could barely wait to see Sarah every afternoon, and he sensed that she knew it. She smiled at him as his eyes followed her around the room. Whenever he asked her if she could stay, just for a minute, just for one glass of wine, she shook her head, but she wasn't cruel about it.

Len wasn't oblivious to the pattern of her refusals, but he pretended to be. Even knowing what her response would be, he asked anyway, because he even liked how she refused him, shaking her head just slightly, her eyes kind. And then, one Thursday evening, when he had invited her to dinner for the umpteenth time, she lifted the lid of the pot on the stove and sniffed at it appraisingly. Len held his breath.

"Okay," she said at last. "I'll stay."

Len could not contain his delight. "Great!" he said. "Jessie! Sarah's going to stay for dinner."

"Yippee!"

Sarah lingered after dinner, sipping her wine, and when Jessie asked if she would read their bedtime books that night, she nodded.

"I'd love to," she said.

While she was in the bedroom, reading to the girls, Len quickly cleaned up the kitchen, his heart pounding. By the time he finished the dishes, she still had not emerged. He poured himself another glass of wine, and then, after a pause, he filled the empty glass that Sarah had left on the counter. He took both glasses out onto the tiny deck behind the apartment, leaving the door open so that he would hear her. He set her glass down on the railing and stood looking out into the night. It was October already, not that anyone could tell, Len thought. He had learned to accept that in Arcata the shift in seasons meant little more than a dip of a few degrees, the summer fog giving way to winter's rain. Len looked up, surprised to see a few stars winking in the dark sky. A light wind blew, rustling the high limbs of the sequoia in the yard.

Suddenly, Sarah was at his side, startling him.

"Sorry," she said. "I didn't mean to scare you."

"I didn't hear you."

"I was being quiet."

An awkward silence descended. Sarah tipped her head back and her eyes followed the massive trunk of the sequoia up into the night. Len let his gaze rest for a moment on the pale thumbprint at the base of her throat.

He swallowed. "Sorry," he said at last, gesturing toward the interior. "I didn't mean to subject you to that."

"Oh, no. It was nice."

"It took a while. Were they okay?"

"Yes. I sat with them for a bit afterwards. Just until they fell asleep."

"I never do that."

"That's what Jessie said. I said it was a treat."

Len smiled. "They're asleep already? That *is* a treat."

"Why?"

"Oh, usually Jessie will be up and down for a while before she settles. 'I need to pee. I need a drink of water. I need another kiss.'"

Sarah nodded, shifting beside him. She reached for her glass, took a sip, and set it deliberately back on the railing. Her arm brushed his.

Len's heart raced. Was it possible that Sarah had sat with the girls until they fell asleep so that . . . ? His mind could barely form the thought, it was so unlikely. But could it be?

He set his glass next to hers on the railing, and as he withdrew his hand, he brushed her arm with his. She did not move away. He could feel how hard his heart was beating; surely, she could hear it, too.

"Sarah," he said, and that was all, but somehow the two soft syllables managed to contain all the weeks of his loneliness and longing. He saw Sarah turn her face up to look at him, her skin pale and luminous in the light from the still-open doorway.

"Sarah," he said again, and it was almost a whisper this time. And then, unbelievably, he was kissing her. At first only their lips touched, dry and soft and tentative. But then Len felt Sarah's fingers on his arm and with her touch something was released between them. Len reached out for her; his hands were on her back, her sides, her face. Her mouth tasted like white wine and something else, something unidentifiable but delicious. He never wanted to stop kissing her, but after a minute he forced himself to pull away.

He looked down at her. "Is this okay?"

She laughed softly. "What do you think?"

She couldn't kiss him; he was so much taller than she was. But she took a little half step closer and reached for his arm again, and that was all the invitation he needed. He kissed her again, more deeply, while his hands moved across her back. She was so slender—he could feel the ridges of her spine. He traced them all the way down, then moved his hands up her sides. He felt the give at her waist, the hard rise of her ribs. As his hands moved up along her sides, his wrist brushed against the outer curve of her breast. He stilled his hands and pulled back reluctantly to apologize; he was so nervous that he might overstep. But Sarah gave a little sigh and seemed to lean, just a little, into his hand, and after that he did not hold back.

There were three more evenings like that. Each time, Sarah put the kids to bed and sat with them until they were asleep, while Len cleaned the kitchen, his heart pounding in anticipation. Despite their desire, they were restrained. Their hands went everywhere, but their clothes stayed on; it was an unspoken understanding between them.

After a while, her breath hot against his ear, Sarah would whisper, "We'd better stop now," and, with an effort, he would. It killed him, but he didn't hold it against her. He felt grateful simply for being allowed to touch her.

Twice, they were together on the deck. And then the dry weather ended and the days grew rainy and cool; it was too wet to be outside in the evenings. Shyly, Len suggested his bedroom, but Sarah shook her head. They made out on the couch, instead, but Len could sense how wary she was. She kept glancing at the hallway that led to the girls' room.

"They're asleep," he reminded her gently, and she nodded, but he could tell she was not at ease. After another moment, she pulled away for good. "I'd better go."

She did not stay again after that night. Something had changed in her. She still greeted him warmly when he came from work. Once, she even agreed to stay for dinner, but when Len pushed back his chair and said, "Bath time, girls," she rose to go.

"How come you're not going to put me to bed this time?" Jessie said, and Len wanted to hug his daughter for asking what he would not presume to ask.

"I've got to get back to my own house, sweetheart," Sarah told her. "I have to take my own bath and get ready for my own bed."

She spoke kindly, and Len could see Jessie's eyes widen with the idea of it: that Sarah, too, had her own bedtime rituals to attend to. But Len felt that all the *owns*—my *own* house, my *own* bath, my *own* bed—were really meant for him. They fell on his ears like bricks, the heavy base of the wall that he could sense she was building between them.

Sarah glanced at the cluttered table, the dishes in the sink.

"It's rude of me to leave you with this mess," she said. "Let me help you clean up."

But this was just a formality, it was clear. Sarah had to know that with the girls to put to bed, Len wouldn't begin on the kitchen until later. And Len, still tender from the sting of her rejection—for that is what it was, she could not deny it—was suddenly irked by her insincerity.

"It's fine," he said brusquely. "I've got it under control." He wiped the worst of the food from Emma's face and lifted her from her high chair. "Come on, Jessie. Bath."

His voice was wounded; Sarah looked at him sadly. Len looked away, burning with emotions he dared not name.

"I don't need your pity—" he began, and then made himself stop, because Jessie was looking up at him curiously.

"Len, I'm not—" Sarah began.

"No?" he said. He couldn't help himself. But they had to stop this now. He would not talk like this in front of his daughters. He took a breath.

"Thank you for having dinner with us, Sarah. Goodnight." His tone had changed completely; he spoke in the voice he used with her when the girls were listening.

"Jess, give Sarah a hug goodbye." He took Emma's sticky hand in his and made it wave at her. "Goodnight, Sarah."

That had been on Thursday. On Saturday, they had plans to go together to an orchard in Fortuna. Len spent Friday in a state of resigned dread, sure that Sarah would not go after all. But when he brought it up that afternoon, steeling himself for her excuses, she only nodded slowly.

"That's right," she said, "I said I would go, didn't I?" She, too, was using the voice she used with the girls, and just like her politeness from the other night, it too felt barbed, intentional: another layer of bricks laid between them. "What time?"

In the morning, she met them at the house, but she didn't come inside. She wanted to drive herself, she said. She would follow them in her car, since she didn't know the way.

"Sarah, this is silly. Just ride with us," Len said, exasperated. "We don't bite, do we, girls?"

And then they all laughed, because they had all looked immediately at Emma, who chewed incessantly now on anything and everything, and who, at that very minute, was gnawing at the corner of a wooden block.

So Sarah rode with them, and at first it seemed that perhaps it would be fine, because their shared laughter at Emma had put them all in a lighthearted mood, and the gray autumn days had finally given way to the kind of day that Len felt fall *should* be, with a sky so deeply blue you could swim in it.

Their expedition started out well enough. They were given a little wooden wagon to take into the orchard, and at this, Jessie jumped up and down excitedly. She wanted to pull it at first, and then ride in it, but once they had picked a bushel of apples in no time at all, both were impossible. The apples were unreasonably heavy. Jessie plodded down the grassy aisle between each row of trees and sulked, kicking at the fallen fruit. The ground was littered with apples, so many that it was all Len could do to stop himself from filling their basket from the ground. But to do so would hardly make a dent—there was so much waste. The sickly smell of too-ripe fruit hung in the air, making him queasy and irritable.

Oh, the whole outing was a waste. There was Sarah, wordless and withdrawn, struggling to push the stroller over the uneven ground. And Jessie, poised for a tantrum; he could see it in the way her eyebrows pulled together. She was simply waiting for an excuse.

"Come on, Jessie," he called to her as she lagged farther and farther behind, knowing he was provoking her.

"I don't *want* to walk," she whined.

He looked to Sarah, who was bent over the stroller, unfastening the strap.

"Would the stroller go in the wagon?" she said. "It's not much use on this ground."

Surely, she hadn't meant to sound accusatory, but Len felt wounded nonetheless. After all, it was his stroller, his baby, his choice to bring them both along.

He nodded and shifted the basket of apples to one side. Sarah put Emma on her hip, and Len folded the stroller and wedged it, as well as he could, inside the wagon.

"Why can't I ride in the stroller?" Jessie said, watching them. "If Sarah is gonna carry Emma?"

Len didn't answer. He continued lugging the wagon down the row. He felt overheated, not from the effort of it, but from the shame. But why? What, really, did he have to be ashamed of? It had seemed like a good, wholesome idea. He had pictured Jessie running excitedly from tree to tree, marveling at all the apples. He had pictured himself strolling along behind her with Sarah, the light golden in the changing leaves, her smooth hand in his.

He had not pictured this. Len felt both cheated and embarrassed by his own delusions. He glared at the basket of apples in the wagon. They would not eat this many in a month.

Ahead, he could see the little shed that served as the register. When they finally made it, the girl inside took their wagon and weighed the apples they had picked. Then she rang up the sale on an old-fashioned cash register. When the numbers flicked up, Len waited; surely, that was too much. He held his wallet in his hand, waiting for the girl to tell him the correct price.

"Sir?" she prompted finally, gesturing at the register. "It's seven seventy-five."

Len's mouth opened. Eight bucks for a bag of apples? Bristling, he opened his wallet and pulled out the bills.

"What a rip-off," he muttered as they trudged back to the car. "You pay less in the store."

Sarah sighed, conciliatory. "I guess you're paying for the experience."

Len laughed mirthlessly. "Some experience."

They were almost across the grassy lawn that served as the parking area when they were passed by an elderly couple headed to pick their own overpriced apples.

The woman pushed up the brim of her hat and smiled at them. Len had Jessie by one hand now, the string from the bag of apples cutting into the other. Beside him, Sarah pushed the stroller with Emma restored inside.

"What a beautiful family you have," the woman gushed. "And what a beautiful day for the orchard."

"Oh, we're not . . . I'm not . . . ." Sarah began, just as Len nodded tersely in acknowledgement. The blood rushed to his face. Because what did it matter? They were nobody to this woman; why bother to explain? Still, he noted how quickly Sarah had jumped to exclude herself, and his mood grew darker than ever.

When Jessie's tantrum finally came—she wanted to sit behind Sarah, not Daddy!—it was almost a relief to him to hear it. His daughter knew no reason to contain her malaise. If she felt irritable, tired, sad—well, the world ought to know it. The tiny thing that set her off was inconsequential, but her anguish was real. She wailed it out unfiltered. Len buckled the seatbelt around her, his ears humming with her screams.

In the car, Jessie cried herself out, then fell silent at last. After a few minutes, Sarah glanced back.

"They're both asleep," she said quietly.

Len sighed. "Thank God."

She smiled at him sympathetically, and they rode in silence for a while. Len waited, his breath shallow. Finally, she spoke.

"Len," she began. "I need to talk to you."

He nodded, his eyes not leaving the road.

"Is it okay to talk now? Since—" She gestured with her head toward the back seat.

"Of course."

"Len, I . . . I can't do it."

"Can't do what?" He knew he was being obtuse, but he didn't care. Let her say it.

"Whatever there is between us. I just can't do it. Not like this."

They were both silent for a moment, staring out the windshield.

Finally, Len said, "Like this?" He shook his head. "*This* is what I have, Sarah. It's what I have." He knew she meant the girls. She was young and beautiful. She wanted a real romance, of course, not diapers and tantrums. Resignation washed over him, leaving in its wake a sad stillness. He let out his breath. "I understand."

"I don't want to have to put your kids to bed so we can have some time together."

"I said I understand."

"I don't want to pretend that there isn't anything between us when there is."

Of course, she had to explain, for her own sake. But he found himself being drawn in, despite himself.

"Why do we have to pretend?"

But Sarah wasn't listening to him. She had opened the dam. Now it would all come out.

"I'm not going to be your daughters' babysitter and your . . . your . . . whatever I am." She paused for a moment, and then took a breath. "I'm not going to be your Maria von Trapp."

Len said nothing.

"I'm sorry, Len. But I just can't."

He nodded, not trusting himself to speak. He managed, at last, a tremulous "Okay." He was relieved to be driving, and not looking at her, so he wouldn't have to see the awful pity in her eyes.

Neither of them spoke. Ahead of them, the road curved through beautiful countryside, the trees along the shoulder gleaming in the afternoon sun. It felt almost like a betrayal, that the external world could glow so brightly. His own private darkness was of no account. It would be a relief, he thought, to get back to Arcata—its soggy grayness was a better fit.

He felt Sarah's eyes on him, and then her light hand on his where he held the stick shift between their seats.

"Len? I'm sorry. I know it's—" She paused a moment, searching for words. "Inconvenient for you."

He glanced at her sharply, pulling his hand away. "Inconvenient? Sarah, you must have absolutely no idea how I feel about . . ." His voice cracked. It was over. What was the point in suffering though all the words? But he gathered himself. "How I feel about you."

She laughed softly. "I think I have *some* idea," she said. "That's why I think it would be a good idea for you to find another babysitter. So we can see where this is going. Where it might go, I mean."

Len was mute. "Another babysitter?" he managed at last.

"Don't you think?"

"So we can see," he repeated.

"If you want to, I mean," she said. She sounded tentative suddenly, unsure if she had misread him after all.

Len said nothing. Slowly, he eased the car to the side of the road. He left the engine running, for the girls. Then he turned to Sarah.

She smiled at him, still tentative. "*Do* you want to?"

He laughed. "Are you crazy?" He snaked his hand under the loose hair that fell to her shoulders, cupping his fingers around her nape. He felt her head shift a little, leaning into his hand. His throat was so full he didn't think the words would come. When they did, they were half whisper, half croak.

"I don't think I have ever wanted anything more," he said.

She laughed, looking toward the back seat. "I doubt that."

He shook his head. "Don't."

He pulled her face toward his and kissed her. Her lips were warm and giving, but after a moment she pulled away.

"Len, it's no guarantee, you know. I said, 'to see where it might go.' It might not go anywhere."

She was trying to warn him, he knew. He might still be hurt. But it was too late. She had let the light in; there was no damping it now. His heart soared.

But then he thought of Jessie, and of Emma, and how crushed they would be to lose her. He could picture Jessie's strained face when he told her, the tears she would try to hold back. And Emma. She might not understand in words, but she would understand her sister's tears. Like Jessie, she would feel the hole that Sarah would leave in their lives.

Laurel had left them, and now it would be Sarah. How much abandonment was he willing to let his daughters suffer?

But Sarah wouldn't be leaving them, Len protested to himself. She just wouldn't be their babysitter anymore. She would be his . . . his . . . *Girlfriend* was too trite a word for what she would be to him. He would get to have Sarah, but only if he made his daughters give her up. Unless . . . But he would not let his mind even form the thought. *It might not go anywhere*, she had said.

But—it might. It might! God forgive him. He couldn't help the hope that surged through him. Because *what if . . . ?* Maybe the girls wouldn't lose her after all.

We are not meant to be happy. Those were the words that had come to him when Laurel had told him she was pregnant, when he had thought that Laurel would be his lot in life. How false they sounded now. He didn't, he *couldn't* believe that now, not when happiness seemed to offer itself to him, so that he had only to reach out and grasp it, pull it toward him and cling to it with all his might.

Leonard was a father; wasn't he supposed to put his children's happiness before his own? But who was he to judge what would make his children happy? Even if he gave this up, it would be no guarantee of his daughters' happiness. Sarah might leave them anyway; already she had said that she couldn't go on the way they were. And even if she didn't . . . Even if she stayed on for another year, another two . . . Eventually she would leave and they would lose her. *He* would lose her.

No, he could not give her up. How could he give it up—this chance at joy? Even as he argued with himself, he knew how it would go. He burned with the shame of it. For it was shameful, this selfishness. He couldn't help it: he would put himself first. He was a father, true, but wasn't he also human? Wasn't he also a man? He would clutch after happiness despite himself, despite the loss it would mean for his girls. For what else could he do? He felt that it was hard-wired in him, this need to love and be loved, this drive to scrabble and strive for happiness, whatever the cost.

"It might not go anywhere," he repeated, meeting her eyes at last. "But that means it might, too. I think . . ." He paused, studying her face. "I think we should at least give it a shot, don't you?"

"Do you think I would do this to those girls if I didn't think so?"

Without dropping his gaze, she reached for her seatbelt; he heard the click of the mechanism as the buckle released. In another instant, she was in his arms. It was awkward and perfect, the way her lithe body reached out for him across the console. He held her and held her, his cheek against her hair, breathing in the scent of her. She smelled of shampoo and apples and sunshine. She smelled *right*. Something settled in him.

He held her until he heard Jessie stirring in the backseat. Then he pulled away and eased the car back onto the road.

Jessie woke up a few minutes later. She gazed out at the trees sleepily.

"Are the trees on fire, Daddy?"

"No, Jess. It's just the light."

She was silent a moment, considering.

"Are we home yet, Daddy?" she said at last.

He beamed at her in the rearview mirror. "Not yet, sweetheart. But soon."

CHAPTER 19

Three Years Later

Sarah

Sarah awoke early one morning in May with a rock of anxiety in her belly. She immediately listened for her son's cries, thinking it was he who had woken her. A week ago, she had been up several times a night, trying to soothe the cough that had wracked his small lungs and kept her constantly on edge. Now she listened hard but heard only the rush of air from the air-conditioning vent above her. Then the thermostat clicked off, the fan stopped, and from behind the closed windows came the muted calls of sparrows from a tree out in the yard.

Around the edges of the blinds, the morning light was bright. A jolt of nerves shot through her. Immediately, her eyes sought out the clock on her bedside table: it was not yet six. Letting out her breath, she closed her eyes. *Please go back to sleep*, she willed herself, knowing it was futile. She would never sleep now that she had woken, now that she had remembered.

Today was Saturday. Three weeks ago, Sarah had circled the date on the calendar and marked the square with two faintly penciled letters, *LW*. She had not dared to write Laurel's name. Jessie, at six, read anything she could. And although Sarah knew her daughter would have to be told soon enough, she had not trusted Laurel not to change her mind. Every time the phone rang, Sarah's heart leaped to her throat.

Secretly, Sarah had hoped that Laurel *would* cancel. It had been nearly two and a half years since she and Len had moved to

Bakersfield with Emma and Jessie. Two and a half years in which Laurel had not been seen by any one of them, not even once. And each day that had passed with no word from Laurel, no mention nor hint that any visit was to come, Sarah had felt equal parts relief and trepidation—relief that their lives had been allowed to proceed with such clear simplicity, and a mounting, intractable fear that such simplicity could not last.

Laurel's lack of interest in seeing the girls both baffled and infuriated Sarah. Her own son, Jay, was nineteen months old, and there were times Sarah's love for him came over her so ferociously she felt her teeth clench like an animal's. She would put her nose against the sweet-smelling silk of his head and her love for him would surge in her, so fierce that her jaw ached.

It was almost terrifying, this love. Never, even at her most passionate, had Sarah felt more bestial. More than once, a picture she had seen years ago in an old *National Geographic* came to mind. In the photograph, a mother croc stood with her mouth ajar; her baby, perched inside, peered out from between her jagged teeth. If motherhood had a picture, Sarah thought, that was it.

For me, Sarah corrected herself. *That's motherhood for me.* Because if Laurel had felt the same way, how could she possibly have given up the girls? Back then, Emma had been only slightly younger than Jay was now. Sarah could not understand how Laurel had been able to endure even a day of that arrangement, never mind the years that had now passed.

Sarah shifted in the bed, pulling the light comforter around her. Len was on his back beside her, snoring softly. She moved her leg under the sheet so that it rested against his, and her thoughts turned to Emma. Would Emma even remember Laurel today? It seemed impossible. Emma was barely four; she had spent the greatest part of her life not with Laurel, but with her.

Sarah gave a small groan of frustration. As soon as they were married, Sarah had suggested to Len that she adopt the girls outright. Already they had begun to call her Mommy. With

Laurel almost completely out of touch, she had felt herself to be all the mother that they had. And what if, God forbid, something happened to Len? She would have no claim to them at all.

But Laurel had been outraged in her refusal, accusing Len of trying to strip her of the only thing she had left of motherhood. How *could* he? Wasn't it enough that he had taken her daughters?

Oh, how indignant Sarah had been. *Laurel's* daughters, *Laurel's* motherhood? Sarah had seen firsthand what that motherhood looked like, and, frankly, the girls were better off without it. But there had been nothing they could do, and with time, Sarah's sense of urgency about the matter had eased. The first year had passed with barely a word from Laurel. She had sent a gift for each girl at Christmas, but that was all. Sarah had written her a thank-you card on the girls' behalf, but her polite words belied the turmoil of her emotions. For she hardly knew whether to rage against Laurel for abandoning her daughters or to thank God that this was all they might expect from her: that Laurel would keep her distance and Sarah would keep her girls.

Sarah knew, or guessed, that most stepmothers did not feel this way. But most stepmothers were not like her! They had not cared for their children as she had. Her thoughts drifted back to her early days with Emma, when she had been nothing more than the nanny. She could remember clearly the moment she first saw Emma. As soon as Sarah arrived at their door, Jessie had taken her hand, pulling her to the edge of the bassinet where the newborn baby lay.

"My baby," Jessie had said proprietarily, pointing at the swaddled lump, and Laurel and Sarah had both laughed.

Sarah had not been prepared for the longing the newborn raised in her. For the first few months of Emma's life, Sarah had pretended—without admitting it even to herself—that Emma was her own. And then one afternoon, when Sarah handed Emma back to Laurel, the baby had begun to cry. Perhaps Emma had objected to nothing more than the momentary interruption of her comfort, the cool air that had come against her skin. But it had been all Sarah could do not to snatch her back and comfort her. Her baby needed her.

After that, she was more cautious. What before she had felt as love, she reframed as longing. Not *this is my baby* but *I want a baby*.

"I want a baby," she had told her boyfriend Pete pleadingly, pretending not to see the fear that had leapt to his eyes.

"Whoa," he had said. "Aren't we getting a little ahead of ourselves?"

Sarah had felt chastised, ashamed. After all, she was so young; there was so much time.

What about their dreams? Pete had said playfully, wielding the cliché to hide how serious he was. Pete did not dream about having babies.

"I meant someday," she had hedged. "Someday I'd like to have a baby."

But the dissembling had changed her toward him. The chisel had found its notch, so that what began as hardly a crease between them became a crack and then a fissure and then a breach so great they both knew there was no hope. They had parted without rancor, but on the day he left, Sarah had felt a bubble of despair rise to her throat, that Pete was so much closer to his dreams now, and she so much further from her own.

At Laurel's house, too, Sarah had felt herself change. Outwardly, she was the same affectionate nanny as always; only Sarah knew how deeply she had withdrawn her heart. It was not until she finally allowed herself to fall in love with Len that the girls had become her children, too. It was ironic, really, how she had insisted that Len find another sitter when so soon afterwards she would become the girls' mother. Sarah grimaced, remembering. She had known, even then, how cruel it was to them.

Sarah knew she had gambled on their happiness, hers and

Len's, and she had won. Still, the memory of it—"No, Sarah, no!" Jessie had wailed, clinging to her legs. "I want *you!*"—made her mind swim with guilt. But hadn't it been for the best in the long run? She and Len had each other now. And their happiness— surely the girls were better off for that, too?

Sarah shifted on the bed so that her side rested against Len's. He stirred, but did not wake, and Sarah felt a rush of tenderness for him. She smiled to herself, thinking of how Len used to hold her tight against him, his nose pressed against her hair.

"You just *smell* so right," he would say, as if the vastness of his love for her could be reduced to that single kernel of truth, a visceral knowledge of belonging that left no room for doubt.

Perhaps Len simply "smelled right" to Sarah, too, and yet she knew her choice had been about something more than that. It had been the dawning realization that here it was: a man she loved, the life she wanted. She would have been a fool to pass it up.

Sarah *was* a fool, her mother had said.

"Life gets messy enough on its own, Sarah. You don't have to go looking for it."

"I wasn't looking for it," Sarah had protested. "It just happened."

"Sarah, there are plenty of men out there. Men who aren't divorced. Men who don't have two children by some crazy, promiscuous—"

"Mom, please," Sarah said, silently berating herself for ever having confided in her mother.

"Look, Sarah. You're young. You have plenty of time. There's no need to rush into this."

"I'm not rushing, Mom. It's what I want."

"There's a difference between wanting something and liking the way it feels to be needed."

Sarah was silent. She had known Len didn't exactly need her: he was managing fine with the girls on his own. And yet, there was something to what her mother said after all. Len just seemed so grateful—like her presence in his life was hardly short of miraculous. It *did* make her feel needed. Was that so bad?

"Jessie and Emma," she had said, turning the conversation. "Those girls need . . . They should have a mother."

"Sarah, they're not orphans. They already have a mother."

They need a different kind of mother, Sarah thought, but she didn't say so.

Instead she said, "I love Len, Mom. And I love those girls. They're my family."

Her mother sighed. "You'll never really be their mother, Sarah. Just you wait and see. It will be different when you have a child of your own."

Sarah had said good-bye through gritted teeth, not even trying to hide her irritation. What could her mother possibly know about it? Of course Sarah would be their mother! And hadn't she proved herself right, after all? She *had* become a mother to the girls. With Laurel's persistent absence, and the girls' hunger for a mother's love, it had been like wading into water so warm you didn't know where your skin ended and the water began. She loved Jessie and Emma like her own flesh and blood.

Only when Sarah became pregnant did she begin to worry, remembering her mother's words. What did Sarah know of flesh and blood, after all? What if the love she bore her daughters turned out to be but a pallid thing, compared to the love she would feel for this new child?

She needn't have worried. That was the thing about love: you didn't have to carve it up. Yes, her love for her newborn son was a corporeal passion that could take her breath away. But then, he was an infant, wasn't he? He came from her body; he nursed at her breast. It was just different, that was all. It didn't mean she didn't love her girls. Watching the three of them in the bath together, or seated around the kitchen table, she felt like a mother hen with her brood, and her heart swelled with love for each of them.

Sarah's body jerked suddenly, startling her back from the edge of sleep. Immediately, her thoughts turned to the day ahead, and the rock returned to her gut. She dreaded Laurel seeing the home that she and Len had built here; Laurel had a knack for belittling whatever was most dear to others. But even more than that, Sarah dreaded handing her two little girls over to Laurel—Laurel who would claim them as her own. Laurel, who believed that blood and breast were all it took to make a mother.

Sarah sighed and swung her legs out of bed. She glanced at the clock, surprised to see how little time had passed since she had first awoken. There were still more than two hours to get through until Laurel arrived at nine to pick up the girls. Now that the day was here at last, Sarah simply wanted to get it over with. Gently, she pulled the covers over Len's shoulders and rose from the bed.

At quarter to nine, the girls were ready. Sarah had ironed their best dresses and polished their best shoes. She had carefully braided their long hair, tying matching ribbons around the end of each braid. At last, she was finished. She took a step back to look at them. They stared back at her, serious looks on their scrubbed faces.

"Do we look good?" Jessie asked. "Will she like us, do you think?"

Tears sprang to Sarah's eyes inexplicably. She had to turn her face away.

"Oh, yes," she said, her voice unnaturally high. "She'll be amazed at how beautiful you are."

"Who will?" Emma wanted to know. "Who'll be amazed?" She pulled at her braids. "They're too tight, Mommy."

"Oh, Emma. Let them be. They'll loosen up soon."

"But why do I have to wear them? Can't I just have a ponytail?"

"Don't you remember?" Sarah said cheerily. "I want you to look nice. Laurel's coming to visit today. Laurel—" she hesitated. "Your biological mother."

Emma narrowed her eyes at her. "But you're our mother," she said.

"Yes, sweetness," Sarah answered, her heart lurching. "But Laurel gave birth to you. She carried you in her belly before you were born."

"You mean, like you did? Like you did with Jay?" Jessie asked. Sarah nodded.

"I was in your belly, too," Emma said, her brow furrowed. "I don't have a 'logical mother."

Sarah took a deep breath and closed her eyes.

"I'm sorry, Em, but you do. I just don't think you remember her."

She took the girls by the hand then, and led them to the living room, where Len's old photo albums were stacked on a bookshelf in the corner. She took one down and flipped through it quickly, then pulled a photo from behind the plastic and showed it to them. It was a Christmas picture. Jessie, as a toddler, was tearing into a wrapped parcel, while Laurel looked on, baby Emma in her arms.

Jessie studied it carefully. "I *think* I remember her," she said.

"I don't," Emma said, and she leaned a little into Sarah's leg.

Sarah sent the girls to Jessie's room to play, telling them she would call for them as soon as Laurel arrived. But by nine-thirty, there was still no Laurel, nor had she called to say she would be late. Sarah called the hotel where Laurel had said they would be staying, but no one picked up when they put her call through to the room.

At ten forty-five, there was still no sign of Laurel. Sarah let the girls go outside to play in the yard, making them promise to keep their dresses clean. She watched them for a moment through the window, the bright sun shimmering on their hair. From a distance, and with both in braids, Emma looked like a smaller version of her older sister; the girls shared the same slim build and strong legs. It was only when you were closer that it was easy to see how different they were. Jessie's hair was darker, her skin less fair. In the Bakersfield sun, Emma's round face was perpetually freckled, her hair streaked with blonde.

Sarah still couldn't help being amazed by how much sun there was here. When, soon after they were married, Len had first applied for the professorship in theoretical mathematics at California State in Bakersfield, Sarah had been skeptical. Who but a farmer would move to Bakersfield? But Len had grown weary of Arcata's rain and fog; that there would be sun was enticement enough for him. And he had been right, Sarah thought. So much sun *had* seemed to add a brightness to their lives.

Sarah lifted Jay from his playpen and set him on her hip. She took a final glance at the girls outside and went to find Len. He was at his desk in the office, the month's bills spread out before him, but he looked up as soon as she walked in.

"Still no sign of her?"

Sarah shook her head. "I can't believe this."

Len grimaced. "I can. This is classic Laurel."

"But Jessie and Emma . . . They know she's coming. They're *waiting* for her. It's cruel."

Len nodded grimly. "To Laurel, only one person matters. And that person is Laurel."

"Oh, Len."

"It's true. Here," he said, holding out his arms. "Let me take Jay for a while. It's not like I'm getting anything done here, anyway."

She set her son down, and he immediately toddled toward his father. Len scooped him into his lap.

"Len? What should we do?"

Len looked up at her miserably. "What can we do, Sarah? There's nothing we can do."

It was almost eleven thirty when the girls appeared at the back door.

"Is Laurel here yet?" Jessie asked.

"Not yet."

"We're hungry."

Sarah glanced at the clock as if she had not been studying it every few minutes all morning.

"Well, it's practically lunchtime."

"Are we eating here? I thought you said Laurel was taking us to Camelot," Jessie said.

"What's Camelot?" Emma asked.

Sarah sighed. "Well, here it's an amusement park. With rides and things." She turned to Jessie. "I did say that. Because that's what Laurel said. But maybe something's happened. Maybe she isn't able to come."

She sent the girls to wash their hands and called to Len. He came into the kitchen with Jay on his hip and lay his hand on Sarah's back where she stood at the counter slicing bread.

"What can I do?"

"Get Jay set up? Drinks for the girls?"

Len was fastening the toddler into his high chair when the two girls galloped back into the kitchen and climbed into their seats beside him. Jay babbled at them happily.

"Watch this, Daddy," Jessie said. "Watch."

Len was pouring milk into two small cups. "I'm watching," he said, setting them on the table. "What?"

Jessie hid her face behind her napkin and turned to her little brother.

"Where's Jessie?" she said. "Where's Jessie?"

Jay squealed in anticipation.

"Here she is!" Jessie said, dropping the napkin from her face. Jay bounced in his seat, laughing.

"I want to do peek-a-boo, too!" Emma said. Quickly, she reached for her napkin and knocked over her cup of milk.

"Oh, Emma," Sarah said. "Careful."

Jay watched as the pool of milk spread. "Uh-oh! Uh-oh!" he said, pointing.

"I'm sorry! I didn't meaned to," Emma stammered.

Len wiped up the puddle with a kitchen towel, then patted his daughter's shoulder.

"It's just milk, Emma. No point crying over it."

"But I'm not crying," Emma said, her face red.

"It's just an expression, Emma," Sarah said quickly. "We know you're not crying."

"What's an expression?" Jessie wanted to know, but at that moment, there was a knock at the door. Sarah started visibly. How could she have been waiting all morning for this moment and still feel so surprised? She looked, not at the door, but at the clock. It was 11:43.

Len turned toward the door, but the handle was already turning, the door opening. In another instant, Laurel appeared in the doorway. Her eyes swept over the room quickly before coming to rest on her daughters.

"Hello, girls!" she said.

Jessie and Emma stared at her, wide-eyed and silent.

"Can't you say hello?" she asked.

"Hello, Laurel," Len said dryly. "You finally made it."

Laurel glanced at her bare wrist as if she were wearing a watch. "What? Am I late?"

"It's almost noon."

"Well, I said eleven-ish, didn't I? I think this counts—"

"Nine," Sarah interrupted. "You told me nine."

Laurel studied her. "Well, excuse me. I was sure I said . . . I was sure we'd said eleven."

Sarah sighed. "We were just getting lunch ready."

Laurel nodded, surveying the table. "Ah, the baby. What's his name? Jeff, or . . . Jason, isn't it?"

"Jay," Len said. "Would you care to join us, Laurel?"

Laurel frowned. "I can't. Kent is waiting in the car." She turned to Emma and Jessie. "You two ready to go to Camelot?"

Jessie nodded.

"Come on then. Kent's probably medium-rare out there already."

"The girls haven't had their lunch yet," Sarah said quickly.

"Well, here," Laurel said, taking two slices of bread from the basket Sarah had just set on the table. "Why don't I just take some food for the girls to eat in the car? I told Kent we'd just be a minute."

Laurel made a move to reach for the plate of cheese, but Sarah snatched it off the table.

"I'll do it," she said. "Just give me a minute."

"Or, you know, we could just eat there? I'm sure they have food there, don't they?"

"Just wait a minute, Laurel," Sarah said curtly. "The girls are hungry, and it'll take you at least twenty minutes to get there, and then you'll have to park."

Quickly, Sarah made two cheese and lettuce sandwiches, wrapped them in foil, and put them in a paper grocery bag. She got two apples from a bowl on the counter, put four cookies in a little baggy, and pulled some napkins from their holder on the kitchen table.

"Mommy, is the cheese thin?" Emma asked, watching her. "I only like it when it's thin."

"I know you do. Now, eat your sandwiches first, girls," she told them, handing Laurel the paper bag.

Jessie nodded dutifully. She had been uncharacteristically quiet since Laurel's arrival, but now she looked up at Laurel and said quietly, "I think I remember you."

Laurel beamed. "Of course you do."

Suddenly, Jessie slid down from her seat. "I do! I remember you! Are we going now? To Camelot?"

Laurel nodded and Jessie gave a little yelp of excitement. She turned to her sister, who still sat uncertainly at the table.

"Come on, Emma. Let's go!"

Emma looked first at Jessie, then at Laurel. Finally, she turned to Sarah. "Mommy?"

"It's okay, Emma," Sarah said. "This is Laurel. You know, who we talked about? She's your . . . She's going to take you to Cam— She's going to take you to an amusement park. It will be fun, sweetheart."

"Come on, Emma." Jessie said again. "Let's go. We're gonna ride the rides."

Slowly, Emma slid out of her chair.

Laurel reached out for her. "My baby. You're all grown up."

Emma shifted away from her. "I'm *not* a baby," she said. She held up four fingers. "I'm four years old."

"Of course you are," Laurel said. "I know that. I'm your mother."

"Mommy said you're just my . . . my . . . my 'logical mother."

Laurel looked up at Len and Sarah. "She did, did she?"

"Emma's very attached to Sarah, Laurel," Len said. "I'm sure you understand."

Laurel snorted. "Of course." She turned back to Emma. "Well, aren't you a lucky little girl," she said. "You have two mommies."

"But you're just my 'logical mother! Mommy is my mommy," Emma insisted.

Laurel scoffed audibly. "I see. Well, Emma, do you know what *bio*logical means?"

Emma nodded seriously. "It means I was in your belly." She looked up at Laurel's waist.

Laurel smiled. "That's right. You were in my belly for nine whole months. And then—oh geez, I forgot about Kent. He's probably dying of heat stroke out there. Seriously, I don't know how you can stand the heat down here. We'd better go. You girls ready?"

"Yes!" Jessie shouted excitedly. "Bye, Mom. Bye, Dad. See you later." She grabbed her sister's hand and pulled her toward the door.

"Bye," Laurel called. "We'll be back . . . I don't know when, but we'll be back."

When Laurel brought the girls home late that afternoon, Sarah and Len met them at the door. Both girls looked tired, and Emma's freckles stood out darkly against her sunburned skin. Her eyes were red, too; Sarah could see that she'd been crying.

"Oh, Emma," she said, rushing to her. "Are you okay?"

Emma collapsed into her arms, burying her face in Sarah's chest. Sarah felt her little body shuddering against her.

"What's wrong with her? What happened?"

Laurel tossed her head. "Nothing."

"But she's been crying."

Laurel scoffed and turned to Jessie. "She said she wanted to go, didn't she?"

Jessie nodded solemnly.

"Go where, Laurel?" Len asked. "What happened?"

"She got scared," Jessie said. "We went on a scary ride, and she got scared."

"What ride?" Sarah asked. "What scary ride?"

"It was the pirate ship," Laurel said. "It's not that scary. The guy said she was big enough if she had an adult with her."

"You took these girls on the pirate ship?" Len said, his voice low. Even without seeing his face, Sarah could feel his anger rising.

Laurel rolled her eyes. "Why not? They wanted to."

Sarah glared at her, then turned to Jessie again. "Jess, what happened?" she said. "Please tell me."

"I wanted to go on the pirate ship, and she—" Jessie gestured at Laurel. "She said it was okay. She said she would go with me. So Emma was going to stay with that man, you know? That man?"

Sarah nodded.

"But Emma didn't want to," Jessie went on. "She said she

wanted to be with me. And so then she—" Jessie pointed again at Laurel. "Then *she* said why didn't Emma just come with us on the ride."

Sarah looked hard at Laurel, her eyes narrowed. "So she *didn't* say she wanted to go on it."

Laurel threw up her hands. "Yes, she did. I asked her, 'Do you want to come on the ride with Jessie and me or stay here with Kent?' And she *said* she wanted to go with Jessie and me."

Sarah threw back her head and groaned. She opened her mouth to speak. "Laurel, I know you may have meant—"

But Len interrupted her. "Jesus Christ, Laurel! You took a four-year-old on the pirate ship? What the hell were you thinking?"

"I was *thinking*," Laurel said, mimicking his tone, "that she wanted to go. Since she said so."

"She wanted to be with her sister," Sarah said, exasperated. "Couldn't you see that?"

Laurel shrugged. "I'm not a mind reader. If she says she wants to—"

"But the pirate ship?" Sarah shuddered. She had never liked rides, but she had been on a pirate ship ride once. She and Pete had been to the county fair in Eureka, and he had cajoled her into joining him. She had to admit it hadn't looked so bad from the ground. A swinging boat—how scary could it be? But she remembered clearly how terrified she had felt, with the ship swinging higher and higher above the midway, so high that she had been sure that something was wrong. It had broken, somehow. It another moment it would come unmoored from its base and they would all be launched through the air. She had screamed so loudly her voice had been hoarse for days.

And she had been a grown up. She clutched Emma to her.

"Oh, sweetness," she said, holding her daughter against her chest. "That must have been so scary." She put her lips against Emma's head. Little wisps of blonde hair had come loose from her braids; one ribbon was missing.

"Are you okay now?" she asked her daughter gently, murmuring into her hair.

Emma nodded almost imperceptibly. Without showing her face, she moved her head up until her mouth was next to Sarah's ear.

"Mommy," she whispered. "It wouldn't stop. I wanted it to, but it wouldn't stop."

"Oh, sweetness," Sarah said, hugging her tight. "I know, I know. But, it's over now, darling. You're home now."

PART TWO

1982-1988

CHAPTER 20

Three Years Later

Emma

Emma was already down in the pasture when the rust-stained pickup rattled up the gravel driveway.

"Emma," she heard Laurel call. "They're here. Bring her on up now."

Emma didn't move. At her side, a small, brown Shetland pony stood placidly in her green halter, one back hoof resting on its tip. Emma stepped closer and pressed her face into the pony's wiry mane until her nose rested against the sleek coat below. She breathed in Raisin's familiar scent, fighting back her tears. She could not imagine the rest of the summer in Mendocino without the pony, never mind all the years to come.

"Emma! Bring her on up now," Laurel called again.

Emma moved so that she and Raisin stood face-to-face. She had to bend down only a little to bring her head level with the pony's. Then she touched her nose to Raisin's and exhaled gently into her velvety nostrils. Raisin's muzzle was the softest thing in the world, the warm air she breathed back at Emma sweet and grassy and delicious.

"Good-bye, Raisin," she whispered. "I'll miss you."

Raisin looked back at her serenely from under her long, dark lashes, and Emma's throat felt so tight she could not swallow. She threw her arms around the pony's neck.

In another minute, Emma heard her sister's footsteps on the

path that led down to the pasture from the house, but she didn't look up.

"Em?" Jessie said. "Mom says to bring her up. They're here."

"I know."

"Want to ride her? I'll lead."

Emma shook her head. "No. I'll walk her."

Her voice was not right, and Jessie met her eye and then looked away again.

"I'll get the gate then."

Emma blinked, grateful to her sister for all she didn't say. One kind word from Jessie and she would not be able to hold back her tears.

At the fence, Jessie opened the gate, standing on the lower rung as it swung open, and Emma led Raisin through. The pony let out a gusty sigh as they walked up the hill. Emma held the lead rope loosely in one hand, the other resting on the pony's withers.

Laurel stood in the gravel driveway, a hand on one hip, watching them come.

"Finally," she said. "What took you so long?"

Emma said nothing. She looked not at Laurel, but at the large man leaning against the driver's door of the white pickup now parked in the driveway.

"That your pony?" he asked.

Emma nodded.

The man walked a circle around Raisin, letting his hand trail along her coat as he moved. He pulled back her rubbery lips to look at her teeth and ran his huge hands down her legs. Raisin picked up each foot obediently, and he tapped at her frog with his index finger. Then he stepped back, hoisting his jeans up on his hips.

"She a good one?" he said, looking at Emma. "Ride okay?"

Emma nodded again, not trusting herself to speak.

"Shetlands can be pretty stubborn."

"She's not."

"I'll have to take your word for it, I guess." He grabbed his enormous pot belly with both hands and chuckled to himself.

Emma frowned. Once, during the first summer she had spent at Baymont, when she was only five, Raisin wouldn't do what Emma asked. Laurel had ordered Emma to dismount and then climbed into the saddle herself. On Raisin's back, Laurel's legs reached almost to the ground. The little pony had staggered under her weight, her eyes wide and nostrils flared.

"Don't hurt her," Emma had called out desperately. "You're too heavy."

"I'm not," Laurel had said. "I'm teaching her who's boss."

Now, Emma glanced up at the man. Laurel was not thin, but this man looked almost twice her size. She stepped closer to the pony and laid her hand protectively on Raisin's neck.

The man saw her and understood. "Oh, don't you worry, sweetheart. I'm not gonna ride her. She's for my grandbaby."

He turned to Laurel. "You were asking seventy-five?"

She nodded.

He reached into the console of his truck and handed Laurel a wad of bills. Then he took the lead rope from Emma and led Raisin to the back of the pickup. He lowered the tailgate with one hand. There was no ramp, but he didn't hesitate. He squatted next to Raisin, wrapped one large arm around her rump and the other beneath her chest. With a low grunt, he lifted her into the back of the truck.

Emma heard Raisin's hooves scrambling for purchase on the metal truck bed, saw her eyes go wide with surprise, so that the whites showed at the corners.

"It's okay, Raisin," she called, finding her voice at last. "You're okay."

And she was. The man had put a flake of hay in the bed behind the cab, and Raisin found it immediately, tossing it with her muzzle before beginning to eat.

Emma turned away, hurt by the pony's incomprehension.

Almost she preferred her wild eyes and clawing hooves to this calm indifference. Emma had been soothed countless times by exactly this placidity, the soft rhythm of Raisin's grazing never faltering as Emma sobbed against her neck. But now—how could Raisin eat at a time like this? Emma's throat ached at the thought, and as she stood there, holding back her tears, a piercing thought went through her.

Here in Baymont, Raisin was Emma's refuge, the only being, other than her sister, to whom she could turn for solace. And suddenly every other distress that Emma had ever felt here—the homesickness, the persistent unease of not belonging, the awful ache of longing for her parents—paled in comparison to the magnitude of this loss. In a moment, Raisin would be gone, and then who would there be to comfort her?

Emma turned abruptly and headed for the barn, her back burning with all their eyes.

"Everything all right, ma'am?" she heard the big man ask, and at the kindness in his voice Emma felt her tears come. She quickened her step, keeping her face turned away.

"Emma, what's wrong?" Laurel called after her. "It's okay that we're selling Raisin, isn't it?"

Emma's steps faltered. Of course it wasn't okay. Surely Laurel knew that. But what if Emma said so? Would the man lift Raisin back out of the truck bed, pieces of hay still half-chewed in her mouth, and return her lead rope to Emma's hand? Would Laurel return his wad of cash and apologize for his trouble? Even at seven, Emma knew when a deal was done. Answer a question that did not want an honest answer, and she would be made, not just a cry-baby, but a fool.

She didn't answer, but started to run instead, suddenly desperate for the darkness of the barn.

"Emma? Don't you want to say goodbye to Raisin?" Laurel called after her.

"Just leave her alone, Mom," her sister said sharply. "Can't you see it's hard enough?"

The following Saturday morning Emma was awake in her twin bed, the soles of her feet resting on the sloped ceiling above her head, when she heard Laurel calling from across the hall.

"Jessie? Emma? You girls awake? Come see this."

On the other side of the attic room they shared, Jessie swung her legs to the floor. She had slept in her ponytail, but half of her long, brown hair had come loose during the night, and she brushed it from her face with both hands.

"You coming, Em? Let's go see what Mom wants."

Beneath their bare feet, the rough-hewn floor boards creaked with each step. Across the narrow hallway, the door to Laurel's room was ajar. Inside, a dresser stood against one wall, a dozen perfume bottles arranged on top. A black bra hung from the knob of one of the drawers, and Emma stared and then looked away. Laurel was in the large bed pushed against the adjacent wall. Her legs were hidden beneath a tangle of sheets, but her chest was bare. An electric fan whirred on the bedside table.

"Look, girls," she said, putting a hand to her breast. She squeezed one broad, brown nipple between her thumb and forefinger, and a bead of yellow milk formed on the puckered skin. "See that? That's the milk you used to drink, Emma."

Emma cringed. "Me?"

"Of course."

"Why not Jessie?" she said.

"Oh, Jessie had milk, too," Laurel said. "But she's older, so she was first. This—" She coaxed another drop of milk from her breast. "This was your milk, Emma."

Emma looked away quickly, her stomach churning. She hated the thought of having suckled those hanging breasts, hated its insistence on some old intimacy between them, a bond to which she would never have agreed.

"But *how*?" Jessie asked, puzzled. "Mom . . . Sarah, I mean. She used to give Jay momma's milk too, but now he's bigger she doesn't have any left. Mom . . . I mean, Sarah. She says it goes away when the baby doesn't need it anymore."

Laurel raised one eyebrow.

"Well, I guess your father just isn't interested in that kind of thing," she said archly.

"What kind of thing?" Jessie insisted. "Dad isn't interested in *what* kind of thing? And what does Dad have to do with *that*?" She gestured, clutching at her throat and sticking out her tongue, at the bead of milk now dripping down the side of Laurel's dimpled breast.

Laurel wiped the milk away with her finger, and then leaned back against the pillows, so that her large breasts splayed out to either side of her body.

"Well, I'm not going to spell it out, Jessie," she said. "But you're a smart girl. I'm sure you can figure it out."

Emma watched her sister's face. She saw the moment when her sister understood.

"You mean Cactus . . . *Gross*."

"Not only Cactus, Jess. But yes."

"What?" Emma asked Jessie quietly. Cactus was Laurel's boy-friend, but what did *he* have to do with this? "Not only Cactus *what*? *What's* gross?"

Laurel grinned. "Why 'gross'? It's just milk, isn't it? You drink milk, don't you?"

Jessie made a face. "Not milk for babies. And not from there."

Emma did not say a word. She suddenly darted from Laurel's side, crossed the narrow hallway between their rooms, and climbed back into her twin bed, pulling the covers over her head. Her stomach felt queasy. When she and Jessie had first begun to visit Laurel in Baymont, Laurel had been married to a man named

Kent. Emma had only been five, then, but she remembered him. He'd had a tattoo of a snake on his forearm that would wriggle when he clenched his fist. She didn't like him. Once, when he sat next to Laurel on the couch, his fingers on her bare leg had looked like the hairy appendages of an animal, and Emma's skin had crawled.

Cactus was better; even Laurel agreed.

"Why do you call him Cactus?" Jessie had asked Laurel a few days ago, as if it had just occurred to her to wonder. "That's not his real name, is it?" Jessie was standing at her mother's dresser, choosing a perfume for Laurel, while Laurel rummaged in her drawer for underwear.

Emma, lying on the bed, had opened her mouth to answer. She knew. She had asked Cactus himself once, and he had taken her hand and rubbed it against the shorn hairs on his crew-cut head.

"Prickly, isn't it?" he had said, smiling.

And it was, sort of, but soft too, not like a real cactus at all.

"Because his head—" she began.

But Laurel had cut her off. "No, not his *head*," she had said, laughing. "Let's just say a certain part of his body—" She paused, slapped her thigh, and laughed again.

"Well, you could say his head, I guess," she said, chuckling. "His *head* is very prickly."

Emma felt her face go hot, remembering. Already she was too warm with the covers over her; she could feel her breath crowding out the air. She didn't like it when Laurel laughed at her and she didn't understand. And she didn't want to see Laurel's stupid milk, either. She lifted one hand to make a window with the sheet and moved her mouth in front of it to breathe the cooler air.

Soon she heard the door open, her sister's footsteps on the creaky floorboards.

"Em?" Jessie said. "Are you under there?"

"Uh huh."

"What are you doing?"

"Nothing."

"Why're you under there then?"

"I just feel like it, okay?"

Jessie sighed. Emma could see the blue fabric of her sister's pajamas through the gap she had made in the sheet.

"Want to come down and have breakfast?"

"Jessie," Emma said. "That is not my milk."

Jessie was silent for a moment. "Well, I guess it must be, since you were born last. But it doesn't matter. Come on."

Emma pushed the sheet from her head and looked at her sister. "No, it isn't."

"Actually—"

"Jessie, it isn't. It's not my milk if he . . . If Cactus . . . No, Jessie, it's not. It's . . . It's so . . ." Emma grasped after words. "It's so *gross*," she said at last, knowing it was Jessie's word, that she had said it first.

Her sister was silent for a moment. "Yeah," she said at last. "It is. But come on out, Em. Please. Let's have cereal and then I'll let you ride Summer if you want."

Summer was Jessie's horse in Baymont; Summer hadn't been carted off in a pickup truck for seventy-five measly dollars. But Emma was sweltering under the covers now, with the morning sun streaming in the dormer windows, so she threw off the blankets and followed her sister down the stairs.

CHAPTER 21

Emma

L aurel lived in Mendocino County, in an old, two-story house that had belonged to her grandparents. As a young man, her grandfather had logged the redwoods in the forest around the house; the woods there now were mostly second-growth, but a few of the ancient trees remained. A logging road, now little more than a trail, still snaked its way up through the woods, but after about a mile both road and woods came to an end.

Emma never stopped being surprised by this: how one minute she could be standing in the cool shade of the redwoods, the forest lush around her, and the next she would be looking out on miles of sun-bleached hills, dotted with the stubby shapes of bay laurels. Laurel's grandfather had named the place Baymont after those trees. And many years later, his daughter Pearl, homesick for a place that was no longer home, had named her own baby girl after the same trees: Laurel.

Emma could not picture Laurel outside of Baymont. She knew that Laurel had come to Bakersfield once, when she was very little, and had taken her sister and her to an amusement park. But the only part of that visit that she could remember was a ride she had gone on, a pirate ship ride that had gone on and on while Emma had sat hunched over in fear, clutching at the metal bar that crossed her lap, too scared even to scream. Emma knew that she had gone on that ride with Laurel, because she had been told that that was true. And she was not surprised, because the dry-mouthed, tangled-belly unease of that memory was exactly how she felt every summer when she stepped off the plane in the

Sacramento airport and saw Laurel, waiting to take her and Jessie to Baymont.

Baymont itself, Emma couldn't help but love. She loved the damp, piney smell of the woods, and the sunbaked, spicy scent of the hills. She loved the green, spring-fed pond near the house, and she loved the golden pastures where the horses grazed. Once Laurel had overheard her call them that—"the golden pastures"—and had laughed derisively.

"They aren't always 'golden,' you know," she had said, making the word sound ridiculous even to Emma's ear. "Just come in the spring sometime and you'll see them green. A green like you wouldn't believe."

But Emma and Jessie did not go to Baymont in the spring. They went once a year, as soon as school let out for the summer. Laurel waited for them there, with that shrill, mocking voice that Emma dreaded. Emma, although shy, did not feel herself to be a stupid child. And yet as soon as she arrived at Baymont, she became one. Laurel spoke words that Emma understood, and yet so much of what she said seemed to have a meaning Emma could not grasp.

At Baymont, Emma grew used to withdrawing inside herself, Laurel's voice a high-pitched buzzing in her ears. She grew used to the feeling that the true Emma was hiding inside her—a smooth, impenetrable nugget—while the outer, Baymont Emma did what she would. The Baymont Emma would start the summer saying "Laurel" but end with "Mom," the betrayal of it sour on her tongue. During the first few weeks at Baymont, Emma would cry for her true mother and beg, long distance, to go home, but it was only a matter of time before Baymont seduced her. When that happened, the Baymont Emma would forget for long hours, days even, how much she longed for her parents, how much she hated those summers away from home.

But the true Emma remembered her loyalties. She did not belong to Laurel, not at all, no matter what worn memory Laurel fished up from her infancy. She was Mommy's; she was Dad's.

Laurel had not wanted her when she was a baby; she could have no claim to her now.

But even the true and loyal Emma understood how the Baymont Emma could be seduced. Because Baymont was Baymont, after all. There were the woods and the horses. There were gallons of blackberries waiting to be picked, and endless miles of lonely hills. On weekends, Laurel would take them on all-day rides through countryside so beautiful it made Emma's throat ache.

Laurel with the horses was easier; Emma could almost love her then. Laurel had taught them both to ride, spending hours in the sand in the middle of the ring, while Emma and Jessie circled her on their ponies.

"Touch your mount between the ears. Now above the tail. Ok, trot on. Touch your right toe. Keep trotting, Emma. Now your left toe."

At Baymont, Emma learned to post while trotting, learned to keep her seat while bareback riding, learned how to urge her mount into a canter with a gentle squeeze, a simple *cluck, cluck, cluck.* She learned to pick hooves, to use a curry brush, to pull a mane, to slip a bit into a horse's mouth. In truth, she hardly learned these things. At Baymont, Emma was a horse girl—they were just the things she knew.

Even with Raisin gone, Emma loved the horses. She began to ride an old paint mare named Penny, and although she could never love her as she had loved Raisin, still she could appreciate the softness of her muzzle against her hand, the prehensile ears that flicked at every sound.

Laurel would often sing in the saddle as they rode, and the songs seemed to capture a longing that ran deep in Emma. *Let me straddle my old saddle underneath the western skies, wander over yonder 'til I see the mountains rise . . .*

In Mendocino, such lonesome freedom seemed so close—*there* were the mountains rising, and *there* the dusty roads to wander under deep blue skies. At home in Bakersfield, Emma had to conjure up such wildness, seeking it out in the empty lots of their suburban neighborhood, where it was always unbearably hot and the flies would not leave her alone. At home, Emma kept imaginary horses in the grassy, irrigated patch in the backyard, groomed them with a cleaning brush she had found beneath the kitchen sink, and galloped them around the cul-de-sac at the end of their road. But none of that could hold a candle to Baymont. At Baymont, it was *real*.

How Emma loved the barn at the end of the day, Penny's sigh as she uncinched the girth and pulled the saddle from her sweaty back. How she loved tending to her afterwards, watching the crusts of sweat dissolve under the stream of water from the hose, the damp imprint of the saddle slowly fading until her whole coat gleamed smooth and wet. Most of all she loved the moment when it was all done, the tack returned to the barn, the hooves checked for stones, the thanks whispered into soft, quivering ears. The pasture gate would squeak as it opened, and the horses, invigorated by their freedom, would toss their heads and head for a bare spot on the hill.

"One hundred, two hundred, three hundred," she and her sister counted, as the horses rolled on their backs in the dust. Laurel always said you could tell a horse's worth by how many times it rolled over all the way. Only when the last horse had risen and gone to graze would the sisters head inside for lemonade.

But that was not every day. Monday would come, and so would the babysitter, and Laurel would go to Ukiah, the nearest town but still twenty minutes away, where she worked the desk at a walk-in clinic. The babysitter's name was Candace, but everyone called her Candy. Candy was fifteen when she started watching them, the first summer they spent in Baymont. She was long-limbed and smooth-skinned, with dark, permed hair that hung just below her jaw. The moment Laurel's car rattled away, she turned the television on. The morning news was followed by *The Price is Right, Family Feud, As the World Turns, All My Children*—a gauntlet of daytime television that would leave Emma feeling woozy and hollow-headed. She and Jessie escaped as soon as they could.

The sisters picked berries, explored the woods, waded in the pond. Forbidden to ride without Laurel, they would visit the horses in the pasture, bringing them carrots and apple cores. Better yet, they would slip through the barbed wire at the bottom of the lower pasture to visit the consignment sales, first seeking out the animals waiting in their pens, then scouring the ground under the stands for discarded bottles and cans. While the auctioneer chanted away above them in his thrilling tongue, they would lug their loot to concessions and trade them for an order of fries or a Snickers, which they ate together, sitting in the stands. Emma loved to watch the silent ranchers, how still they sat, so that the slightest motion of a finger was a flag waved, and then the auctioneer's voice would rise and pulse and carry on.

Those were the good days, the days Emma needed no one but her sister, the days Mendocino was nothing less than magic. But there were days enough when Emma felt her longing for home just beneath the surface of her skin, days when she would have given up all that Baymont offered just to have her mother near.

And yet it was not Sarah's absence in Baymont that was the worst of it, although Emma missed her painfully. The worst part was the knowledge that Sarah was at *home*, with her father and her little brother, that life in Bakersfield simply carried on without her.

Emma loved her brother; this she did not doubt. At home, she would help him push his trains down the floorboards in the hallway, or put on little plays for him with his stuffed animals. She loved his lopsided smile when she made his bears and lions talk, the way he clapped his chubby hands together. But when she was in Baymont, a terrible envy rose up in her, so that she had to swallow hard to choke it down: Jay was *home*. He had her parents all to himself; he was getting all the good love. When she thought of her brother by himself in Bakersfield, it was her own absence that she saw: at the table, in the bath, in the backseat of the car. She should have been there with him, but she wasn't, and the aching emptiness she felt was almost more than she could bear.

CHAPTER 22

Two Years Later

Emma

"**H**ell, yeah," Candy said, hanging up the phone in the kitchen. She brushed her hair back from her perfectly tanned shoulders. Candy was seventeen that summer and liked to lay out on the deck, her bikini top unfastened in the back, while her new *Like A Virgin* album spun on the record player in the living room. She had grown out her hair that year and cut her bangs, which she wore hair-sprayed in a donut above her forehead. She patted them gently with her palm while she looked around for the girls.

"You two wanna go swimming?"

"Yes!" They were not supposed to go swimming in the pond alone, but if Candy came . . . The girls raced upstairs to get their suits.

"I thought you didn't like the pond," Jessie said, pulling her T-shirt back on over her one-piece.

Candy laughed. "Not the pond. A lake."

Emma was skeptical. "Where's there a lake?"

"Just hurry up, will you? Our ride's gonna be here in a minute."

And soon enough there was the crunch and spit of gravel in the driveway and a red pickup pulled up beside the house. There were three teenagers in the cab, and more in the bed, but they shifted to make room when Candy pulled the girls up after her. Once they were settled, Candy immediately transformed. She was no longer their perpetually annoyed babysitter but a bona fide teenager, talking and laughing with her friends. Jessie watched her, mesmerized, but Emma could not take her eyes from the ground that whizzed beneath them, the trees blurring along the side of the road. She hunched down in the bed, one hand clinging to her sister, the other clenching the side of the truck.

After more than an hour, they arrived at a large lake, and Emma scooted off the tailgate onto the ground, relieved. Looking toward the blue-grey water, she saw a small gravel beach, and, for the first time since they had left Baymont, she felt a thrill of anticipation. This water wasn't the murky green of the pond, where her feet sank up to the ankles in slimy, gelatinous goo every time she touched the bottom. This water was clear and blue. Even the small, makeshift beach beckoned, with its hundreds of little stones just waiting to be skipped.

Behind her, the teenagers were leaping out of the back of the pickup, pulling off their T-shirts and shorts and tossing them into the truck. But instead of lifting down the cooler and heading toward the water, they began climbing a steep embankment in the opposite direction. Jessie and Emma stood uncertainly by the truck.

"Come on," Candy called. "This way." Dutifully, the girls fell in behind, clambering up the hill behind them.

Where are we going? Emma wondered, but was too shy to ask. In any case, the answer was soon clear. As they gained altitude, she saw where they were headed: an enormous dam that formed one edge of the lake. For it was not a true lake, she realized now, but a reservoir, with a giant cement wall that held the water in. It was to the top of this dam that they were going, the group now almost in single file, led by a young man with dark hair whose bare back glistened in the sun.

When they arrived at the dam, at last, he paused, turning to smile at the gaggle of teenagers that followed him.

"Voilà," he said.

"Wow," a girl marveled. "How high is it?"

"*Fucking* high," someone answered.

"Fifty feet," said the young man, fiddling with the drawstring on his red trunks. "And watch your language. There's a couple of young ladies present." He nodded toward Emma and Jessie at the back of the line.

The group tittered.

"Just jump out and you'll be fine, I promise. It's awesome."

"You've done this before?" another girl asked Candy.

Candy shook her head. "No. But I'm going to." Then she turned to Jessie and Emma.

"Want to wait here? I'll come back up and get you."

"You're going to *jump*?" Jessie asked incredulously, and as she did, Emma's stomach seemed to fall all fifty feet to the glimmering water below. For if Candy was going to jump, Emma had no doubt that Jessie would want to, too. Her sister was not one to be one-upped.

"Jessie," she said, her voice desperate. "You can't."

Don't leave me here alone, she thought.

"Come on, Emma," Jessie said. "You heard him. Just jump out and you'll be fine." In her voice was a new note of nonchalance. Emma was not reassured.

She watched her sister pull her T-shirt over her head and fling it to the ground. Under it, her blue one piece stretched tight against her flat chest, her lean arms crisscrossed with scratches from picking blackberries.

"Come on," she said again, beckoning for Emma to follow. "It'll be fine."

The dam was perhaps eight feet across, wide enough to walk along, wide enough that from Emma's short height, she could not see clearly what lay below. On the left side, she knew, was the reservoir, but what about to the right? Carefully, she dropped to her knees and began to crawl toward the edge. Peering down, what she saw paralyzed her. For if the dam was fifty feet high on the reservoir side, it looked twice that on the other, the rocks and eddies so far below that her head swam with vertigo.

"Jessie," she called out, her voice high-pitched with fear. *"Jessie."*

Her sister glanced back at her. "Emma, what are you doing? Just stand up and come on."

But Emma could not stand. She crawled along on all fours instead, her fingers clinging to the concrete surface of the dam even as her mind held tight to the image of the river below and would not let it go. She was trapped. God, how she longed to be off that dam, to be *down*, and yet turning back on her own was inconceivable.

"Jessie," she tried again. But her voice was barely a whisper, and by now her sister was twenty feet ahead. The group had clustered there, the girls clinging to each other, giggling. Suddenly, as Emma watched, someone tore himself from the group and flung himself off the edge. Emma listened to him scream as he fell, her stomach in knots and her eyes clenched tight. His scream seemed to go on and on, until at last she heard a distant splash. There was a moment's silence, and then a whoop, and then the nervous, tittering laughter of the girls.

Emma did not rise from her knees to look, but instead lowered her body fully, so that she was now lying belly down on the dam, her cheek against the concrete, her eyes closed.

One by one, they jumped, and screamed, and laughed, until it was just Emma and her sister left up on the dam, alone with the young man in the red trunks. He was encouraging; Jessie was hesitant. He was solicitous; her sister was coy.

Just jump if you're going to jump, Emma thought bitterly. She didn't believe her sister could be scared; Jessie was *never* scared. More likely she was enjoying having his full attention, now that the bikini-clad girls had all jumped off the side of the dam like lemmings.

"Come on down, Emma," Candy yelled up, treading water in the lake below. "The water's great." But Emma would not budge.

"You don't have to jump, you know," Candy yelled, the

annoyance back in her voice. "Just walk down the way we went up."

But Emma couldn't. She was paralyzed. "Somebody help," she whispered, knowing no one would hear her. Her sister was yards away, only occasionally glancing back to where Emma lay. "*Please* help."

Emma wanted to cry but couldn't let herself; her whole body was clenched against disaster.

At last, Candy gave up and swam to the beach, then trudged again up the hill. She strode along the dam toward Emma as if it were any sidewalk in the world. Emma had no choice; she let Candy coax her back to all fours. Then ever so carefully, ever so slowly, while Candy dripped impatiently onto the hot concrete of the dam, she turned her body around.

Emma crawled all the way back to the end of the dam like a cat, leaving her sister alone with the young man. She lost sight of her as she and Candy skidded down the dusty hillside, but when she reached the little beach and looked up, they were still there.

Emma walked out into the lake until the water touched her chin. A few yards from her, the other swimmers were getting impatient.

"Come on, Adam," someone called up. "She's not going to do it. Just jump. She can walk down like the other one."

But Emma knew her sister. Jessie would jump. Emma watched as she took a step back, gathering her momentum. And then there she was, launched into the air, her blue bathing suit falling, her tan limbs flailing, until she disappeared with a splash beneath the shimmering surface of the water.

I am alone, Emma thought. An emptiness shot threw her, so piercing that she ducked her head under the water to hide her tears. When she came up, there was Jessie in the lake, her eyes wild, laughing. Emma raised her arm to catch her sister's eye, but Jessie did not turn toward Emma or the little beach. She took a few quick strokes toward the dam.

"Adam," she yelled, gasping. "Adam, I did it!"

Emma took a deep breath and let herself sink beneath the surface of the water. When she came up at last, Jessie was swimming toward her, grinning, but Emma found that she could not meet her eye.

CHAPTER 23

Two Years Later

Emma

By the time Jessie and Emma came in from the barn, Laurel was already showered and dressed and in the kitchen, pouring macaroni out of a white box into a pot on the stove. Jessie looked at her outfit skeptically.

"Where are *you* going?" she asked.

"Cactus is taking me out to dinner, remember?" Laurel said. "What took you two so long?"

Jessie shrugged and headed for the fridge. "Nothing. We were just watching the horses."

She opened the fridge door and pulled out the plastic pitcher full of lemonade. "Want some?" she asked Emma.

"Yes, please."

Laurel set a timer for the macaroni and then turned to Jessie.

"Can you pour me some, too, Jess?" She reached into the cabinet beside the stove and pulled out a half-full bottle of vodka.

Jessie hesitated, glass in hand.

"You're not going to put that in your lemonade, are you, Mom?"

"Why not?"

"Because you'll ruin it. And Dad says you shouldn't be drinking if you're going to be driving."

"For Christ's sake, Jessie. It's one drink. And I'm not driving. Cactus is." She took the glass of lemonade from Jessie and poured in vodka straight from the bottle. "You two going to be okay on your own tonight?"

"Mom," Jessie said, exasperated. "I babysit for Emma and Jay all the time at home. Dad even pays me."

"Oh really?" Laurel snorted. "Well, don't expect that here."

The timer went off, and Laurel drained the macaroni over the sink with the lid, then returned the pan to the stove.

"Can I put the cheese in?" Emma asked.

"Sure." She handed the packet to Emma. "Jessie, pass me the milk, would you? And put the lemonade away."

"I'm not done with it yet," Jessie said, pouring herself another glass. "I was so thirsty on that ride I thought I was going to die."

"Yeah, well, that's enough. Drink water after that. I can't believe I just bought that and it's almost gone already."

Laurel spooned macaroni and cheese into two bowls and set them on the kitchen table. "You girls want anything else?"

Emma eyed the table, empty but for the two lonely bowls. "At home we have a vegetable with dinner," she said quietly.

Laurel rolled her eyes. She went to the refrigerator and looked inside. "What the hell happened to all the carrots?" she asked.

Jessie grinned. "Summer likes them."

"Oh, for heaven's sake. Well, Emma, there *are* no vegetables. But you'll survive, I think. Get your own forks, okay? I've got to finish getting ready." Laurel plopped some napkins on the table and went upstairs with her vodka and lemonade.

Five minutes later she was down again. Emma could smell her perfume as she brushed past the table.

"Can I have some more macaroni and cheese, please?" Emma asked.

"When did your last slave die off?" Laurel said. "It's on the stove."

She pulled the phone book from beneath a pile of clutter on the counter and flipped through the pages, squinting at the small print. Then she jotted down some numbers on a piece of paper and stuck it to the fridge with a magnet.

Jessie watched her. "What's that?"

"It's the number at the restaurant where we'll be, *if* there's an emergency," Laurel said. "And the number for the Jacksons next door, too."

Jessie nodded importantly and Emma felt a flash of annoyance. Jessie was just two years older than her—why did *she* need a babysitter if Jessie didn't? Now Jessie got to feel all high and mighty, when Emma could take care of herself just fine.

"We should be back by nine," Laurel said. "Ten at the latest. But you two should be in bed by then. No horses when I'm not here. And no swimming."

Jessie rolled her eyes. "We know, Mom," she said. "Plus my butt's so sore I don't think I want to ride for a week."

Laurel smiled and emptied the rest of the macaroni into an empty bowl, put a saucer on top, and set it in the fridge. "The rest is in here if you want it," she said.

She was running water into the dirty pot when the screen door squealed. Emma watched as Laurel startled.

"Geez, Cactus. You scared me."

"Should I have knocked?" Cactus strode into the room in black cowboy boots, and Jessie and Emma grinned at each other. Secretly they made fun of Cactus' boots. What was the point of boots if he wouldn't ride a horse?

"Hey, girls."

"Hi," Jessie and Emma said in unison. Cactus stopped by the table where the sisters sat, their uneaten macaroni congealing in their bowls.

"That looks good," he said, although Emma knew it didn't, not now anyway, with all the sad little noodles uncurling in their chalky sauce. A wave of Cactus' cologne broke over her, and the smell of it, mingling with the remnants of Laurel's perfume that still hung in the air, stopped Emma's throat. She gagged and pushed her bowl away.

Jessie waved her hand in front of her nose. "Phew. You guys *stink*."

Laurel laughed. "Well, at least we don't smell of horse like two girls I know."

"But horses smell good," Jessie said.

"Take a shower anyway," Laurel said. "Both of you. Sure you'll be okay?"

Jessie groaned in mock annoyance. "Just go, why don't you? We're fine."

"Got a teenager on your hands now, I see," Cactus said dryly, and Laurel rolled her eyes.

"Alrighty then. Have a good night." She headed out the door, Cactus behind her, his boots clomping loudly on the wooden floor.

When the door had shut behind them, Jessie put her bowl in the sink and opened the fridge. She pulled out the pitcher of lemonade.

"Want some more?"

"But Laurel said . . ."

"Oh, Emma, you don't have to be such a goody-two-shoes all the time."

Emma felt her face turn red. "I'm not."

"Look, I'll only have half, okay? Do you want some more?"

Emma shook her head.

"Want to play Scrabble?"

"No. You always win."

"Monopoly?"

"No."

"Uno?"

"I guess."

They played Uno for half an hour, then turned on the TV. Jessie stood at the set, turning the knob, until Emma saw Arnold from *Diff'rent Strokes* and called out, "Stop."

Jessie flopped down beside her on the couch, but the next minute, she was up again, heading down the hall.

"Where are you going?" Emma called.

"Just to pee," she said.

Jessie was gone a long time. When she came back, something in her expression made Emma look twice.

"What's wrong?" she said, moving her feet on the couch so that Jessie could sit down.

"I don't know," Jessie said. "I couldn't pee."

"Maybe you didn't have to."

"Well, I feel like I do," Jessie said. She started to lean back on the couch but grimaced and moved to her side instead, curling her legs to her chest.

They finished *Diff'rent Strokes* and started *Three's Company*. Emma felt a little thrill when it started; at home her mother would be sending her to bed.

But five minutes in, Jessie was up again. "Now I *really* have to pee," she said. "It's all that lemonade."

Emma had to pee, too, but she held it, waiting for the commercial. When it came, she walked down to the bathroom at the end of the hall. Jessie was sitting on the toilet, her face pale.

"I still can't pee," she said. "And it hurts."

"Well, can you just get up for a sec?" Emma asked. "I've gotta go."

"Go upstairs in Laurel's bathroom, will you? Oww . . ."

Normally Emma would have argued. Why should *she* have to go upstairs? But the look on her sister's face worried her.

"Is it . . . Is it your period?" she asked. Jessie had started her period earlier that summer, and the fact of it was still a novelty for the girls.

"No," Jessie groaned. "I don't think so."

Quickly, Emma went upstairs to the bathroom. When she came back down, the commercial was over but she checked on Jessie anyway.

"Did you pee yet?"

"No." Jessie's face was white; she had begun to sweat. "I can't. And, oh God, I have to."

"Maybe if you took a shower?" Emma suggested. "Sometimes that makes me need to pee. Want me to start it?"

"I guess." Jessie's face was twisted in pain.

Emma reached past the shower curtain and turned on the tap. "Jessie, maybe we should call Laurel?"

Jessie shook her head. "No, I'm . . . I'll just try this."

Slowly, Jessie peeled off her clothes. Emma noticed how she didn't straighten as she did so, but kept her body curled around her bladder.

The shower curtain was clear plastic, streaked with mildew. Emma watched as Jessie stood hunched in the stream, not washing, just hunched there, moaning softly.

"Oh please," Jessie muttered. "*Please.*"

Jessie stood in the shower until the water ran cool.

She glanced at her pile of clothes on the floor, the jeans and T-shirt she had worn all day with the horses.

"Em, do you think . . . Could you get me some clothes?"

Emma passed her a towel, nodded, raced up the stairs, and yanked open Jessie's drawers. Underwear, bra, T-shirt . . . She paused at the shorts, imagining her sister struggling to button the waistbands over her painful bladder. She dug through the drawer, tossing shorts on the floor. Finally, at the bottom of the stack was one she thought might do, a pair of polyester blue athletic shorts with a worn-out elastic waist. She grabbed the clothes and ran back down.

"Jessie, I got these—"

She stopped short at the door of the bathroom. Her sister was lying on the bathmat, naked. No, not lying, writhing.

"Oh God," she said. "Oh God."

"Jessie. That's it. I'm calling Laurel."

Jessie nodded slightly. "Help me get dressed first."

Emma held her underwear so her sister could get her feet through the holes, then helped her pull them up.

She held up the bra, but Jessie shook her head urgently. "Forget it."

She managed to get her head into the T-shirt, but when she had to raise her arms to get them through the arm holes, she winced and cried out.

"Jessie!"

"I'm okay," Jessie said. "*Oh God.*"

"I found these," Emma said, holding up the soft shorts. "I thought they'd be better . . ."

Quickly, she slid Jessie's feet through the holes, pulled them up her legs. With Jessie lying on her side, she had to stop when she reached her hips.

"Can you just—" she began.

"No," Jessie said, sobbing. "No, it hurts. God, it hurts. Oh, please make it stop. *Please.*"

Emma left her sister on the bathroom floor with the shorts still around her knees. She raced to the kitchen and grabbed the paper with the numbers from the fridge.

The phone rang five interminable times before someone answered.

"Giovanni's," a man's voice said.

"My mother's there," Emma croaked into the line. "I need to talk to her. Please. It's . . . It's an emergency."

"How old are you?"

"Eleven. Please. I need to talk to my mother."

"All right. All right. What's her name?"

"Laurel. She's there with her boyfriend, Cac—" Oh, God, what was Cactus' real name?

"She's there with her boyfriend. He's got really short hair. He's . . . He's wearing cowboy boots."

"I'll see if I can find them."

Emma waited for what seemed like forever. She could hear Jessie moaning in the bathroom and longed to go to her.

Finally, the voice was back.

"I'm sorry, but the waitress said they just left. They're probably on their way home now."

Trembling, Emma hung up the phone and dialed the other number. Oh, *please*. But the phone at the Jacksons' rang and rang. She hung up and tried again, but after six, seven, eight rings, there was no answer.

She ran back to the bathroom. Jessie still lay there, writhing, her face white.

"Jessie, she's not there. And the Jacksons won't answer."

Her sister looked at her, her eyes wide and strange.

"The horses . . ." she said. "Take Summer . . . He's fastest. Get help."

Emma stared at her. She imagined herself racing down to the pasture with a halter, the darks shadows of the horses in the field. She'd have no time to saddle up, but she knew Summer would neck-rein with his halter and lead. She saw herself leading him through the gate in the dark, then vaulting onto his back and galloping up the street to the Jacksons', her fingers tangled in his mane.

It is what Jessie would do. That was why she had thought of it. Even now, out of her mind with pain, there was something in it that Jessie could revere: her sister and her trusted steed, galloping through the night in search of help. But Emma knew, even as the vision passed through her mind, that it was impossible. She couldn't leave her sister like this. And what if the Jackson's weren't home? Even if they were, what could they possibly do?

They'd call an ambulance, Emma thought. That's what they would do.

In a second, she was back in the kitchen, dialing 911.

"My sister needs an ambulance," Emma said, struggling to keep her voice calm. "Please hurry."

"Address, please?" the operator asked her.

"315 . . ." Emma began and then panicked. No, that was her address at home. What *was* the address here? Sequoia Road, she knew, but the number? Quickly, she searched through the clutter on the counter for an envelope. There.

"Eight Sequoia Road. Oh, please can they hurry? My sister." Emma started to cry, then. "Please tell them to hurry," she pleaded into the phone.

She heard clicking on the other end of the line. "They're on their way, sweetheart. Everything's going to be okay. The ambulance is on its way. Now, tell me. How old are you?"

"Eleven."

"And is someone there with you?"

"My sister. She was . . . She's babysitting me."

"And how old is she?"

"Thirteen."

"And what's wrong, sweetheart?"

"She can't pee. I don't know why. She drank a lot of lemonade but she can't pee. And she's in there on the floor . . . I've got to go to her—"

"Don't hang up the phone, sweetheart."

"I'm just gonna go tell—" Quickly, Emma set the phone on the counter and raced back to the bathroom.

"Oh God Oh God Oh God," Jessie was groaning, her eyes closed. She was still on her side on the floor, both arms curved over her middle. The shorts had slid to her ankles. Quickly, Emma pulled them off.

"The ambulance is coming, Jess. Don't worry. The ambulance is coming."

Jessie opened her eyes. "You called an ambulance? I thought . . . I thought you had gone to the Jacksons' . . . on Summer."

"Oh, Jessie. There's no time for that. And they would have called an ambulance, wouldn't they have?"

Jessie didn't answer. She closed her eyes. "Emma. It hurts so bad. Do you think . . . Do you think I'm going to die?"

"No. Jessie, no. The ambulance is coming."

"But it hurts. It hurts so much."

"Jessie . . . I've got to . . . The phone."

Emma raced again to the kitchen and picked up the phone.

"Are you there?"

"Yes, I'm here."

"Are they here? Are they coming?"

"They're on their way, sweetheart. Just hang on. Stay on the phone."

"But my sister."

"Just don't hang up, okay?"

"I won't."

Again she left the receiver on the counter and ran back down the hall. She paused just before the doorway, dreading what she would see. This was the worst day of her life. To see Jessie like this, and to be able to do nothing. Not one single thing to make it better. Oh God. When would they come?

In the bathroom, Jessie was the same, no, worse . . . She moaned and winced and did not seem to see Emma. Emma sat down on the floor by her head and began to stroke her hair.

"You're going to be okay," she said softly. "They're coming. You're going to be okay . . ." God, where were they? What was taking so long? Emma pictured the dark road that lead to Baymont. How far was it to town? It was twenty minutes to the grocery store, twenty-five to the clinic where Laurel worked. Where was the hospital? *Was* there even a hospital in Ukiah? Emma didn't know. Oh, God, when would they come?

"Jessie, you're going to be okay . . ." Her voice was calm but she could feel the tears dripping off her cheeks and into Jessie's hair. "It's going to be okay . . ."

Even in the windowless bathroom, Emma could feel the darkness of the night outside pressing in on them. There were no streetlights on Sequoia Road, no neighboring houses with their windows aglow. Usually, Emma loved that darkness, the brilliant spray of stars it allowed in the pool of sky above the pond. But tonight the dark was different, sequestering her in the empty house, her sister ensconced beyond the wall of her private pain. Utterly alone, Emma longed for two things: the lights of the ambulance that would cut through the dark, and her mother—not Laurel but Sarah—who would know what to do, who would put her calm hand on Emma's shoulder and make everything all right.

Emma started when she heard the door. The ambulance!

She jumped to her feet and raced to the living room. They were here, at last.

But no. Not the ambulance, and not her mother. Laurel. Laurel and Cactus, brushing through the living room, laughing.

"Why is the phone off the hook?" she heard Laurel say, saw her striding toward it.

"No!" Emma yelled. She had no idea if the 911 operator was still on the line; it seemed like hours since she had last heard her say, "Don't hang up." But that phone was Emma's one minuscule point of comfort, her one connection to the world, to someone—anyone—who could help.

"Emma, what are you still doing up?"

"It's Jessie! The ambulance is coming . . ." Suddenly Emma was sobbing wildly. "They said they were coming. I don't know why they're not here."

Laurel's face went white. "The ambulance? Oh my God. Where is Jessie? Emma, where is she? What happened?"

"She couldn't pee . . . I called the ambulance . . . They said they were coming." Emma followed Laurel down the hallway, Cactus at her heels.

"Oh, Jesus." Laurel said. "Oh, Jessie. What's wrong?"

But by now Jessie was speechless with pain. Her eyes were pinched tight, her moans low, awful growls.

"Emma. What happened? What's wrong?" Laurel turned to her urgently. "Why didn't you call me? Oh, God, I left the number."

"I tried," Emma sobbed. "They said you'd left already . . . And the Jacksons didn't—"

Suddenly, they heard the squeal of the screen door and then urgent voices in the living room.

"Hello?"

"They're here," Emma sobbed. She pushed past Cactus and rushed to the front of the house. "She's here! She's down here. She's in the bathroom. You've got to help her!"

After that, everything happened so quickly that the relief Emma felt was overwhelming. The awful, awful waiting—listening helplessly to her sister's cries, with each minute stretching on and on impossibly—was over at last.

"Clear the way, folks, please." She felt Cactus grab her shoulder and gently push her out of the way, saw the men in uniforms come through the hall with the stretcher.

"Out of the way, please, ma'am," one of them said.

"I'm her mother," she heard Laurel say. "I need to know what's going on."

"We need you out of the way so we can get this young lady some help."

Emma heard the rattle of the shower curtain and knew that Laurel had stepped inside the stall rather than back down the narrow hallway to where Emma stood with Cactus. Then there was shuffling and voices and her sister's cries. In another moment, there they were again, coming through the living room with the stretcher, but this time Jessie was on it, still curled on her side, whimpering.

Emma searched her sister's face for some sign of her own relief. Jessie would be okay now. But her sister's face was contorted and colorless and if she saw Emma standing there, she gave no sign.

Laurel followed the stretcher, her face pale and drawn. Emma could smell the faint scent of her perfume as she passed.

Laurel was almost to the door when she turned.

"Cactus . . . you'll stay with Emma?

"No, I want to go! Jessie—"

"No, Emma. You have to stay here."

"But—"

But the stretcher was out the door now, and Cactus had his hand firmly on Emma's shoulder, rooting her in place.

"I have to go with her. I have to make sure she's okay—"

"She'll be okay, don't you worry," Cactus said. "She's in good hands now. You did the right thing, Emma. You did good."

Outside, there was the crunch of gravel and the sweep of lights as the ambulance pulled out onto the road. Emma heard the siren go on and pictured the ambulance rushing down the dark roads to the hospital.

"Will they . . . ? Will they be able to help her in the ambulance?" she asked, her voice cracking. "Or will she have to wait for . . . for the hospital?" She thought of how long it had been until the ambulance arrived, the pain piling up on her sister, crushing her. Surely, she couldn't stand to wait all that time again. Surely, they could do something in the ambulance . . .

"I don't . . ." Cactus began, and then he paused and studied Emma's face. "In the ambulance," he said. "Don't worry, sugar. She'll be fine. Here, why don't you sit down for a while?"

He steered Emma to the couch. To her surprise, she realized the television was still on; it had been on all this time.

"You want to watch something?"

Emma shook her head, so Cactus walked over to the set and clicked it off. Emma watched the picture shrink into a little brown rectangle, then vanish. The house was suddenly very, very quiet.

"How long do you think it will take them to get there?" Emma asked.

"About twenty minutes, I'd think," Cactus said. "There'll be no traffic."

"And what . . . what can they . . . what will they be able to do for her?"

"Well, she can't pee, you said? I expect they'll put in a catheter."

"What's that?"

"It's a little tube. It'll let the pee out."

Emma felt her body relax infinitesimally; she could almost feel her sister's relief.

"And the . . . the catheter? They'll do it in the ambulance?"

Cactus looked away. "Yeah."

"But why couldn't she pee? What's wrong with her?"

"That, I have no idea. But the doctors will know. Don't worry about that. They'll make it right."

They sat in silence for a moment.

Finally, Emma said, "I want to call my mom."

Cactus let out his breath in a quick burst. "Sugar, I'm sorry, but there's no way . . . She'll call from the hospital when they're situated. When they know something."

"I mean . . . my mom at home. In Bakersfield."

For a moment, Cactus just looked at her. "I don't know, sugar. Maybe you should wait until we know . . . Maybe you should wait until your mother . . . Until Laurel calls and we know something."

But now that the ambulance had come at last, Emma's longing to talk with her mother was overpowering. She stood up. "I'm going to call. I want—I need to talk to her."

Cactus looked at Emma's face. Her tears had traced pale tracks down her cheeks, still grimy from the afternoon's ride. "I guess you should go ahead and call her then," he said.

Emma was supposed to call collect; that was the agreement. Long distance was just way too expensive, Laurel had said. Dutifully, she dialed the operator, gave her number. She heard the phone ring, once, twice . . . What time was it? It seemed the middle of the night; would her parents be in bed? She pictured the brown phone on her mother's night table ringing, ringing.

"Hello?" Emma heard her mother answer the phone, and she breathed a little sigh of relief.

"You have a collect call from Emma Walters. Will you accept the charges?"

"Oh, Christ!" she heard her mother say. "Of course."

"Thank you," the operator said. "Hold the line." Then there was a click and she was gone.

"Mom!" Emma said. "Mom!"

"Emma? What's wrong? What time . . . It's after eleven! Where are you? What happened? What's wrong?"

Emma heard the panic in her mother's voice. She felt like crying again, but knew she had to get the story out.

As quickly as she could, she relayed the events of the evening. Part way through, she heard her father pick up the downstairs phone and her mother asked her to start again.

"So Jessie's at the hospital now?" her mother asked urgently when she had finished. "Which one?"

"I don't know. I don't know," Emma said. "They took her in the ambulance. I hope . . . I just hope she got there already. Mom?"

"Oh, sweetness."

"It was awful, Mom. I didn't know what to do." Fiercely she brushed away her tears. "She was hurting so much and I didn't know what to do."

"Oh, sweetness," her mother said again. "You did the right thing. You called 911. And you were there with her." Suddenly, her mother caught her breath. "But what about you? Where are you?"

"I'm at home—at Baymont. Cactus is here."

"Cactus?"

"Laurel's boyfriend."

There was a pause. "Honey, can I speak to Cactus for a minute? Then you can get back on."

Emma held the phone out to him. "Cactus, my mom wants to talk to you for a sec."

Emma listened as Cactus talked to her parents. She could tell what they were asking because of what he said, could sense their growing frustration as he repeated, "I promise I'll call as soon as we know something."

At last, he handed the phone back to Emma.

"Honey," her mother said. "We'd better hang up now. We want to call the hospital and see what we can find out. But you did the right thing, sweetheart. Thank you."

"Mom," Emma croaked. "Don't go." They couldn't hang up now. They couldn't leave her alone again. "Mom. I . . . I don't want to be alone."

"Cactus is there, honey. He's not going anywhere."

"But I don't want to be here alone, Mom," Emma sobbed. "I want to . . . I want to come home."

"Honey, sweetness, shhh. I know. I know. And I promise I will call you right back. But we're worried about Jessie. We want to find out—"

"Okay," Emma managed at last. "I know."

"Bye, Emma. We'll call right back, okay?"

"Okay."

Emma hung up the phone and collapsed onto the couch. She pushed her face into one of the cushions, smelled the lingering scent of her sister, of horses. Awkwardly, Cactus reached down and put a hand on her shoulder.

"You okay, Emma?"

She nodded, not looking up, but the tears wouldn't stop.

"I just want to go home," she said again.

"It'll be okay, sugar, don't you worry. Jessie's gonna be okay, and your mom's gonna be home soon."

CHAPTER 24

One Year Later

Jessie

"Laurel, please," Jessie begged over the phone. "Please don't."

"I have to."

"Why? She doesn't want to come, Mom."

Her mother snorted. "Emma's twelve."

"So?"

"She's *twelve*! Who lets a twelve-year-old make a decision like that?"

"But she doesn't want to!"

"Jessie, it doesn't matter. I'm her mother. I deserve visitation—at the very least. And if Len and Sarah deny me that, I have to take action. I can't just sit back and let them take my daughter away from me."

"But Mom! They're not taking her away. Emma doesn't want to come. Aren't you listening?"

The line went silent for a moment.

"Mom?"

"Jessie, it was not *my* fault you had that cyst. What happened last summer—Emma is not *allowed* to blame me for that!"

Jessie moved her hand over her abdomen instinctively, her fingers probing at her scar.

"Mom," she said quietly. "It's not about the . . . It's not about what happened with me."

"Of course it is. Emma has always been perfectly content to come visit before."

"No, Mom," Jessie said quietly. "She hasn't."

Jessie closed her eyes, awaiting her mother's disbelief. How, she wondered, could this possibly be a revelation to her mother?

"What do you mean?" Laurel said. "You girls . . . You love it here."

Jessie sighed. It was true. Even Emma, she knew, loved Baymont.

"Mom, it's not about that. It's—" she hesitated. It seemed impossible to put into words. "Oh, Mom. It's just *everything*. Everything that's ever happened. The pirate ship. Raisin. The dam. The things—"

The things you do, she was about to say, but stopped herself.

"Well," Laurel said stiffly. "I had no idea you blamed me for all of that."

"I don't. But Emma—"

"Oh, but Emma does."

"No. That's not what I was going to say."

Emma is just *different*, she thought.

"Mom, it's not that she blames you. She . . . She just doesn't want to go anymore, okay? Why can't you just let it be?"

"*Why*? Because I am not about to let Len and Sarah take my daughter away from me a second time!"

"Mom! Please! Please, just don't do it, okay? Please don't take Dad to court. *Please!*"

"I'm sorry, Jessie. I'd fight for you, too. You know that, right?"

Jessie and Laurel didn't speak again until the summons came. Jessie knew it had come because her father's face went white when he saw it.

"Sarah!" he yelled. "Oh Jesus."

He left all the other mail on the kitchen counter and strode down the hall with that one envelope. She could hear him tearing it open as he walked.

Jessie followed him down the hall, but he didn't notice. He walked into the office where Sarah sat at her desk, and swung the door closed behind him.

Jessie stood listening outside the door as he began to read the letter aloud. She heard "summons" and "complaint" and "custody" and her stomach plummeted. Oh, why hadn't Laurel listened to her? She ran to her bedroom and flopped onto her bed. How could her mother do this to her?

"Hey Betty Boobs! Can't you winch 'em up any better than that?"

Jessie stared at the oily green bus seat in front of her, pretending she didn't hear.

"Come on, leave her alone," she heard another voice say, and for a moment the awful twist in her stomach loosened a little. She strained her ears. Was someone really going to stick up for her? She wanted to turn around to see who it was, but stopped herself. She knew better. Best not to look, not to react, not to show any sign of having heard.

"Leave her alone," he repeated. "You know cavemen never wore bras."

The two boys laughed loudly, and it was worse now, because of that little bit of hope she'd had.

Suddenly Jessie turned in her seat, knowing that she shouldn't, that it would only make it worse. But there she was, raising her middle finger at them and telling them to shut up, why don't you.

"Oooooh!" they laughed, clutching each other. "We're scared now! What you gonna do, titty-drop us?"

"Ha! She'd knock you out. Ka-boom! Thirty pounds of hairy titty right on your head. Bam!"

Jessie blinked back her tears. If they saw her cry, it would only be worse next time.

"Hey, Crow Magnum? What you doing tonight? My friend here wants you to titty-drop him."

"Neanderthals," Jessie muttered.

"What'd you call us?"

"Neanderthals," she said, louder. "Crow Magnum was way more advanc—"

Their laughter buried her words. "I know you are, but what am I? What is this, fucking third grade? Go buy a bra, why don't you? I hear Kmart's having a special."

Again, the awful laughter. "Attention Kmart shoppers: Boulder Holder Blue Light Special, aisle two . . ."

How could they not grow bored of their own stupidity? No, it went on and on and on, until at last the bus reached her stop. She had stopped her tears, but her face was burning. Even worse, there was a dampness between her legs that Jessie hoped desperately was sweat. But when she stood up, she felt the blood leaking out of her.

She was off the bus as fast as she could, not even listening to their taunting now, just hoping, oh God *please*, praying that nothing was showing through her jeans. If she had bled through her pants, she would never hear the end of it. Please, just let her off the bus without anything showing and she wouldn't care what they said ever again.

As soon as the bus turned the corner, Jessie started to run. Her backpack held three textbooks and a novel; it bounced uncomfortably against her back as she ran. In front, despite her bra, her breasts bounced, too. She held one arm against her chest to steady them. With each step, the scar on her abdomen ached, and she felt the blood seeping out of her, soaking her underwear.

By the time she reached the house, there were damp patches of sweat beneath the straps of her backpack, sweat dripping between her breasts, sweat dampening the hair that now clung to her temples. Stepping into the air-conditioned kitchen at last was like diving into the pool on a hot day. She paused for a second, relishing the cool, then peeled off her backpack. In another second she was racing for the bathroom.

"Jessie?" she heard her father call. "Is that you? I need to talk"

"Just a second!" she called back. "I've got to go to the bathroom."

"Oh God," she said, after she had fought her jeans off her hips and could see. Her underwear was saturated with blood, a red oval in the crotch of her jeans, too. Quickly, she pulled them off. Had the blood gone through? Yes, but not much. She could see some blood where it had seeped through the fabric around the seam, but surely that had happened while she ran home? Surely no one on the bus could have seen . . .

She put in a tampon and rinsed the underwear out at the sink, watching the water run red, then pink. There was a sharp ache in her abdomen now, not her scar but deeper, like someone was scraping out her insides with a grapefruit spoon.

She rinsed out her jeans after the underwear, then hung them both in the shower to drip. She would have to ask Sarah if she could do a load of laundry later.

She wrapped a towel around her waist and opened the door.

"Jessie? Will you . . . Oh, sorry."

It was her father again, standing in the hallway, waiting for her. "Sorry, Jess. But I do need to talk to you. Just as soon as you're ready."

She nodded and went to her room, found clean underwear and a pair of shorts. Her bra was damp with her sweat and felt clammy against her skin, so she pulled off her T-shirt and changed that, too.

She looked away from the sight of her breasts in the mirror while she changed. She could still hear the boys' taunting voices, their vulgar words and innuendos, and her throat tightened. Why couldn't they just leave her alone? There were seven more months of ninth grade. Seven months of riding the bus, seven months of their relentless bullying. Jessie could see no way out but to wait, and yet the waiting . . . How would she stand it? She didn't think she could.

When Jessie emerged from her bedroom, her brother Jay was in the hallway. Four lines of green army men stretched from one wall to the other. Jay stood with his back to her, fiddling with the house plant in the corner.

"What are you doing, Jay?" she asked.

He jumped. "Nothing. Just setting up an ambush."

"I nearly tripped over all those guys."

"Sorry."

He didn't sound that sorry. He sounded just like he always did: a regular nine-year-old boy, who loved battles and baseball and Super Mario Brothers. Not one of those things should have mattered to Jessie, and yet somehow they all did. Jay was just so *normal*. Jay didn't get picked on at school; he got invited to birthday parties and swimming pools and sleepovers. Recently he'd even cut his hair in a spike; he used hair gel, for Christ's sake. *Gel*, in the fourth grade.

"I don't see why it bothers you so much, Jessie," Sarah had said when Jessie had pointed this out. "Just let him be who he is. He lets you be who you are."

Jessie knew Sarah was right, but *still*. She couldn't help imagining what Jay would be like five years from now. There was no doubt in her mind that he'd be one of the *in* kids: popular and athletic, with clothes that were just right. She couldn't stand those kids.

To be fair, she knew Jay wouldn't turn out like those boys on the bus. Despite all the clichés that made him so infuriatingly normal, Jay was a sweet kid. He never killed bugs, for example, which she supposed was another nine-year-old, boys-will-be-boys stereotype. Little green army men the exception, Jay didn't like to see anything get hurt.

Jessie knew that her half-brother was kind, funny, and smart, and yet not one of those qualities made her want to be closer to him. He was also perceptive enough to sense her disdain, and so he kept his distance from her, too.

With Emma, he was different. When they were younger, he and Emma had often played together, making houses out of blocks for their stuffed animals, or cities for his cars. Jessie had overheard Sarah say once that Emma hadn't gotten to enjoy a healthy infancy—because of Laurel—so that after Jay was born, Emma had regressed, talking baby talk and crawling around with him under the kitchen table.

But it wasn't just because of *Laurel*, Jessie had thought bitterly when she'd heard this. Laurel hadn't wanted a divorce. She hated it when Sarah said things like that, when she made it sound like everything had been Laurel's fault.

Jessie was the only one in her family who defended Laurel. Of course, Sarah and Dad wouldn't, and Jay hardly even knew her. But Emma . . . She didn't know why Emma couldn't see Laurel the way she saw her.

Jessie remembered one summer in Baymont when she was eight or nine years old. The phone had rung in the early morning, waking Jessie. When she tiptoed into Laurel's room, her mother was already getting dressed. The call had been from the Jacksons; the horses had gotten out. Jessie followed her mother while she pulled on work boots and headed to the barn for gloves and wire cutters.

"What are you going to do?" Jessie had asked, skipping behind her, still in her pajamas.

"Well, what do you think? I'm going to fix the damn fence. And then we'll catch the horses."

They had followed the fence from the gate until they found the place where the horses had broken through. And then Laurel had fixed it, while Jessie looked on. *That*, Jessie had decided then and there, *that* was the kind of woman she was going to be one day. The kind that could fix a fence by herself when one needed fixing.

But when they had arrived back at the house, her sister had greeted them at the door, wide-eyed and pale.

"I woke up and no one was here," she said tremulously.

"The horses got out," Jessie had explained to her importantly. "We were fixing the fence."

Emma had probably told Sarah about that morning, and Sarah had almost certainly told Dad. And so, in their minds, it became just another instance of Laurel's poor choices, her unfitness as a mom. Only Jessie knew what it had really been like, that crystal-clear moment of revelation when she had understood for the first time that no man was necessary, that a woman could do anything she put her mind to.

Jessie stepped over Jay's army battalion and went to her parents' office at the end of the hall. Inside, Len sat at his desk, his red grading pen in hand, but Jessie knew that he had been waiting for her by the way he pushed the pile of papers away when she walked in.

"What are you doing?" she asked.

"Just grading."

"Your students' tests?"

"Yes."

She craned her neck to see. Her father taught math at the university, but whenever she looked at the students' work he brought home, it looked like no math she had ever seen: all shapes and symbols and letters, with very few numbers at all.

"How'd they do?"

He snorted. "Not great. How was your day?"

She hesitated. She could barely remember the day before the bus ride. Really, it hardly mattered. Even the best days could be ruined during the fifteen-minute ride home.

"Okay," she said. She took a breath. What point would there be in telling her father? What could he possibly do that wouldn't make it worse in the end? And yet she still longed to tell him, just so she could feel that there was someone on her side. "Dad, I—"

"Jessie," Len said quickly, "I'm not sure what you know. But Laurel is demanding . . . Laurel has taken me to court for joint custody."

Jessie swallowed hard and looked away. She could sense her father watching her, waiting for her reaction. She didn't know what to say, didn't know how she was supposed to look. Finally, she nodded, a barely perceptible dip of her head.

"So you knew?"

"No," Jessie said. "I didn't know for sure. I knew maybe. I asked . . . I begged her not to."

"Well, she did anyway."

Jessie glanced up at him. "So now what?"

"I've hired a lawyer," he said, watching her closely. "But I'm not going to fight for something you don't want. So I have to ask you. Do you want to . . . ? Are you happy . . . ? Do you want to keep on living here, with us?"

For a second, Jessie felt as if her heart had stopped. She tried to breathe but couldn't. She had a choice? Jessie had never imagined that it would come to that. When Laurel had said she was going to take her father to court, Jessie had envisioned only conflict— bitter testimony and hard feelings. She had never thought it would mean that she would be asked, for the first time, what *she* wanted.

I want them to leave me alone, she thought, the torment of the day still hot on her skin. That wasn't what her father had meant, she knew, but wasn't that part of it? Moments ago, she had seen no possible way out. But now . . .

For years, the idea of living year-round in Baymont had been like Jessie's imaginary friend. Whenever her life in Bakersfield had felt hard or unfair—when her classmates teased her, or Sarah scolded her, or her father seemed to love her brother more—

the alternate life she could be living with Laurel was her secret consolation. In Baymont, the clothes she wore to school would never matter, nor would she be punished for inconsequential things, like a capless marker left on her bed which had bled onto her quilt. In Baymont—and this was the crux of it, the one thing she knew positively but would never, ever admit to knowing—it was *she* who was the favored one.

She thought of Baymont then, with its conifer-scented woods and rolling pastures, its lonely dirt roads and thickets full of blackberries. In the woods above the pond, she had found a perfect ring of redwoods, where saplings had grown up around the mother tree. The saplings now were thicker than she could circle with her arms; the mother tree had long since returned to the earth. The ground in the center of the ring was spongy and soft, and fine red needles blanketed the ground. Jessie loved to lie on her back there, with the trees towering above her. In those moments, she felt, not alone, but *whole*.

There was *nothing* like that here. In Bakersfield, Jessie's only glimpse of wildness was of the hazy, orange mountains beyond the farms. In Baymont, there were horses, woods, long rides down abandoned roads so lovely they made her heart ache. And here? Here there were bus-riding bullies and awful, hair-sprayed girls, all the usual taunts and name-calling, plus a daily gauntlet of disapproving stares. Surely ninth grade in Mendocino could not be so cruel.

"Jessie?" her father said. "You don't have to decide—"

"There," Jessie said quickly. "I want to live there."

Later, in her room, Jessie felt ashamed of how quickly the words had tumbled out of her. She had thought only of Baymont, as if the wild beauty of the place alone would be enough to save her. She hadn't thought of what it would mean to her father, or Sarah, or Emma. She hadn't thought of her best friend or her little brother.

She had been asked what she wanted at last and she had thought only of herself and her tormentors, while no one that mattered to her had even entered her head. Her face burned with the shame of it and her belly ached. She knew it must be her period, but it scraped away at her gut like guilt.

She swallowed two Advils and lay down on her bed, curling her knees to her chest and closing her eyes. She tried to recapture the vision of Baymont she had had in the office with her father, but it felt now as it always did, a fantasy so worn its edges blurred, a dream so familiar and so impossible it couldn't hold her faith.

CHAPTER 25

Emma

Emma and Jay were both upstairs in their rooms, Emma with her homework, Jay on Atari, when they were called down to the kitchen.

"Okay!" Emma bellowed down the stairs. It was too early for dinner, she thought, but she was glad to be called away. She paused at the door to her brother's room; he was playing Galaga, she could tell by the sounds.

"Mom called. You coming?"

"I'm just gonna die first," he said. He glanced up at her. "You want a turn afterwards?"

She shrugged. "Okay."

She didn't like playing video games, but she liked that Jay had asked her. They had little in common these days—he with his friends and his little league, she with school and track—but whenever they did spend time together, she felt the ease of their old closeness.

"Any idea what Mom wants?" she asked.

"Nope."

"Think we're in trouble for something?"

"Like what?"

"I don't know."

She waited for him to die, and then they raced each other down the stairs and up the hall to the kitchen. She slapped her hand against the doorframe seconds before Jay.

"I win."

Her mother and father were standing side by side in front of the sink. When she saw their faces, her stomach flip flopped inside her.

"What did we do—" she began, but then she saw Jessie seated in her place at the kitchen table and went quiet. Her sister's face was red and puffy; she clutched a sodden tissue in one hand. Emma breathed a quick, inaudible sigh of relief. Whatever it was, it wasn't them— it was Jessie.

But what had Jessie done? And why, if Jessie was in trouble for something, had she and her brother been invited in to witness her shame? That was not like her parents. "You have your own behavior to think about," her mother always said when one of them wanted to spy or gloat.

Emma studied her sister's face, trying to guess. Then again, maybe it wasn't what she thought. Maybe some actual tragedy had occurred. Had her sister's hamster Snowflake died? He had a big lump on one side of his head and one eye was permanently closed. She tried to catch her sister's eye, to get some hint of what was going on, but Jessie wouldn't look at her.

"Emma. Jay. Jessie has something to tell you," Sarah said quietly.

Jessie hesitated only a second. "I'm going to live at Baymont."

Emma stared at her in disbelief. "With Laurel?"

"Yes."

"For . . . For forever?"

"Well—"

"I mean, all the time? For school and everything?"

"Yes."

"But what about us? What about—"

"I'll come and visit sometimes."

At her side, Jay didn't move. She glanced at her parents; both their faces were masks of stone. Emma couldn't speak. She couldn't ask the one question that was screaming in her head: *Why?* For how could Jessie answer with their parents looking on like that? Emma knew what drew her sister to Baymont, for those things drew her, too. But beneath all those reasons—the horses, the beauty, the extraordinary fact of actually *living* in such a place— there was only one possible, unspeakable answer: Jessie liked Laurel more than she liked Mom. But how *could* she? To Emma, it seemed impossible. Laurel as a mother—that was too high a price to pay.

As soon as they were dismissed from the kitchen, Emma cornered Jessie in her room.

"Jessie, why?"

Immediately, Jessie threw herself face down on her bed and began to cry again.

Emma did not relent. "But *why?* Jessie, how can you—?"

"I just want to, okay?"

Emma stood on the rug by the door and watched her sister cry. Normally, she would have gone to her in an instant, but now she stood as if rooted to the spot.

After a moment, Jessie looked up and regarded her with teary eyes. "Don't you *know?*"

Emma shrugged noncommittally and looked away. Did she know? Emma had seen Jessie in Baymont; she had seen her with Laurel. At times, she had even envied her sister for how well she fit there, when Emma herself felt ill at ease and traitorous. Jessie was right: she did know. Emma felt that she understood all of it, all except for that one huge, undeniable piece: Jessie was choosing Laurel to be her mother.

This she did not, *could not* understand.

"But how—?" she began. "Laurel—"

"Oh, Emma. Don't you get it? Life here *sucks*. Every day it's the same thing, and I'm sick of it."

"Those boys still?"

Jessie met her eye and nodded.

"So . . . why don't you tell Mom and Dad? I mean, they could do something—"

"What? What could they do?"

"I don't know. They could talk to the bus driver."

Jessie snorted. "Right."

"They could drive you home from school."

"It's not just on the bus, Em. It's everywhere."

"Well, they could . . . I don't know." She looked at her sister hopelessly. "You could just tell them."

Jessie sighed. "It's not just the bullying, Em. You know what it's like at Baymont. It's . . . It's just different, isn't it? I mean, can you imagine actually living there? I *want* to go."

"But what about Laurel?" At last she had said it.

Jessie looked hard at her. "What about her? She's our mom, Emma. It's not so crazy that I want to go and live with her."

Emma shook her head. "No, she's not. She's not *my* mom, at least."

Jessie sighed, exasperated. "Well, technically, she is. But whatever."

Emma studied her sister, who had propped herself up on her elbows on the bed and was wiping at her cheeks with the backs of both hands. Suddenly Emma felt how far Jessie was from her. They had always been so close, and yet here was this colossal piece of her sister's heart that she did not know and failed to understand. Already she looked different to her: the sister who would be a different kind of sister now. An absent sister, a partial sister, a sister who could choose to leave.

Emma did not cry or beg her sister to change her mind. She could feel a new distance opening up between them. She did not contemplate, then, what Jessie's absence would mean: this bedroom empty of her sister and all her things, the way her own life would shift and shrink without her sister in it. Her sister was a part of her, her love for her so deep that she hardly needed to call it love. And yet even then, on the precipice of losing her, Emma did not think to tell Jessie that she loved her, or plead with her not to go. Instead, an awful greed loomed up in her. When Jessie left, she and her brother would be alone. They would be the faithful ones. They would be loved best.

Does every child feel this horrid thing? This secret, sucking need to be loved more? Emma loved her sister—she *knew* she loved her sister—and yet, during those long moments in Jessie's room, she felt that love trumped in her. There it was, undeniable but awful. Horrid, yes, but thrilling: Jessie would leave, and Emma would be loved more.

CHAPTER 26

Jessie

One afternoon a few months later, Jessie burst through the back door into the kitchen, her backpack halfway off her shoulders already. She unzipped it and plunged her hand inside, pulling out a slightly crumpled piece of paper. She held it out to Sarah, who stood at the counter, unloading the dishwasher.

"I need you to sign this form," Jessie said.

Sarah looked up.

"What's that?"

"I want to run cross country next year. They made an announcement today at school—there's a meeting next week. All I need is to get a physical and for a parent to sign this form."

"Could you close the door please, Jessie? The air-conditioning's on."

"Would you sign it?" Jessie said, holding the paper out to Sarah with one hand and pulling the door closed behind her. "So I can run cross country in the fall?"

But Sarah didn't reach out for the paper. She simply turned, a coffee mug in each hand, and looked at Jessie sternly, her eyebrows arched and forehead wrinkled.

"Mom, I said is it okay if I run cross country next year?"

Sarah stared at her, silent.

"Mom, I—"

"Next year?"

"Yeah, it's a fall sport. It'll start next—"

Jessie stopped. Suddenly, she understood the odd expression on Sarah's face. All at once, she remembered—she wouldn't be here next year. She wouldn't run cross country for Spelman High School next fall. She wouldn't even go to that school anymore. And she wouldn't, she realized, need her mom and dad's permission for anything. Her breath caught in her throat.

"Oh," she mumbled. She felt too ashamed to add, "I forgot." The blood rushed to her face and she scuttled to her room, throwing herself onto the bed.

"I just forgot, okay?" she muttered into her pillow. "I just *forgot*." She pushed the heels of her hands into both eyes, hard, and clenched her teeth. She was so tired of crying, and what was the point, anyway? Nobody here even cared.

That Friday evening at Leah's house, Jessie reported to her best friend what had happened. They were lying side by side on their backs on the shaggy rug in Leah's room, staring at the ceiling.

"I just forgot that I was going to leave, you know? But I felt so stupid. Asking Mom if I could run cross country when I won't even be here." Jessie was dry-eyed now, nonchalant, but the urge to cry was still lodged in the bottom of her throat, even now, two days later. Oh, she just couldn't wait for it all to be over. But everything seemed to be moving so *slowly*. The court date had not been set; weeks passed with no word from the attorney. When Jessie had first told Laurel she wanted to live with her, Laurel had called her every few days for two weeks, full of questions and plans and gratitude. But now weeks might pass with no phone call from Laurel—as if nothing had happened at all, Jessie thought. As if her whole world was not about to change.

No one at home seemed to understand Jessie's impatience for the suit be resolved. After all, she had made her decision, and her father had said he would not cross her. Next summer Jessie would go to Baymont for good. But what would the judge say about Emma? The question hung over all of them. Jessie had, more than once, overheard her father and Sarah speaking to each other in tense voices, but to Jessie and Emma they said almost nothing.

"I mean," Jessie said to Leah now, "everything just feels pretty much the same as it always has. Except Mom and Dad . . . I don't know, they seem different somehow. But they never talk about the court case. I don't even know what's happening."

"I still can't believe you forgot," Leah said beside her. "That's so weird."

"Yeah," Jessie agreed. "But how can they blame me? I felt stupid and everything, but I don't know. Everything just feels so *normal* that I forgot for a second."

"Well, technically a lot longer than a second, if you asked your mom to—"

"Come on, Leah. You know what I mean."

"Yeah."

Leah had been Jessie's best friend since they were both five years old, when Jessie had started kindergarten in Bakersfield. They had been together through all six years of elementary school; it was only in retrospect that Jessie understood what a difference that had made. Jessie had never been easy with her peers, but with Leah there—fearless, gregarious, likeable Leah—the other kids had hardly seemed to notice Jessie. Back then, it had only been Leah who had teased her, calling her "Brainy Smurf" good-naturedly whenever the teachers praised her.

"Okay, Smurfette," Jessie had retaliated. With her perfect blonde hair and her ballet lessons, Leah had always been the kind of girl that Jessie had no wish to emulate, no matter how many times her friend talked her into painting her toenails or curling her hair.

Everything had changed after fifth grade, when Leah's parents decided to send their only daughter to private school. Leah and Jessie had managed to stay friends, but it was different now. Jessie had often wondered how her life might have been if she and Leah had gone to the same school. Would Leah's friendship have been enough to keep the other kids at bay? Or would Leah—so popular now, so *cool*—have understood immediately what a social liability her best friend was and kept her distance? Jessie wouldn't have blamed her, if she had. Who'd want to be best friends with Crow Magnum, after all?

Jessie rolled onto her stomach and propped herself up on her elbows. She looked around at the familiar room. There, on Leah's bookshelves, were all the romance novels that Leah loved but that she disdained, although she had borrowed and read most of them. There, on the dresser, was the shoebox where Leah saved every wrapper from every piece of gum she had ever eaten, all the shiny, silver pieces of paper neatly folded and stowed away. On the walls hung half a dozen pairs of old ballet slippers and pointe shoes.

Jessie gestured to them now. "If you can't wear them anymore, why don't you just throw them away?"

Leah shrugged. "I like how they look."

Jessie lowered her head to the rug and closed her eyes. When she left, would Leah just ask one of her friends from school to sleep over on Friday nights? Would it all go on exactly the same—the Domino's pizza Leah's parents always ordered for dinner, the voices on *Dallas* filtering in from the den, the trundle bed pulled out for some other girl who might actually like the pink comforter that Jessie hated? Would it all go on just the same, but without *her*? She felt her presence like a ghost in the room, already fading.

When she opened her eyes, she saw that Leah had turned onto her side and was looking at her seriously.

"What?" Jessie said.

"You don't have to go, you know."

"What?"

"You don't have to go to Mendocino. You don't *have* to go live there. Stay here. Run cross country."

Jessie laughed nervously. "But I already decided."

"So change your mind. It's your life. You can just . . . *stay*. Plus, if you run cross country, you won't have to ride the bus, right? Somebody's gonna have to pick you up."

"But I've already said—"

"So say you've changed your mind."

"But—"

"Oh, come on, Jessie. Do you really want to go and live up there? How can you want to live there?"

"You don't understand. It's different there."

"Fine. I don't understand. I'll never understand." She paused for a minute, and when she spoke again her voice was different, less petulant but sadder somehow.

"You're right, Jessie. I don't understand. I don't understand how you can just decide to leave everything. Everything! Emma, Jay, your mom, your dad. Snowflake. Me."

"What?"

"Geez, Jessie. I mean, come on. How can you just *decide* to leave your best friend like it's nothing?"

"It's not that it's nothing. It's just—"

"It's just *what*? It's just that Baymont is so *different*, blah, blah, blah. There you can blah, blah, blah. Laurel lets you blah, blah, blah. Well, what about us? Don't you care about us? How can you just *leave* everyone like that?"

Leah got up suddenly. She tore a Kleenex from the box on her bedside table and wiped her nose. She stared at the ballet shoes hanging from the wall. When she spoke again her voice had softened.

"Look, I'm sorry." She closed her eyes for a moment and sighed deeply. "I'm just really going to . . . I'm just going to miss you."

Jessie couldn't speak. The room was quiet except for the muffled voice of JR coming through the walls and the hum of the air-conditioning unit just outside Leah's window. Jessie looked at Leah and then buried her face in her arms. Her friend knelt beside her on the floor and put a tentative hand on her back.

"Jess, I didn't mean to make you cry. I'll just miss you is all. But you can visit, I guess, right? Jessie? What's wrong?"

Jessie was sobbing hard now, her face hidden in her arms.

"Jessie?"

"I don't think I want to go," she mumbled through her sobs.

"What?"

"I don't want to go." Jessie looked up finally, her eyes puffy and nose running. Leah offered her the Kleenex she still had balled up in her hand, and Jessie took it and wiped her own nose fiercely. When she spoke again, her voice was calmer.

"I don't want to go and live in Baymont. I want to stay here."

There was a long pause.

"Really?"

Jessie nodded.

"Why? I mean, what changed your mind? I thought—"

"You did."

"Jessie, I didn't mean . . . I was just talking, you know? I didn't mean to make you—"

"It's not that. It's not what you said about how I didn't have to go and everything. It's just—"

Jessie hesitated, not wanting to repeat it. It felt too precious to repeat; she didn't want to spoil it.

"Then what?"

"What you said about . . . about missing me. You're the only one who's said that."

"Oh." Leah plopped down on the bed. "That can't be true. Everyone is going to miss you."

Already Jessie could feel her friend backing away. Leah was not one to gush. Instinctively, Jessie backed off, too. Leah had said it; that was enough.

"I mean, I can imagine myself being there," she said. "Mostly. I just never imagined myself not being *here*. You know?"

"Yeah, I guess."

"And I honestly never thought about how anybody might miss me."

"Honestly, Jessie, that's just stupid."

Jessie smiled through her tears; this was more familiar ground. She gave a little shrug. "Maybe."

"Of course everybody's gonna miss you. What did you think?"

Jessie shook her head. "I don't know." Then she shrugged again. "Maybe you're right. I guess probably Emma will, anyway." But inwardly she was thinking, *But you're the only one who* said *it*. And suddenly the realization that until now not one person in her family had said that they would miss her seemed monstrously sad. Jessie began to cry again, covering her face in her hands. "I'm sorry."

"Oh, Jessie. Please stop. Here." Leah got the Kleenex box from beside her bed and shoved it at her friend. "You've got to stop. My mom's going to come in here soon to tell us to go to bed, and if she sees you crying she'll be worried and call your parents and . . . Are you really not going to go, do you think?"

Jessie looked up. Leah looked uncharacteristically serious.

Jessie nodded. "I really don't think I want to anymore." Suddenly the prospect of going to live in Baymont with Laurel seemed ludicrously far-fetched. How had she missed that, before? She'd been so caught up in the fantasy of it. She would go to Baymont, escape her tormentors, gallop through the hills with the wind in her hair . . . She let out a little burst of laughter.

"What?" Leah wanted to know, but Jessie just shook her head. That was just the kind of thing Leah would tease her about. "The wind in your hair? Oh, *come on!*"

Jessie laughed again, almost giddy with the relief of it, a dark mass suddenly loosened from her gut. Her life was here. She couldn't just leave it. Her family was *here*—all but Laurel, at least. How had she thought she could just opt out? She saw it all differently now.

Yes, she would tell her father that she had changed her mind. She would tell him she wanted to stay. Tomorrow, as soon as she got home. At the thought, a nervous excitement shot through her gut. How surprised he would be, she thought. How glad. She smiled to herself, imagining.

"Well, call me as soon as you tell them," Leah said. "I want to know exactly what they say."

CHAPTER 27

Sarah

Sarah and Len were sitting on the couch watching *Out of Africa* when Sarah heard the living room door swing open behind her. She didn't turn around.

"Jay," she said, her voice firm. "Go back to bed."

"Mom, it's me," Jessie said. She left her hand on the door handle uncertainly. "Can I talk to you guys for a minute?"

Sarah shifted on the couch so that she could see Jessie. "Right now?" she said. "Your father and I were just sitting down together to watch a movie."

Jessie winced visibly, and Sarah immediately regretted how exasperated she had sounded. She pulled her feet from where they rested in Len's lap and sat up. "But it's fine. We rented it, so we should be able to stop it. Len, do you know how to stop it for a minute?"

Len reached for the remote and studied the buttons. In a moment the screen went black.

Sarah turned to Jessie. "Come on in."

Jessie pulled the door closed and took a few steps into the room. She glanced at the love seat, but did not sit down. She stood beside the coffee table, looking down on Sarah and Len as if she were on stage.

"Well, um, I've been thinking. A lot. And I just wondered . . . Would it be okay if I changed my mind?"

Sarah had been watching Jessie's face as she began, but now she looked quickly away. Beside her, she heard Len let out his breath. "Jesus, Jessie," he muttered.

Sarah forced herself to meet Jessie's eye. "About?" she said slowly.

"About where . . . About Baymont . . . About where I'm going to live." She paused for an instant, and then went on in a rush. "I've done a lot of thinking and I've changed my mind. If . . . If it's okay, I'd like to keep living here. I mean, I want to stay here. With you guys."

An awful silence descended, and Jessie looked anxiously from Len to Sarah, and then at the floor. "If you don't mind, I mean."

"Can I ask what made you change your mind?" Sarah asked, and Jessie shrugged.

"I don't know. I mean, my life is here. I can't . . . I shouldn't just leave it. And the family—"

Sarah and Len simply watched her, saying nothing, so Jessie went on.

"I guess it's that . . . I mean, things have been really hard at school lately, and I guess at first going to Baymont seemed like an easy way to get away from it all. But then I started thinking about everything else I was going to leave, like Leah, and Emma, and you guys."

"And Jay," Sarah said, a note of bitterness in her voice. It had always irked her, the lack of closeness between Jessie and her son.

Jessie nodded. "Yeah. And Jay."

Sarah pressed her lips together and let out her breath quickly through her nose. "I can't help saying, Jessie, that it seems strange to me that all those things didn't occur to you before."

Jessie looked away. "I know. And I'm sorry. I really am. But now . . . now they did. Last night . . . Leah helped me to see that. And I want . . . I want to stay here."

Sarah felt Len stir beside her. Even without looking at him, she could feel his temper rising. She placed her hand on his leg to calm him.

"Jesus, Jessie," he repeated, louder this time, so that Jessie winced again. "Do you have any idea what you've put us through?"

Sarah watched the shock in Jessie's face as she registered her father's words and heard the anger in his voice. She felt a flash of irritation: how dare Jessie look so surprised! Len had given so much to raise her, to keep her safe. What did she expect? After everything he had done for her, all the years he'd cared for her . . . Did she really think that she could tell him that she would rather live with Laurel and everything would be the same between them?

Sarah herself was not surprised—not at Len's anger, nor at how little Jessie seemed to expect it. Jessie was fourteen; she had thought only of herself. Her daughter was little more than a child, presented with a choice no child should have to make. Still, Jessie's decision had twisted something inside of her, because so many years ago and in all the years since, Sarah had chosen to be a mother to Jessie, but when Jessie was given a choice, she had not chosen Sarah.

For days, Sarah had not been able to look at Jessie without swallowing hard against the bitterness that rose in her throat. She had tried so hard to make them a family. She had not understood, for one minute, how Jessie could simply choose to walk away.

And now she said that she'd changed her mind? *Goddamnit, Jessie*, she thought. *You could have spared us.*

Sarah took a deep breath and looked up at Jessie's guarded, uncertain face. None of this was Jessie's fault, and yet here she was in the midst of it, struggling for a foothold.

"I'm sorry," Jessie said again, and her voice cracked. "But I do want to stay here. If . . . If it's still okay?"

"Jessie—" Sarah began, but Len cut her off.

"Jessie, I absolutely refuse to go through this all again," he said angrily. "So you had better be damn sure. You can't keep doing this, you know. You *can't* keep changing your mind, jerking us all around like this—"

Jessie's face crumpled and tears rose to her eyes. "I know," she mumbled. "I'm sorry."

Sarah watched as Len looked pointedly away. She heard Jessie begin to sob and knew that Jessie had seen it, too: her father, turning away from her, when surely she had counted on his open arms. A bleak despair pooled in Sarah's stomach. It was so easy to see it as Jessie must: she had humbled herself, and her father had turned away. But Sarah knew what had made Len turn: Jessie, breaking down in tears, had looked—even to Sarah—so much like Laurel that it had stopped her breath.

"Stop crying," she wanted to say to Jessie, not cruelly, but because she knew her sobs would only make it worse. Len did not like tears. She had seen before how they hardened him. He had watched Laurel cry one too many times, he had told her once.

Beside her, Len got to his feet. Without looking at Jessie, he said, "I'll call the attorney on Monday morning and tell him you want to stay. You've got until then to change your mind, and that's it."

The next morning, Jessie was red-eyed at the kitchen table, eating her pancakes in silence. As soon as Emma and Jay went to brush their teeth, she rose, too, as if she could not stand to be alone with her parents. Len watched as Jessie went to the sink to rinse her plate. Then his chair scraped across the linoleum as he stood up quickly and went to stand beside her.

"It's okay, Jessie," he told her quietly. "We're glad you're going to stay, you know. I should have said so last night, I guess, and saved you a rough night. I just . . . It was just that I was ang—"

"No, Dad. It was *my* fault," Jessie interrupted him, her voice cracking. "Daddy, I'm really sorry. I never should have—"

Len put one arm gently around her shoulders. "Don't worry about it, Dessie. We all make mistakes. God knows I've made my share." He sighed deeply. "Unfortunately, you're in this mess because of some of them."

Jessie grimaced and shook her head. Then she turned toward her father and put her arms around his waist. "I love you, Dad."

"I love you, too, Jess," he said.

At the table, Sarah sat motionless, her chest tight. It was so easy for him: a hug, an *I love you*, a tender nickname. And now there they were, holding onto each other, as if the breach had never been. Sarah felt a ripple of longing for an earlier time, when the children were still little, when they still launched themselves into her arms whenever they skinned a knee or got their feelings hurt. Back then, it had been second nature to kiss their scraped elbows or crumpled faces. They had told her countless times a day, "I love you, Mommy!" and she had never missed a beat with her own "I love you, too."

It was easier with children. To hold an infant close or cuddle a toddler, to drop down and hug a child who had wrapped her arms around Sarah's knees—all of that felt like the most natural thing in the world. But her children were so big now. Jay, at nine, came up to her chin; the girls were taller than she was. It didn't come naturally to Sarah to cuddle them as she once had, to whisper sweet nothings.

A few months ago, Sarah had taken Emma and Jessie to see the film adaptation of *Anne of Green Gables*. Beside her, both girls had cried rivers when Anne's beloved guardian, Matthew, died in the fields. But it was the next scene that nearly undid Sarah, when Marilla went to Anne's room in the night to comfort her. "You mustn't think I don't love you as much as Matthew did," she told her. "It's never been easy for me to say the things from my heart."

Sarah had looked over at the girls then, wondering if they had understood, if they *could* understand. Sarah was like Marilla. She loved her children ferociously; she would have given the world for each one of them. But it wasn't her nature to snuggle and fawn.

She remembered the time, years ago now, when her college friend, Kim, had come to visit them in Bakersfield. Jay had been a toddler, then, the girls five and seven. In the morning, Kim had sat at the counter with her coffee, watching Sarah do the girls' hair for school.

"Wow," she had said admiringly, as Sarah parted Emma's hair into three neat sections and began to twine them through her fingers. "You girls are lucky your mom does your hair so lovingly. I wasn't allowed to have long hair until I was ten."

Kim's words had struck her: so *lovingly*. Kim had been among those who had marveled at Sarah's sacrifice when she had married Len: just imagine, a newlywed and already the mother of two. That morning, Sarah had been glad to show Kim how wrong she'd been. She was proud of her love for her girls, and pleased that Kim had seen it so clearly.

Remembering her friend's words now, Sarah felt a tinge of resentment. Braiding hair, putting on a Band-Aid, nursing a baby— it was so easy for others to see the love in things like that. But cleaning out the inside of a lunch bag that's been left inside a locker for two weeks? Or scrubbing the blood stains out of period-soaked underwear? Wouldn't you call that love, and then some?

But children didn't see those things in the same way that parents did. Sarah knew she had been no exception. She, too, had always taken her mother's acts of love for granted. She remembered how her mother had always packed her favorite sandwiches in her lunchbox, even when they'd been abroad and American cheese was hard to find. And she had always been there when Sarah got home from school, ready to hear about her day, even though it meant she'd had to pick up evening and weekend shifts at the telephone switchboard where she worked, connecting the soldiers' calls to their families and girlfriends back home.

Sarah understood now the sacrifices her mother had made, for she had made them, too. When they had moved to Bakersfield, she had decided to wait until all the children were in school before she looked for work of her own. Jessie and Emma had gone through so much separation already; she didn't have the heart to leave them with yet another babysitter, or drop them off at daycare every morning. Several years ago, when Jay had started first grade,

Sarah had finally gotten a job as an adjunct in the anthropology department, but even now she didn't work full-time. She wanted to be home in the afternoons when her children came home from school, just as her mother had been for her.

Sarah knew that compared to Len's, her career might seem a paltry thing, but she didn't begrudge her children the choices she had made. She had all her life to work if she wanted; this was her one chance to give her children a home.

A home that Jessie had wanted to leave. Sarah swallowed hard against the bitterness that rose in her throat. All these years, building this life for them, and Jessie always with one foot out the door, yearning for horses and forests and freedom—all the things that Sarah couldn't give her—and never seeming to see all the things she gave.

Len shuddered when he hung up the phone.

"What is it?" Sarah asked, laying her hand gently on his back. "What did he say?"

"He said that since mediation has failed and we'll be going to court, we need the girls to be 'evaluated by a neutral third party.' I think those were his words."

"What, like a psychiatrist?"

Len nodded.

Sarah sighed. "Well, it's probably not the worst idea."

Len looked at her. "You think so? I don't see—"

"It might be good for them to have someone to talk to. Someone who's not involved. And he's probably right, you know. The judge will be more swayed by a psychiatrist's assessment than by anything we say."

"God, I just hope . . ." He shuddered again.

"What?"

"I just hope we don't go through all this and then the judge—"

Sarah reached up and put her hand over her husband's lips.

"Len, we can't think like that. You just have to put that out of your head."

"I'm trying, Sarah, but—"

He turned to her then, and his face was so anxious, so despairing, that her chest ached.

"Oh, Len," she said, wrapping her arms around him. "It's going to be okay, I promise."

She held him tight, pressing her cheek against his chest. She could hear the muted thump of his heart within. She closed her eyes and let out a deep breath. She would not . . . She could not let her own fears rise.

Please let me be right, she thought. *Please just let us keep the girls.*

It was Dr. Haskin's idea that Laurel be invited for a joint ses-sion. It wouldn't be right, she told Len, for her to give the court her professional opinion without ever having met Laurel herself.

"We don't need your opinion on Laurel," Len countered. "Just an 'evaluation' of the girls."

"Well, I can't very effectively evaluate their inner state with respect to their mother—"

"Biological mother," Len corrected.

"With respect to their biological mother, of course," Dr. Haskin said. "I simply cannot evaluate their inner state with respect to Laurel without seeing them together at least once."

So it was agreed, at last, that Dr. Haskin would extend the invitation. Soon after, she received Laurel's reply, and arrangements were made for a joint session one Friday afternoon in the middle of May.

CHAPTER 28

Emma

The day came, the afternoon sky so white with sun it hurt Emma's eyes to look at it. She and her sister sat together in the back seat, their father at the wheel. The ride felt long, with Friday traffic already clogging the roads, but at last Len pulled the van into a small parking lot. Stepping out of the air-conditioned cool of the car, the heat on Emma's chilled skin felt wonderful, like a warm blanket draped across her. By the time they had crossed the parking lot, however, she could already feel perspiration tingling just beneath her skin, and she welcomed the rush of cool air as they entered the building. Inside, Emma stood blinking in the foyer, blinded by the dark of the lobby after the afternoon's glare. When she could see again, she took in a row of upholstered chairs, a few artsy lamps on end tables, a wicker basket full of magazines.

"Hi, Jessie. Hi, Emma."

Emma's eyes swept around. There was Laurel, rising from a chair on the far side of the lobby. A novel hung from one hand, her thumb between the pages, marking her place.

Her eyes rested on Emma for only a second. "It's good to see you. Both."

"Hi, Laurel," Jessie said, glancing at her father.

"Hi," Emma managed.

"Laurel," Len said. "Hello."

"Hello, Len. Or should I say Dr. Walters now?" She laughed nervously.

Jessie sat down in a chair in the middle of the row. Emma took the leeward seat, putting her sister between her and Laurel. Len stood a moment more and then sat down beside Emma. Emma had her math homework in the backpack she held between her feet, but she made no move to get it. Instead, she studied the dark hairs on her father's arm. No one spoke.

Finally, Emma could stand the stillness no longer. She reached down to open her backpack, and at that moment, the door to Dr. Haskin's office opened.

"Ah," the tall woman said, taking in the four of them. "I apologize for running late."

They stared up at her, motionless.

"Jessie. Emma. Ms. Black." Dr. Haskins held the door open. Then she nodded at their father, who pulled a magazine from the basket and opened it on his lap.

"Perhaps the girls would be more comfortable if . . ." Dr. Haskin began.

Len rose, slid the magazine back into its place. "Of course. I'll come back. Goodbye, girls."

As her father opened the door to leave the lobby, the threshold seemed to glow with light. Emma felt a wave of heat break over her. Then the door closed behind him, the light was gone, and the cool resettled itself against her skin. She followed Laurel and her sister through the door Dr. Haskin held for her.

Once inside her office, Dr. Haskin sat down in a straight-backed chair beside her desk. Angled in the far corner of the room was a small couch, and facing that a striped armchair.

Laurel, Jessie, and Emma stood in the center of the room uncertainly.

"Have a seat?" said Dr. Haskin. She smiled slightly.

Jessie was the first to move. She plopped down on the couch; Emma sat next to her. Laurel sat down in the armchair opposite but did not lean back.

"Well," said Dr. Haskin when they were finally settled. "Thank you all for being here. Ms. Black, I'm glad you could make it."

"Of course," Laurel said. "I'd do anything . . ." Her voice trailed off, and again there was silence. Emma studied the rug in front of the couch. She could feel the cushions move as her sister shifted beside her.

"I suggested that we meet like this before the hearing. To give the girls and you, Ms. Black, the chance to—"

"Yes. Yes," Laurel interrupted. "The chance to talk. Because I never get to see Emma, you know. Len won't let her visit anymore."

Emma's head shot up. Laurel was looking right at her, hungrily. Emma looked quickly away.

He'll let me, Emma thought. *I just don't want to go.* But she kept her mouth clamped shut.

"And why?" Laurel went on. "What did I *do*? What did I do to have my child taken from me? So that I never even get to talk—"

"But," Emma said, the word coming out as a squeak. All eyes turned to her; she lowered hers to the rug again while she spoke.

"But I wasn't *taken* from you. You didn't want us. You *gave* Daddy custody. Nobody forced you. And it was my choice not to go to Baymont anymore. Mom and Dad didn't tell me to stop, I just . . . I just . . . I just *chose*. I just didn't want . . ."

She didn't finish the sentence. She had been going to say, "I just didn't want to see you anymore," but even with her eyes on the rug, she could feel Laurel's presence in front of her, and she couldn't say it. It sounded too unkind.

"I just didn't want to go anymore," she finished quietly.

"But why?" Laurel's chin began to quiver. She looked pleadingly at Dr. Haskin. "Why? What did I do?"

"Now, Ms. Black," Dr. Haskin said sternly, but her voice was not unkind. "Do you really not understand that there were choices you made that may have made Emma feel uncomfortable? Even unsafe?"

Laurel let out a disbelieving puff of air that was almost a laugh. "What? Raisin? I sold a pony, for Christ's sake. I'm sorry, okay? I'm sorry, Emma, that I sold that damn pony. Forgive me for thinking you'd be over it by now."

Her tone was belligerent, and Emma found her eyes drawn to Laurel's face despite herself. Laurel had been watching her, but now she looked quickly away.

"What else? What else did I do that was so awful?" She meant the question to be rhetorical, perhaps, but Emma heard herself whisper, "The dam."

"What? Oh, the dam. The goddamn dam."

"Ms. Black," Dr. Haskin interrupted. "Please watch your language. I understand that you are upset. But you are with your children."

Laurel snorted. "Of course. I'm sorry." Her voice quieted. "Look, the dam wasn't my fault. The babysitter . . . I even got rid of the babysitter after that."

"It is my understanding that it was Dr. Walters who insisted that you find a more responsible babysitter or he was going to come and get the girls."

"The summer was almost over, for crying out loud. And Candy was seventeen. It was her last summer anyway, so I would have had to find—"

"Ms. Black," Dr. Haskins interrupted gently. "I think this is all beside the point. Which is, that the girls were in your care. Is it so hard to understand that Emma might have been frightened? Felt unsafe?"

Laurel laughed humorlessly. "Okay. She felt *unsafe*. But that was *one* day out of how many summers? For that I'm going to be denied my rights as her mother?"

"Ms. Black," Dr. Haskin interrupted. "No one is trying to deny you anything. I, for one, am merely looking at the best interests of the children."

Laurel seemed not to hear her. "Because of that, I'm going to lose all—"

"Ms. Black," Dr. Haskin said sternly. "We are speaking of the best interests of your daughters."

"But I didn't *do* anything," Laurel pleaded. "I just want the chance to be with my girls. I'm their mother, for Christ's sake."

Suddenly Laurel's tone changed, softened. "Shouldn't I be allowed to be with my own daughters?" Her chin began to quiver violently. Watching her, Emma felt her jaw grow tight, then begin its own answering vibrations. She clamped her teeth hard against each other, horrified. She wanted nothing to do with this soft, emotional, needy woman in front of her. She didn't want to hear the echo of her shrill voice in her own. She didn't want her wobbly chin. Emma had a sudden vision of herself sobbing in her bed, while Sarah perched, dry-eyed and rational, on the edge of her chair. Is this how Emma looked to Sarah: dramatic and tearful, her emotions practically dripping from her sleeve? She shuddered at the thought. She was not like Laurel—she couldn't be.

She snuck another glance at her mother. Laurel was slumped back in the armchair now, sobbing into a crumpled tissue.

". . . and some inappropriate behavior, Ms. Black," Dr. Haskins was saying. She paused to pass Laurel a box of Kleenex.

Dr. Haskin's voice went on and on, but Emma found she could register only occasional phrases: "not acknowledging . . . not the best choices . . . it isn't about blame . . . Emma and Jessie's best interests . . ." Instead, Emma watched, horrified, as Laurel cried. Was her mother really crying about *her*? Why would she? How *could* she? *You didn't want us*, Emma thought. *When we were little, you didn't want us . . .*

"Oh, Mom," Emma heard Jessie say from beside her on the couch. Her voice sounded almost exasperated. "Stop crying. It's all going to work out."

Laurel looked at Jessie through her tears and gave her a small smile. "Really? Do you think so? Because I really don't know." She blew her nose loudly.

Emma sat on the couch stone-faced, staring again at the whirling design on the rug, the erratic colors like a mirror of the turmoil inside her. There was no denying it: Emma knew what it was like to cry like that. The thought disgusted her, that from Laurel she had inherited those hideous tears, that indeed there was anything at all that linked them.

"You are *not* my mother," she wanted to say. But for Laurel's garish emotion, it could be so simple: she need not visit her—need not, in fact, have anything to do with her at all. Sarah was her mother; Laurel was not.

But Laurel's sobs unnerved her. Despite her gaudy tears, her ridiculously quivering chin, it was undeniable: Laurel was sad. And as unbelievable as it seemed—for never had Emma felt that Laurel held much real affection for her—it was clear that she was sad about *her*.

But what can I do? Emma thought. She wanted nothing to do with this sobbing woman who claimed to be her mother. And yet, inside her stubborn heart she felt her pity rise, unbidden. She could make Laurel happy. She could go to her now. She could say that she had changed her mind, that she would go to Baymont again. For a moment, she let herself remember the pastures and the pond, the smell of horses on her hands. But just as quickly, the other memories came. Laurel looking on as Raisin was lifted into the truck. Laurel splayed on the bed, milk leaking from her bare breast. Laurel . . .

No. Inside her chest, she felt the stone valves close. Laurel was wrong. It *was* her fault. She had made her bed, let her lie in it. Her mother had not wanted them as babies. She did not deserve her now.

Laurel might be sad, but it wasn't Emma's fault. No one could deny this, and now Emma clung to it. *It's not my fault. It's not my fault* . . . The words cycled in her head. No, she would not betray her parents by faltering now. Any show of compassion for this quivering woman before her seemed to Emma a back-handed blow to her true mom and dad. Emma straightened on the couch. Laurel could cry all she wanted; she was not Emma's mother. She would never be.

It was almost four-thirty by the clock on her desk when Dr. Haskin finally rose.

"Would you like a hug from your daughters perhaps, Ms. Black?" she asked kindly. At the unexpected compassion in her voice, Laurel's wobbly chin began again. She clenched her jaw and nodded.

Jessie stepped forward. "Bye, Mom," she said. "And I mean it. It's going to be okay."

Emma stood where she was, her face hard, her heart harder.

"Emma?" Dr. Haskin prompted. "Do you want to give your mother a hug? She's come a long way to see you."

Emma shook her head imperceptibly and did not move. *She is not my mother.*

"A handshake, maybe?"

Laurel looked at Emma plaintively and held out her hand. Emma stepped forward unwillingly and took it.

Laurel's hand in hers was warm despite the coolness of the room. Her flesh felt pudgy and damp, so unlike the smooth firmness of Sarah's small hands. Laurel's grip was soft, almost liquid, pleading. Quickly, Emma withdrew her hand and looked away.

Dr. Haskins sighed. "Emma, you don't have to love someone to give them a hug, you know," she said. "You don't have to love someone to have a Coke with them."

Then she opened the door that led back to the waiting room, where their father sat in the same chair as before, waiting for his daughters.

You don't have to love someone to have a Coke with them. You don't have to love someone to have a Coke with them. You don't have to love someone

to have a Coke with them. All the way home through rush-hour traffic, the car air-conditioner blasting, the late afternoon light as harsh as noon, Dr. Haskin's words rattled in Emma's brain. *You don't have to love someone to have a Coke with them.*

How could Dr. Haskin's not understand? Emma wanted her family to be her *family*. They were perfect; Laurel had no place. She *had* a mother—a dear, wonderful mother. She didn't need Laurel. She didn't want her. Oh, *why* had Dr. Haskin said that? Emma didn't *want* to have a Coke with her. She didn't want to have anything to do with her at all. Emma sat in the back of the silent minivan and hid her face against the torn vinyl of the seat in front of her.

That night, Emma dreamed she was on a ship with Laurel and her sister.

"Let's go get ice cream," Laurel suggested, smiling. She took Jessie's hand in hers, then turned to Emma. "Emma? Let's go."

Emma stood there, unmoving, her face of stone, her legs leaden.

"Don't you want to get ice cream?" her sister asked.

Emma shook her head.

"You know, Emma, you don't have to love someone to have an ice cream with them," Laurel snapped, turning away.

The dream shifted, and now Emma was alone at the railing of the ship, the waves breaking against the hull below her. Across a narrow stretch of water there was another ship, and Laurel and Jessie stood on its deck, their shoulders almost touching, each holding an ice cream cone.

"Jessie!" Emma yelled. *"Jessie!"*

But her sister didn't hear her. Their ship was pulling away, the water between them widening, their figures shrinking as the distance grew.

"Wait!" she screamed. "Okay, I'll have an ice cream. *Wait!*"

But the ship did not stop, and at last Emma's cries woke her.

"Mom," she called. "Mom!" But it was the middle of the night, and Sarah was fast asleep and did not hear her through all the doors that separated their rooms.

CHAPTER 29

Emma

"Ouch," Emma said. "Geez, Aunt Margie, I can do it myself."

Aunt Margie tugged the elastic band roughly from Emma's ponytail, so that her blonde hair cascaded around her shoulders.

"There," she said, running the brush through it. "That's better. Your hair is so pretty, Emma. You should wear it down more often."

"But it's so hot, Aunt Margie. And I don't see what difference it makes. It's not like the judge is going to care about my hair."

Margie shook her head. "Maybe not, but there's nothing wrong with trying to make a good impression."

Emma reached for the brush. "At least let me do it," she said. "I'm about to turn thirteen, Aunt Margie. I think I can do my own hair."

But Aunt Margie moved the brush out of Emma's reach. "Just let me," she said, positioning Emma's head with her hands. "Your parents asked me to be here, so I might as well make myself useful."

Emma caught her aunt's eye in the mirror. "Are you nervous, Aunt Margie?"

"Of course I'm not—" Aunt Margie began and then stopped. "Yes, I suppose I am, a little." She held the brush aloft and studied her niece. "Are you?"

Emma looked away. "Yeah. I guess."

Aunt Margie sighed. She smoothed Emma's hair with her fingers. "Well, it will all be over soon."

"But what if—?"

Aunt Margie shook her head. "There's never any point to what-ifs, Emma. We'll just have to wait and see."

Emma had expected a courtroom like in the movies, the stands full, a podium where she would have to raise her hand and pledge to tell the truth, the whole truth, and nothing but the truth.

But she never saw a courtroom. She walked with her sister and Aunt Margie down a long, tiled corridor, and then into a small, empty room with brown walls and straight-backed chairs.

"Where are we?" she whispered to Aunt Margie, but her aunt just shook her head.

Emma felt overheated and uncomfortable in the pantyhose her mother had told her she had to wear. The crotch had inched down as she walked like it always did; she could feel the material tugging at her thighs. She longed to reach down into her skirt and hitch them up. She wanted to gather up her loose hair into a ponytail again, just to get it off her neck.

"I have to go to the restroom, Aunt Margie," she whispered. The elastic waist of her pantyhose pushed uncomfortably against her bladder.

Her aunt sighed. "Can it wait?"

She shook her head.

"Do you need to go, too?" Aunt Margie asked Jessie. Emma's sister sat stone-faced two seats away. She shook her head.

"Well, stay right here, then" Aunt Margie said. "We'll just be a minute."

In the stall, when she had finished on the toilet, Emma bent down and tried to coax the stockings up her legs. But the material clung stubbornly to her skin and was hard to get ahold of.

"Hurry up, Emma," Aunt Margie called to her. "The judge will be asking for you soon."

Emma reached for the fabric where it gathered, a bit more loosely, at her ankle.

"I *am* hurrying. I just need to—" Emma began. She felt her finger go through the thin fabric of her pantyhose. "Shoot."

"What happened, Emma?" her aunt asked anxiously.

Emma stared as the run wasted no time in creeping up her leg. In a moment, there was a long ladder from her ankle to her knee, her flesh pale and freckled between the rungs.

"Aunt Margie," she said. "My—"

But at that moment there was a knock at the outside door and a woman's voice.

"Excuse me? The judge will see the girls in her chambers now."

"Emma," Aunt Margie hissed. "Come on."

"But my stockings—"

"Just *come* on."

They hustled back down the hallway. Emma could feel the uncomfortable pull of the pantyhose between her legs, hobbling her. She could feel the air against her skin where the ladder crept up her thigh. Her face burned.

Back in the room where they had waited, her sister was gone.

"Where's Jessie?" Aunt Margie said, and Emma could hear the panic in her voice. "She was right here—"

"She's with the judge," said the woman who had retrieved them from the bathroom.

"Oh God, I was supposed to be with them."

"It's fine," the woman said kindly. "She's in with the judge now. It may be a few more minutes. Perhaps I was premature in coming to find you. Would you like to have a seat?"

But neither Aunt Margie nor Emma moved. Aunt Margie held Emma's hand tightly. Emma tried to keep her leg turned so that the woman would not see the run.

In another minute, Jessie was back. She met Emma's eye for an instant, then gave the briefest smile.

"Don't worry, Em," she said. "She's nice."

The woman led Emma into the judge's chambers. The judge was seated behind a large, wooden desk, but she rose as they entered. She nodded at the woman, who excused herself, closing the door behind her.

"Please have a seat, Emma," the judge said, gesturing to an upholstered chair.

Emma sat. It was impossible to hide the run now, but she pulled her skirt down over her knees.

"How are you, Emma?"

Emma shrugged. "Okay. I just . . . There's a run in my panty-hose."

The judge smiled. "It happens to the best of us. You look very nice."

Emma shrugged again and looked away.

"So, Emma," the judge said, settling in the chair across from her. "I'm sure you understand why you are here?"

Emma met her eye for a second, then nodded. "I guess so."

"Well, I would just like to hear from you . . ." The judge paused. "I'd like to hear from you what you would like. With respect, of course, to your parents."

Emma spoke quickly. "I just want Mom to be my mother. I don't want—"

"When you say, 'Mom,'" the judge interrupted, holding up her hand. "You mean—?"

"I mean Sarah," Emma said quickly. Her mother's name on her lips felt strange, as it always had. She didn't like the distance it seemed to carry.

"I call her Mom," she said. "I consider her my mother. I always have."

The judge nodded. "I understand. But you realize, of course, that your birth mother, Laurel, would like joint custody. Would you like to live with Laurel, even if only for part of the year?"

"No."

The judge looked up at the vehemence of her response. Then she nodded slowly. "I'm sorry, but I need to ask." She paused. "Can you tell me why?"

"I just don't . . . I don't consider her my mother. She didn't raise me like Mom did. She didn't want me. She didn't take care of me. She's just not my mother," Emma said. Her stomach felt sick. What would the judge think of her, denying her own mother? *You don't have to love someone to have a Coke with them.* Maybe it wouldn't matter to the judge that she didn't love Laurel. Maybe the mere fact of her biological connection to Laurel trumped all that. She studied the judge, who was jotting something on her pad. She could see the tiny clumps in her mascara behind her glasses.

The judge looked up. She smiled sympathetically and Emma let out her breath.

"So you want to live with your father and stepmother . . . Sarah, I mean, who is, to you, your mother," the judge said. Emma nodded.

"But with respect to visitation? Do you want to visit your . . . Do you want to visit Laurel as you used to?"

Emma shook her head. "No."

"Could you explain?"

"I just . . ." How could she say it all here, in this room? How could this woman possibly understand? How could she understand about Raisin, about the afternoon at the dam, about that awful night waiting for the ambulance with Jessie writhing on the floor? That wasn't Laurel's fault, everyone had told her again and again, but it didn't matter. Because it wasn't about any one of those things. It was because every time she was around Laurel, she felt something inside her shrink; she felt her true self wither and grow cold. No, she didn't want—

"I understand you had some frightening experiences while at her house," the judge said kindly, interrupting her thoughts.

Emma nodded, felt her tears rise at the sympathy in the judge's voice.

"What happened with your sister there. That wasn't your mother's . . . That wasn't Laurel's f—"

"I know!" Emma snapped, her voice cracking. "I know it

wasn't her fault. But what about the rest of it? She never wanted
. . . Oh, she never loved . . . I just don't want to go there!"

Emma felt the judge go motionless. She looked up, met her
eye, waited.

There was the briefest moment of silence. Then the judge
clicked the end of her pen with her thumb. "Fair enough," she
said.

Emma held her eyes. "You don't think I'm—" she began, but
she couldn't finish. Cruel, a bad daughter . . .

"Oh no," the judge said, shaking her head. "I'm just sorry to
have upset you. But I had to ask. And I believe I understand. Here,"
she said, reaching for the Kleenex box on her desk. "Take one of
these. We can wait while you . . . while you pull yourself together."
She smiled gently at Emma. "It shouldn't be much longer now."

Back in the lobby, she could feel Jessie studying her face, felt
her unspoken question: "What did you say?"

Emma shrugged, managed a smile. She sat down next to Aunt
Margie. She felt deflated, hollowed out.

"Are you hungry?" Aunt Margie asked anxiously. "We could
see about some lunch—"

Both girls shook their heads.

"The judge told me it wouldn't be long now," Emma said.
"Let's just wait."

Emma was sitting in one of the straight-backed chairs, her eyes
closed, her head leaning back against the brown wall, when she
heard her mother's voice.

"Jessie! Emma!"

Emma's head snapped up and her eyes opened. She felt her
aunt startle beside her.

And there were her parents in the doorway, coming toward
them, their eyes bright but their faces so serious—

"What happened?" Aunt Margie asked, before Emma could open her mouth. "Is it over?"

"It's over," Sarah said. "'Len will retain full custody. Supervised visitation in accordance with the wishes of the girls.'" Suddenly, her voice caught in her throat and Emma gaped, open-mouthed, as her mother burst into tears. It was the first time she had ever seen her cry.

"Mom," she said, alarmed. "What's wrong?"

But already Aunt Margie was in motion beside her, stepping forward to take Sarah in her arms. Sarah hid her face in the other woman's neck. "I'm sorry, Margie," she muttered. "It's just—"

"Shhh," Aunt Margie hushed her. "It's over now. It's all over now."

Emma looked at her sister. Jessie's face looked pale, stricken. Suddenly, Emma felt light-headed; she sat down again heavily, her mind muddled. The judge's decision—wasn't it what she had wanted? Yet there was something in the cool finality of it that took Emma's breath away. Laurel had no claim to her. *Supervised visitation in accordance with the wishes of the girls.* That meant that Emma would never have to see Laurel again. The judge had said that she—that they!—could choose.

But *supervised visitation*? What would that mean for Jessie? Emma understood at once: no more summers alone at Baymont. Suddenly, she understood her sister's face. Jessie, in choosing not to leave the family—had she lost Baymont?

No, Emma wanted to call out. That was not what this was all about. This—this whole court case—it was about *her*, Emma. It was all because she hadn't wanted to go to Baymont anymore. But not Jessie. Jessie loved Baymont. Jessie loved . . . Jessie *loved* Laurel. It was the first time Emma had ever admitted this to herself. For her sister, Baymont and Laurel—they were inseparable. Jessie loved them both.

How Jessie could love Laurel, Emma could not understand.

Except—well, maybe she could, a little. For Emma, Laurel was nothing that a mother should be. She was neither sympathetic nor loving, offered neither safety nor solace. But to Jessie, Laurel was something else entirely. To her sister, Laurel was independent and free-thinking, strong-limbed and strong-minded. She was . . . she was . . . the best parts of her anyway . . . She was a little like Jessie, Emma thought.

Emma looked back at her sister in dismay and tried to meet her eye. But Jessie was staring at the floor. She looked instead to her parents who were embracing now. She wanted to share in their relief, but instead she felt a small bubble of despair. Oh, why could it never be clear? She had thought that if she could shut Laurel out of her life, things would be simple. That was all she had wanted. She had just wanted them to be an ordinary family, without Laurel's awful presence looming over her like Darth Vader: "Emma, I am your mother." She hadn't meant for Jessie to lose Baymont. She hadn't meant for her to lose Laurel.

She looked at Jessie again and finally caught her sister's eye.

"I'm sorry," she mouthed. "I'm so sorry."

But Jessie just shook her head and looked away.

PART THREE

1998-2003

CHAPTER 30

Ten Years Later

Jessie

Jessie was grading biology tests on the small deck behind her house when the phone rang. She had rented the house almost two years ago now, when she had moved to Pendleton, Oregon from Albuquerque the summer after she turned twenty-four. She had thought the house would be temporary, just until she got her bearings, but she had never moved. The little house suited her, with its large garden plot in the back yard and the gnarled cherry tree that shaded the desk.

Now, hearing the phone, she rose from her chair and went inside to the kitchen. But the receiver was not on the wall mount, and it was several rings before she found it on the dresser in her bedroom.

"Hello?" she said breathlessly, racing the answering machine.

"Jessie? It's your mother."

"Laurel? Oh, Mom, thank God. Why haven't you called? Are you okay?"

"Don't be ridiculous. I'm fine."

"Mom, I've left you a gazillion messages and you never called me back. Where were you?"

Laurel laughed gleefully. "Oh, I had to go out of town for a few days."

"You could have let me know. I was worried about you."

"Well," Laurel said. "It was nice of you to be concerned, but you needn't have been. I'm absolutely fine. Wonderful, actually."

Jessie shook her head in surprise. *Wonderful?* Until five days ago, Laurel had called her practically every day in tears. Jessie did not begrudge Laurel her grief—Laurel's mother, Pearl, had passed away suddenly of heart disease three months ago—but still she had been surprised by how much Laurel had included her in it. After all, it could be no secret to Laurel that between Pearl and Jessie there had been little love lost.

Pearl had moved to Baymont to live with Laurel in 1993, when she lost her Los Angeles apartment. Jessie had been a junior at UC Davis then and had visited Baymont—just two hours away—as often as she could. But when Pearl arrived, a little of Baymont's magic had been lost. Cantankerous and lazy, Pearl rarely rose from her recliner, a cigarette pinned between two yellowed fingers, her ashtray balanced on the chair's overstuffed arm. Jessie had never gotten used to coming downstairs from the attic bedroom and seeing her grandmother already slouched in her seat in the living room.

There had been a time when Jessie had thought that Baymont had been lost to her. After the judge's verdict, Jessie had thought with despair that she would never be allowed to have another summer there. And it had seemed, for a while, that this would be true. The summer after the custody battle, she had not gone to Baymont. Her father, perhaps trying to make it up to her, had taken the family on a long road trip that summer: The Grand Canyon, Mesa Verde, Arches. Jessie had learned to love the desert on that trip. But it had not been Baymont.

The next summer, she had pleaded with her father to let her go, if only for a few weeks, but he had refused. *Supervised visitation,* the judge had said; Baymont was not supervised. The next year, however, he gave in, and by the following year she was eighteen and could do as she pleased.

Being at Baymont with Laurel had been strange at first, a new distance between them. Jessie felt sheepish about her change of heart, and Laurel, feeling herself slighted, did not forbear from playing the martyr. But in time the old ease had returned, and with it a new bond: Jessie was the loyal daughter now, without whom Laurel would have no one.

Jessie had never outgrown Baymont's joys. Even as a teenager, she had never stopped loving the cool of the pond closing over her head, the *plunk* of blackberries in cut-off milk jugs, the ache in her thighs after a day in the saddle. In Baymont, she was no longer the Jessie of the dirty nails and unstyled hair, the never-quite-right clothes. In Baymont with Laurel, she was just herself—brave and burly and rugged.

But then Pearl had come to Baymont. Laurel's mother had come close to tainting it all. Jessie had never managed to completely squelch the revulsion she felt for the older woman, with upper arms like loaves of unbaked bread dough and a yeasty, sour smell that wafted from beneath her faded muumuus. She had always tried her best to ignore the similarities between Laurel and her grandmother: the ease with which their bodies plumped to fat, their sharp judgements of anyone but themselves and those they loved. But Pearl was lazy, slovenly, a whiner; how could Laurel have chosen to share her home with such a woman?

But as the years went on, Jessie could not deny the affection Laurel clearly felt for Pearl, nor the strange affinity that bonded the two women. Pearl had had Laurel young and raised her almost single-handedly; she was the only family, other than Jessie, that Laurel had. Jessie knew that Laurel would take her mother's death hard, but still she had not been ready for the cavernous depths of self-pity that Laurel's grief had opened up in her.

Everyone leaves me, Laurel had wailed to Jessie on the phone day after day. Two husbands. Her daughter. Now her mother, too. *So this is what it is like to be a motherless child,* she wept, her voice cracking into breathless sobs. Even Jessie had left her; why had she moved so far away? Jessie tried to be sympathetic, but it irked her that her mother had included her in the list of abandoners. Hadn't she been the steadfast one?

For over a month, Laurel's almost daily phone calls had continued. Then, abruptly, they had stopped. Worried, Jessie had called Baymont again and again, leaving message after message until the tape on Laurel's answering machine had run out. That had been four days ago. And now Laurel had called at last, her voice startlingly bright, and said that she was *wonderful*.

Jessie carried the phone back out to the deck and glanced at the stack of tests on the table. It was nearing the end of the spring quarter at the community college where she taught, and Jessie had planned to give the tests back to her students tomorrow. But it wouldn't kill them if they had to wait until Wednesday.

"Okay, Mom," she said, capping her red pen, her curiosity roused. "Why don't you tell me what's going on?"

"Well," Laurel said, her voice girlish. "You are never going to *believe* what I'm going to do."

"What are you going to do?"

"I'm going canoeing."

Jessie sighed. "Really," she said dryly.

Laurel laughed. "I don't just mean I'm going canoeing, Jessie. I'm going on a canoe *trip*."

"You mean like overnight?" Jessie asked skeptically. "Camping?"

On the other end of the line, Laurel pealed with laughter.

"I know. You can't believe it, right? I couldn't either. I *still* don't really believe it."

"Believe what?"

"I told him I know absolutely *nothing* about canoeing. Well, except once when your dad and I were married, but that was just for an hour or maybe not even that long—"

"Mom, I have no idea what you are talking about. Can you back up a little?"

"Jim!" Laurel said triumphantly. "Jim knows all about canoeing. He even has a boat. A canoe, I mean."

"Mom, who is Jim? I don't even know who Jim is," she said.

"Of course you do."

"No, I don't."

"You don't?" Laurel laughed again. "I can't believe I haven't told you. But it has all been happening so fast—"

"Mom," Jessie interrupted her. "Who is Jim?"

"Jim? Jim is my new . . . my new lover!"

Jessie was stunned into silence. "Oh," she managed to say. How was it possible? Laurel was overweight, with a mullet of long, dingy hair. Even for a more attractive woman, the dating prospects around Baymont were surely limited. Most of the men that Laurel knew were the petty criminals she met in the small law office where she now worked as an office manager. As a rule, they were not good catches.

"Is he a . . . Did you meet him at work?" Jessie asked.

"No," Laurel giggled.

"So how did you meet him?" Jessie asked impatiently.

"Well," Laurel said. "If you must know, I answered a personal ad."

Jessie sighed. That Laurel had answered the ad did not surprise her. Laurel was lonely; she could imagine her answering an ad. What surprised her was that whoever had placed the ad had reciprocated Laurel's interest.

"Well?" she asked. "What's he like?" She tried to imagine the kind of man who would be eager for Laurel's attention. "Is he older?"

"*No.*" Laurel was indignant. "He's actually quite a few years younger than I am. Forty-five, I think."

"And . . . ?" Jessie prompted.

"Well, he lives in Northfield. Near Minneapolis."

"He lives in Minnesota?"

"Is there another Minneapolis?"

Jessie shrugged this off. "I meant, isn't that sort of far?"

Laurel ignored this. "He's a chemist. At Carleton. Didn't you think of going there at one point? It's a very good school."

"Wow," Jessie said. She tried to think of something else to ask, but the only question that came to her was "What's wrong with him?" Because why would a young, normal, Carleton professor be interested in her mother? He must be extremely—

"He's polyamorous."

Jessie never finished her thought. "He's *what*?"

"You know, *polyamorous*." Laurel was giggling again. "Many loves."

"Yeah, okay, Mom. But what does that really mean? That you'll be one of many? That he isn't looking for commitment?" Jessie wondered if that was a line he fed to everyone: "I'm polyamorous" code for "Don't be surprised when I cheat on you."

"That's actually a common misconception of polyamory," Laurel was saying, her voice suddenly serious, pedantic. "But actually we are very committed—just not to a single partner."

"We? Are you polyamorous now, too?" Jessie immediately regretted the sarcasm that had flooded her voice.

"It's not that I'm polyamorous *now*, Jessie," Laurel said. "I've always been polyamorous. I just didn't have a word for it, and there *is* such social stigma, you know. Your father always said I was promiscuous, and he didn't mean it as a compliment. But really . . . I don't think I've ever been cut out to be in a relationship with only one person. And who made that rule anyway? Do you know that humans are the only mammals who mate for life? And they're terrible at it. It's an unrealistic expectation. Look at chimpanzees. They share ninety-nine percent of our genes, and they have multiple partners . . . Jessie, are you still there?"

Jessie rolled her eyes. "Yes, I'm here. But I'm not sure that's right, Mom. What about gibbons and prairie voles?"

"What? They don't share ninety-nine—"

"No, they're mammals who mate for life. You said—"

Laurel laughed. "Well, almost the only mammals then. And you get my point."

"Okay. Fine. So—so you're polyamorous. That should work

out nicely with Jim, especially since you live, what, at least a two-day drive away from each other? You can both see other people—"

"Well, that's not exactly what he's looking for," Laurel said.

"What is he looking for?"

"Another primary."

"Another primary what?"

"Oh, Jessie. Don't be obtuse. Another primary partner."

"Another? He has one primary already?"

"Yes. Sue. They've been together almost twenty years."

"Wow. And where does Sue live?"

"With Jim, of course. In Northfield. They have this amazing log house right on the river. You'd love it."

"You've been there? To Minnesota?"

"Well, of course. He couldn't really consider me as a primary without Sue meeting me, could he? That's where I've been these last few days."

"You interviewed with Sue, too?"

Laurel laughed. "It wasn't an interview. Jim and I met first. And then, because we liked each other, he invited me to meet Sue."

"And she gave the thumbs-up?"

"Pretty much. She said we could try it out."

"God, Mom. I can't believe you haven't told me any of this. Wait, let me get this straight. Jim and Sue want you to be part of their . . . their threesome." Jessie immediately disliked the sound of this. "Their relationship."

"Yes."

"And will you and Sue be . . . involved, too?"

"Oh, no," Laurel said.

"I was just asking," Jessie said. "I'm not sure how it all works."

"Well, to be honest, I wondered the same thing at first. But no, Sue is not interested in that. In fact," Laurel's voice turned conspiratorial. "Sue's not very interested in sex. That's why they placed the ad."

"Oh."

"She and Jim have very disparate sex drives. They thought another primary would help."

"Oh."

"So, when we get back from the Boundary Waters—"

"What? Where?"

"The Boundary Waters. Where we're taking the canoe trip."

"Oh, right." Jessie had already forgotten about the canoeing. "Is Sue going, too?"

"Well, she normally would," Laurel said. "But she couldn't get the time off work."

"So it will be just you and Jim."

"Yes."

"How romantic."

"I know!"

"When do you leave?"

"In two weeks. Jessie, I'm so excited."

"Mom, I don't mean to rain on your parade, but don't you think you should be a bit more cautious? I mean, you really don't even know this Jim person at all. And you're going to go who-knows-where in a canoe with him? What if he's—?"

"Oh, Jessie."

"What? It's dangerous, Mom."

"Well, I appreciate your concern. But you wouldn't think like that if you met him. Plus, by my age, I've learned to trust my instincts."

"Mom, I'm just worried about—"

"Well, I thank you very much for your concern," Laurel said perfunctorily. "But I'm not going to let you ruin this for me. I haven't felt this happy in years."

Jessie sighed. She could tell there would be no talking her mother out of it. "Just be careful, okay?" she said. "And take bug spray. I hear the mosquitos can be bad there this time of year."

Laurel laughed. "Oh, I will. Jim has it all planned out, don't worry."

Later, Jessie had to admit that Laurel's instincts had been un-characteristically trustworthy. Laurel had come back from her trip to the Boundary Waters bug-bitten and in love. Two months later, she called Jessie to tell her that she was moving to Minne-sota.

Again, Jessie tried to reason with her. What about her house? Her job?

"Well, I don't have to be here to sell the house, you know. It's probably better if I'm not."

"Mom, you can't sell the house."

"Why not? It's not like I've been very happy there, especially since Mom died."

"But . . ." How could Jessie say that it was not her mother's memories she was thinking of, but her own? That house, those pastures, the barn . . . the best parts of Jessie's childhood were there. Laurel couldn't just sell them. She tried, haltingly, to explain this to Laurel.

"Well, it's not like you spend any time here anymore," Laurel argued. And she was right; Jessie rarely visited Laurel at Baymont now. There were just too many other places to explore.

Jessie shook her head; this was all beside the point. Every relationship Laurel had ever been in had ended in heartbreak and disaster. If this one was no different, and Laurel had given up both house and job to make it work, where would she be? She urged her mother to reconsider.

"What would you say if I was giving up everything for a man I'd only just met?" she asked finally.

"Oh, Jessie. We are hardly in the same position. You have your whole career—your whole life—ahead of you. And I'd been thinking of leaving the office anyway. It's time for a change. And I'm not that far from retirement, you know."

"Mom, you're only forty-nine."

"I'm almost fifty, Jessie. And that's not the point. If it was what you wanted, I'd support you. You know that."

Jessie had to admit that she was right. Laurel had never been the voice of caution. So she said nothing more, listening as Laurel talked about Jim and Sue's house, with its myriad of bedrooms and large front porch. When, at last, she had told her daughter everything, silence settled between them on the line.

"Jessie? Are you still there?"

"I'm here."

"Well?" Laurel said. "Do I have your blessing?"

"Okay, Mom," Jessie acquiesced after a pause. "If you think it will make you happy."

CHAPTER 31

Jessie

After Laurel moved to Northfield, Jessie rarely heard from her. Still, during their occasional phone calls, her mother sounded cheerful and relaxed, and slowly Jessie began to relax, too. She stopped waiting to hear her mother's weeping voice on the other end of the line, telling her that it was over, that it hadn't worked out. Then, one Sunday afternoon late in October, Jessie was kneading bread dough at the counter when the phone rang. She answered it with hands caked in dough.

"Jessie, I have to talk to you. Do you have a minute . . . a few minutes?" All of Jessie's trepidation about her mother's new relationship returned in a rush. She clutched the phone to her ear with her shoulder.

"Just a second, Mom," she said. She set the phone down on the counter, rubbed the biggest clumps of bread dough off her fingers, and sat down at the kitchen table.

"Oh, Mom," she said. "What is it? What happened?"

There was a hesitation on the other end of the line, and Jessie sighed audibly.

"Oh, Mom," she said again. She spread her hands in front of her, studying the broken nails and ripped cuticles visible beneath the white of the flour. "What happened? You can't start a conversation that way and then beat around the bush."

"Well," Laurel began. "I feel, I don't know, shy about it."

"Shy?" Jessie had never known her mother to be shy. "About what?"

"Well," Laurel said again. "We're trying to conceive . . ."

Jessie waited for her mother to finish her sentence. "Conceive of what?" she prompted finally.

"Oh, Jessie. You know this is hard for me to talk about. Conceive a child, of course."

It was impossible not to laugh. Laurel was, what, fifty-one now? Hadn't she been menopausal for years?

"Isn't that sort of impossible?" she finally asked, as kindly as she could.

Laurel laughed, clearly enjoying Jessie's confusion. "You're right. I can't *physically* have a child at my age," she said. "But I can still *have* a child."

Jessie waited in silence for her mother to go on.

"Oh, Jessie. Don't you get it?" Laurel said at last. "Sue will have the child. Jim will be the father. I'll be . . . well, I'll be a co-parent."

"Oh," Jessie said flatly. "I see."

"Well?"

"I thought you were done having kids, Mom. Isn't that why you had your tubes tied?"

"Well, I thought I was, too. But that was then, this is now." She giggled nervously. "And things change, don't they? Sue wants a child—there are lots of health benefits, you know. Lower rates of cervical cancer. And breast."

"Sue wants to have a baby so she won't get cancer?" Jessie asked dryly. "Come on."

"Well, that's not the only reason, of course. She wants . . . you know . . . the experience—"

"Oh." Jessie did not know. She had always assumed, growing up, that she would have children, but recently the idea of trying to steer her life in that direction filled her with a strange mix of inertia and dread, as if she were on a raft adrift in the doldrums and her supplies were running low. Better, she had decided recently, to let the wind take her where it would. She did not mind the thought of being an old maid. She could almost imagine the cottage where she would live in her dotage, the counters cluttered with canning jars while the daylilies bloomed outside her window.

"And Jim's on board. So honestly I didn't have a lot of choice," Laurel was saying. She laughed again nervously. "It was either get on board or . . ."

"Get on board or abandon ship?" Jessie offered. "And you don't want to leave."

"No. I don't want to leave," Laurel said.

"I see." Again, silence descended between them.

"Wow, so you're going to have a kid," Jessie said at last. "I can't believe it." Her voice sounded deflated and hollow even to herself, but Laurel did not seem to notice.

She laughed shrilly. "Well, we're not pregnant yet."

"Don't you think it might be a little . . . a little odd for the kid?"

"Jessie!" Laurel was indignant. "I'm surprised at you. Lots of children have two mommies, two daddies. There are thousands of kids in this country with only one parent. Ours will have three. Who can argue with that?"

Now Jessie laughed. "Well, I think there are a lot of people who would argue with that, Mom, and so do you."

"I know!" Laurel said. She sounded gleeful. "But we'll show them."

When she hung up the phone, Jessie's stomach felt raw, her thoughts muddled. Her first instinct was to call her father and tell him what Laurel had told her. She could almost hear his booming laughter. He would see it, she guessed, as yet another of Laurel's theatrics. In her father's mind, Laurel lived her life as if her every experience were to be headlined: *Grief-stricken mother loses daughters in sexist custody battle; free-thinking polyamorous triad raising healthy, well-adjusted child.* It would be comforting to collude in his amusement, rather than attempt to comb through the tangle of her own reactions.

For a few moments, Jessie returned to kneading the bread

dough on the counter, but even the rhythmic motion of her hands in the soft dough did not soothe her as it usually did. Quickly, she plopped it in a bowl, covered it with a kitchen towel, and looked around the room for a warm place to let it rise. It was cool in the house; the weather had changed today, but Jessie had not yet brought in wood for the woodstove. Jessie turned the oven to warm and placed the bowl with its towel inside. Then she quickly rinsed the caked dough from her hands and found her running shoes in the bathroom where she'd kicked them off the night before.

Outside, the skin on her arms tightened against the cool of the evening. She began running at once, knowing she would not be cold for long. Soon enough, the work of her cells turning adenosine diphosphate to triphosphate would warm her body, the endorphins released by her pituitary gland would calm her mind. Even as the thought formed, she laughed at herself; no wonder Leah called her a geek. But it soothed her, this knowledge of her body's inner workings. Life could be a difficult thing to make sense of; she might as well understand what she could.

Jessie looked up at the desert sky. The moon, almost full, slid dramatically from behind a film of clouds, and Jessie felt her chest filling with the beauty of it. She kept her face tilted toward the sky as she ran, trusting her feet to find their own way along the gravel road. Only when she had run a half a mile or so from home did she permit her thoughts to return to what Laurel had told her.

Really, it was no concern of hers. She thought of the objection she had half-raised to Laurel on the phone, but she knew that what other people might think of her mother's choices was not what troubled her. Was she worried for the child? She had never met Jim and Sue, but she sensed they might be a little odd. Still, children were resilient and adaptive; surely the child would be fine.

As she ran, Jessie felt her thoughts circle in on the one reaction she had not allowed.

"Are you jealous, Jessie?" she asked herself aloud.

For that was it, she realized suddenly. She *was* a little jealous. *She* was Laurel's daughter. For all intents and purposes, she was Laurel's only daughter. It had not been an easy nor a simple path—not one, certainly, that she would wish on any child. But it was part of who she was. On a day-to-day basis, she rarely thought of her mother, and Laurel, caught up in her own life now, rarely called her. Yet despite the infrequency of their communication, Jessie never doubted that Laurel valued her. Jessie had been the faithful one. She alone had not refuted Laurel's claims to motherhood.

All that would change now. Laurel would claim this new child with all the passion of her convictions. This child would be her flag to wave to the world: Look at us! Look at what we can do! But she—or he—would also be Laurel's personal chance at redemption, her last shot at sterling motherhood: the child that she would not leave.

So that's it, Jessie thought. *I'm jealous.* And simply in the naming of it, the feeling began to disperse into the cool night air. Jessie's head felt clear again, her thoughts transparent. She smiled to herself as she ran. Laurel was going to have a baby, and Jessie would be an aunt. Unlike motherhood, being an aunt was a role she could imagine. She would send the child books at Christmas, *A Fish Out of Water* and *The Velveteen Rabbit*, and all her other childhood favorites. Later, when the child was bigger, she would teach her how to play cat's cradle, to build a fire, to tie a slip knot . . .

It wasn't until Jessie was almost home that she thought to correct herself.

"I won't be the aunt," she said aloud, coming to a stop on the dark road. "I'll be the sister."

The realization deflated her. She sprinted the last seventy yards to her house, trying to recapture the calm she had felt. She opened the front door, her heart still pumping hard. Inside, a strange burning smell hung in the air. She had forgotten to turn off the oven before she left, and the towel draped over the bowl inside was crinkled and warped at the edges, the oven filled with gray smoke.

"Shit," Jessie said, tugging the towel off the bowl and burning her fingers. The dough inside had risen to a plump, soft ball, its surface just beginning to crust. Jessie sniffed at it. Then she greased a baking sheet with a paper towel she'd wiped in butter and plopped the loaf on top to bake.

In the morning, she had toast for breakfast with homemade blackberry jam, ignoring the slightly singed taste of the bread. It would be a waste to throw it out.

CHAPTER 32

Jessie

T he plane dipped as it began its descent into Minneapolis, and Jessie's stomach dropped with it. She clutched at her armrest, and then immediately let go, embarrassed by her fear. It made no sense. Jessie had flown on an airplane at least once a year since she turned seven, she and her sister departing for northern California almost as soon as school was out in June. How Jessie had loved those flights as an unaccompanied minor. While her sister had cried and clutched at Sarah while they waited to board, Jessie had felt charged with anticipation. In another moment, the stewardess would lead the sisters onto the plane alone. *Alone.* For an hour and a half, she and Emma would be parentless, and, oh, the thrill of that.

Usually their flight to Sacramento had been nonstop, but a couple of times they had changed planes in San Francisco for a puddle jumper. Jessie had loved hurrying through the unknown airport, the stewardess' heels click-clacking beside her, all the people streaming by. She could still remember vividly the impulse that had come over her then: to pull her hand free and disappear into that river of people. She had not given into it, of course—she would not have missed the summer at Baymont for anything—but still it had been exhilarating to feel so close to such utter freedom, to be separated from it by nothing more than the stewardess' thin fingers wrapped gently around her hand.

Never once, in all those years of flying, had Jessie felt afraid. But now, as the plane shook violently from side to side and then dropped suddenly through the sky, Jessie couldn't help her sharp gasp for breath. The man next to her smiled sympathetically.

"Nervous flier?" he asked.

"Not usually," she muttered. She turned to the window, but all that she could see beyond the rain-streaked pane was the fuzzy gray-white of clouds.

"It's just the storm that's creating turbulence," the man reassured her. "It's not really dangerous."

"I know that," Jessie said, more sharply than she'd meant to, then snuck a glance at him, hoping he hadn't noticed her tone. "Is Minneapolis home?"

"Yes. For you?"

"No, I'm—" For a moment, Jessie was tempted to say too much, just to take her mind off the violent tremors of the plane. *I'm going to visit my polyamorous mother in Northfield. She moved there five months ago to live with her primaries, and now they're trying to have a baby.*

"Just visiting," she said.

"Look." The man gestured toward the window. "We're through it now."

The gray beyond the window had transformed into a brilliant green. Rain drops still splattered against the glass, but beyond them the trees were clearly visible. Such green! Jessie had lived in one desert or another for all of her adult life. The desert suited her, she thought. She was not an indulgent person; she did not like to take even her most basic needs for granted. But now, looking through the rain-splattered window to the ocean of green beyond, Jessie felt the tightness in her muscles give way. She put her hand to the glass, wishing she could feel the moisture on the other side. In another moment, the wheels had touched the tarmac and the plane was roaring along the runway.

Laurel was waiting for her at baggage claim, looking anxious. Her gray hair was cut short on the top and sides, but in back it hung past her shoulders in straggly strands. Her face looked puffy, deep creases around her eyes and mouth. Instinctively, Jessie's hand moved to her own face. Would she look the same, she wondered, when she was her mother's age? Like Laurel, Jessie eschewed the trappings of femininity, and yet only rarely did she doubt her own attractiveness. Seeing Laurel now, however, she wondered how much of that confidence came from youth alone: her body strong and firm, her large breasts pushing out beneath her T-shirt.

When Jessie was fifteen, Sarah had gently suggested breast reduction surgery. Jessie had recently joined the cross-country team, and the straps of her sports bra made deep, red welts in her shoulders when she ran. Sarah had taken pictures and sent them to Blue Cross Blue Shield, but the insurance company had deemed the procedure cosmetic and would not pay.

Jessie had been secretly disappointed, not because she felt any great attachment to the idea, but because she had, without even admitting it to herself, enjoyed Sarah's attention and concern, the rare sense that she and her stepmother were a united front.

A few years later, it had seemed that the insurance company might be persuaded if they pushed the matter, and Sarah had asked Jessie if she wanted to try again, but Jessie had refused. By then, Jessie was seventeen, and her breasts had long since ceased to feel new; they had become a part of her. She also had a boyfriend and was beginning to sense, with no small amount of surprise, that her generous bust might be an asset not to be underrated.

Looking at Laurel now, with her pendulous bosom hanging almost to the kangaroo pocket of her sweatshirt, Jessie wondered if she finally understood the reason behind Sarah's concern. She shifted her backpack on her shoulder and surreptitiously hoisted her breasts, feeling the perspiration beneath her bra momentarily cool with the air she'd let in.

"Mom!" she called, waving. "Right here."

"There you are," Laurel beamed, holding out her arms.

Jessie smiled and stepped into her mother's embrace. She put her arms around her mother's back and felt the spongy softness beneath her touch; her mother's shoulder blades seemed sunken in doughy flesh.

Laurel stepped back and gestured toward the baggage claim.

"Any bags?" she asked.

"Just this one," Jessie said, slipping her other arm through the strap of her backpack.

"Good. Jim and Sue are right outside. It seemed silly to park."

Jim and Sue were not where Laurel had left them at the curb, but Laurel was unconcerned. "They must have circled around. We'll just wait."

After a few moments, a blue Honda Civic came into view. Laurel grinned and waved wildly. "There they are!"

The car pulled up and Jessie followed Laurel into the backseat, cramming her backpack into the foot well between her legs. Jim was at the wheel, but he turned partially in his seat and extended a cool, limp hand for her to shake.

"Welcome to Minnesooota," he said, clearly forcing a Minnesota accent. "Glad you could make it."

"Thanks," Jessie said. Jim's face was pale and lightly freckled; hazel eyes peered at her from behind large, plastic-framed glasses. She leaned forward to get a better look at him, but he turned away at once to watch for a break in the traffic, and a curtain of straggly red hair shielded his face from view. Sue was sitting next to him in the passenger seat. She wore a red baseball cap over short, dark hair, and her face below the bill was square and tan, strong-jawed. She smiled at Jessie and waved.

"Sorry," she said. "I'd shake, but I've got carpel tunnel and it hurts."

"We tried to tell her she was working too much," Laurel said, settling back against the vinyl seat. "Where's Mrs. Weasley?"

"What?" Jessie asked. Who?"

Laurel giggled. "I was talking to Jim and Sue. Well, where is she?"

"She's in the hatch," Jim said, pulling the car into the moving traffic.

"And she's staying there?" Laurel laughed again. "How unlike her."

"Well, it's not like she has much choice," said Sue. "We had to put her in a cage."

"What?" Laurel said with mock indignation. "Cage Mrs. Weasley? Whatever for?"

"Vet's orders," Jim said.

"Ah." Laurel glanced at Jessie, who had to stop herself from rolling her eyes.

Yes, Yes, Jessie felt like saying. *I see what a tight little family you are.*

"What are you talking about, Mom?" she said instead, trying to keep the annoyance out of her voice. "Who's Mrs. Weasley?"

Laurel's face lit up. "Oh, didn't I tell you? Mrs. Weasley's our ferret."

"Your what?"

"Our ferret. Our pet. Well, really she's more like another member of the family." She lowered her voice conspiratorially. "We think she might be a wizard. You know, an *animagus.*"

"A what?"

"An animagus. Oh, come on, Jessie. *Harry Potter*?"

"I only read the first one."

"And you call yourself my daughter."

Jessie shrugged and looked out the window.

"Jessie, please. I was joking. But yes, we have a pet ferret. She had to go to the vet in Minneapolis for her checkup this morning, so she's along for the ride. Just wait 'til you meet her. She really is a remarkable little animal. So much smarter than a dog."

Laurel's voice was animated, almost giddy.

"That's great, Mom," Jessie said. She almost felt embarrassed for her mother now; it was clear how desperately Laurel wanted to show off her new life. "I didn't know people kept pet ferrets."

"Oh, yes," Laurel said. "Just not very many. There are probably less than a dozen in all of Minneapolis."

"Fewer than a dozen," Sue said, glancing back.

"That's what I said."

"No, you said 'less than.' But ferrets are a count noun. Less milk. Fewer ferrets."

Jessie glanced at her mother and saw her roll her eyes.

"Okay, Sue, you got me," she said cheerfully. She turned to Jessie. "Sue's a grammarian," she said. "In case you haven't noticed."

"But a good-natured one," Sue said.

Jessie didn't know what to say to this. "You didn't tell me you had a pet ferret, Mom."

"Well," Laurel said. "I suppose she's really Jim and Sue's. Jim's and Sue's?" She laughed uncertainly. "I mean, they had her before I, um . . . joined them."

"Jim and Sue's," Sue said. "You were right the first time. But don't be ridiculous, Laurel. Mrs. Weasley is yours, too. We're family, aren't we?"

Jessie glanced at Sue, wondering if she was making amends for calling Laurel out before.

Laurel beamed. "We are indeed," she said. "Oh Jessie, just wait until you see the house."

The house where Jim, Sue, and Laurel lived was just outside of Northfield on a wide, slow-moving river.

"There's the river now," Laurel said, leaning across Jessie in the backseat and pointing. Jessie, peering through the rain-streaked window, could just make out flashes of silver water between the houses that lined its edge.

"It's supposed to clear up by tomorrow," Laurel reassured her. "So you'll be able to swim, if you want. Or we can go canoeing. But look! Here we are."

Jim turned the car onto a gravel driveway that led to a large log home. As soon as the car was parked, he got out and opened the hatch to retrieve Mrs. Weasley. Jessie watched him curiously. He wore a black Carleton T-shirt that was too big for him, and his arms, lifting out the cage, looked skinny and pale in the gaping sleeves. Jessie, hoisting her backpack to her shoulders, had to resist the urge to reach out to help him.

She caught only a glimpse of the brown ferret inside the carrier as Jim turned toward the house.

"Sorry," he called over his shoulder. "But Mrs. Weasley really doesn't like the cage."

Jessie stared up at the house. It was constructed of large varnished logs which crisscrossed at the corners, just like the fairy houses she and Emma used to build with sticks in the woods at Baymont, except that the ends of these logs were as big as Frisbees instead of dimes.

She turned to Sue. "Did you guys build this house?"

"Well, not personally. But yes, we did have it built. Years ago now."

Jessie felt Laurel watching her.

"Don't you just love it?" Laurel said.

Jessie nodded, trying not to think about the small forest that must have given its life to yield all those perfect logs. She looked up at the house appraisingly, shielding her eyes against the light rain. High above her she could see a small balcony.

"The view must be pretty nice from up there," she said sincerely.

Laurel face lit up. "It is! And guess what? That's where you're going to stay. Just wait 'til you see it. And the deck. The deck is amazing."

Inside, the house seemed even bigger. The dining and living rooms opened onto an enormous deck that fronted the river.

Standing under the shelter of the awning, Jessie could see a wide staircase on the other side that led down to a wooden dock. Two kayaks lay overturned along one side, and a canoe was moored in the water. The surface of the river was slate gray and dimpled with rain.

"Wow," she said. "You weren't kidding. You really are right on the river."

"I told you it was amazing, didn't I?" Laurel said. She reached for Jessie's hand. "Come on," she said, pulling her back inside. "I'll give you the tour."

The rest of the house was a maze of rooms on multiple floors, all connected by narrow, wood-paneled hallways, the planks worn so smooth that Jessie couldn't resist letting her hand trail along the honey-colored wood as they walked. Leading her throughout the house, Laurel was giddy once again. She pointed out each of their rooms as they came to them.

"This is Sue's room," she said. "And this one is Jim's."

"And yours, too?" Jessie asked.

"Oh, no," Laurel said quickly. "We have our own rooms. Mine's upstairs."

"Oh. Sorry. I just thought—"

Laurel let out a small breath. "I know. At first it didn't seem fair," she said. "I mean, if we're both primaries, why should Sue be the one with the room right next to Jim? Especially since, you know . . ." she trailed off.

"Since I know what?" Jessie said.

"Oh, well. Just that Sue doesn't really like sex that much. I thought I told you."

Jessie suppressed a shiver. Laurel had mentioned something about this before, she remembered, when she had told Jessie about the personal ad that Jim and Sue had placed. But now Jessie had met Sue. She was downstairs in the kitchen. Surely, this was not Laurel's confidence to share.

"Although I have wondered, you know," Laurel went on, her voice turning conspiratorial. Jim is . . . Well, let's just say Jim has rather specific tastes. In bed, I mean. I *have* wondered if maybe Sue just wasn't so keen to—"

"Mom."

"What? I mean, not every woman wants to—"

"Mom! That's enough."

"Oh, Jessie. You're, what, twenty-seven years old? I would have thought by now we could have an honest conversation about—"

"Mom, stop. I do not need to know—I do not *want* to know— what Jim likes or doesn't like in bed. I am your daughter. And it's none of my business. We're not . . . we're not supposed to talk about stuff like that."

"Well, pardon me," Laurel said, looking wounded. "I'll just keep my mouth shut then."

An awkward silence followed. Laurel would not look at her.

"Mom," Jessie said at last. "You don't have to keep your mouth shut, okay? I want to hear about your life here. I'd just rather not hear the gory details, okay?"

Laurel nodded tersely. "Let's go upstairs. I can show you my room. It's nice—nicer than these, even."

Laurel's was a nice room. It had a high, rough-planked ceiling and windows on two sides that looked out over the river. The wood floor creaked pleasantly as Jessie walked across it. Outside, the rain had let up at last and steam rose from the surface of the river.

"You know," Laurel said. "It's not like I'm the lone ranger up here. Look at this." She gestured to an intercom panel by the door. "It's such a big house; it can be awfully hard to find each other. So Jim and Sue had these put in. It's also convenient for—" She hesitated. "Well, you know. All Jim has to do is push the button and voilà!"

Jessie sighed. "I didn't expect you to all have separate rooms," she said.

"What? You thought we'd all sleep together?"

"No, I guess not. I suppose I thought you'd be with Jim, since you said that Sue and he were mostly just roommates—"

"That wouldn't have been very fair to Sue, would it?" Laurel interrupted. "I mean, the only way polyamory works is if there's total equality."

"I didn't mean that Sue wouldn't be—"

"Oh, I know you didn't. But think about it. It's not just the s— the part you don't want to hear about. It's the dynamic it sets up. If Jim and I shared a room, and Sue didn't . . . Well, it just wouldn't feel equal. Plus, there are other reasons."

"Like what?"

"Well, for one thing, Jim doesn't like to sleep with anyone." She giggled girlishly. "I mean, he likes to *sleep* with people, he just doesn't like to actually—"

"Okay, Mom. I get it."

"Plus, this way, if I want to have a secondary sleep over, it makes it easier."

"A secondary? You mean, like someone else?"

"Of course. I mean, Jim and Sue don't sleep together often, but they do sleep together. So it wouldn't be fair if I didn't have someone else, too."

Jessie glanced at the bed. "So everything's got to be totally fair," she said, aware even as she said them how mocking her words might sound to her mother.

Laurel nodded emphatically. "Well, it helps. Biamorous relationships are hard enough. Imagine how complicated it can get when there are more than two people involved."

Jessie nodded vaguely, backing out of the room. "Is there more?"

"Well, at the moment, Jim is happy with just Sue and me as

primaries. But if he were ever to want a secondary, too, well then I would have to—"

"To the house, Mom! I meant more to the house."

"Oh! Sorry," Laurel said, laughing. "I thought you meant . . . But yes. Just wait until you see the third story. I picked the perfect room for you."

Jessie fell in love with her attic room immediately. The floor was rough-hewn hardwood, and the ceiling sloped down on either side almost to the floor. At one end of the room was a glass door that opened onto the small balcony that she had seen from the driveway. As soon as Laurel left her to get settled in, Jessie stepped outside. A rush of deliciously cool air greeted her; she wanted to lick the moisture from the dripping trees. To her right was the river, its dark water now almost completely concealed beneath a blanket of steam. To her left was what appeared to be forest, although Jessie instinctively mistrusted it. How much true forest could there be so close to Minneapolis, after all?

The street by which they had arrived at the house stretched out in front of her, following the river, and in the distance she could see the spire of a church rising above the trees. The entire vista— the shrouded river, the lush woods, the church spire— was so picturesque that Jessie stood gazing at it for several minutes. Then she laughed; she couldn't help it. It all seemed so old-fashioned, and the irony of that—of Laurel's postmodern love affair unfolding in such a quaint setting—tickled her.

No doubt Laurel would not call it postmodern at all. She would say that it was monogamy that was constructivist and unrealistic, a distasteful remnant of a patriarchal society that ensnared women in the name of romance. But then Jessie thought of Jim, with his two primaries and his intercom button, and she cringed. So what if Laurel got to have her—what had she called them—*secondaries* on the side? Jim still had his little harem, didn't he? She didn't know how her mother stood it.

Jessie sighed, and for an instant she could see her breath suspended in the moist air. She suspected Laurel could stand it only because she saw Sue as no real threat. If Sue didn't want to sleep with Jim, and Laurel did—well, of course Laurel would feel she had the upper hand. *Not every woman wants to . . .* her mother had said. Jessie shuddered, remembering. But at least it was a little clearer now why Jim had wanted Laurel on board; Jessie could stop feeling so puzzled by it.

Still, it all seemed so . . . so precariously balanced. What if Jim did take on a new partner? Laurel had made it clear that then she would feel she needed to have another one, too. And what about Sue? It didn't sound like Sue had a secondary. Did she not care, like her mother so obviously did, about things being "fair?" Jessie let out her breath and gave her head a little shake. It wasn't her business, was it? Laurel seemed truly happy for the first time in years. Wasn't that enough? Jessie took one last look at the mist-shrouded river and went inside.

Back in her room, Jessie quickly unpacked her backpack. Laurel had emptied the top drawer of the dresser for her, seemingly into the other drawers, as the lower ones were crammed so full they barely opened for her to peek inside. When she had finished, she pulled off her boots and lay down for a moment on the quilted bed. The planks of the ceiling sloped over her, and she lifted her legs and pressed her feet against the boards.

The sloped ceilings reminded Jessie of the house at Baymont. Jessie and Emma had shared an upstairs room there, too, and at night they would both lie in bed with their sheets kicked off, their feet propped up against the peeling boards. During the first weeks of every visit, Emma had always cried after Laurel came in to wish them goodnight.

"What's wrong?" Jessie would ask.

"I just miss home," Emma would gasp, her voice so tight and thin she could barely speak. "I miss Mommy."

Why? Jessie thought to herself. Sure, home was okay, but it would still be there when they got back. And Baymont—Baymont was better. Why couldn't Emma just enjoy it?

Still, she never said any of those sorts of things. Instead, she would walk barefoot across the gritty floor, perch on the edge of her sister's bed, and stroke her heaving back.

"It's okay. You'll go home soon," she would say. She never said, "We'll go home soon," because that would have meant that she, Jessie, was not at home at Baymont either, and she felt, almost desperately, that she was. Sitting on Emma's bed like that, the slope of the ceiling was only centimeters above her. She would rest her head against it until Emma's cries ceased, or until she grew so sleepy that she simply stretched out beside her sister in the narrow bed.

CHAPTER 33

Jessie

Jessie went downstairs on a narrow, honey-colored staircase near the back of the house, and then found her way to the kitchen. Sue and Laurel were both there; Mrs. Weasley, Jessie noticed, was curled up on a cat bed in the corner.

"There you are," Laurel said, seeing her. "Want some tea?" She gestured to the steaming kettle.

When Jessie nodded, she opened a cabinet crammed with boxes. "Take your pick," she said. "We're tea drinkers ourselves, as you can probably tell."

Jessie chose a decaf chai that looked as if its extraction would not cause an avalanche. Then she looked around the kitchen.

"Something smells good."

"There'll be banana bread to go with your tea in a minute," Sue said.

"Sue loves to bake," Laurel said proudly.

Jessie nodded and looked at Sue. She was medium-height and stocky, with strong forearms and short, unstyled hair. She was dressed as Jessie herself might dress, in thrift-store jeans and a button-down flannel shirt. In fact, Sue reminded Jessie a little of herself: sturdy and unadorned, and comfortable in her own skin.

Had Jessie met Sue anywhere else, she might have taken her for a lesbian, just as people often mistook her for one. Jessie's mind turned again to her mother's unwanted confidences; according to Laurel, Sue simply wasn't that interested in sex. Sometimes people suspected the same of Jessie, she knew—mostly other women who simply did not get how Jessie could so blatantly flaunt the norms of female sex appeal and still feel sexy.

Oh, but she could, Jessie thought. *And how!* It was simply a matter of finding the right kind of man—a man who liked his woman a little burly, her strong legs around him, the great heft of her breasts in his hands. Maybe the magazines and movies could convince all those people that men wanted their women to look like prepubescent girls, with slippery legs and shaved pubes, but Jessie knew differently. Other men were out there, wanting what they wanted. Wanting her.

Standing in the warm kitchen, Jessie felt herself grow flushed with her thoughts. She put her tea down on the cluttered kitchen island and went to stand in front of the large picture window that looked out on the river. The red and yellow kayaks that she had seen on the dock seemed almost to float in the steam rising from the water.

Laurel followed her gaze. "You can go out in one of the boats whenever you want," she said. "Sue goes out every morning."

"Not this morning," Sue corrected. "Too wet and cold. Would you like some banana bread?"

Jessie nodded and returned to her tea and the piece of banana bread that Sue had set down beside it on a chipped saucer. She ate it quickly, suddenly aware of how hungry she was.

"Want another?" Sue asked. "Here, just help yourself." She held out the wooden cutting board on which she had upturned the bread. "We don't go much for formality around here."

Jessie smiled. "I'll fit in just fine then." Already she could tell she was going to like Sue.

"Do you mind if I go out with you in the kayak in the morning? I mean, if you prefer to go alone, I don't—"

"I go alone often enough. But just to warn you, I do get up early."

"That's okay. I do, too," Jessie said.

"I knew you two would hit it off," Laurel said, grinning at them. "I tried to tell Sue. I just knew you would."

When Jessie had finished her tea and a third sliver of banana bread which she cut from the loaf directly into her hand, she investigated the kitchen. Its disorder pleased her, the clutter reminding her of her own small home. The refrigerator was covered in pictures, most curling up at the edges, as if tugging against the magnets that held them in place. There was a picture of Sue in a kayak, and another of Jim and Laurel paddling a canoe. In another, a skinny young man stood next to a woman with thick hair that fell almost to her waist.

"Who's that?" Jessie began, but as soon as the words were out she knew. "Oh, that's you, Sue. Isn't it?"

Sue glanced over, nodding.

"And Jim," Laurel said. "That's Jim, too. Didn't you recognize him?"

Jessie moved closer to the picture, studying the young man. In truth, she saw little resemblance between the man in the photograph and the scrawny, long-haired, middle-aged man whom she had barely seen since she'd arrived.

"Oh, right," she lied. "Wow, Sue, you two must have been together a long time."

"Twenty years this August," Sue said. "Since grad school."

"And was it . . . just the two of you then?" Jessie asked.

Sue smiled dryly. "For a while. But it didn't really work out too well that way."

"So, before Laurel, there were other . . ." Jessie searched for the right word, and Sue grinned.

"Partners?" she offered.

Jessie nodded.

"Just two. One while we were still in grad school. Another after we moved here."

"What happened to them?"

Sue shrugged. "Nothing, really. They moved on. I still keep in touch with Beth. She got married and has a kid. I heard Jean's a lesbian now." She shrugged again, then grinned. "Neither one of them was as enthu . . .Well, as committed as your mom is."

Jessie looked at Laurel, who was watching Sue closely. She smiled broadly.

"I'm definitely not going anywhere," Laurel said.

Jessie glanced surreptitiously at Sue. She had a deadpan tone that was hard to read, and Jessie couldn't help feeling puzzled by her. She knew that her mother had told her too much about the other woman, and yet, having heard it, she couldn't help but wonder. Why had Sue stayed—for twenty years!—with a man she didn't want to sleep with? It seemed suddenly even more bizarre to her, that Jim and Sue had chosen to a use a third person to save their relationship, rather than simply go their separate ways. Still, twenty years was a long time. Clearly it was working; this wasn't just a passing fad. And yet Jessie couldn't help but wonder: what was in it for Sue? She glanced around the kitchen, as if it might hold some clue.

On the wall next to the pantry, two calendars hung side by side. One was from the Nature Conservancy; Jessie had received the same one in the mail herself, accompanied with the usual plea for a donation. In its squares were printed regular sorts of calendar things—her arrival this morning, for instance, and, a few squares later, "Jessie leaves." The other was printed from a computer program, and it was blank except that at the bottom of every other square was a capital letter—*L* or *S*, but mostly *L*. The only other writing was a series of numbers, *97.8, 97.9, 97.8,* written by hand on each square. There was no number on today's date, or on any of the squares that followed.

"What's this?" Jessie asked, pointing to the second calendar.

"Oh, shoot," Sue said suddenly. "I forgot. Laurel, write 97.8 for today, will you?"

"What is it?" Jessie asked again.

"Just my temperature," Sue explained. "I mostly remember to take it. I just forget to write it down."

"Your temp . . . Oh, yeah," Jessie said, remembering. Sue was trying to get pregnant. "Is it helping?"

"Well, I've been doing it for three, four months now. Jim graphs them on the computer. They're textbook, really. But—" She shrugged. "No luck yet."

Jessie nodded, suddenly uncomfortable. She turned away from the calendar, feeling as if she had been caught spying.

Laurel's voice stopped her. "Don't you want to know what the letters are?"

"What?"

"These letters, here." She pointed to the Ls and Ss printed in the squares.

Jessie glanced at Sue, but her back was turned. Her mother gazed at her expectantly.

"Sure," she said. "What are they?"

Laurel smiled. "Well, L is me, of course. And S is for Sue." She paused. "We tried keeping this calendar separate from the basal body temperature one, but it just got too complicated. Especially since we have to work around Sue's cycle now." She looked at Jessie knowingly.

"Sorry, Mom," Jessie said. "I'm not following you."

"Oh, Jessie. This is our . . ." She smiled lopsidedly. "Well, not to put too fine a point on it, our 'intimacy' calendar."

Jessie turned back to the calendar, almost unwillingly. It was obvious to her now. Every other day, there was an L, but in the middle of the third week, Ss were printed in three squares in a row.

"That," Laurel said, pointing, "is when we think Sue will be ovulating. So she and Jim have to—"

"Mom," Jessie said, the harshness of her tone surprising her. "I told you."

"Oh," Laurel said, screwing up her forehead. "What you said before, right? You don't want—" She grimaced. "Sorry."

Jessie sighed. "It's okay."

There was an awkward silence.

"And you just keep it in your kitchen like that? For anyone to see?" Jessie said finally.

Sue grinned. She seemed completely unembarrassed by the turn the conversation had taken.

"A lot of people don't understand what it is," Sue said. "And, anyway, most of the people who come into our kitchen . . . well, they're friends. They're like-minded." She looked out the large window. "Want to go out in the canoe now? I think the rain has finally stopped."

Jessie glanced at her mom. Laurel nodded emphatically. "That's a great idea. You two go have fun, and I'll make dinner."

Jessie looked back to Sue, who was watching her expectantly, and suddenly, she understood. Sue got to live in this house, this beautiful log home on a river, with canoes and kayaks only steps away. She had her own lovely room, a man to sleep with occasionally, two partners to help pay the bills and cook the food and do the chores. Sue had . . . Well, she had a family. She had companionship and belonging. But she had solitude, too, and independence. She could do as she liked and yet she was not alone. Jessie smiled a little to herself. Maybe it wasn't such a bad deal for Sue after all.

"I'd love to," she said.

That night, Jessie and her mother sat on the floor in the living room, playing Scrabble. It was a tradition; they had played Scrabble together almost every evening during those summers in Baymont. When Jessie was a child and even a teenager, Laurel had beaten her without fail. Laurel knew all the obscure little words that allowed her to rack up points even on a crowded board, words Jessie had never heard of but had quickly learned not to challenge. Her sister had never liked to play Scrabble with them, and Jessie could understand why. Laurel always wore an annoyingly gleeful look whenever she used an X on a triple letter score, or arranged a word to reach one of the coveted triple word squares at the edges of the board. Their mother had never believed in going easy on them.

She watched now as Laurel used an S to turn *liver* into *sliver*, and then laid out the letters for *simile* over a double word score.

"Very nice," Jessie said appreciatively, as Laurel counted her points aloud.

"Thank you," Laurel said, smiling. She reached for the score pad.

Jessie took a sip from her water, studying her letters.

"Mom," she said suddenly, looking up. "You're not drinking."

Jessie's water glass was alone on the coffee table; for the first time she could remember, Laurel had no cocktail within arm's reach.

"No," Laurel said.

"Mom, that's huge."

Laurel smiled. "Well, thank you."

"You finally realized you had a problem?"

"Oh, I didn't have a problem." She narrowed her eyebrows at Jessie. "Is that what you thought? That I was an alcoholic or something?"

"Well—"

"There's nothing wrong with having a drink or two to take the edge off."

Jessie shook her head, confused. "So why did you stop?"

Laurel shrugged noncommittally. "I don't know. Jim and Sue don't drink much, and, well, I didn't want them to think—"

"That you had a problem?"

Laurel shrugged again and Jessie nodded, understanding. Her mother wanted so much to fit in here that even her beloved vodka and tonic had not been too high a price to pay.

"And, you know, since we're going to be pregnant soon . . ."

"Mom, it's Sue who will be pregnant."

Laurel looked at her sharply. "I know. But the baby will be mine, too. And I'm planning to co-nurse."

Jessie startled. An old memory surfaced suddenly: Laurel's nipple between her thumb and forefinger, a bead of yellow milk on brown skin. Surely, she didn't still . . .

"Mom, how? That's not even poss—"

"The science these days is remarkable, Jessie. I've already spoken with a lactation specialist. She said it might be possible, with hormone therapy, to induce lactation. Adoptive mothers sometimes try it."

"Oh." Jessie's mind churned. A woman wanting to nurse an adopted newborn—that made sense to Jessie. But this baby, if they had it, would presumably have a lactating mother already.

"And Sue's okay with that?" she asked skeptically.

"Well," Laurel said quickly. "I'm sure she will be. We've just been so preoccupied with getting Sue pregnant, we haven't . . . I figure we'll cross that bridge when we come to it."

"Oh," Jessie said again. With an effort, she tried to refocus her attention on the board, but her mind wouldn't settle. Quickly, she laid out the letters for *lean*, using the *e* in simile.

"There. Four points. Your turn, Mom."

"Jessie, really? That's the best you can do?"

Jessie nodded, reaching for the silver bag of letters. For a few moments, neither of them spoke.

"Now, Jessie," Laurel said at last, her eyes on her tray, feigning nonchalance. "You haven't mentioned your sister the whole time you've been here. How *is* Emma?"

Jessie moved her letters around, not looking up. "She's fine."

"Yes? And?"

"And nothing. She seems fine."

"Come on, Jessie. How is Emma, really? What's she up to these days?"

"Mom, you know I hate being in the middle."

"I'm not putting you in the middle. I just want to hear a little about my other daughter. How is that putting you in the middle?"

"I just don't know how much she'd want me to—" Jessie paused. She glanced at her mother, who was looking at her hungrily. "Look, she's fine, Mom. Okay? She's living in Berkeley. I'm sure you knew that already. She got a job teaching language arts at a middle school. In Oakland, I think. She seems to like it okay."

"In Oakland? That must be quite tough, wouldn't you think? And what about grad school? I thought when she moved to Berkeley, she might . . . She's always been such a good student, you know."

Jessie nodded and studied her letters. Suddenly Laurel put a hand over her mouth dramatically. "Oh, I didn't mean . . . You have, too, Jessie! You know you have. *Both* of you are such smart girls. You always have been."

"It's okay, Mom. I wasn't offended. I just—"

"I suppose," Laurel said, interrupting her. "I suppose I have to give your father at least *some* of the credit for that."

"For what?"

"For how smart you girls are."

Jessie rolled her eyes. "Mom—"

"But Emma? Is she there alone? She must have a boyfriend."

"No, I don't think so. She's actually—"

Jessie stopped, unsure of what—or how much—to say. She tried to picture her sister as she had last seen her: her long, blonde hair cut shoulder-length, beige cargo pants hanging low on her hips. It wasn't easy to picture her like that. Whenever Jessie thought of Emma, she imagined her as she had looked in high school: her ponytail swinging as she sprinted around the track, the way she'd smile whenever they passed each other in the halls, Emma carrying her books in a stack against her chest just like all the cool kids did. Jessie herself hadn't seen the point in that; she had always used a backpack. She shook her head, remembering how even such a trivial thing as that had been fodder for the other kids' teasing: "Double-strapper," they had called her.

Had they thought that they could shame her? By then, Jessie had begun to feel nothing but scorn for their taunts. Why did they *care* how she carried her books? How could they not see their own pettiness, the dumb conformity they adhered to at all costs? It was clear to her even then that their jibes were not about her backpack—not really. The backpack simply let them see it clearly: how different she was from them.

Jessie let out a little snort of a laugh. The college kids in the classes she taught now all came to class with backpacks, the straps over both shoulders. Presumably "double strapping" was the fashion now.

"What?" Laurel asked.

Jessie looked up. "What what?"

"You laughed."

"Oh," Jessie said, shaking her head. "I was just thinking about something."

"About Emma?" Laurel busied herself laying out her word: *eclat*.

"Not really. Well, sort of. High school. Doesn't *eclat* have an accent mark?"

"Not necessarily. You were saying?"

"Nothing really. Just how the kids used to tease me for wearing a backpack, and now it looks like it's the cool thing to do."

"Ah, well. You've always followed your own path, Jessie."

Jessie shrugged. "I guess so."

"You have. You're like me, Jessie. We are who we are, and we're not afraid of that."

Jessie glanced at her mother. She opened her mouth to object, then immediately changed her mind. Instead, she picked up six letters from the little wooden tray in front of her.

"Take a look at this," she said, carefully arranging them on the board. "That's thirty-four points with the triple letter."

"Now that's more like it," Laurel laughed, picking up the pencil and score pad. "I was worried about you there for a minute, Jess."

CHAPTER 34

Emma

E mma didn't feel like a lesbian. Or maybe she did. She noticed that when she went into the coffee shop on Piedmont Avenue, her eyes sought out the dyke behind the counter; she hoped that she would be the one to take her order.

"So, do you *like* her?" she could almost hear her sister asking. "If you like her, you should ask her out."

Emma considered this. No, she didn't *like* her, not like that. Nor did she particularly want the other woman's interest. Emma just enjoyed the feeling that that woman might look at her and *know*.

It was the language that always tripped her up. Know *what*? That Emma was a lesbian? She didn't feel like a lesbian. In high school, when she had first started making out with her boyfriend, she had been shocked at how wet her underwear would be afterwards. The third time it had happened, she had snuck into Jessie's room and secretly borrowed her sister's copy of *Our Bodies, Our Selves*, then stayed up late that night reading until at last she had figured it out. Afterwards, she had felt slightly peeved to have been so in the dark. All that talk about blood and periods, but no one ever bothered to tell you what desire felt like.

Later, in college, when Emma had started having sex, it was never like that again. It was as if the act itself stifled the desire that had always risen in her so easily before. But the desire had been there, she couldn't deny that.

So how could she claim to be a lesbian?

She couldn't. She *didn't*. Mostly, she avoided the language. *Bi* felt too wishy-washy; *dyke* too burly. *Queer* was better—broader, anyway. And yet still it didn't fit right.

"I just feel more into women right now," she had told her sister recently, and really, that was the best way to put it. Emma would sit on the BART train on her way to work and quietly check the women out: their small, smooth hands, especially, and the lovely ridge of their collar bones. She loved the taut skin of their bellies where it disappeared into their jeans, the push of their breasts against their shirts. The irony wasn't lost on her; in college she would have reared up with indignation if a man had dared to objectify her so. And yet now she sat with her unread book open on her lap, secretly staring. It made her mouth go dry, watching those women, imagining.

"We're going to a show tonight," Meg told her over the phone. "Want to come?"

"Where?" Emma asked, although it didn't matter, really; she knew already she would go. Meg and her girlfriend, Becca, had been together since college, and Emma jumped at any chance to be with them. How she envied Becca. Becca had told Emma once that she had known that she was a lesbian since she was four years old. It had not been an easy road. It had taken her parents years to accept their daughter's sexuality, and of course high school had been a living hell. And still Emma envied her the easy knowledge of who she was, the unequivocal direction of her desires. Meg's path had been more similar to Emma's own, with a series of boyfriends that had ended only when, drunk at a basement party, she had found herself in Becca's arms.

That had been three years ago. Afterwards, Meg—whom Emma had known since their freshman year—had seemed almost entirely unchanged. If her new relationship with Becca had unleashed any crisis of identity, she had not let it show. Meg had stuck a rainbow sticker to the rear bumper of her pickup; occasionally, she had gone with Becca to meetings of the Queer Alliance at the student center. But, for the most part, Meg had appeared totally unaffected by the new direction her life had taken.

Emma had dared to ask her about it once. How did she explain it to herself? But Meg had only shrugged. "I'm only surprised I never saw it before," she'd said.

Emma thought back to her own younger days, wondering what hints she, herself, might have missed. There had been a few. An older girl in the advanced class at gymnastics whom ten-year-old Emma hadn't been able to keep her eyes off. A role model, her mother had said, smiling, when Emma had told her about the girl.

In junior high there had been another one. Tiffani had been Emma's classmate for years, although she could not have been called a friend, for Tiffani was in the "in" crowd and Emma was decidedly not. But Tiffani had always been nicer to Emma than the other popular kids were, and Emma's loyalty to her was absolute. With Tiffani alone would she share the answers from her homework, and, in return, Emma would get to stay close to her while she copied, close enough to smell her hairspray and admire the perfect smoothness of her shaven legs.

At the time, Emma had thought nothing of it. Tiffani was a role model, just like her mother had said of the other girl: a model of perfect girl-ness. Why shouldn't Emma admire that?

It was not, she thought, so very different from how she felt about Becca now. Becca was a bona fide lesbian. Emma was sure that Becca did not waste time agonizing, as Emma herself did, about why, or who, or for how long. Becca was tall and slim, with long, wavy blonde hair that she sometimes twisted into a knot at the back of her head. Emma guessed that Becca did not stare at herself in the mirror, wondering how a lesbian should wear her hair.

"I'd love to go," she told Meg now. "What kind of show is it?"

"You know, I'm not really sure," Meg said. "Becca knows more about it, and she's not here. Maybe drag? Erotica? No, really, I have absolutely no idea. But good, I'm glad you're going to come."

Emma suspected that Meg was just being polite. She rarely saw the couple now. Meg and Becca lived in the city; they had a large circle of friends through Becca's job which did not include Emma. But Meg occasionally reached out to her, inviting her to the parties they hosted periodically at their enviable, rent-controlled apartment on the edge of Pacific Heights. Still, Emma knew that her friendship could never be as valuable to them as theirs was to her, and this knowledge disheartened her a little. But Emma was not proud. She was glad to be included; she had no other lesbian friends. She would be happy to go to this show with them, whatever it was.

The club was in the Mission. When Emma entered, the show had not yet begun, although the room was already full. She scanned for Meg and Becca among the clusters of women gathered around the stage, but saw immediately that they were not there. Feeling self-conscious, she weaved through the crowded tables toward a small empty one she had spotted along the wall. She sat down and began to survey the crowd.

It was mostly couples, Emma noticed. All over the club, women had their arms draped around each other or their fingers jammed into the back pockets of their girlfriends' jeans. Emma sat alone. At a table near her, a slender woman with a pixie cut sat with her back toward her. Emma watched the soft feathers of hair at the base of her neck, the way they moved across the pale skin of her nape every time she turned her head. Beyond her, she could see the door of the club. She watched it, waiting uneasily for Meg and Becca to appear.

"Waiting for someone?" a voice said. Emma started.

She nodded. "Just some friends."

"Can I buy you a drink?"

The woman was heavy-set, with a broad face and a boy's cut. Emma hesitated.

"What, bull dykes not your type?" she asked seriously, but with a note of belligerence in her voice. Then, before Emma could even think how to respond, the woman burst out laughing.

"I'm kidding! Boy, you should have seen your face. No offense, but you're not my type either, so don't get all worked up. You just looked lonely. And, from the looks of it, we're about the only single girls in here."

Emma smiled. "Yeah. I noticed. Why is that? I'm Emma, by the way." She extended her hand.

"Lily. Nice to meet you."

As her hand disappeared in the other woman's, Emma let out a little laugh.

"What? Don't I look like a Lily to you?" The large woman batted her eyelashes.

Emma shook her head. "Not really. But seriously, why is it only couples in here?"

"How did you find out about it?"

Emma smiled. "From a couple."

"It's lesbian bed death."

"What?"

Lily grinned. "Pardon my asking, but are you a dyke?"

"I . . . I don't know. I guess so."

"I thought as much. Baby dyke, right? May I?" Lily gestured to the empty chair at Emma's table, and Emma nodded.

"Lesbian bed death, my dear," she went on, sitting down, "is the unfortunate but widespread phenomenon endured by lesbians across the country—perhaps the world? Some of us, unfortunately, just seem to stop doing it."

Emma glanced back at the neck of the woman she had been watching. She imagined tracing her tongue along the feathery line of hair, her hands cupping the ample breasts beneath her shirt. A flash of desire shot through her. Lesbian bed death—no, it wouldn't happen to her.

Lily was watching her. "Mind if I ask . . . Ever had a girlfriend?"

Emma nodded, blushing.

"Her first, too?"

Emma nodded again.

"How long?"

"Five months."

"And what happened?"

Emma shrugged. "It was when I was in college. We went our separate ways, I guess." She was embarrassed by the truth. The semester had ended; she and Ana had had different summer plans. Ana had returned to her hometown on the coast to work at a bookstore. She mentioned casually in an early letter that her high school flame was also in town. When the letters turned chatty and infrequent, Emma had read between the lines. There had been no drama, no hard feelings. When she and Ana saw each other back on campus in the fall, they had hugged like old friends, but that had been the end of it. Their paths had rarely crossed again.

"No time for bed death then, I guess," Lily said.

"No. But what does, um, what does lesbian bed death have to do with—" Emma thrust out her chin at the room. "With this?"

"Oh, come on. It's porn. You know. Spices things up a little."

"This is going to be porn?"

Lily laughed. "Porn, erotica—what's the difference?"

"Emma!" It was Meg. She was holding her black, curly hair back from her forehead with one hand and maneuvering her way through the tables to where Emma sat. Becca, behind her, was almost a head taller. She wore a tailored, button-down shirt that accentuated her lovely chest. Lucky Meg, Emma thought, glancing at the buttons.

"Hey," Meg said. "Sorry we're late. Becca wanted to drive and it took us forever to find parking." She turned toward Lily. "Hi. I'm Meg. And this is my girlfriend, Becca."

Lily stood up to shake Becca and Meg's hands, then gestured toward her chair. "You guys can have this one. Emma, it was nice meeting you."

"Wait," Meg protested, "you don't have to—"

"That's okay. I was just keeping Emma company. But the show's about to start. I'm gonna rush the stage." She winked at Emma and made her way through the crowd.

"Who was that?" Meg asked, watching her.

"Lily," Emma said. "We just met."

Later, Emma supposed she should have been more prepared. After all, Lily had called it porn. Emma wasn't sure what she had expected, exactly—some lesbian version of a strip club, she supposed, with half-naked dancers getting dollar bills stuffed inside their panties. But she had *not* expected the enormous strap-on dildo that the performer in the first act released from her pants.

Her partner—*in life, or just the act*? Emma wondered—dropped to her knees in front of her and took it into her mouth. The crowd roared while the woman on her knees licked and sucked and groaned. Emma winced involuntarily. She searched the faces of the women in the crowd. Most were grinning, some laughing, a few shouting encouragement. Emma didn't get it. The last thing she would want to do with a woman in bed was give her fake penis a blow job. She glanced at her watch. It was already close to eleven. If she had stayed at home tonight, she would already be in bed.

The next act was tamer. A curvaceous woman with a head of wild black curls did a burlesque-style striptease. She worked the crowd easily; it was an easy crowd to work. Emma clapped and smiled when clapping and smiling were appropriate, but instead of feeling one with the audience, she felt somehow set apart. She saw the back of Lily's head near the stage, could imagine the uncomplicated enjoyment on her face as she watched the act. Emma glanced back up at the dancer, who was spinning the tassel pasties on her two enormous breasts. The crowd whooped.

Again, Emma looked at her watch. She suddenly wanted desperately to be home. She regretted her decision to take BART. It would take her at least forty-five minutes to get home, longer if she had to wait for a train. As the act ended, she swallowed the last of her drink and tapped Meg on the shoulder.

Both she and Becca turned. "I'm out of here," she said.

"What? Why?"

"Just tired, I guess. And I'm on BART, so it'll take me a while to get home."

"If you want to hang out for a while, we can take you home," Becca said. "It's not a problem."

"That's okay. I'm happy to take BART."

Becca nodded. "Just be careful."

"I will."

Emma paused at the door to the club, looking back to where Lily stood by the stage. She wanted to at least wave good-bye, but the woman's broad back was still toward her. She pushed through the door into the cool evening air.

Outside, Emma was surprised by the number of people on the streets. She buttoned up her jean jacket and felt her pocket for her wallet. As she walked to the station, she passed three panhandlers and heard one casual catcall, but she didn't feel unsafe. There were so many people.

At the station in Berkeley, it was different. The few people who had gotten off at her stop headed in the opposite direction, and Emma walked home on empty streets. She tried to walk quickly, purposefully. When she passed a man alone, his hands pushed deep into the pockets of his corduroy jacket, she made eye contact and nodded hello, but after they passed each other, she glanced

back, just to make sure he hadn't turned. She picked up her pace
a little, hating her nervousness, how it jarred with the peace of
the evening air, ruining it. She wished she had left her bike at
the station. She imagined how much better she would feel if she
were biking home, free from these ridiculous nerves. This was *her*
neighborhood, she chided herself. Why did she feel so nervous in
her own neighborhood? She didn't want to feel this way.

It was only when she turned onto her short block that she felt
herself relax. She glanced up, hoping to see stars, but there was
only a low canopy of clouds, tinted gray-yellow with the lights
of the city. She ran up the three steps to her stoop and let herself
in.

It was almost eleven the next morning when Emma's phone rang.

"Hello?"

"Emma? It's Becca. I just wanted to make sure you made it
home okay last night." Her voice sounded gravelly.

"I did. Are you sick?"

"No, I just woke up. We ended up staying out later than we'd
planned. You missed a great show."

Emma shrugged. "Yeah? Oh well . . . Honestly? I wasn't that
into it. I mean, do you get it, Becca? Why would . . ." There she was,
tripping over the words again. But she went on anyway. She still
felt unsettled by what she had seen the night before, and wanted
to talk about it with someone. She had called her sister earlier that
morning, but Jessie had said little more than, "Wow, that *is* weird,"
and "I can't even imagine," as Emma had tried to describe to her
the two acts that she had seen.

Becca, on the other hand, had been there. And she was a lesbian. Emma plowed ahead.

"Why would lesbians . . . Why would women who love women
want to suck a dildo? Actually, why would *anyone* want to suck a
dildo? I just don't *get* it."

There was a pause on the other end of the line. "I mean—" Emma began again, but Becca interrupted her.

"It's just play, Emma," she said. "Personally, I don't want to blow a dildo either, but I do get it. It's . . . Look, it's just a . . . it's an appropriation of male power, right? It's a way to, you know, reconfigure the power dynamics of sexuality."

Emma sighed. "You sound like a women's studies textbook," she said.

There was another pause. "Yeah? Well, anyway, I'm sorry you didn't like it. But, I'm gonna go, okay? I need to make some coffee. We just wanted to make sure you'd gotten home okay."

"Thanks. Yeah."

Hanging up the phone, Emma felt worse. She knew she had somehow offended Becca without meaning to. For what did she know, really, of lesbian sex? Lily was right. She was a just a baby dyke; all those heated make-out sessions with Ana didn't count for much, really. She worried that she had sounded belittling, and almost called Becca back to apologize. But then she thought of the phone ringing in their light-filled apartment, Becca making coffee, Meg probably still lounging in bed, her dark curls mussed and sexy, and she dismissed the idea at once.

The picture that had formed in Emma's mind—of Meg and Becca's lazy Sunday morning, together in their apartment, loath to be disturbed—did not lighten her mood. Emma could feel her spirits sink. Usually, Emma cherished living alone; it was a rare thing here in the Bay Area, with rents as high as they were, and Emma did not take it for granted. In general, she loved the freedom of her tiny studio apartment, each day hers to do with as she would. But there were times, like this morning, when she felt her solitude not as a buoy but as a weight. Glancing out her window, she could see people in the street below, walking in twos and threes, heading to brunch or church or who knows where. Even to the solitary figures her mind gave some purpose or destination: a friend waiting at a bakery or café, a partner at home.

She could hear noises in the apartment below her, too—footsteps and muffled voices. On a morning like this, the city seemed made up of millions of little clusters. Meg and Becca, the couples on the streets, her downstairs neighbors doing whatever it was they did. They were all like little molecules, each person linked to another by an invisible bond, while she was an atom, alone.

Emma shook her head at the thought. She knew she had no reason to feel sorry for herself. She was not friendless; her solitude here had been her choice, and it was a choice she knew she would make again. Yet the sense of otherness she had felt at the show last night still colored her mood and gave an unfamiliar weight to her aloneness.

Throughout the morning, she thought of Becca's words on the phone, and gradually, her mood lightened. Maybe what she had seen last night wasn't about trying to be something else, as Emma had thought at first. It had seemed to her, then, that the performers had been merely simulating roles—roles that Emma had assumed most lesbians eschewed. But maybe, ultimately, that wasn't the point. Maybe they weren't simulating the roles as much as claiming them. Maybe it was just a way to turn erotica on its head, to take some small portion of its power for themselves.

When she looked at it like that, she could understand what Becca meant. She could even begin to see what Lily, and the others, had seen in the show. It didn't turn her on, but at least she was getting it, she thought.

CHAPTER 35

Jessie

Months passed. Laurel's phone calls grew more frequent as the conception of a child did not proceed as planned. Jim's graphs of Sue's temperature still looked reassuringly like the ones in the back of the fertility book they had bought at the local bookshop. So what was the problem? They didn't understand it. Sue began to use ovulation predictor kits, and when the blue smiley face appeared on the stick, Sue's initial was immediately penned in on the intimacy calendar. But even with these perfectly timed efforts, Sue's temperature continued to dip on the twenty-eighth day of her cycle, her period arriving predictably the next morning. Increasingly frustrated, the threesome did not wait long before making an appointment at the Center for Reproductive Science in Minneapolis. Sue was forty-five; time was of the essence.

When Laurel called Jessie the evening after the appointment, Jessie was already in bed, struggling to keep her eyes open to finish an article on the role of microbes in digestion in one of the scientific journals piled on the floor by her bed. When she had moved into this house, she had intended to buy a frame for the futon mattress where she slept, but she had never gotten around to it. Sleeping on the floor also meant she hadn't needed to buy a bedside table. She picked up her new cell phone from the floor beside the magazines and fumbled with the buttons.

"Hi, Mom," she said, moving the phone to her ear.

"Jessie? How'd you know it was me?"

"I finally got a cell phone. It tells you who's calling."

"Oh. Interesting. I woke you, didn't I?"

"No. I was just reading." Jessie laid the magazine on its pile by the bed and leaned back on the pillow she had propped against the wall.

"Well? How did it go?" she asked.

There was a brief pause. "Not well. But . . . you sound tired. We can talk about this in the morning."

"No, it's fine. Tell me. What did the doctor say?"

"Well, to make a long story short, it turns out Sue has endometriosis."

"When the uterine lining grows—"

"Yes," Laurel interrupted her. "Uterine tissue grows outside of the uterus. Sue has always had very painful periods, you know." She said this as if she had known Sue for years, and Jessie felt a twinge of irritation with her mother.

"And so? Can they treat it? Do they think that's why she's not getting pregnant?"

Laurel sighed. "No, and well, yes. Surgery is an option for some women, but the doctor didn't think Sue was a good candidate."

"No?"

"Well, her age, you know. He didn't think that even if they did the surgery, which can be very invasive . . . Well, the odds don't look good."

Now Jessie sighed. "Oh." Was that a hint of relief she felt? "I'm sorry, Mom. That must have been hard to hear. Especially for Sue."

"Yes, it was. We are very disappointed."

"I bet." Jessie cast around for the right thing to say. "Tell Sue I'm sorry," she said, and she meant it. She scooted down on the pillow until she was almost horizontal. She knew that after she hung up the phone she would not pick up the magazine again.

"You know, Mom," she said. "Maybe it just wasn't meant to be."

"What wasn't?" Laurel's voice sounded surprised, defensive.

"Oh, you know. You three having a child."

Laurel snorted. "Oh, we're still planning on having a child."

"You're going to try to adopt?"

"Oh, no. Sue may not be able to conceive naturally, but she can still carry a child."

"Mom, I'm sorry. I'm not following you." Jessie glanced at the clock by her bed, calculating how many hours until her alarm went off, how much sleep she'd get if she were to fall asleep right now.

"The doctor recommended in vitro. Fertilization. They make an embryo and implant it in the woman's—"

"Mom, I know what in vitro is."

"Oh. Of course you do."

"Well? Go on."

"Well," Laurel hesitated. "Even though Sue is technically still fertile, human eggs are just not that . . . that . . . that *robust* at her age."

"Really," Jessie said dryly. She was amazed that they hadn't considered this before. A woman's eggs, formed inside the female fetus while still in utero, were precisely the age of the mother. So Sue's eggs were forty-five, almost forty-six. It wasn't impossible, but Jessie did not doubt the doctor's reluctance.

"So, what did he suggest?" she asked. She smiled to herself, imagining the scene at the doctor's office. All three of them would have been there, of course. Jim, with his wiry frame and straggly red hair, Sue in her formless jeans and thrift-store button-down, Laurel in a monochrome, polyester-blend sweat suit and her gray mullet tied back into a ponytail. What had they told the doctor, she wondered? Absolutely everything, she was sure; they would not have considered anything less than full disclosure.

"Well," Laurel said. "We'll need an egg donor."

Jessie pushed herself back up to sitting and took a sip of water from the Nalgene bottle she kept by her bed. She suddenly felt much more awake.

"Oh?"

"Yes."

There was a pause.

"And?" Jessie prompted.

Laurel laughed uncomfortably. "Well, we are very picky, you know. We don't want our child to have the genes of just anyone."

"Well, it . . . the baby, I mean. It'll have Jim's genes anyway, won't it?"

"Well, of course. But that's just half, isn't it?"

Jessie shrugged. "It's better than nothing, right?"

"Ha. You sound like the doctor."

"Why? What did he say?"

"He said all humans share ninety-nine point nine percent of their DNA anyway."

Jessie laughed. "Well, that's true, isn't it? It's a good point."

"Well, as Sue pointed out to him, we share ninety-nine percent of our DNA with chimpanzees, too. But that's not the point either. It's the point one percent we care about." There was a brief pause. "Wouldn't you?"

"Wouldn't I what?"

"If you were going to have a child, wouldn't you want to know she had your genes?"

"Honestly, Mom, I don't know. I've never given it much thought. But I know that lots of people do in vitro with egg donors. And you can look at profiles of the donors, I'm sure. You can try to match—"

"Oh, we don't care about hair color."

"What then?"

"Oh, Jessie. Don't be obtuse. It's just that not everyone is as . . . We don't want just anyone's . . . Oh, come on. Don't you understand?"

Jessie sighed. "I guess."

"Thank you."

"So? If Sue's eggs aren't viable, and you don't want to use an egg donor—"

"We're not opposed to using an egg donor. We just don't want eggs from an *unknown* donor."

"So you want someone you know, someone smart enough—"

"Jessie."

"It's okay. I get it. You want someone—someone whose genes you wouldn't mind your child inheriting—to donate her eggs."

"Exactly."

"Well, do you have anyone in mind? They'd have to be pretty young, wouldn't they?" How many young women did Laurel know well enough to ask for this kind of thing?

"Yes."

There was a moment's silence on the line. "Jessie? I hope this isn't too much to ask. And of course you can say no. We would totally understand. But we did think of you."

"What?" Jessie said reflexively, although she had understood immediately. Laurel wanted her to donate her eggs. She saw instantly that it made perfect sense to her mother. Jessie was young. She was healthy. She was bright. She was a known donor. But more than that, Jessie shared half her mother's DNA. If Jessie was the donor, this baby would be—genetically, at least—even more related to Laurel than it would be to Sue. Laurel would get her stake.

"Jessie? You don't have to answer now, of course. All I am asking is that you think about it."

Jessie didn't know what to say, so she said nothing. Her mind reeled.

"Are you there?"

"Yes."

"Jessie, you don't have to do it if you don't want to. But just think about it. It would be so perfect. Jim would be the father—we know he's got good genes. Sue would carry the baby. And—if you say yes, of course—I'd be the genetic grandmother and co-parent. Plus, we'd love to have your genes, you know."

"They're half yours, Laurel," Jessie said dryly. "That's why you want them."

Laurel laughed shrilly. "Well, that's part of it. I won't deny it. But your father's a smart man, too. I'll give him that."

"Well, you certainly didn't mind passing on his genes the first time around."

"What's that supposed to mean?"

"Nothing. Just that you must have thought his genes were good enough for your children the first time you got pregnant."

There was a brief pause, which made Jessie doubt, not for the first time, that her mother had given much thought to getting pregnant at all. Jessie did not regret her birth—how could she? Still, she knew a small part of her blamed her parents for it. How could they have been so foolish as to have a child when they were not committed enough to make their marriage work?

"Of course I did," Laurel was saying. "And I was right, wasn't I? You two girls turned out perfectly. You're beautiful, athletic, brilliant . . ."

Jessie snorted. "You don't have to flatter me, Laurel."

"I mean it. Just look at you."

"Okay, Mom."

"Will you at least think about it?"

"Yes. I'll think about it."

"That's all I ask. Just think about it."

"I said I would."

Again, there was silence on the line.

"Mom?"

"Yes?"

"It's late. I was about to go to bed."

"Of course. I'm so sorry. And you sounded so sleepy. Is everything okay? I should have asked before. I was just so preoccupied with all of this—"

"I understand, Mom. Everything's fine. I just want to go to sleep now."

"Okay. Well, goodnight, then."

"Goodnight."

"Jessie?"

"Yes?"

"Thank you."

"For what?"

"Oh, I don't know. For considering it. For being such a wonderful daughter."

"Okay, Mom. Goodnight."

"Goodnight."

Jessie silenced her phone and turned off the light. She lay back against her pillow and closed her eyes, but all her sleepiness was gone. Her mind raced. With a sigh, she turned the light back on and picked up the copy of *Science* she had put down when Laurel called. But even as her eyes dutifully followed the lines of words, her brain refused to register them. Instead, it returned again and again to her mother's question. She glanced at the clock again. It was almost midnight, and even if she managed to fall asleep in the next half hour, she'd get barely six hours. She anticipated the exhaustion she would feel tomorrow afternoon—she had a microbiology lab to teach from one until four—and felt a stab of irritation at her mother. Laurel could have waited until the morning, at least.

Twenty minutes later, Jessie was still awake, the microbe article unfinished on the floor. Sighing, Jessie climbed out of bed and walked into the dark kitchen. She heated some milk on the stove and sat with it in the large armchair she had been thrilled to find at the Salvation Army. It had big armrests where the upholstery had worn smooth, and she rested the mug of steaming milk there while she pulled a blanket over her legs.

Now that she was up, Jessie didn't mind how late it was. She liked the silence of the night at this time of year, the busy chatter of summer nights behind them. The living room was dark except for a soft glow from behind the glass of the wood stove. The fire she had lit this evening had burned down to a few red embers, but she did not get up to add another log.

She plucked the dimpled skin of the hot milk with her thumb and forefinger and dropped it into her mouth. The film stuck to her teeth; she took a small sip of milk.

She settled back in the chair, cradling the cup in her hands, blowing on it softly. For a moment, she saw herself as an outsider would: the cozy chair and steaming milk, the dying fire and warm throw, and she thought of how serene she must look. She did not feel serene. Again, a flush of anger at Laurel swept over her. Why had she brought this up tonight?

But Jessie knew she could not wholly blame Laurel for her own thoughts. She could not blame her for the memories that would not let her sleep. For Laurel's question had stirred up the mire of Jessie's past, and now a memory bobbed again and again to the surface no matter how she tried to turn her thoughts.

Three years ago, she was dating a man she had met outside of Albuquerque. She had been hitchhiking home after a weekend backpacking trip in the Sandia Mountains. She was wearing the one pair of clothes she had brought with her, and they were grubby and rank. Her fingers were streaked with soot from the temperamental backpacking stove she had had to disassemble yet again that morning before it had begrudgingly heated the water for her morning cup of tea and bowl of instant oatmeal. Her unwashed hair hung heavily from her scalp.

Jessie did not mind these things for herself. Indeed, she relished in them, the same way she relished in her sweat-soaked clothes after a hard run, the satisfying grime that clung to her after a morning digging in the garden. They were the tangible imprint of two days spent the best way she knew how, the shower that awaited her at home the exclamation point to her weekend. And yet, Jessie had to force herself to hold out her thumb as she hiked along the highway. After all, she could not walk the fifty miles home. It was not the risks of hitchhiking, even alone, that gave her pause; long ago she had resolved not to be afraid. But she did not welcome the self-consciousness that she knew would come unbidden once she was in another's presence. By herself, she felt wild, burly, free. But enter another human being and she knew the high would end. She would immediately be transformed from glorious wood sprite to smelly hitchhiker. However inevitable, it was not a prospect that she relished.

Jessie walked along the shoulder of the road with her back to oncoming traffic, her hitching hand almost at her hip. She hoped a pickup might stop, so that she could ride in the back, the wind in her greasy hair, alone. When a motorcycle stopped instead, she felt a rush of anxiety. She was, at once, embarrassingly aware of her body odor, her unwashed hair.

The motorcycle rider flipped up the visor on his helmet. Brown eyes took her in. "Hey. Where you headed?"

Jessie felt another stab of discomfort. He was young—her own age, more or less. She looked down the highway ahead of them.

"Albuquerque. But it's okay. I've got my backpack, so . . . Thanks anyway."

At that moment a truck appeared on the highway, approaching them. Jessie stuck out her thumb deliberately, hoping the gesture would underscore her point: he could be on his way.

"I'm headed there, too," he said instead. "And we can strap your pack to the back, no problem."

Reluctantly, she agreed to the ride. She shrugged the pack off her back and stepped away as the air circulated under her arms where the straps had clung. She blanched when he pulled a leather motorcycle jacket and spare helmet from the motorcycle's small storage compartment, holding them out to her.

"Maybe this isn't the best idea," she wavered. "I'm filthy." She put her hand to her hair self-consciously.

"Oh, don't worry. They've seen worse, I assure you. I'm Mike." He held out his hand.

"Jessie." She was surprised by how heavy his gloved hand felt in hers.

She put the jacket and helmet on reluctantly, but once they were on, she felt better. The leather of the jacket emitted a pleasant, animal smell, and she felt contained inside it, safe and separate. The helmet, she realized with increasing relief, would make conversation virtually impossible. This would not be so different from riding in the bed of a pickup after all, she thought. She felt her body begin to relax, and when Mike finished fastening on her pack and motioned for her to get up behind him, a thrill of anticipation ran through her.

The ride home took her breath away. The wind whipped against her face, scouring her skin; she forgot about how dirty she was. She felt wild and adventurous, even sheepishly cool inside the borrowed badassed-ness of the leather jacket.

When Mike pulled up in front of her little house and she awkwardly climbed down off the motorcycle and handed the helmet back to him, she was beaming.

He grinned at her. "Makes you feel like a different person, doesn't it?"

"Yeah."

He seemed to hesitate so she just stood there, grinning back at him, until she realized she was still wearing the jacket. She didn't want to take it off. An hour ago, she had wanted nothing more than to be home, alone with a cup of tea and a novel. Now, she didn't want her adventure to be over.

"Are you in a hurry?" she asked suddenly. "I could shower . . . I'll buy you dinner if you want. As a thank you, I mean. There's a great taco truck near here."

"Sounds great," he said, his eyes sweeping over her. "I love tacos."

CHAPTER 36

Jessie

Mike the Motorcycle Man, as Jessie had first called him to herself, was not her type. But neither, it turned out, was he the type she would have expected from his motorcycle and black leather. His hands, when he took off his gloves, were soft, almost pudgy. He was not the rugged, back-to-the-earth type she usually fell for, but neither was he the badass motorcycle man she had first taken him for. It seemed, in fact, that he wore his bike gear as little more than a costume, a convincing enough disguise for a twenty-something-year-old man who still lived in his parents' suburban basement, had a meaningless job in a warehouse, and spent most of his free time playing what, as far as she could tell, was basically the computerized equivalent of Dungeons and Dragons. Although it would be months before she would admit it to herself, the more she learned about Mike, the less appealing he became.

Nevertheless, for a few months she relished in the thrill of leaning into curves taken at breath-catching speeds, the delicious moment when she pulled off the borrowed helmet and shook out her hair. When she was with Mike, she referred to herself, half-mockingly, as his motorcycle bitch, and oddly, when she zipped up the black leather jacket he soon let her borrow full-time, she felt more feminine than she had in her life.

Jessie knew enough about herself to recognize all of this for the performance it was. The jacket and helmet were little more than a costume she enjoyed losing herself in on a Friday night. But just as with all costumes, there was also the lightness she felt when she took it off and donned again the Goodwill jeans and old road race T-shirts that were her usual attire.

Still, the thrill she felt in those first months had easily encompassed Mike, and she had looked forward to their time together. She recognized in him the awkward, nerdy boys whose friendship was the only thing that had made high school tolerable for her, and even once his allure had begun to fade, she felt for him a sympathetic affection that fueled them through another few months together. And although Mike had almost zero interest in the things that inspired her—mountains, gardening, science—he was, like her, a voracious reader, so they never lacked for things to talk about.

Jessie was not, in general, judgmental about the bodies of others, sensitive as she was to the ways her own body might be judged. She looked away from the hairy, white-pink belly that pushed out from beneath Mike's T-shirt, the squishy feel of his upper arms. For a while, she relished in the unexpected pleasure of being in bed with a man on his way toward fat: the way, in bed with him, her own body seemed especially lithe and firm, the gasping thrill of his weight on her. And Mike was good in bed in the way she had found most nerdish men to be: attentive, eager to please, almost grateful in his pleasure.

Still, after five months together, it was all wearing thin. She still enjoyed riding through the desert hills on the back of his bike, and their sex made up for in reliability what it lacked in passion. But Jessie had begun to feel a stab of annoyance when she heard his voice on her answering machine. She was ready to move on, she knew, but, disinclined to confrontation, she bided her time. The spring semester was winding down, and come June she would be moving to Missoula for the summer for an internship at the University of Montana. It would be a natural break.

And then one day, she found she couldn't stand the smell of him. There was a sickly odor emanating from his left ear; she gasped in disgust when he hugged her. At the end of their evening, she did not invite him in, exaggerating how early she had to be up the next morning, how tired she was. She watched him peel away down her street with an overwhelming sense of relief. But a few minutes later, when she opened the compost container to take it outside, she gagged at the smell. Her heart raced as an unwelcome thought immediately took shape in her mind.

She took the calendar down off the kitchen wall. When had she last had a period? As she counted the squares, she felt somewhat reassured; she was not due for another few days. Still, she tossed and turned as she lay in bed that night. Maybe Mike's ear did smell bad—hadn't he complained of an earache only a few days before? But Jessie was not squeamish; compost had never made her gag before. Finally, she pulled on some sweatpants and rode her bicycle to the 24-hour Walgreens a mile from her house.

She almost reconsidered when she saw the cost. Almost twenty dollars for the early-detection pregnancy tests, and on the twenty-fourth day of her cycle, they promised only sixty percent accuracy. She and Mike hadn't been that sloppy with birth control, she thought. Surely her period would come. Still, there was no point ruining her weekend with needless worry. She paid cash for the test, not meeting the cashier's eye.

She read the entire instruction booklet when she got home, and even though it recommended testing with the first urine of the morning, she decided to use one of the two enclosed sticks that night. She followed the directions exactly, catching her pee in a plastic cup, then submerging the stick in her urine. She perched on the edge of the tub, watching the seconds pass on her digital watch. She did not look at the test until the requisite two minutes had passed, but when she did, her heart sank. The pale blue cross was unmistakable. She was pregnant.

She barely slept that night. The kitchen wall calendar was on the floor by her bed. She'd marked the date when she'd gotten her last period, then counted forward. She stopped when she reached thirteen, and her stomach lurched. The thirteenth day of her cycle had been last Wednesday; the timing couldn't have been worse. That afternoon Mike had been waiting for her outside the biology building when her class let out. She had been looking forward to the walk home, alone in the cool of the evening, but had done her best to hide her disappointment at the sight of him.

"It's such a nice night. I thought you might like a ride."

It *had* been exhilarating to race down the empty road, the pavement glowing almost silver in the moonlight. When they reached the BLM land north of town, he had slowed the bike and turned, without speaking, down an unlit gravel road. Jessie had said nothing, nor did she protest when a few minutes later, he stopped the bike and spread out a fleece blanket between the sage bushes. She recognized the blanket from his parents' house, which annoyed her; beneath it, the ground was lumpy and hard. But the moon hung in the sky like a polished silver dollar, and the cool desert air was scented with sage. She tried to put out of her mind all the reasons that she should be home by now, and to squelch the persistent irritation she felt with Mike. She recognized this drive, with the blanket under the full moon, as his best attempt at romance. She could sense him watching her for her reaction, and it had seemed cruel to ruin it for him. Soon enough it would all be over; why not try to enjoy the night?

And she had enjoyed it. She couldn't deny that, even now. But during the sleepless night after the pregnancy test, she groaned aloud in frustration—at herself, for putting off the breakup she knew was coming, and for foolishly acquiescing to Mike's desire, even when he had whispered apologetically that he'd forgotten the condoms. The condoms, she thought now with disgust, but not the blanket.

It was only nine days since that night, but, incredibly, she knew she would be counted as three and a half weeks pregnant. The zygote inside her was a microscopic raspberry, burrowing into the lining of her uterus, its cells relentlessly dividing. By nine o'clock tomorrow morning, when she told herself she could realistically expect the Planned Parenthood clinic to open on a Saturday, it would have almost twice as many cells as it did now.

She cried when, the next morning, her anxious call was picked up immediately by a recording. The clinic was open one Saturday morning a month, but today was not that Saturday.

The weekend felt endless. Jessie buried herself in her work. She turned off the ringer on her cordless phone and worked her way through the stack of grading for the Intro to Biology class that she was TAing that semester. When that was done, she forced herself to meticulously outline the journal articles her dissertation advisor had recommended. When she couldn't focus on the work, she cleaned her house or went for long runs, pushing herself harder than she ordinarily would, so that all her attention was required merely to make her legs keep up the pace. On Sunday evening, she tried to read but couldn't concentrate, so she biked the three miles to the video rental store and rented a documentary about the making of the Panama Canal. Forty minutes in, she fell into a dreamless, exhausted sleep.

She woke at seven and was immediately suffused with gratitude that the waiting was almost over. She called the clinic at ten until nine, thinking maybe someone would be in early and answer the phone, and, when they weren't, she called again at nine. At three minutes past nine, she finally reached a human being.

"We can get you in on Thursday at nine-thirty," the receptionist told her.

"Thursday! You don't understand. I've already waited . . ." She found she could not put into words the agony of the weekend.

"But isn't it best to take care of this as soon as possible?" she said instead.

"When was the date of your last period?" the woman asked.

"April nineteenth," she said, then waited impatiently through the silence.

"Ma'am? Even if you are pregnant, you're not even at four weeks. A few days won't make a difference."

"The zygote is doubling cells every twelve hours."

"Excuse me?"

"The cells in the zygote are constantly multiplying. After twenty-four hours, it will have four times the number of cells it does now. That means that by Thursday, it will—"

"Well, that may be," the receptionist interrupted her, "but you do realize that we're talking about something the size of a poppy seed? If that."

Jessie groaned. "Of course I realize. That's why I want to do it now."

"Well, I can put you on our cancellation list, if you'd like."

"Please. And, um, you'll . . . I mean, the doctor will do the procedure on Thursday, right? I just want to make sure—"

"Actually, Thursday is just for the consultation. They'll do an exam and a pregnancy test, but you'll have to come back for the—"

"Jesus. I thought you guys supported early—"

"Ma'am, I understand your sense of urgency. But no doctor would perform the procedure without doing an exam first. Plus, you have to be offered counseling, and there is a twenty-four hour waiting period."

Jessie sighed. She felt suddenly exhausted. "Fine. But can I go ahead and make the other appointment for Friday?" She could not stand the thought of enduring another weekend like this one.

After she hung up, she went to retrieve the wall calendar from the floor by her bed. She printed the times of her appointments on their respective squares. She had a meeting with her thesis advisor on Friday afternoon; she wondered if she should call and reschedule. But her advisor was a meticulous and impatient woman who always sounded vaguely irritated. She intimidated Jessie, who was not easily intimidated. No, she would keep the meeting. Jessie had made the appointment for ten o'clock; surely she would be fine by that afternoon.

Jessie had been fine, she remembered now, although the meeting with her advisor had not gone as she'd expected. It was that

Friday afternoon that Dr. Hartley, leaning back in her rolling chair and bringing her fingertips together, had said that she was disappointed with her. Jessie sat uncomfortably in front of her desk while her advisor flipped through the laboratory log.

"I was surprised, Jessie, by how seldom your name appears. My other doctoral students spend, on average, thirty percent more time in the lab than you. I have wondered about the discrepancy before, but I waited to speak up. You were such a promising candidate, Jessie. But I cannot dissemble. You are not, I am afraid, living up to your promise. You seem to . . . how should I put it? You seem to lack a *passion* for science."

Jessie had bristled at the insult. Of course she was passionate about science! But poring over the minute details of her research did not inspire her. She'd rather spend her Saturday in the woods of the high-country, appreciating science, than freezing in the over-air-conditioned lab, giving herself a headache with the minutiae and the measurements. She would rather be teaching cellular structure, Punnett squares, photosynthesis—anything at all, really—to confused and eager undergraduates than doing research. It wasn't just that she disliked the research, although that was certainly a part of it. It was that she had begun to suspect recently that she wasn't actually very *good* at it, and to wonder if her gift lay elsewhere.

Jessie didn't want to drown in the details of some narrowly focused research project. She wanted to paint the big picture of biology so that it came alive. She wanted to break it down and build it up again, so that her students saw, not the tedium of science, but the precision, the wonder, the beauty of it. Not passionate about science? Oh, Dr. Hartley had no idea.

Suddenly, sitting there in her advisor's office, burning with shame and indignation, a low ache deep in her gut, she understood. This wasn't what she wanted. It wasn't the science she wanted to give up; Jessie would never forsake the science. But what was the point of going on like this, of struggling for years in a lab to complete a dissertation, only so that she would be qualified to do more research? No. What she wanted was to teach; she was already more than qualified for that. And she was good at it. Her students had told her again and again: *This is the first time I've really understood . . . You make it all so clear . . . Will you be TAing anatomy, too?*

Walking home that afternoon, her mind had raced. She had made some excuse, some apology, to Dr. Hartley, but all the time she had been thinking that sooner or later she would have to tell her: this was over. For Jessie knew immediately, with a sweet certainty that cleared her mind, what she had to do. She would cancel the internship in Missoula. The prospect of two and a half more months in a lab now seemed intolerable. She would turn her unfinished doctorate into a master's and look for a teaching job at a community college. She was willing to go anywhere if it meant that she could make a career of teaching.

As she walked she put her hand to her belly, remembering her appointment at Planned Parenthood that morning. She felt a prick of guilt that it was today, of all days, that she should have the epiphany that would change the course of her career. But maybe it wasn't so coincidental after all, she thought. This morning she had chosen to keep her life her own; this afternoon she had decided to make that life match her truest self. It was both the least and the most that she could do. And it was, she realized with another ripple of guilt, a welcome relief to have something else to turn her mind to.

The abortion itself had quickly faded from her mind. Her biggest regret from that time was making such a hash of her relationship with Mike. She hadn't told him about the pregnancy; doing so would have required an intimacy that no longer felt tolerable to her. He had been baffled by her sudden change of heart, and had left weepy, desperate messages on her answering machine for weeks, which did not endear him to her.

"Oh, be a man," she had muttered once as his voice droned on, surprising herself with the sentiment, since she generally did not hold men to manliness any more than she herself aspired to femininity.

She had thrown away the "what to expect" literature the clinic had thrust on her as she'd left. Now that it was behind her, she felt no reason to be mournful. The tiny ball of cells aspirated from her uterus that Friday morning was not even an embryo yet. Every day fertility clinics across the country disposed of hundreds of similar blastocysts, treating them as they would any other clump of cells. Oh, there were a zillion things that happened every day in the name of science that could give you pause. Jessie would not allow herself to lose sleep over this.

But as the years had passed, she had sometimes found herself calculating. "How old would the child have been?" They were idle thoughts, mostly, that had only served to reassure her of her choice. She had been too young, and too selfish: she was just setting out on her own true path. And then there was the undeniable fact that she and Mike together would have been a disaster. If anything, she felt relieved at the collective misery that had been averted.

Mike, she knew, was married now. They were not in touch, but he included her on the electronic Christmas letter he e-mailed each December, which was always accompanied by a digital picture of him and his wife on a motorcycle. The first year he sent it, Jessie was sure she recognized the leather jacket his wife wore, and she felt a momentary pang of loss, not for Mike himself, but because it felt startlingly clear to her that she would never again be that girl.

Once, a few months before she left New Mexico, she had found a motorcycle jacket at her favorite thrift store. Its price tag, even secondhand, had surprised her, but she had fished a twenty-dollar bill out of her wallet and taken it to the register, suddenly eager to feel again that thrill of impersonation she had felt the first time she had put one on. But standing on the sidewalk outside the store in her hiking boots and black leather, she had felt conspicuous, foolish, and much too warm. The jacket had stayed on its hanger in the back of her closet. When, several months later, she had packed to move to Oregon, where she had been offered an adjunct teaching position at a community college in Pendleton, she had thrown it into the pile of clothes to take to the same thrift store where she had bought it.

CHAPTER 37

Jessie

The milk in the bottom of Jessie's mug was lukewarm now, the window of the wood stove dark. Jessie put the mug down and pulled the throw blanket up to her chest, snaking her arms beneath it.

"I did the right thing," she said aloud, as if to close the floodgates on the memories that washed over her.

Jessie was not religious, nor New Agey. Science was her religion, and if there were things that science could not explain, still this did not shake her faith. There would always be new frontiers, new revolutions of understanding. Her friends, even her colleagues, sometimes spoke of the universe as a kind of God, as in, "The universe offered me this opportunity, so I had to take it." She did not begrudge them this; we all make sense of our lives the best we can. But in her heart Jessie knew the universe to be indifferent to the struggles and aspirations of anyone. The universe merely provided the raw materials; it was up to us to build the life we wanted.

And yet, there was that cluster of cells that she had chosen to . . . Her mind would never settle on the right word for what she had done by not continuing with her pregnancy. She had no moral qualms about it; those were *her* cells, no more separate from her, no more human, than the egg that every month slipped undetected out of her body in a flood of menstrual blood.

Still, she could not deny that her choice had averted a life that could have been. And what was Laurel asking her but to make possible a life that otherwise would not be? She could not, in good faith, believe this, but still it felt to her as if she were being offered a chance for balance, the embryo she could make for Laurel standing in for the one she had disallowed. She did not need redemption; it wasn't that. And yet, strangely, the idea that she could help to bring about a new—and wanted—life calmed a disquiet in her that she could not name.

Jessie woke sometime before dawn shivering and with a crick in her neck, her body still sprawled in the armchair. She wrapped the throw around her and walked down the short hall to her bedroom, purposely thinking only of the warmth of her bed. Despite this, her mind immediately reached for all the thoughts that had kept her awake the night before. But once her body was horizontal at last and the sheets began to warm against her chilled skin, her mind stilled and she slept.

When she woke again the sky was bright and cloudless outside her window. She cringed when she saw the clock, vaguely remembering waking just enough to silence her alarm. Now, it was almost nine-thirty. In general, Jessie disliked sleeping late, disliked the feeling that she had missed the best part of the day. But today Jessie felt grateful for the extra hours of sleep. Despite her late night, she felt clear-headed and rested, her mind quiet but alert.

She made tea, carried it out into her small yard, and drank it while she studied her garden plot. The kale and spinach seeds she had planted last weekend were just beginning to sprout. Her small fall crop of greens always moved her, how they grew even as the days shortened and the light waned, as if racing in their slow and steadfast way the coming of the cold.

Only when she had gone back inside and finished her usual bowl of oatmeal, topped with blackberries she had picked herself, did she allow her mind to return to her mother's request. In the daylight, it did not seem as fraught as it had the night before. Her mother was asking her a favor, that was all. It was, she granted, a favor of some magnitude, but, really, was it that much to ask? She couldn't help but be flattered that Laurel wanted her genes. On the genetic level, it even made sense to her. This child, if it was to be, would share Jessie's mother. Generationally, it would be like a much younger sibling. A true biological brother or sister would share, statistically, half of Jessie's DNA. An embryo formed from her egg would also share half of her genes. So what difference was there, really? If she donated the egg for this child, she would be no more genetically related to it than she would be to a true sibling. What did it matter how their shared genes came to be?

Jessie stood at the sink for a long time, her dirty bowl in her hands, gazing through the small window above the sink. *Would it matter to her?* she wondered. If she did donate the egg, would she feel some maternal connection to the child? She forced herself to imagine a baby in Laurel's arms. Would she feel, in some undeniable way, that it was hers?

It was an effort to keep the picture in her mind, and almost immediately, she let it go. No, she felt no stirring of possession. Instead, she felt almost a repulsion, not of disgust, but as if she and this theoretical baby were similar poles on a magnet, gently pushing back against each other. No, Jessie thought, feeling strangely comforted by this image. No, the baby would not be hers.

Now Jessie's thoughts turned to Laurel. How much had it taken for her mother to ask her for this? She remembered the nervousness in Laurel's voice on the phone the night before; it had not been an easy call for her to make. Jessie felt a sudden surge of tenderness for her mother, for the chain of losses that had unraveled throughout Laurel's life. She thought of her mother's failed marriages, first to her father and then to Kent, and of her mother's despairing tears when Cactus had left her, too. Out of the chasm created by that last separation had crept a fear that Laurel would not allow to be assuaged: in the end, she would be unloved.

Jessie thought of her own solitary life. She had not had a serious relationship since she had moved to Oregon. Instead, she had her little house and garden, her students, the habits that sustained her: backpacking, running, reading, gardening. When she felt lonely, she crammed one of her two flowing skirts into her backpack and biked to the contra dance held at the college on Saturday nights. The music, the easy flirtation on the floor that lasted only until the end of the dance, the exhilaration of being swung almost off her feet—these things elated her. When she unlocked her bike at the end of the evening, the anticipation of the dark ride home alone elated her, too. Often she could feel her joy pushing so hard against her chest that she wanted to shout it out into the night.

Laurel, she knew, also knew such moments. Jessie remembered how they would both whoop after a long canter, grinning widely at each other until their cheeks hurt. Her sister knew them, too. "Like a bubble of life love in your throat," Emma had called the feeling once. Whether other people experienced life in quite that way, Jessie wasn't sure—perhaps they did. And yet, thinking of her mother and her sister, Jessie felt the web of their shared DNA, connecting them despite all the ways they had been severed from each other.

Still, that *joie de vivre* did not sustain Laurel as it did Jessie. Underneath there was always that gaping need for love. To such a need, Jessie could not relate; Jessie herself needed so very little beyond what she, alone, could provide. And yet Jessie saw what a powerful force it was for her mother. Again, she felt flooded with sympathy for Laurel, for the losses she had endured, yes, but even more for that deep well of need in her which seemed never to be filled.

And now, at last, Laurel seemed to have found her niche. She spoke of Jim and Sue as kindred spirits; she felt they understood her as no one had before. Miraculously, Laurel had stumbled across a family in which she felt that she belonged. And now they wanted to have a child.

Jessie thought of what it would mean to Laurel if she denied their request. Almost certainly, they would go to another egg donor. And if they did that, Laurel would be set, inevitably, just a little bit apart. Laurel would surely parent the child all the same, and yet Jessie did not doubt that her mother would forever feel the tenuousness of her ties to it. It might make no difference to Jim and Sue where they got the egg, so long as they were confident that their intelligence would not be diluted. But it would, Jessie knew, make all the difference in the world to Laurel.

Jessie could give her mother that. With one small cell, she could give her mother the chance to have her stake, to feel connected to her new family in a way that she would not feel without it. Jessie could imagine no gift her mother would value more, and thinking of it, she felt an excitement slowly rise in her. It was the perfect gift.

As with all perfect gifts, Jessie couldn't wait to give it. She put her bowl in the dish rack at last and went to find her phone.

On Sunday evening, Jessie's phone rang again. This time, it was Emma.

"Hi, Em," she answered. Jessie's heart beat a little faster. All weekend she had wondered if she would tell her sister about her decision, but she had not picked up the phone. Suddenly, an irrational fear seized her that Laurel had called Emma, that somehow Emma knew.

"Do you have a minute?" Emma asked, and Jessie's stomach lurched.

"Of course."

"Good. Because I really want to tell you something." Her sister's voice was bright with excitement, and Jessie breathed easier. Laurel never talked to Emma; of course she hadn't told her.

"Well? What is it?" she asked.

"Jessie, I met someone!"

"Really?" Jessie grinned. "Tell me."

"I can't believe it, Jessie. I really can't. She's just too perfect. Honestly, I didn't think it was possible."

"Oh! So she's a she."

"What? Why? Are you surprised?"

"I don't know. But . . . it doesn't matter. Go on."

There was a brief pause. "I forgot what I was saying."

"You didn't think it was possible."

"Oh yeah. Well, that's it, I guess. I just never thought I'd meet someone like her. I mean, I honestly never thought I'd meet a woman I liked who was also interested in me."

"But you did before, right? You met Ana."

Emma snorted. "Yeah, I guess. But that was in college, you know? Everyone's a L.U.G. in college."

"A lug?"

"Lesbian Until Graduation."

"Oh. I wasn't."

"OK, not everyone. But you know what I mean."

"I guess."

"Anyway, I always sort of thought Ana was an aberration. I never thought I'd meet someone else."

"Emma, don't be silly. It just takes time. Everyone feels that way."

"No, Jess. That's not what I mean. It's just . . . Do you remember that movie *Chasing Amy*?"

"I don't think—"

"You know, about the guy who starts dating the lesbian?"

"I don't think I saw it, Em."

"Well, there's this guy who starts going out with this really beautiful lesbian, and his roommate can't believe it. So he asks him, 'What do a lipstick lesbian, the tooth fairy, and Santa Claus all have in common?'"

"And?"

"That they don't exist. That there's no such thing as a lipstick lesbian. I saw that movie with Ana, and God, we were indignant. *We* were fem, and *we* were lesbians. But since then, I've wondered. I mean, how many really fem girls out there really *do* want to be with another woman? I mean, *be*, you know? Not just fool around 'cause they're bi-curious."

"Bi-curious?"

"Yeah, you know. Want to know what it's like and all that."

"Oh, right. But, Em, tell me about this woman you met. You still haven't said anything."

"That's just it, Jess. Katherine's *totally* fem. I mean, when I met her, I couldn't even believe she was a lesbian. We've laughed about it. She kept trying to come out to me—"

"Come out how?"

"Well, for example, she told me that she had written her senior thesis on lesbian poetry. You know, Audre Lorde, bell hooks? But I still wouldn't believe it."

"So what happened?"

"Well, Meg had introduced us. You know Meg, my friend from college?" Emma paused. "Come to think of it, Meg and Becca are both pretty fem."

"Emma, you were telling me about Katherine."

"Right. So I asked Meg later, 'Is Katherine queer?' And she asked me what planet I was living on. So, well, then I just called her."

"And?"

"And we went out to dinner last night." Emma sighed happily. "And then we kissed."

"And?"

"And nothing. But it was great." There was a momentary silence. "Jessie? You wouldn't believe her skin. I still can't believe it. It's *unbelievable*."

Jessie laughed.

"Seriously, her skin is . . . It's just so smooth. I don't think I feel like that."

"Feel like what?"

"So soft."

"Oh, Emma, stop."

"I'm serious. But anyway, Jess, what's going on with you?"

Jessie thought about her conversation with Laurel and her appointment at the fertility clinic in Portland next Monday, when they would do a baseline hormonal screening and an ultrasound of her ovaries. If everything went smoothly, the woman on the phone had told her, they would start her on meds as soon as her next cycle began, and harvest her eggs twelve to fourteen days after that. That was the verb they had used—harvest—as if her body were the earth, bearing fruit. Jessie felt slightly overwhelmed at how fast it would all happen. Within a month her decision would no longer be theoretical, an embryo formed from her egg implanted in Sue's womb.

It was on the tip of her tongue to tell Emma all of it, but she held back. She felt that she had spent the last few days in a bubble of clarity, of goodwill. When she had told Laurel that she would donate the eggs, her mother's gratitude had overwhelmed her. Even Sue had called to express her thanks. Never before had Jessie felt such magnanimity.

But Emma, she guessed, would not see it that way. And Jessie did not want her sister's perspective muddying the waters of her own clarity.

"Not much, really," she said vaguely. "So, what's Katherine like?" she added. "Besides soft?"

It was so easy to change the subject; Jessie would keep her secret to herself.

CHAPTER 38

Emma

Katherine and Emma had kissed just once before, as they stood in the narrow entryway of Katherine's apartment. They had met for dinner last Saturday in Bernal Heights, and though Katherine's apartment was in the opposite direction of the BART station where Emma would catch the train home, she had insisted on walking her home.

"That's ridiculous," Katherine had scolded her, laughing. She shook her head slightly, her straight blonde hair glancing across her shoulders. "I don't need you to walk me home. I do it all the time."

"I know," Emma had protested. "I don't mean it like that. But can't I just walk with you? I'm not ready to say goodbye yet."

Katherine had smiled and held out her hand. "Well, if you put it like that."

The feel of Katherine's hand in hers, so soft and small, had preoccupied Emma all the way to her apartment. They had walked in silence, which Emma was glad of, for she was unable to concentrate on anything but the smooth, narrow fingers laced inside her own. By the time Katherine gestured with her free hand to a small Victorian house, divided into duplexes— "That's where I live."—Emma was already wet with desire.

They had kissed easily that night, each moving toward the other without awkwardness, but after a few moments, Katherine had pulled away and smiled at her.

"Call me?" she had said.

Emma had nodded vigorously, trying to hide the disappointment she felt. She felt elated by their kiss, and yet the fact that Katherine had been the first to step away had wrenched something inside of her. She had had to bite her tongue to keep from asking if she could go inside with her. Instead, she had reached for the other woman's hand, kissed her palm, and hidden her face in it.

"Don't go yet," she had wanted to say then, but knew better. She couldn't let Katherine sense the need that had suddenly opened up in her. Instead, she had smiled lightly and said good-bye, turning to go even before the door had fully closed. She had walked to the corner without looking back, but once she was out of sight, she had let out a loud whoop of joy. "Katherine," she whispered. She could not believe her luck.

Their next date was a week later, in the East Bay, where they had dinner at a Thai restaurant on Piedmont Ave. It was still light when they left the restaurant, so Emma led Katherine to the small rose garden a few blocks away, hidden in a residential neighborhood.

"Wow," Katherine said. "This is beautiful. How did you find it?"

Emma grinned. "Isn't it? I was just running in this neighborhood one day, and I thought I'd see what was down this street." She was glowing with pride, as if she had planted the roses herself instead of merely stumbled upon them. "I love it here," she said, and bent down to smell an orange rose. She could not stop smiling.

As they meandered through the small garden, Emma kept sneaking glances at Katherine. She was petite, like Emma, with slender arms and legs. Her blonde hair was perfectly styled, her skin golden and smooth. As they walked, Katherine's hand found hers, and Emma felt her heart beat faster. She glanced around the garden; there was no one else there. When Katherine followed a path toward a mossy fountain, pulling Emma gently along with her, she felt her mouth go dry. She stopped and tugged on Katherine's hand, so that the other woman swung around to face her.

"What?" Katherine said, but her green eyes were bright and inviting: she knew. She parted her lips as Emma kissed her. Emma let go of Katherine's hand, releasing it only so that she could hold her face with both hands. Softly, she stroked the fine hair behind her ears, followed the smooth curve of her jaw with her thumbs. Almost of their own accord, her hands moved down Katherine's neck to trace the raised ridge of her collarbone, the neckline of her tank top. She could hear Katherine give an almost inaudible gasp beneath her kiss, and Emma felt she couldn't stop. She slipped her fingers beneath the fabric of the tank top, felt the silky fabric of Katherine's bra against her fingertips.

"Emma," Katherine whispered against her lips. "Stop."

It took all of Emma's will to stop her fingers, to bring them back to rest on the sides of Katherine's neck, where she held her gently. "Why?"

"We can't. Not here."

"Why?" Emma said again. She looked around them. "There's no one here." She moved one hand down the side of Katherine's body, felt her palm graze the outer curve of her breast. She heard Katherine's sharp intake of breath, and taking it for assent, she began to cup her hand around it.

Katherine's hand stopped her, and for a second Emma felt the first dark tendrils of despair. Was it to be over so soon, she thought. It had been impossible to believe, really, that a girl like this would let Emma touch her.

But Katherine did not let go of her hand, just moved it gently to her waist. She moved in to kiss Emma, her tongue dipping between her lips. "Not here," she whispered.

"Where?"

As soon as Emma's apartment door closed behind them, Katherine was in her arms, her body pushing against her. Emma's hands reached for her: her face, her neck, her shoulders. She moved them down the sides of Katherine's body to her waist and left them there. Emma did not want to be rebuked again; she felt she couldn't bear it. When, after a moment, Katherine touched her hand, Emma's stomach fell, but she was not surprised. Katherine's face against hers, her rapid breaths, the tight curves of her body beneath her hands—it was all the stuff of dreams. If this were to be the end so soon, well, that was the way of dreams.

But Katherine did not step away. Instead, she moved Emma's hand with her own until it was pressed against the fullness of her breast. She let out a soft moan, and Emma felt Katherine's nipple harden beneath her palm. Emma let out her breath.

"I can't believe it," she said softly.

"Can't believe what?"

"You. You're so . . . beautiful."

"Shhh."

"You are."

"Shhh."

Emma smiled and whispered in her ear, but after that neither of them spoke.

That night, after Katherine had gone, Emma lay awake in bed. She felt electrified. It was all real, it had happened right here, and yet it all felt so incredible, so unlikely. That Katherine—so petite, lithe, feminine, soft—that such a woman should have been here, in Emma's bed, offering herself to Emma, pushing against her, wanting her . . . Emma had never expected it. Her skin prickled, remembering. It didn't make sense to her, this desire. Every part of Katherine that she had ached to touch was known to her, and yet nothing had ever felt so forbidden, so unexplored.

Katherine had let Emma touch her everywhere. She had wanted her to. Emma's heart beat fast to think of it. When Emma had slipped her finger inside her, Emma had gasped at how wet she was. It was a marvel to her, that Katherine could want her so.

But then in the middle of things, Emma had had to pee.

"Don't move," she'd said. "I'll be right back."

Katherine had pulled her back down next to her and slid her hand beneath the crotch of Emma's underwear, moving her fingertips softly against the wetness there.

"Wait. I just have to—" Emma murmured.

Katherine smiled. "I know. Just don't wipe all this away, please."

Emma shook her head, remembering. All the adjectives that came to mind—incredible, marvelous, fantastic—seemed suddenly so literal, so apt. That Katherine might delight in Emma's desire as she delighted in Katherine's was impossible to believe: a marvel, the stuff of fantasy. Emma switched on the light. She felt giddy with joy and awe. She glanced at the clock, reached for her phone, and dialed her sister's number. She had to talk to somebody or she would burst.

CHAPTER 39

Emma

Emma thought that Katherine was far better at being a girl than she was. She shaved her legs every other day and washed her hair and blew it dry on the days she didn't. She kept a bin full of skin creams and hair products below her sink, a good pair of tweezers in her medicine cabinet. Most of her bras were trimmed in lace and she owned several pairs of thongs, which she wore to work when her pants were sheer and she didn't want the outline of her underwear to show.

Emma discovered this by surprise one evening when Katherine agreed to meet her in the Mission after work for dinner. Katherine had a job in the city, editing websites for a new dot-com, often not leaving the office until close to six.

That evening, she had come straight to the Salvadoran restaurant where they had agreed to meet, putting her work bag on the chair beside her and smiling at Emma across the table.

"Did you order for us already?" she said.

"Yes. Pupusas. And fried plantains."

"Good girl."

Back at Katherine's apartment afterwards, Emma slipped her hand up Katherine's skirt. She started when she felt the bare skin there.

"Are you wearing a thong?" Emma asked in surprise.

"Yeah. Don't you ever?"

"No."

"Why not?"

"What's the point?"

"So you don't have panty lines."

"Oh." Emma had never once given a thought to panty lines. She ran her thumbs over Katherine's bare skin. "Aren't they uncomfortable?"

"You get used to them."

Emma pulled Katherine's skirt up and held her bottom in both hands. Katherine kissed her deeply.

"You know what else?" Katherine asked, pulling away, her face close.

"What?"

"They're also sexy."

Emma smiled. "You're such a good girl," she murmured. "But I want to spank you anyway." And she gave Katherine's bottom a soft swat with the palm of her hand.

Please let this never end, she thought.

Katherine loved lots of girl things, too: poetry and yoga, soy lattes and cashmere sweaters, swing dancing and the ocean. She had a younger sister who lived in San Jose, and one weekend a month Katherine would drive to the South Bay to visit her.

"What do you two do together?" Emma asked one Sunday evening in March as they sat together on the couch in Emma's apartment. Katherine had just gotten back from San Jose, and Emma still felt a little stung that she had not been invited to join them. She was used to spending Sundays with Katherine; the day had felt long and empty without her.

"Nothing much," Katherine said. "Go to brunch and get pedicures, usually."

Emma glanced at Katherine's perfect toes. She had thought she painted them herself.

"Can I confess I've never had a pedicure?" she said.

Katherine's eyes widened. "Are you serious?"

"Completely."

"Wow. Well, what kinds of things do you do with your sister, then?"

Emma smiled, imagining Jessie's reaction if she suggested they get pedicures. "A bike ride? A hike? Definitely not a pedicure."

The next morning, Emma stayed in bed, watching Katherine get ready. Normally, Emma would be out the door for work before Katherine even rose, but today was a rare teacher workday. She stretched out on the crisp sheets, savoring the leisure of a morning when she didn't have to be in front of the school for bus duty at quarter till eight.

She watched as Katherine fingered some sort of product into her hair.

"Katherine," she said. "You really are good at being a girl. I still can't believe you're a dyke." She had heard Katherine refer to herself that way countless times, but Emma still stumbled a little over the word.

Katherine glanced at her in the mirror. "That's exactly what my mom says." She laughed wryly. "But *you* should know better. Dykes *are* girls. Just girls who like girls."

"I know, I know. But you know what I mean. You're not your typical dyke."

"Why? Because I'm fem? You're fem, too. You just don't do your hair."

"Or get pedicures."

Katherine laughed. "I'm sure there are lots of fem dykes who don't get pedicures. Trust me, you're fem."

Emma shrugged. "Maybe. But I'm not as fem as you."

"What are you talking about?" Katherine said. "I think you are."

"No way. I don't wear makeup."

"I only wear lipstick," Katherine protested. "And eyeliner."

"I don't wear thongs. And I don't shave my legs."

"You don't?"

"What?"

"You don't shave your legs? At all?"

"You haven't noticed?"

"Not really . . . You really don't shave?"

"Why is that so surprising? I just wax them every once in a while."

"Really?"

"Yeah. I had a friend in high school who was an exchange student from Spain. We ran track together. She told me that none of the girls shaved in Spain, just waxed. I said I wanted to try it, so she showed me."

"Doesn't it hurt?"

"Not once you get used to it." She grinned at Katherine. "Sort of like thongs, I guess."

Katherine shot her a look. "And did anything ever happen between you and . . ."

"Crisanta? No. It wasn't like that. I never thought about it."

"But she waxed your legs? That's pretty intimate."

"She just helped me, the first time. But it wasn't like that. Not what you're thinking."

It was true; there had been nothing more than friendship between her and Crisanta. But Emma could clearly remember her friend sitting next to her in her underwear, her long brown legs stretched out in front of her, the muscles of her calves tensing as she ripped off the muslin strips. She could almost hear the little wince of pain she had made and then her voice, "Like this? See? It only hurts one moment. Do you want that I do it?"

Emma had nodded, watching as Crisanta had carefully spread the hot wax down Emma's leg with a wooden spatula and then put the strip of muslin in place.

Crisanta had run her palm up and down the strip several times, pushing the fabric firmly against Emma's skin.

"*Lista?*"

Emma had nodded again, and Crisanta had gripped the corner with her fingers and quickly torn it away. Immediately, she had clasped her cool palm over the skin where the wax had been.

Emma had called out with the pain. "Jesus!"

"It hurts only one moment."

Crisanta had kept her hand on Emma's leg, pressing firmly against the tender skin. "Okay now?"

Emma had nodded, and as Crisanta took her hand away, she had felt a surge of tenderness for the other girl. It hadn't been desire. Back then, Emma had not even thought to wonder if it were. But there was something about how unabashedly Crisanta had pulled off her pants in front of her, the easy, automatic way she had reached out to ease Emma's pain. Katherine was right— it *had* been intimate. The intimacy of it had thrilled Emma even then, who had felt that she had never been touched in quite that way before.

Katherine stepped closer to the bed, brushing Emma's cheek with the back of her hand.

She smiled. "Where'd you go?"

Emma looked up at her. "Sorry. I was just thinking."

"About Crisanta?" Katherine teased.

Emma shrugged, grinning. "Not like that, Kat," she said. She reached up and grasped Katherine's wrist. "What time do you have to be at work?"

Katherine showed Emma a new way of existing in the world. Frugality had always come naturally to Emma. When she went out to eat, she invariably chose the cheapest thing on the menu, and she never ordered a drink. She shopped at Goodwill, mostly, and discount stores, occasionally; most of her pleasure in the things she owned came from how little she had paid for them. She almost never shopped for the specific ingredients of meals she planned to make; she bought what was on sale and then invented dishes from the things she found in the fridge.

But it wasn't just money that she was frugal about. If she bought a bagel, she scraped off most of the cream cheese; she never put butter on her toast. She did indulge her sweet tooth, but even that she did sparingly: when she ate M&Ms, she bit them in half and ate the pieces one by one. She didn't scoop ice-cream into a dish; she carved a spoonful directly from the carton and licked it off the spoon, making it last.

Katherine, on the other hand, knew how to indulge. She had less money than Emma but spent it more easily. She wore a nice pair of black leather boots and drove a newish black Toyota Camry. The first time Emma rode in it, she had marveled at the glossy paint and clean interior and had guessed that Katherine had money. Only later did she learn that, no, she had car payments.

Emma also learned that other people—even people with limited funds—did not follow the strict rules of deprivation that governed her own life. When she and Katherine met once for coffee at her favorite coffee shop, Katherine ordered a double decaf soy latte. Emma ordered mint tea, which Katherine insisted on paying for.

"It's only a dollar, for goodness' sake," she said when Emma protested, digging in her wallet for change. "I think I can afford it." The first time Katherine watched her scrape the cream cheese off her bagel, she added it to her own.

"You're crazy," she said. "That's the best part."

Every Tuesday morning, Katherine stopped for coffee at a small Chinese-owned donut shop on her way to work.

"It gives me something to look forward to on Monday," she explained, pulling up to the curb. "Do you want anything?"

Emma shook her head and waited in the car while Katherine went inside. She came back with a lidded paper cup and a small brown bag.

"I got you a donut, anyway," she smiled.

Emma could not remember the last time she had had a donut. It might have been in junior high, when the cafeteria ladies sold donuts in the morning as a school fund-raiser.

"That's okay," she said. "You have it."

"I got myself one, too. And I definitely don't want to eat both of them. Come on. Just try it. Here," she said, popping the top off the steaming coffee. "Dip it in here. It's really good."

Obediently, Emma dipped the donut in the coffee and quickly took a bite. It dripped coffee on her jeans, but, oh, was it good.

"Okay," she said. "You're right."

Katherine smiled at her. "I told you." She took her own bite of donut. "You know, Emma, you really ought to let yourself enjoy life a little more."

"What do you mean?" Emma asked, indignant. "I enjoy life plenty. I think I enjoy life more than most people do."

Katherine considered this for a moment. Finally, she put the last of her donut into her mouth and said, "I guess you're right. In a lot of ways, you do. But, come on. You liked it, right?"

Emma smiled. "I liked it."

CHAPTER 40

Emma

One Wednesday evening, two months after they had first met, Katherine came over to Emma's apartment for dinner. Later, making out on the bed, Emma moved so that she lay on top of Katherine, then pushed her pelvis hard against her.

"God," she muttered, her teeth clenched. "I just want to fuck you."

Afterwards, as they lay together, Emma traced circles around Katherine's bare breasts with one fingertip. Katherine drew in her breath.

"You can if you want, you know."

"Can what?"

"Fuck me."

Emma raised herself up on one elbow.

"Didn't you come?"

Katherine laughed. "*Yes.* I didn't mean that." Then she hesitated. "What you said before . . . 'I want to fuck you.' I wasn't sure what you meant. I just thought maybe you meant . . . you know."

"You mean, I could fuck you with—"

"A dildo? Yeah."

Emma sat up in surprise. "Do you have one?"

Katherine shook her head. "No. But we could get one."

Emma lay back down beside Katherine. "Okay. If you want to."

"Do *you*?"

Emma grinned. "I think so. I mean, yeah."

"Okay then. Let's."

The following Sunday afternoon, they went to Good Vibrations on Shattuck Avenue in south Berkeley.

"I've biked by here before," Emma said. "I always thought it was a surf shop."

Katherine laughed. "You're funny."

Inside, a petite woman with delicately spiked hair and a nose ring greeted them.

"Hello, ladies. Can I help you find anything?"

Emma glanced at Katherine and took a small step back.

"We're just going to look around, if that's okay," Katherine said. She reached for Emma's hand.

"Of course. Just let me know if you need anything."

Katherine seemed totally unembarrassed. She led Emma past the edible underwear, the feminist porn, and a display of brightly colored vibrators with little white placards that said, "Try me!"

"They can't mean—" Emma said.

"Of course not, silly. They just mean turn them on."

"Turn them on?"

Katherine laughed. "Yes, turn them on. Like you turn on an appliance."

They found the dildos along the back wall. There were over a dozen to choose from: big ones, little ones, straight ones, wavy ones, plain ones, colorful ones.

"Well," Katherine said at last. "What do you think?"

"I don't know about this." Under each dildo was a little description, complete with the material the dildo was made from, and the price. Emma looked closer. *Eighty-seven dollars!*

"I don't know about this," she said again.

Katherine turned to face her. "I thought you wanted to."

"I did. It's just . . . I didn't expect so many choices, I guess."

Katherine stepped forward. "Well, look. What about this one?"

She picked up a large, dark blue dildo from the display. Despite the color, it was very realistic. And big.

"Um, doesn't it seem a little big?"

Katherine shrugged. "I like big."

"You do?" Emma was unprepared for the rush of jealousy that flooded her. Her cheeks burned.

"What's wrong? Why? Don't you?"

"I can't talk about this here."

Katherine sighed. "Okay. Well, I like this one."

"It's the first one you looked at. What about these?"

Emma walked over to a corner display and picked up a more moderately sized gray dildo. The material felt different, not hard rubber like the other one. Like suede, almost.

"Here, feel this. I like this better, I think."

Katherine nodded. "Okay."

Just then the spiky-haired woman appeared beside them. "Those are from our new silicone line," she said.

"I like the way they feel," Emma said, forcing her voice to sound nonchalant. "The material, I mean."

The woman nodded enthusiastically. "Yes, they're designed to be more realistic. Sort of like skin. But, just so you know, you do have to use a condom."

Emma and Katherine looked at each other. Emma put the dildo back on the display.

"I know," the woman said. "Most people have the same reaction. It's a major disadvantage."

In the end, they settled on the blue dildo Katherine had picked out initially and a simple black harness.

"We can get something different for you, you know," Katherine whispered, but Emma shook her head.

"That's okay."

"But if you think it'll be too big—"

"It's okay, Katherine. Let's just stick with this one for now, okay?"

When the cashier rang up their total, Emma was shocked. With the harness and the lubricant that the spiky-haired woman had recommended to them, the total was one-hundred sixty-nine dollars. Katherine reached inside her purse, but Emma elbowed her out of the way.

"I'll get this," she said.

Katherine put the plain brown paper bag on the back seat of her car, then opened the door for Emma to get in. When she got into the driver's seat, she buckled up but didn't start the car.

"Now what?"

"Could you drop me off at BART? There's a station right up there," Emma said.

Katherine looked at her strangely. "You're going home now?"

Emma shrugged. "I guess. It's almost three already. And I wanted to run. And get some grading done for tomorrow."

Katherine sighed. "All right."

"What?"

"Nothing. I just thought . . ."

"What?"

"Nothing. That's fine. But I can just take you home, you know. You don't have to take BART."

"I really don't mind. It's not on your way."

"It's fine. It'll save you some time."

They rode in silence for a while. Finally, Katherine asked, "Is everything okay?"

Emma put her hand over Katherine's on the stick shift. "Of course."

Katherine glanced at her. "You're acting . . . I don't know. I thought you *wanted* to do this."

"I did. I do."

Katherine sighed. "It doesn't seem like it."

Suddenly Emma understood. "You thought we would . . . Right now?"

"I just thought—"

"Well, we can. I'm sorry. I didn't realize."

"No, it's fine. You've got stuff you want to do. I get it."

"No, Katherine. It's okay. I'll run tomorrow. You can come up."

"No."

"Why not?"

"It's fine. Just do your stuff. It doesn't matter."

"Katherine, please. Just come up. You wanted to—"

"And now I don't."

"Katherine. I'm sorry. I just didn't think we had to try it all out right away."

"We don't."

"But you wanted to."

"And now I don't. Will you drop it already?"

"Fine."

Neither of them spoke as they drove the last few blocks to Emma's apartment. When they arrived, Katherine stopped the car but did not turn off the engine.

Emma reached for the door, then paused. "You sure you don't want to come up?"

"Yes."

"Well, when will I see you?"

"I don't know. This week is pretty packed."

"What about Wednesday?"

"I wanted to try out that yoga class."

"Thursday?"

"Let's just see, okay?"

Finally, Katherine turned to look at her. "Bye."

Emma opened the door and climbed out. "Bye." She was already moving away from the car when she heard Katherine call her back.

"Emma."

Emma's heart gave an extra little beat of expectation.

"Yeah?"

"You forgot the bag." Katherine tossed her head, gesturing to the back seat.

"Oh. That's okay. You can hold onto it for us."

"But you paid for it."

"So what?"

"So it's technically yours."

"Just keep it, Katherine," Emma said, turning away.

The rest of the afternoon, Emma's gut felt hollow, like a pumpkin that has been scraped out before carving. She ate peanut butter on toast for dinner, but afterwards, when Katherine still hadn't called, the feeling was worse. She made herself some decaf tea and forced herself to sit down with a pile of her students' essays, but her mind kept slipping back to those last few moments in the car with Katherine. She could hear Katherine's words—*Let's just see, okay?*—and the coolness in her voice, as if Emma had no claim to her. Emma was glad that she had not agreed to take the bag. Simply knowing that it was in Katherine's possession was a small comfort to her. At least there was that: some tangible thing that connected them, the anonymously wrapped package a small assurance that Katherine would not, now, be able to slip out of Emma's life as quickly as she had slipped into it.

Emma fell asleep in the armchair, waking when the pile of essays she had been grading fell from her lap. It was only 9:20 p.m., but she went to bed anyway, although not before checking her answering machine. Its double zeros peered at her in the dark like two empty eyes.

By Tuesday, Katherine still hadn't called. On Tuesday evening, Emma finally dialed her number and waited through all six interminable rings before leaving a forcedly cheerful message on her voicemail. Katherine did not call back.

On Wednesday morning before she left for work, Emma

opened her laptop and searched for the phone number of a florist in Bernal Heights. When she got home, there was still no message from Katherine. She called the florist and ordered a dozen stargazer lilies to be sent to her at work.

"Would you like a personalized message, dear?" the woman asked her.

Emma hesitated. "I'm sorry," had come first to mind, but a stubborn part of her would not permit it. What had she done, after all, to be sorry for? There was also no way of knowing if Katherine's three days of silence meant anything at all. They had not been in the habit of speaking every day.

Perhaps everything was completely normal, Emma thought. Perhaps their parting Sunday afternoon had simply been a single note of discord, and Emma alone was guilty of replaying it again and again. She could almost hear Katherine dismissing her anxiety of the last several days: "Silly, you thought I was leaving you over *that*?"

"Did you want to include a message, dear?" the florist asked again.

"Uh, yeah. Um, 'I'm excited to see you.' No, wait. 'I can't wait to see you.'"

"Any name?"

"No." Emma wasn't sure if Katherine was out to her colleagues at work. "No name. And—" Emma hesitated. "Actually, could you change the message to 'Thinking of you'?"

"Thinking of you. Of course."

All three versions were equally true, but Emma didn't like how eager the first two sounded. If Katherine was taking a step back, Emma didn't want to be the one who couldn't wait to see her again.

CHAPTER 41

Emma

Emma couldn't wait to see Katherine again. That night as she lay in bed alone, she thought of how soft Katherine's skin was when she rubbed her cheek against her belly, the weight of her breasts in her hands, the nub of her clitoris against her tongue. Emma shut her eyes and felt her desire billow up in her and then settle against her skin, like a sheet hovers in the air above a bed before coming to rest at last.

"Katherine," she whispered into the empty room. "Please call me."

The next morning, the fog was so thick she could not see the end of her street. As she rode her bike to the BART station, she could feel the tiny droplets colliding with her face. By the time she got to the station, her eyes and nose were streaming. She found a crumpled napkin in her backpack and blew her nose.

The train was crowded and warm, and Emma felt herself begin to sweat as she maneuvered her bicycle through the car.

"Sorry. Excuse me," she said again and again, as she jostled her way through the crowd. She tried to ignore the looks of annoyance the other passengers gave her as they dodged the handlebars of her bike and moved their bags out of the way of its wheels.

Eventually Emma made her way to the end of the car, where she could push her bike against the wall and keep it out of everyone's way. She steadied it with one hand and grabbed a handle that hung from the ceiling with the other. Her underarms felt damp.

"Would you like to sit down?" she heard someone ask. "I can move over so you can still hold your bike."

"I'm fine," Emma said, glancing down, but the owner of the voice had already gathered up her bag and was sliding over, making room for her at the end of the row.

"Thanks," Emma said, sitting down next to her. The young woman wore faded jeans that had a swirly design snaking its way down the side of her thigh. Her short hair was bleached blond with black roots, and a tiny diamond stud glittered in her nose. She bent over suddenly and reached into her bag, then handed Emma a small rectangle of pink paper.

"I don't know if you like punk, but here."

Emma glanced at the paper. "Sorry?"

"It's for my band. We're playing tonight at the Black Bird. Do you know where it is?"

"Yeah," Emma lied. Girls like this intimidated her with their easy style and perfectly unkempt hair.

"Actually, no," she admitted. "But my girlfriend probably does."

The woman nodded. "Good. Bring her, too. We need as many fans as we can get. I'm Samantha, by the way."

"Emma."

"Nice to meet you," Samantha said, rising. She put one arm up to brace herself against the slowing train, and, when she did, her shirt rose up. Another jewel blinked at Emma from inside the perfect well of her navel. She glanced down at Emma. "Nice bike."

"Thanks. Nice belly button ring."

Samantha laughed, tugging her T-shirt down.

"No, really," Emma said. "It looks great."

The train stopped. "Don't forget the show," Samantha said. She flashed Emma a smile. And then she winked. It was a perfect wink, the lid closing effortlessly over a startling blue eye.

Emma was too startled to respond, and in another instant, Samantha was gone. *She was flirting*, Emma thought. She almost laughed aloud. There she was, feeling sweaty and awkward and decidedly uncool. And then someone like Samantha flirted with her. She leaned back in her seat and grinned.

When Emma got back to her apartment late that afternoon, there were two messages on her answering machine. Emma hung up her helmet and unpacked her lunch bag before she hit play.

"Hi, sweetheart. It's, um, six-thirty or so. A.M. Sorry I never got back to you yesterday. Work was crazy, and then I had to rush to make it to yoga, and then afterwards I just passed out. But I was hoping I'd catch you this morning. I miss hearing your voice. Call me."

Six-thirty? Emma was sure she had still been home at six-thirty this morning. How had she missed the call, and then not noticed the message? But it didn't matter. Katherine had called, and her voice, although sleepy, sounded perfectly normal. There was none of the coolness Emma had dreaded. Emma did a little dance around her tiny kitchen.

The other message was from her sister. "Hey, Emma. Just wanted to talk to you about something. Call me when you have a chance."

She was still dancing when the phone rang. She dove for it, collapsing into her armchair.

"Hello?"

"Hi. It's Katherine."

"Hi."

"Is this a bad time?"

"Of course not." Emma's heart dropped. "A bad time for what?"

"I don't know. You just sound out of breath."

"Oh. I was just . . . dancing."

Katherine laughed. "You didn't have to do that, you know."

"What? Dance?"

"No, silly." She hesitated. "They *were* from you, right?"

"Oh, right. The flowers."

Katherine laughed again. "You forgot you sent them?"

"No. Well, just for a minute. Are they okay?"

"They're gorgeous. It was very sweet of you."

Emma grinned. A moment passed; neither of them spoke.

"So, how's your week been?" Katherine said at last. "I'm sorry I never called you back on Tuesday. Every time I had a chance, I knew you wouldn't be home. I wish you'd just get a cell phone already, Em. It would make it a lot easier. Did you get my message this morning?"

"Yeah. Just a minute ago."

There was another silence.

"Do you know where the Black Bird is?"

"Isn't it that place on Telegraph? Next to the bookstore? Why?"

"This girl on BART invited me to go to her show there tonight."

"What girl?"

"I don't know. I just met her this morning on the train. Her name's Samantha. She's in a band, I guess."

"So . . . are you going to go?" Katherine asked. The coolness was back in her voice. Emma sat up so quickly the blood rushed to her head.

"Katherine! I didn't mean it like that. I meant . . . do you want to go with me?"

Katherine snorted. "I don't think that's what she had in mind, Em."

"But I told her about you. She said you should come, too."

"What did you tell her?"

Emma hesitated. "Nothing. I just said that you were . . . my girlfriend. Well, actually I said that my girlfriend would know where that club was."

"Really?"

Emma let out her breath. "Yeah. Was I right?"

"That I know where it is or that I'm your girlfriend?"

"What do *you* think?"

They both laughed.

"Yeah," Katherine said finally. "You were right. About both."

"Katherine—" Emma said. "I'm sorry about Sunday."

"Don't apologize. It was me. I was just . . . disappointed, I guess. And embarrassed."

"You sounded so cold. I was worried . . ." Emma didn't finish the sentence. She didn't want to let on just how far her fears had gone.

"Yeah. I'm good at cold, unfortunately. Sorry about that."

Emma lay back onto the worn cushions of her chair. For a moment, neither of them spoke.

"So, what about tonight? Do you want to go?" Emma asked at last.

"What time?"

"Hold on," Emma put the phone down and rummaged through her backpack for the little pink flyer. "Eight-thirty."

"Sure."

"Want to just come here first? I can make us some dinner."

Emma and Katherine ate pasta and salad at the tiny table by the window. They spoke of everyday things, of Katherine's job at the dot-com and how dry she found the writing, of Emma's middle school students and the other teachers she was slowly getting to know. They smiled at each other often and nodded earnestly while the other spoke, but as they talked Emma felt a weight begin to settle in her stomach. The ease of their first few months together had shifted. Why were they being so polite?

"Katherine," she said, putting down her napkin.

Katherine glanced at her watch. "You're right. We should go." She took a last sip of her wine and stood up. "That was excellent. Thank you. Let me just go to the bathroom and I'm ready."

Emma waited for her in the kitchen, putting the dishes in the sink.

"Do you want me to help you clean up first?" Katherine asked. Emma turned. Katherine's lips were glossy with lip balm.

"No, that's okay."

"Should we go then?"

"Katherine?" Emma stepped forward. "You look great."

Katherine smiled. "Really?"

"Can I still kiss you?"

"Of course. Why couldn't you?"

"I don't know. It just feels different tonight . . . Like we're trying to be friends."

"Why shouldn't we be friends?"

Emma shrugged and looked away. "We should, I guess." She hesitated. "I *do* want you to be my friend, Kat. But I also want—"

Katherine gave her a look then that eased, in an instant, the heaviness that had weighed Emma down all evening. It was a teasing look, full of knowing and invitation.

"What do you want, baby?" Katherine said, stepping toward her and letting her bag slide down her arm onto the floor. "What *do* you want?"

And then Katherine was kissing her, her cool hands slipping beneath her shirt.

Emma pulled back for a second. "We're not going to be just . . . friends?"

Katherine laughed. "What do you think?"

"I think," Emma said, reaching for her. "That we'd better not go to the show."

"But Samantha—"

"Be quiet, Katherine. You know what I want."

Katherine smiled and moved so that the whole length of her body was pressed against Emma's own.

"Yes," she whispered into Emma's ear. "I know."

A few minutes later, Katherine's shirt was off, her back pushed up against the narrow strip of wall beside the window. Her breasts were deliciously warm in Emma's mouth, but she left them to move down the soft slope of her belly, licking at the skin where it disappeared into her jeans. Then she pushed her face between Katherine's legs, pulling at the button on her fly.

Suddenly, Emma stopped and stood up. "Do you have—"

Katherine nodded. "It's all still in the back seat."

"Give me your keys," Emma said, her voice thick.

The harness was awkward. Emma felt like she was gearing up to go rock climbing, and it broke the mood a little. But when Katherine smiled up at her and parted her legs, all Emma's desire returned in a rush. And when she entered her slowly, her lips against the taut skin of Katherine's shoulder and heard Katherine moan . . .

"Is that okay?" she asked quietly, but Katherine said nothing, rocking against her, breathing. When Katherine came, her cries made Emma come, too, and the surprise of that left her gasping.

"Wow," they both said, afterwards, laughing, clinging to each other. "Wow."

CHAPTER 42

Emma

Emma's mother, Sarah, had delicate hands, the skin across her knuckles so smooth they seemed to have been polished. She kept an emery board in the console of her car, and at red lights she filed her nails into perfect ovals, the cuticles always smooth and perfectly intact. For years, Emma had filed hers, too. "It's the most girly thing you do," her college boyfriend had said once, and Emma had thought she had heard a note of accusation in his voice. Probably he had wished she shaved her legs.

Unlike her mother's, Emma's hands were perpetually desiccated. The backs of them were so wrinkled they seemed the hands of a much older woman, which Emma's middle school students never failed to tactlessly point out.

"You got old lady hands," they told her as she handed back their papers. "How old are you anyway?"

Emma was not ashamed of her hands exactly, but she felt them to be a trial, with their endless thirst for lotion and the way her cuticles hardened and split and demanded that Emma constantly police herself lest she tear them into bloody shreds.

So it surprised her when, one Saturday morning, as she and Katherine walked along the eastern shore of Lake Merritt, Katherine raised their clasped hands to her lips and said, "I love your hands, Emma."

Emma felt her face redden. "What? Why?"

Gently, Katherine opened Emma's hand and traced her finger along the calloused skin of her palm.

"I don't know exactly. They're so rough. Real."

Emma laughed. "Well, I love yours."

And she did. Katherine's hands reminded her of her mother's: the smooth skin, the slender fingers. Lacing her fingers with Katherine's, she felt a peculiar sensation of contentment come over her, a contentment laced with nostalgia. As a child, Emma had rarely spent time alone with her mother, without her brother or her sister, but once a year in late summer their mother would take each of them to the mall in turn, to buy them what they needed in back-to-school clothes.

As soon as Emma and her mother entered through the double doors into the singular smell of cosmetics and new clothes, Emma would take her mother's hand. Even when Emma was in her teens, and knew instinctively that most girls her age did not walk hand-in-hand with their mothers, she did not stop. She loved the feel of her mother's hand in hers, the oiled skin, the affectionate way she rubbed at the bones of Emma knuckles so that they shifted against each other.

It was not the only time Emma sought out her mother's affection. She remembered once when she was nine or ten and their family had been invited to spend the afternoon at the pool of one of her mother's friends. She remembered vividly how she had carefully dried and wrapped herself in a towel before squeezing into the lawn chair next to her mother and taking her hand.

"Aw," her mother's friend had gushed. "You're so lucky. She's so sweet, isn't she?"

Her mother had smiled and nodded in reply, but Emma had known instantly that she was not being truthful. It occurred to her for the first time that perhaps Sarah would have preferred it if Emma were not so demonstrative in her affections. Her mother had never done anything to give her that impression. She had never pushed Emma away or wriggled free. She squeezed Emma's hand when Emma took hers, and she stroked her back or patted her head when Emma snuck her arms around her waist. And yet, in that moment by the pool, Emma felt sure that her mother did not, in fact, count herself "lucky" that Emma was "so sweet."

But even after that moment of insight in the lawn chair, Emma did not change her behavior toward her mother. At first, she had tried, but it did not come naturally to her to rein in her affections, nor was she able to curb her longing for her mother's embrace. Once, when she was thirteen and swimming in adolescent angst, she had vowed to herself that she would stop. She would not hug her mother, or say that she loved her. She would wait. She would see how long it took before her mother reached out to her, or told her that she loved her without Emma saying it first.

Emma had not been able to complete the experiment. One afternoon three days later, as her mother was leaving her room having just delivered a neat stack of folded clothes, Emma had blurted out accusingly, "You never say you love me."

Her mother had paused in the doorway, her arms still full of her brother's laundry. She had looked at Emma for a long moment.

"And you never hug me," Emma had quickly added, since why not? Emma knew that she would never have the courage to say anything like this again, and so the need to say it—to say all of it—was too strong in her for her to hold her tongue.

Her mother had taken a deep breath and let it out slowly, as if to gather the patience to deal with this new ridiculousness. And this summoning of patience had made Emma feel both ashamed and irate. Ashamed, because she knew that to her mother she must seem petulant and nit-picking. And yet it infuriated her, nonetheless, that her mother could, with her sigh of exasperation, so belittle something which was, to Emma, of such monumental importance.

Emma could not remember her mother's exact words that afternoon, but the message was this: that she, Emma's mother, did not show her love in the same way that Emma did, but that that did not mean that she did not feel it. Emma's mother had nodded at the pile of folded clothes she had left on Emma's chair. "I do your laundry. I cook your meals. I take you wherever it is you need to go. I am *constantly* showing you that I love you."

Emma had nodded, contrite. She had not muttered, "But you have to do those things. You're my mother," as she had wanted to. She had sensed her mother's exasperation with her; she knew that she could easily push her over the thin line into anger.

"I know," she had murmured instead, although inwardly she had railed against her mother's cool logic. A pile of clean clothes was not the same as a hug. A meal was not "I love you."

The strange thing was that even while Emma longed for more from her mother—some effusion of affection that would match Emma's own—Emma did not ever doubt her mother's love. It was the scaffold on which their family was built, the underpinning of the narrative that bound them. Laurel, her birth mother, had not loved Emma. If she had, how could she have given her up? In her father's telling, he had offered Laurel all he had if he could keep his girls, and Laurel had not hesitated.

But if her father had been the early hero, it was Sarah who had made them a family. Emma had been only a baby then. She had needed a mother, and Sarah had stepped up. Laurel had not loved her, but Sarah had. She had proved it.

Growing up in the eighties, families fractured by divorce were a dime a dozen; rare were the kids at school who could claim their family as intact. Strangely, Emma had always counted herself among them. She did not bounce biweekly between houses, nor did she feel any affinity with the girls who whined about their stepmothers. She had a *mother*, not a stepmother. She had a brother, not a half-brother. The unequivocalness of her mother's love had saved them. They were a family—intact, inviolable.

Now, holding hands with Katherine by the lake, Emma's chest tightened with emotion. Was this how it felt to be in love? When Katherine took Emma's hand and raised it to her lips, or slipped her arm around her waist, or moved in bed so that she lay pressed against Emma's side, Emma felt an immense joy billow up in her. It was an elated feeling—a feeling of hunger sated, of belonging beyond measure. She squeezed Katherine's slender fingers between her own; she felt that she could never let her go.

Emma stopped suddenly on the path and pulled Katherine around to face her. Katherine smiled at her indulgently.

"Katherine," she said desperately. "I . . . I love you."

Katherine's mouth formed a little pout of sympathy, and Emma's heart missed a beat. She didn't want Katherine's compassion, she wanted—

But then Katherine's arms were around her, her mouth against her hair.

"Silly," she said, her voice low. "I know you do."

Emma tried to pull away without looking at her, but Katherine held her so that at last she met her eye.

"Do you need me to spell it out, Em?" Katherine said, her mouth a half-smile that Emma couldn't read.

Emma shrugged. "Maybe." She tried to smile a little, too. "Okay, yes. I think I do."

Katherine moved so that her lips were by Emma's ear. "I love you, silly," she whispered. Then she drew Emma's hand to her mouth and kissed her fingers. "Are you happy now?"

Emma grinned sheepishly. "Yes. Very. Thank you."

CHAPTER 43

Jessie

The way it all happened shook Jessie's faith a little. Or rather, it shook her lack of faith, her certainty in happenstance. Unconnected events were just that: unconnected. Jessie had always believed that. It was only our human need for meaning that put a celestial shine on them, that colored them as something other than coincidence.

Jessie believed this. And yet she couldn't shake the words that created their own rhythm in her brain: "Give, and you shall receive." For she had given, and how! The scale of her gift had not been obvious to her at first. She had returned home from the fertility clinic minus several cells, and with a strange sensation in her abdomen—not pain, exactly, but as if pain had come and gone and left a shadow. Laurel had driven her home from the clinic. Jessie remembered little of what they had said; her sleepiness was overwhelming. As soon as they got home she lay down on her futon and was asleep immediately. She woke to find the sky already darkening and a note from Laurel on the table. She had gone back to the hotel to be with Jim and Sue.

Jessie felt as if she had slept for days. She wandered the house restlessly before returning to the bedroom. The alcohol pads and needles she had used to give herself injections over the past few weeks were still arranged on the stack of magazines beside her bed. She brought the trash can and swept them in.

"Well, that's done then," she said aloud. Jessie was not squeamish; needles did not faze her. But she was glad her body was her own again, with no added hormones, no crop of eggs crowding her ovaries.

Still, she was restless. She wanted to go for a run, but when she had asked at the clinic if that would be okay, the doctor had said, "Can't you take it easy for at least one day?"

He had been laughing; he didn't understand what it cost her.

But if harm could be done—which she doubted—she didn't intend to do it. She slipped her laptop into her backpack, filled her water bottle, and found her wallet. She rode the few miles into town slowly, taking it easy as the doctor had said. She meant to go to her favorite coffee shop, but found it closed. She glanced at her watch; she hadn't realized how late it was. The ride into town had eased her restlessness, but still she wasn't ready to go home. She doubted that she would be able to sleep again for ages, and she did not feel like being alone.

Jessie locked her bike to a light post and walked down Main Street. The stores were all dark, and as she passed by a donut shop, a street light cast her reflection in the window. She turned to look and immediately wished she hadn't. Her face looked gaunt, and her hair hung heavily in tangled strands around it. A line of poetry she had read once came to mind:

> Sometimes I could be Narcissus.
> Sometimes I turn my own self to stone.

She understood that; today was not a day she wanted to face herself.

There were tables on the sidewalk a block ahead, but as Jessie neared, she saw that it was a bar and her heart fell. The outside seats were all taken, and Jessie knew she would not venture inside. She had never liked bars; they seemed to exist for a different sort of person entirely.

She turned to go, thinking she would head home after all, take a shower and wash her hair. But just as she did so, she saw a couple stand up from a table at the edge of the sidewalk, and after a second's hesitation, Jessie sat down in one of the seats they'd left.

She pulled out her laptop and set her water bottle on the table. She knew she should order something, but no server came and she didn't want to go inside. She found a hair tie in the bottom of her backpack and pulled her hair into a low ponytail.

She opened the computer and created a new document in Word. When she got home and could connect to the internet, she would copy and paste it into an email to her sister.

"*Dear Emma,*" she typed, then hesitated. Even now that it was too late for Emma to try to talk her out of it, she knew she didn't want to tell her sister what she had done. Like her abortion so many years ago, this was a matter for her own private reckoning, a decision that concerned no one but herself. Still, Jessie knew that this was a choice that would not be so easy to put behind her. Already the egg she had given up was no longer an egg. It was a zygote now, and soon would be a blastocyst, an embryo, a fetus . . . If it were to be a secret, it would only get bigger and harder to keep. Jessie began to type with new resolve.

"*It is almost ten-thirty, and I am sitting at a little table on the sidewalk downtown, at a bar of all places, after sleeping most of the afternoon. Doesn't sound like me, does it?*" She paused again. She *had* to tell Emma, but how to begin?

"*Today—*" she wrote, then deleted the word. "*Laurel is here,*" she began again.

"Excuse me? Do you know if they serve food here? Excuse me? Miss? Ma'am?"

Jessie looked up at last, finally understanding that *she* was the miss, the ma'am. A tall man stood at the curb, trying to get her attention. He was dirty and disheveled, an enormous backpack cinched around his waist.

"I'm just coming off the trail, and I'm out of food. Do they serve food here, do you think?"

She shook her head. "I have no idea."

"Do you mind if I leave this here while I go see?"

Strands of brown hair hung in greasy clumps around his face, which was rugged and unshaven. He had clearly been on the trail for a while. Jessie flushed with envy and discomfort. What if he took her for someone who didn't know? Someone who didn't know the gritty simplicity of the backcountry, the containment and completeness, with everything you needed muscled into a dead weight on your back? Jessie guessed what he must be feeling, although she had never owned up to it before: that gloss of superiority, coming in from the woods, that no one in town could even begin to fathom how glorious it was.

She nodded, putting a hand to her hair. "Which trail did you do? Nine Mile Ridge? Or the North Fork?"

She watched him take her in, surprised, and she blushed; he'd caught her showing off.

"North Fork." His brown eyes met hers and he smiled. Then he unclipped the hip belt of his pack and swung it to the ground. Gray rings of salt stained his T-shirt where his shoulder straps had been.

"I'll come right back for this," he said, leaning his backpack against the empty chair. "Thanks."

When he had gone, Jessie quickly saved the letter to her sister and closed her laptop. She was watching for him when he reappeared at the entrance to the bar.

She caught his eye and nodded at the other chair at her table. "You can sit here, if you want."

"You sure? I'm, um, pretty grungy. And I probably stink."

He was right. When he moved by her, she caught his scent. Wood smoke and sweat and unwashed skin. She breathed him in.

"I don't mind," she said.

When his food came, she watched him while he ate. Then she bought them both root beers, because the bar didn't serve dessert, and they talked about the North Fork trail and his job as an archeologist on the Umatilla reservation outside of town. When they were done, he stood up to go, and she wondered where he was headed; the nearest campground was miles away. At this time of night—and looking like he did—hitching a ride would be nearly impossible.

"I'll be fine," he said, when she pointed this out. "I can sleep any old where." He gestured to the sidewalk where they stood.

She grinned. "I can do better than that," she said. "Just wait here, okay? I'll be twenty minutes, max."

Jessie biked back home, quickly this time, and got her car. Together, she and Heath squeezed his pack into the tiny hatch, and then she took him home with her, where he showered for fifteen minutes and then passed out on the couch. When he was asleep, she tiptoed into the bathroom. The mirror was still steamy, and he had left his sawed-off toothbrush on the sink. She noticed how worn the bristles were.

She showered, then, too, and although the hot water ran out almost immediately, she washed and conditioned her hair and scrubbed beneath her arms. In the morning, she made him an omelet with tomatoes from her garden.

Several blissful, heady days passed in which Jessie did not think about the truncated letter to her sister, saved on the hard drive on her laptop. Then, on Tuesday evening, Laurel called with an update: of the two embryos the doctor had implanted in Sue's womb, one had survived. Sue was pregnant. As soon as Jessie hung up the phone with her mother, she called Emma, sensing that already she had waited too long. But when Emma finally answered, she rushed through telling her about the eggs she had donated; Heath now seemed like much bigger news.

When at last she had told her sister everything, Jessie fell silent, waiting for Emma's reaction. But her sister's enthusiasm seemed muted, and Jessie was annoyed. Hadn't she been over the moon for her, when Emma had met Katherine?

"Is something wrong, Em?" she asked. "You sound, I don't know, down or something."

"No," Emma said. "Nothing's wrong. It's just . . . I almost wish you hadn't told me."

Jessie drew in her breath. "About Heath? Emma, this is a big deal for me. I wanted—"

"Not about him," Emma interrupted her. "About the eggs."

Jessie sighed. "Really?"

"Yeah. I mean—now I'm in the middle again, aren't I?"

"How are you in the middle? This has nothing to do with you."

Emma snorted. "Maybe not. But you're not going to tell Mom and Dad, so I'm in the middle."

"That doesn't mean you're in the middle, Emma."

"It doesn't? It feels just like when we were little, and you and Laurel used to talk about how one day you'd tell Mom and Dad that you wanted to move to Baymont. And I wasn't supposed to say anything."

"Oh, Emma."

They were both silent for a moment.

"Look, Emma," Jessie said at last. "I'm sorry. You're right. Maybe I shouldn't have told you. It just—well, it seemed like too big a secret to keep from you."

"But not too big to keep from Mom and Dad?"

Jessie took a breath. "I don't think they would understand."

"I'm not sure I do, either," Emma said. She drew in her breath. "I mean, it is pretty weird, Jess. That Laurel's going to raise your kid."

"It's not . . . It's not going to be *my* kid, Emma."

"Genetically it is. It came from your egg, didn't it?"

"So?"

"So, technically, it's your kid."

"*You* came from Laurel's egg. And you don't consider yourself *her* daughter."

There was silence on the line.

"Emma?" Jessie said at last. "I didn't mean . . . Look, I shouldn't have said that. I was just defending—Emma?"

"I'm here."

"Look, I'm sorry. Okay?"

"For what? You're right. It just feels different to me."

"Okay." They were silent again.

"So," Emma said at last, "do you think you'll ever tell them?"

"Mom and Dad?"

"Yeah."

Jesse hesitated. "I don't know. Maybe when the baby is born."

Emma sighed. "Good. Because I don't want to have to keep this secret forever."

But Jessie didn't tell them. The baby—a girl—was born at thirty-seven weeks. Laurel called from the hospital in Minneapolis to tell Jessie.

"Can you believe it?" she gushed. "Another little girl."

Jessie frowned. "Another one?"

"Well, you and Emma, of course. I must be destined to have only daughters."

Jesse sighed. "Mom, you had nothing to do—"

But Laurel cut her off. "We've named her Elizabeth, after Sue's sister. But we'll call her Liza. Oh, just wait 'til you see her. Our dear, dear Liza."

"*There's a hole in the bucket, Dear Liza, Dear Liza,*" Jesse said dryly.

"What?" said Laurel.

"Nothing. Elizabeth what?"

"I beg your pardon?"

"What's her full name?"

"Oh. Elizabeth Halley Patterson."

"Halley . . . That's Sue's last name?"

"Yes. And Patterson is Jim's."

Jessie hesitated, sure that the omission must be just as obvious to her mother.

"But what about yours?" she asked at last.

"Well," said Laurel cheerfully. "That would be a little much, wouldn't it?"

Jessie was silent for a moment. "I'm very happy for you," she said at last, but she wondered at the sudden darkening of her mood.

"Really happy," she added, to make up for her momentary insincerity. And she *was* happy for her mother, wasn't she? The baby was fine. Laurel had a new daughter, and Jessie had a . . . Her thoughts stumbled amid the terminology. But it didn't matter now, did it? Her part was over.

Despite her best intentions, Jessie couldn't bring herself to tell her parents the truth about Elizabeth. She wished she hadn't waited so long. Now, it all seemed too momentous. It was one thing to say that she had donated her eggs, that Laurel had asked her. It was another to say: this baby, she came from me.

She had to tell them that there *was* a baby, though. Her parents asked her occasionally about Laurel, and this was far too big a development to leave out. But even that had cost her. Her face burned all through the conversation, the phone hot against her ear.

"So, she's Sue's?" Sarah asked, her emphasis unmistakable. "Sue and what's-his-name's? Jim's?"

Jessie was evasive. They had used an egg donor, she hedged.

"But Sue carried her? She's her mom?" There was an urgency in Sarah's voice that made Jessie anxious.

"I guess so," Jessie said. "But the idea is they'll all three be the parents."

"Jesus," Sarah said. "That poor baby."

"Not necessarily," Jessie began, the weight of her lie pressing down on her. "Maybe she'll . . . Laurel is different now, Mom. I think she'll be a good—"

Sarah laughed dryly, cutting her off. "Laurel's never going to change, Jessie. Laurel lives for Laurel, and Laurel alone. That's never going to change." She sighed deeply.

"Poor little baby," she said again.

CHAPTER 44

A Year and a Half Later

Emma

Emma closed the door quietly behind her; she didn't want to wake Katherine. Her heart quickened a little as she heard the latch click into place. Emma couldn't explain it, this little rush of excitement that came over her every time she crept outside in the early morning. It wasn't that she was leaving. That was the worst part of it, really; it was always with an effort that she tore herself away from the warmth of Katherine's side, the scent of her between the sheets. But Katherine would be there when she returned, and here was the cool morning against her skin, with the city laid out before her, rousing itself after the briefest of nights.

Seven months ago, she and Katherine had found an apartment together in Oakland, a detached mother-in-law suite behind a Victorian house in one of the city's older neighborhoods near Lake Merritt. The apartment had only one bedroom, and Emma had worried about putting both their names on the rental application. A family with two young children lived in the main house, and even in the Bay Area, sometimes people's prejudices surprised you. Emma had tried to send Katherine flowers again on the anniversary of their first date, but the bouquet had not been delivered.

"We were busy," the florist had said flatly when Emma stormed in to complain. "I'll refund your money."

Emma thought of the little notecard she had filled out in the florist shop—"Happy Anniversary, baby. I love you."—and had wondered. Still, it was impossible to prove that the mistake had been intentional, and Emma had swallowed her rage and held her tongue. Instead, she had snipped a single rose from the rose garden where she had taken Katherine on their second date, slipping it into Katherine's water glass while she slept.

The family that owned the apartment, though, had chosen theirs from the dozens of rental applications they had received. The dot-com boom was in full swing by then. Apartments rented the same day they listed; people lined up at open houses with their credit history reports and pay stubs in hand. When the landlord had called Emma to say the apartment was theirs if they wanted it, she had thought she would burst with gratitude at their luck.

The apartment was small, but cozy, with crown molding on the ceilings and built-in bookshelves in the living room. Emma still felt a small thrill when she saw Katherine's books there beside hers. Emma loved that when she and Katherine were together now, there was never the looming specter of their parting, with one or the other always having to go home.

But they weren't joined at the hip, unlike so many of the lesbian couples they knew. Often, on Saturdays, they did their own thing, Emma going for long bike rides in the Berkeley Hills, Katherine hiking in Pt. Reyes with some friends she'd made at work. Sundays they spent together. Katherine would be up by the time Emma got back from her morning run, sitting at the kitchen table with her coffee, reading the poetry in *The New Yorker* that Emma rarely understood. They would make breakfast together, and maybe afterwards go back to bed.

Emma smiled to herself at the thought, quickening her pace. She ran along the path that circled Lake Merritt, keeping her eyes up so that she didn't see the trash that crowded in the shallows. Her thoughts turned to her sister as she ran. Jessie had called late the night before, fairly bursting with her news. She was engaged, the date set for the following summer. Hiding in the bathroom with her phone—Katherine was asleep already—Emma had laughed a little when she'd heard. Jessie had always insisted that of the three siblings, she would be the last to marry, if in fact she ever did. There was a kind of arrogance in the way she'd said it, as if, of the three of them, she considered herself the least constrained by convention. Emma and Jay might marry, but she would have more important things to do.

But there Jessie was, giddy as anyone over her engagement, and willing to let herself be teased a little for getting it wrong after all. Emma was excited for her sister, and pleased at the idea of a wedding. Katherine would go with her, and then everyone would know.

She smiled, imagining it; she couldn't help her pride. She felt it swell within her, so that she practically floated down the path around the lake. But Emma knew it wasn't just the anticipation of her sister's wedding that had made her spirits soar. It was that Jessie had found it: the one person with whom she would spend her life. Heath wasn't just one more link in the chain of her sister's relationships. The chain was over; Heath was the final ring. The thought was vertiginous. If Heath could be the one for her sister, maybe Katherine was—

Emma wouldn't let her mind finish the thought, but her heart raced.

Emma ran for forty-five minutes and then opened the door to their shared apartment with as much excitement as when she had closed it.

Katherine was in the kitchen, making coffee. She moved out of the way so that Emma could fill a glass with water at the sink.

"Emma, you're dripping." she said.

"Sorry." Emma grabbed the dish towel from the rack and mopped her face. "You're never going to believe this."

"Please don't put that back."

"What?"

"That towel you just used to wipe your sweat."

"Oh. Okay." Emma draped the towel over the back of a chair. "But guess what?"

"What?"

"My sister got engaged."

Katherine looked up. "Really?"

"Yes!"

"Wow." Katherine poured some soy milk into her coffee and took a sip. "That's big."

"I know. I can't wait for the wedding. It will be the perfect chance for you to meet everyone."

Katherine didn't respond. Emma downed the glass of water.

"I'm going to go take a shower, and then let's make breakfast? I thought we could go to the flea market later."

"I can't, Emma. I'm going hiking."

"But . . . it's Sunday."

"Well, Melinda had family in town yesterday, so I said we could go today. I thought I told you."

"Well, you didn't. And who's Melinda?"

"No one. Just someone new at work." Katherine opened the refrigerator and put the soy milk away, then glanced at Emma. "Look, I'm sorry, Em. But you and I didn't have any plans, so I didn't think it was a big deal. I'd invite you to come, but . . . I don't know. I wouldn't want her to feel like a third wheel."

"It's just the two of you going?"

"Yeah, why?"

"I guess I always thought it was a bunch of people."

"Well, sometimes it is. But everyone was busy this weekend."

"Is Melinda a dyke?" Emma asked suddenly.

Katherine hesitated. "Yeah."

"Katherine." Emma took a step toward her, but Katherine sidestepped away.

"Emma, sorry, but you're disgusting. Don't worry, though. She's got a girlfriend."

"You used to say you liked me this way," Emma protested.

"All sweaty and gross?"

"Yeah. You said it was sexy."

Katherine shrugged. "Oh."

"So why isn't the girlfriend going?"

Katherine turned away. "I don't know. Why don't you go take a shower?"

Emma was almost to the bathroom when she heard Katherine call her. Her heart leaped.

"Yeah?"

"You forgot this sweaty towel, Em. Can you take it with you, please?"

CHAPTER 45

Emma

*O*nly *six tickets left at this price,* the website warned her. *Act fast!*

"Kat," Emma called. "Can I go ahead and get these tickets? I'm afraid the price is going to go up."

"Tickets for what?" Katherine said, coming to stand behind her.

"For Jessie's wedding. Did you get the time off work?"

"Em, it's still months away."

"Only three months. We should really get our tickets. The price will only go up."

Emma felt Katherine go still behind her. She swiveled around in the desk chair so that she was facing her.

"What's wrong? Did you not get the time off?"

"It's not that, Emma," Katherine said. Her voice was very quiet.

Emma's heart stopped. "Then what? Don't you want—"

"I'm just not sure I should go."

"What? Why?"

"Emma, it's just that I know what a big deal it is to you. You want to show me off to everyone. And it doesn't feel right."

Emma felt her whole body go cold. She waited.

"Emma, I just don't think I should go and meet your whole family as your 'girlfriend' when I'm not even sure . . ." She trailed off; she no longer looked at Emma but at the floor.

"You're not even sure what? Katherine, for Christ's sake, say it. You're killing me."

She saw Katherine nod ever so slightly, then take a breath. Emma held hers.

"When I'm not even sure we should be together." She sighed deeply, like it was a weight off, to have said it at last. But still she didn't meet Emma's eye.

Emma leaned back in the chair. She didn't trust herself to speak.

A long, awful moment passed. "Katherine," Emma managed at last. "Why?"

"Oh, Em. We're just so different. And . . . And the passion's going, don't you think?"

She peeked up at Emma's face, as if she expected her corroboration. But Emma shook her head vigorously.

"Katherine, no. That happens with everyone. It's never like it is at the beginning."

"But—"

"Katherine, please. You don't *have* to be sure. It's my sister's wedding, not ours. Everyone has doubts, Katherine. It doesn't mean—" Emma's voice cracked. She couldn't say, It *doesn't mean it's over.*

"Emma, there's someone else."

What was the difference between despair and desperation? Maybe there wasn't one, or perhaps it was only one of degree. Because, with Katherine's words, Emma felt she had been transported from the midst of one to the far edge of the other. The desolation she felt overwhelmed her.

"Katherine, *please*." She had to clench her teeth to stop her chin from trembling, and suddenly a long-suppressed memory of Laurel sprung to mind: Laurel, distraught in that psychiatrist's office so long ago. *"Emma, please,"* Laurel had begged her then. Well, now it was Emma's turn to plead. She braced herself for Katherine's scorn.

"Emma, I'm sorry. I didn't mean for this to happen."

"Who is she? Or he?"

Katherine hesitated. "I don't think I should—"

"Katherine, *who*?"

Katherine shook her head a little. Her eyes went to the ceiling and she sighed again, as if Emma was trying her. "Melinda," she said flatly.

Emma let out a little wail. All those hikes, all those Saturdays . . . God, how had she been so naïve?

"But I thought . . . You said she had a girlfriend."

"She did. They're . . . ending things, too."

Emma hadn't known that pain could be so multifaceted. Each jagged edge led to another. There was the outrage of it, the hot lash of jealousy. And God, the shame. The shame was the worst. Emma hadn't been enough for her; Katherine wanted someone else.

They're ending things, too. It was that one word, *too*, that poked its awful, fatal hole in Emma's disbelief.

She spoke quietly. "So this is the end?"

Katherine nodded. And there it was, at last. That look of pity for which Emma had waited for so long, and then had somehow stopped expecting. It was a look that said that all of Emma's desire was a pitiful thing in the end. Pitiful not because it was small or insignificant, but because it was to be pitied.

"Oh, Em," Katherine said. "I'm so sorry." She reached out for Emma, as if to comfort her.

But Emma couldn't stand her comfort; she was burning with the shame of it. "Don't touch me," she whispered. "Just go."

Katherine did go, and then it was worse, for Emma was sure she had gone straight to Melinda. Emma writhed on the bed, imagining Katherine telling Melinda what had happened, that it was over at last. Melinda would give her a sad little smile, but how pleased she would secretly be. And then they would cling to each other, each comforting the other about the wreckage she had brought. And then they would . . . *Oh God.*

Emma bobbed helplessly between rage and misery. Her face streaked with tears, she crammed Katherine's things into garbage bags and left them on the stoop—she didn't want Katherine in the apartment. She didn't *deserve* to come in. But then she waited anxiously for two days for her to come to retrieve them, desperate to see her, disconsolate when she came home from work one afternoon to find the bags were gone. Out of spite she had not included in the bags a few of Katherine's things: a set of flannel sheets, a cashmere sweater. Let her feel she had lost at least *something*, Emma thought.

Then, a few days later, as Emma was taking a bra from her underwear drawer, she noticed that the dildo and the harness were gone. Rage hit her like a punch to the gut. She doubled over, steadying herself against the dresser. How *dare* she? As soon as Emma could walk, she rushed to the computer and wrote Katherine an outraged email, then clicked "Send" without pausing, knowing even as she did so how pathetic and petty she sounded, how dog in the manger.

The next day she found the dildo on the doorstep, discreetly wrapped in plastic bags. But this only made Emma feel worse, because of course having it back didn't mean that Melinda and Katherine weren't doing it; it only meant that now Melinda knew Emma was a fool. To make matters worse, Emma had missed seeing Katherine again when she had dropped it off, which could only mean that Katherine was purposefully avoiding her, and this knowledge slid Emma right back down into despair.

"There's a beauty to grief," a friend had remarked to her once, years ago, after she had complained of some disappointment, some unmemorable malaise. "You know, doing it right. Eating chocolate cake in your pajamas and all that."

Emma had smiled at his words, thinking he was on to something. Now she realized just how stupid it was. Grief wasn't picturesque; it wasn't poignant. It was a dark place that held you under, that didn't let you breathe.

It was May; there were still two more weeks of school to be gotten through. Emma stumbled through them, shrugging off the condolences offered by the people who knew. The poems she chose for her class were all miserable, gloomy things.

> *Grief is a quiet thing*
> *Deadly in repose*
> *A raging horror, a thunder of abuse*

"Can't we read some happy poems, Ms. Walters?" her students teased her.

But all the same, they seemed to notice her mood and were kinder to her than normal. Then, one day in third period, she opened the textbook to the chapter on imagery and there was "Fog" by Carl Sandburg:

> *The fog comes in*
> *on little cat feet*
> *It sits looking*
> *over harbor and city*
> *on silent haunches*
> *and then moves on*

The tears leaped to Emma's eyes. She had to leave the room lest her students see her cry. She stood in the empty hallway, leaning heavily against the cement block wall, remembering one bright morning in bed. She had held Katherine's instep gently between her thumb and fingers.

"Your little Kat feet," she had joked, and they had both laughed at the pun. She had never thought to remember the end of the poem, but it seemed, now, like a forewarning.

When the two weeks of school were over, Emma rode BART to the Oakland airport and boarded a plane for Bakersfield. In the empty place that grief had hollowed out in her mind, one clear thought had formed: Emma wanted to go home.

It was not new to her, this ache of homesickness in her gut. Every summer of her childhood it had been the same. When Raisin was carted away from Baymont in a pickup, when Emma had crawled, numb with fear, on all fours along the dam, when her sister lay on the bathroom floor, her body curled around her pain . . . Each new trauma had released in Emma the same fierce longing to be home, to be where she was truly loved.

What a fool she had been to ever doubt that love. Emma had always wanted Sarah to *prove* her affection, as if words and embraces were what mattered most. It was only now, sitting in the window seat of the airplane, her forehead pressed against the glass, that Emma felt she understood at last.

Katherine, she thought bitterly, had told Emma she loved her a dozen times a day. And Emma had believed it, had thought that because Katherine touched her—held her, kissed her, made her come—that she was hers for good. But Emma had been wrong. It was another kind of love that mattered, Emma saw that now: the kind that stayed. The kind that gave and gave and did not stop giving even when the next best thing came along.

"It's good to have you home, Em," her father told her the next morning, while she sat at the kitchen table, drinking English Breakfast, and he flipped blueberry pancakes at the stove. "I'm sorry you've had a rough time of it, though."

Emma tried to smile. "I'll survive."

She rose and got three sets of silverware from the drawer. But even once she'd laid out all their forks and knives, their plates and napkins and juice glasses, the table still looked bare. At Christmas, when Emma had last been home, her family had barely fit around the table, with Jessie and Heath visiting from Oregon, and Jay home from college in New York.

"Do you mind it just being you and Mom here now?" Emma asked.

Her father paused, considering. "Well, we miss you kids, of course. But we never really had this time, you know, when it was just the two of us."

He added three more pancakes to a large stack warming beneath the light. "I still make too many pancakes, though. Would you go and get your mom?"

Emma climbed the stairs quietly, then gently knocked on her parents' bedroom door.

"Mom?"

"Come in," her mother said. Emma stepped inside the room. Her mother was not yet up, her face peeking out at Emma from beneath the covers.

"It's time for breakfast," Emma said, her eyes sweeping over her mother's bed. It was just as she remembered it: the same billowy comforter, piled high, with crisp, white sheets beneath. Emma couldn't help herself. Without saying anything, she walked around to the other side, kicked off her shoes, and climbed in next to her mother.

For a long moment, she and Sarah lay side by side without speaking, both gazing at the morning light that flickered on the blinds.

"You doing okay, dear?" her mother asked at last. Emma began to nod, because a second before she *had* been doing okay, maybe for the first time since Katherine had left. But even before the nod was over, the kindness in her mother's voice undid her. She began to cry.

"I'm sorry," she murmured, ashamed. Her mother never cried except in private, and Emma had always suspected that her mother wondered at her, at how easily her tears could come. She squeezed her eyes tight but the tears found their way out, trailing each other down the sides of her face to make damp gray shadows on the white pillowcase.

Her mother said nothing, but Emma heard the rustle of sheets and felt a wisp of warmth as her mother stirred. And then her mother's hand was on her forearm, her thumb stroking back and forth, back and forth.

"Oh dear," she said. "Oh dear."

"Oh, Mom," Emma sobbed, and then she got it out at last. "What if nobody ever loves me?"

"Of course they will, Emma. You just wait and see. Of course they will."

They lay like that for a long time, Emma quietly sobbing, her mother's thumb moving back and forth on her arm, until at last Emma had cried herself out. Her mother shifted in the bed to reach for a Kleenex and then waited while Emma blew her nose.

"You know," she said tenderly. "If Laurel didn't love you when you were a baby, it wasn't because you were unlovable. You were *very* loveable, Emma. You *are* loveable."

She sat up in bed, suddenly matter-of-fact. "And if that Katherine person doesn't have the sense to see that, well then, she doesn't deserve you."

With that, Emma's tears started again.

"Oh dear," her mother said softly. "I didn't mean to reopen the floodgate." She pressed Emma's arm sympathetically and reached again for the box of Kleenex. Emma was laughing through her sobs now, clutching half a dozen sodden Kleenexes, not sure of what to do with them in her mother's perfect bed. But she felt a new lightness inside, as if all those tears had, at last, washed something out of her.

"The pancakes are almost ready," Emma said, pulling the comforter up to her chin.

"We'd better get up then, hadn't we?" her mother said. But she made no move to rise. "I think your dad will understand."

CHAPTER 46

Jessie

The large wooden shelter had a roof but no walls. There was that, at least. Jessie did not want to get married inside, but the rain would not let up. It came down in sheets and then in trickles, awful trickles that gave her hope, then in sheets again. The ground squished underfoot.

When they had chosen this place as their venue, Heath had pointed out the shelter where Jessie stood now.

"That'll be good to have, just in case it rains."

She had nodded distractedly, ignoring him, trying to picture where they would stand in the meadow—by the creek, or by the trees? But there was no chance of that now, even if the rain did stop. The meadow was a wash.

It *is* cozy here, she thought, looking around at the dry platform, resigning herself. Cozy and dry, with the rain dripping down off the sloped roof and the brilliant green of the forest beyond, its colors vibrant with so much to drink.

Jessie zipped up her rain jacket and ducked back into the downpour. She had better go start moving chairs.

Jessie had wanted a small wedding, and they had tried. But even with only immediate family and friends, the guest list had turned out longer than she had expected. She was relieved when the chairs all fit in the shelter.

"Thanks for helping, Em," she said, moving the last one into place.

Emma was toweling off a row of chairs. She straightened. "Of course."

"Em—" Jessie began. "I know we should have talked about this before, but—"

"You want to know what to expect on your wedding night?"

Emma said this with such a straight face that Jessie had to laugh. Emma grinned.

"Seriously, though, Jess . . . What should we have talked about?" she asked.

"Well, you know Laurel's coming right? With Jim and Sue."

"I assumed so."

"They're bringing Elizabeth."

"Oh." Emma looked away. "How old is she now?"

"She just turned two. You . . . You didn't tell Mom and Dad, did you, Emma?"

Emma looked back at her sister sharply. "No, I didn't tell them. I said I wouldn't."

Now Jessie sighed. "I guess I sort of wished you had. And that they didn't care."

"Well, I didn't tell them. And, well . . . it's sort of hard to imagine they won't care, isn't it? But wait . . . You're not planning to tell them today, are you?"

"Of course not," Jessie said. "I just thought you should know that Elizabeth would be here. So you wouldn't be surprised."

Emma nodded. She studied her sister's face. "Jess? Did *you* know she was going to be here? Are you okay with it?"

"Yes, yes, of course," Jessie said, not meeting her sister's eye. "I mean, why wouldn't I be?"

Emma raised her eyebrows. "Well, it is a little odd, isn't it? To have your kid at your own wedding?"

"She's not my kid, Emma. Please don't call her that."

"Well, whatever she is. Are you sure you're okay with it?"

"I'm fine."

In truth, Jessie wasn't sure how she felt. When she had sent the invitation to Laurel, she hadn't expected they would *all* come. And at first it had seemed they wouldn't. Laurel had talked of coming alone with Jim; Sue would stay home with Liza. But then, two weeks ago, they had changed their minds. Laurel had called her excitedly with the news.

"Just wanted to let you know it'll be the whole crew!" she said. "So you can adjust your numbers."

Jessie had sighed, abandoning once and for all any hope she still had that they would keep the guest list under thirty.

"Okay," she said. "That's fine."

"And since Liza is coming . . . Well, I just wondered—would you want her in your wedding? You know, flower girl or something? She would be so cute."

But Jessie had drawn the line at that. "We're not having that kind of a ceremony," she had explained. "It'll just be us and the justice of the peace. I don't even have bridesmaids."

"Well, okay," Laurel said, sounding slightly wounded. "I just thought I'd offer."

"Mom?" Jessie had said. "Dad and . . . Sarah—they still don't know, okay? So can you please . . ." Jessie had flushed, stumbling over the words. She wouldn't call Sarah "Mom" to Laurel; it rang too cruel. But to say "Dad and Sarah" when Jessie had always called Sarah "Mom"—there was a tinge of treason to it, and she felt ashamed.

"Can we please be discreet?" Laurel had finished for her. "Of course!" She sounded almost gleeful at the prospect, as if she had just been granted a leading role. "Not a word."

CHAPTER 47

Emma

E mma's insides felt wrapped so tight she was sure she would have gas. She sat next to her brother on one end of a semicircle of wedding guests, clutching a folded paper in her hand. On it, in her own handwriting, was a little homily to her sister. It was what she would share during the ceremony, when it came time for that. Emma liked what she had written; she was proud of how well she knew her sister. She knew the sensibilities that hid beneath Jessie's eccentricities, the softness and the savage strength of her. If Jessie didn't fit into the mainstream, it was because she didn't *want* to, because, to her, the world was something else entirely. Something grander and more complicated, Emma thought, something Jessie could revel in and wonder about and strive to make better.

Emma felt a flash of pure pride in her sister, washed of envy, and she clung to the feeling, wanting to hold it. For she had resolved—she would *not* feel sorry for herself. She would not let herself be green—or blue—today.

Emma looked around at the gathering guests and felt a stab of nerves. Gently she unfolded the paper in her hand, which had gone limp in the damp air, and began to read it over.

"Wasn't Laurel going to come to this?" Jay said, his voice low, startling her. "I thought she would be here. I wanted to see—you know."

Emma's gut made another twist. Her brother was right—where *was* Laurel? She scanned the small crowd. But just at that moment, the music started; all around her, guests shifted and smiled and strained to see. Suddenly, there was Heath, walking down the path toward the shelter, wearing an REI rain jacket and weathered hiking boots and looking, despite his sheepish expression, almost exactly as if he might be setting off on a hike through the dripping woods.

A low murmur ran through the guests, and Emma smiled. *Everyone's thinking what I'm thinking*, she thought. *He's perfect for her.*

Heath cleared the steps up onto the shelter in two easy bounds, and then stood before the small crowd, grinning nervously. But nobody was looking at him. Suddenly another murmur went up, this one louder than the first. Emma looked back toward the path and smiled when she caught sight of her sister. She was wearing a dress, not white but burgundy. The color was high in her face, and her wet hair, loose to her shoulders, had dampened the fabric so that it was almost black. Emma guessed that she had squeezed a run in, and had just come from the shower. As Jessie passed in front of her, Emma could see drops of perspiration beading up on her forehead, and she had to stifle a laugh. Jessie *had* been running, Emma was sure of it now. Despite the shower, she was still sweating.

Jessie caught her eye as she passed and smiled. Beside her, Jay gave a low chuckle. "Only Jessie," he murmured, and Emma grinned.

Their sister took her place beside Heath and looked out at the guests, smiling broadly. But almost immediately her face grew serious; Emma watched as her sister scanned the crowd.

The tangle in Emma's stomach tightened. Where was Laurel?

Jessie murmured something to Heath, who frowned, shook his head, and mouthed a question. Jessie shrugged and straightened, then nodded at the justice, who cleared his throat and opened a small notebook.

"Welcome," he said.

Emma tried to listen to the justice's words, but found herself instead watching the tendrils of dampness sneaking down the back of her sister's dress. She forced herself to keep her eyes pinned to her sister; otherwise they kept darting down the little path, watching for Laurel's arrival.

But even with her eyes on the ceremony, Emma knew the minute they arrived. She watched Jessie startle at the same moment her own gut lurched. Heath, Jessie, and Emma all turned to look at the same instant; through the woods came the high-pitched timbre of a child's voice, indecipherable, and the lower ones of an adult, answering. Still hidden in the trees, they had no idea how close they were, how much the sound carried.

The justice paused, mid-sentence, as all the guests looked, too, until everyone's neck was craned toward the little path, as if the bride were still to come.

A child's voice again, louder, but now the colors of them were visible through the trees, and they must have seen the shelter, too, standing hushed now and waiting, because the grown-up voice was softer, shushing. In another instant, they were out of the trees, and although there had never been any question of who it was, now it was certain. There was Laurel in the lead, in a long paisley skirt she held in both hands, hitching it up above the dampness of the grass. Behind her came the two other adults. Sue carried the toddler in her arms; Jim walked at her side. The child had gone silent now, hiding her face against her mother's shoulder.

Laurel smiled apologetically as she mounted the stairs.

"We are *so* sorry. A travel nightmare that you wouldn't believe!"

The justice smiled indulgently. "Welcome."

Laurel directed her entourage toward some empty seats in the back of the circle, and slowly heads turned back to where Heath and Jessie stood. Now that she wasn't waiting anymore, the tension in Jessie's stance eased. Emma felt her own stomach soften. She leaned back in her chair a little, suddenly aware of how rigid she had been holding herself.

Emma barely made it through the reading she had prepared. She saw the tears in Jessie's eyes as she spoke, and her own voice cracked. Then they were both crying, and laughing. The guests murmured appreciatively and laughed, too, and suddenly Jessie broke away from Heath's side and crushed her in a hug.

As Emma found her seat, the crowd quieted politely, eyes darting, wondering who would go next. Beside her, Emma heard Jay's chair scrape against the wooden floor as he rose. Jay was six foot two, with black wavy hair that fell artfully across his forehead. He had arrived only this morning on a red-eye from New York, where he was spending the summer doing an internship at a marketing agency, but his shirt was perfectly ironed, his khakis crisp. Beside him, Heath looked slightly rumpled and unkempt. Emma smiled up at Jay. She only saw her brother at Thanksgiving and Christmas now, and it still surprised her a little, to see him so grown up.

Jay cleared his throat. "I'm Jay, Jessie's brother, and as you can probably tell," he began, looking down at himself appraisingly, "Jessie and I are pretty different."

The crowd chuckled.

"Jessie is five-years older than I am, and when we were growing up together, we weren't really that close. In fact, back then I always sort of suspected that Jessie didn't really think that much of me. I was just her kid brother who cared about sports and video games and other trivial stuff like that, *and* she could beat me at running even when she gave me a huge head start." He met Jessie's eye and winked, and the crowd laughed again. "Anyway, it occurred to me today that maybe my sister thought the same thing about me. So I think I'll take this opportunity to set the record straight. Jessie, anyone who knows you at all knows what a powerhouse you are, and I am no exception."

Jay turned to Heath.

"Heath, I hope you appreciate what a pot of gold you have found in my sister. She has aced every test she's ever taken, she's faster than all the boys—or she was in sixth grade anyway—and she is a hell of an arm-wrestler. That's all. I hope you'll be very happy together."

Jay returned to his seat next to Emma, and she looked up at him wonderingly.

"Wow, Jay," she whispered. "Nice job. I didn't know you felt that way."

Jay looked down at her. "Boys have feelings, too, you know. Sometimes we are even able to articulate some of them."

She grinned. "Go figure," she said. "Maybe I'll keep that in mind if this whole lesbian thing doesn't work out."

The sharing came to an end, at last, and the guests murmured as they watched Heath and Jessie take the steps hand in hand and disappear together down the path that led into the woods. When they had gone, there was a restless shifting; chairs scraped the wooden floor, children whispered audibly to their parents, "Is it over now?"

The justice smiled. "Yes, the ceremony is now over. Thank you for your participation. There will be dinner and dancing in the lodge, if you'd like to make your way there and join Jessie and Heath."

Guests soon began to trickle out of the shelter and up the trail; others stood milling about, talking, while a handful of older kids began to leap from the edge of the shelter into the wet grass below.

Emma watched as Laurel separated herself from her clan and walked toward Len and Sarah.

"Leonard," she said, holding out her hand. "Sarah."

"Laurel." They each shook it. "How are you."

It was not a question, but still Laurel rattled on.

"Oh, wonderful. Just wonderful. I'm so . . . proud? Happy? I don't know what I am! But you must know what I mean."

Emma watched her father glance away, her mother nod tersely.

"Jessie was worried, of course, that this might be . . . 'weird' I think was her word. But I told her there was nothing to worry about. We are all grown-ups, I told her. Surely we could all get along now. Surely there wouldn't be—"

"Momma," a tiny voice called out. "Momma!"

Laurel faltered in mid-sentence and turned. "Liza!"

Emma, Len, Sarah—all turned in the direction of the voice. A little girl, more a toddler than a child, was racing across the shelter toward them, holding out her arms.

"Momma!"

Her blond hair was in two pigtails on each side of her head, her small face round and lightly freckled, her eyes blue-green and almond-shaped. She looks familiar, Emma thought suddenly. She looks like . . .

Emma felt her heart stop for one long second, felt the color drain from her face. She looks like *me*, she thought. There was a photo in her bedroom at home, taken soon after their family had moved to Bakersfield. In the picture, she and Jessie sat together in the porch swing of their new house, their legs stretched out in front of them so that their faces seemed to peek out at the camera from behind the little knobs of their toes. Emma's face was round as a cantaloupe, she had always thought, with two pig-tails sprouting like stems from either side.

Oh no, she thought now, her eyes going first to the child, still running toward Laurel, and then to Sarah. She watched her mother register the girl, watched her see the pigtails, the round face, the sea-green eyes. She didn't know if her mother thought, then, of the same photograph that she had immediately called to mind, but she saw her mother's face go white, watched her clutch at her father's hand as if to steady herself.

"Len," she said.

Len looked at her with relief. "Time to go the lodge, isn't it?"

Laurel knelt to catch the girl in her arms. "This is my . . ." she began, then faltered. "This is our Liza. Jessie told you, I guess, that Sue had—"

Sarah frowned down at the girl. "Yes, we heard."

"Glad you could make it, Laurel," Len said. "We should probably—"

"Of course." Laurel scooped the little girl awkwardly onto her hip. "We'll all come along in a minute, too."

In the lodge, Emma immediately found the ladies' room. She stood in the narrow stall, taking deep breaths to steady herself. Suddenly she heard the outer door to the restroom open. There were only two stalls; she couldn't stay inside much longer without being conspicuous. Readying herself to smile at whomever had just come in, she unlatched the stall door and pushed it open. Then she froze. Her mother stood in front of the sink, digging a tissue from her bag.

"Mom."

Sarah looked up, saw Emma, and looked away. She blew her nose.

"That little girl."

Emma didn't speak. She felt herself nod.

"She looks—she looks just like you did, Emma, when you were that age."

Emma's chin dipped again.

"Is she—?" Sarah asked. "Did you—?"

"Mom. *No.*"

Her mother nodded. "I didn't really think so," she said. "Jessie then."

Emma closed her eyes.

"You knew, didn't you?"

Emma said nothing.

"Oh, Emma. It's not fair of her. She can't keep asking you to keep secrets like that."

"Mom, she doesn't *keep* asking."

"Well, it's not fair, is it? To make you carry that around."

"I thought . . . Well, I think she meant to tell you. After the wedding, maybe."

"Yes," Sarah said dryly. "I could see how that would be more convenient."

"Laurel knew it was . . . a secret. How could she not have predicted this? She must have known—"

Sarah laughed mirthlessly. "Oh, I don't know. She didn't see much of you at that age. The resemblance might not be so striking to her."

"But—"

"And even if she had realized, do you think that would have stopped her? I am absolutely certain that Laurel wouldn't have passed up a chance like this to put her 'family' on display—"

"Mom."

"It's true, Emma. She's thrilled to bits at having created a sensation. You just have to look at her—"

"Mom," Emma interrupted. "I'm sorry."

Sarah looked at Emma.

"Why?"

"For keeping it from you. I hated it." Despite herself, Emma could feel her tears rising. God, she was so fragile these days; the slightest thing could set her off.

"Oh, Emma. This is exactly what I meant. You shouldn't have been put in this position. It's just not fair."

Emma sighed. "Well, it's over now."

But her mother shook her head. "I doubt that, Emma. I really do."

Emma was in line at the buffet when Laurel came to stand behind her.

"Hello, Laurel," Emma said, turning. She looked down and

saw to her surprise that Laurel was alone. "Where is—?" She hesitated. "Where's the little one?"

"With Sue and Jim. I saw you here and just thought I'd—"

Emma nodded. "How are you?"

"Wonderful. Wonderful! You wouldn't believe what a blessing . . . what a complete joy this baby has been. Yesterday she said the funniest—"

"I just hope you're grateful," Emma interrupted. The words seemed to have left her mouth before she had even thought them. "Very, *very* grateful."

"Grateful? Of course. Didn't I just say what a blessing—"

"I meant, *to Jessie*. I hope that you appreciate what she did. To give something like that. It's a *very* big deal." Emma heard how schoolmarmy her voice sounded; she felt strangely as if she were speaking to a child. But she couldn't stand Laurel's cheerful flippancy.

Now Laurel's eyes teared up, and Emma had to look away.

"Oh yes," Laurel said, her voice cracking. "Yes, we are very grateful. Jessie . . . Jessie was very generous."

Emma nodded tersely, then looked toward the buffet table. They hadn't moved any closer, and she couldn't stand the thought of trying to make conversation with Laurel as they crept along in the slow-moving line.

"You know, I think I might wait until the line dies down," she said. Across the room, she spotted Aunt Margie. "And there's my aunt. I better go say hi."

She said an awkward goodbye to Laurel and made her way across the room to where Aunt Margie stood. When the older lady saw her, she grabbed her in a fierce embrace.

"You girls are so big, I can't believe it. It seems like just the other day when . . ."

Aunt Margie launched into reminiscing, and Emma smiled and nodded along; she felt her mind grow calmer in Aunt

Margie's steady presence. Then, suddenly, she became aware that Aunt Margie's gaze had shifted. She was no longer looking into Emma's eyes but two inches above them. Emma raised a hand to her forehead, self-conscious, and then immediately understood. Her hair.

"You girls used to have such beautiful, long hair."

Emma laughed. "Yeah, well, I cut it off a couple of weeks ago."

"For goodness' sakes. Right before the wedding? Why on earth . . . ?"

Emma smiled grimly. She had asked herself the same question often enough over the past few weeks, staring into the mirror at her cropped hair. In truth, she didn't know how to explain why she had cut it. It had been a bad day; all morning she had lain in bed, despondent. When she had finally gotten up, she had wielded the scissors recklessly, as if the dull blades might cut away her grief.

Later, she had wished she hadn't. Katherine's leaving had changed her. Emma was not the upbeat, sanguine person that she used to be, and now . . . Now she no longer even looked like herself. Even her own regret depressed her, because she sensed that there was something homophobic in it. She could feel other lesbians notice her now; she saw their infinitesimal nods as they passed her on the street, and she began to understand that in the queer community a short haircut was less a style than a subtle flag: *I'm one of you*. But with Katherine gone, Emma didn't want to look like a dyke. Without Katherine, she felt dismembered, disarranged. She didn't want to be recognized; she wanted to be invisible.

Now she forced herself to smile. "Don't worry, Aunt Margie, it'll grow back."

But Aunt Margie was looking at her seriously.

"Emma," she said earnestly. "Your father told me about you . . . I mean, about your . . ."

Emma's stomach plunged for no reason she could have explained. "He told you about Katherine?"

"Yes."

"What did he tell you, exactly? It wasn't a secret," she added quickly, suddenly sick of the very word. "I would have told you, if . . ." If Katherine hadn't left, she thought. If she were here now.

"He just said that you were dating a . . . dating a girl." She paused, and again her eyes darted upward. "Is that why you have your hair like that, Jessie? Is that lesbian hair?"

Emma laughed. "No. Well, maybe." She paused. "Katherine . . . My girlfriend left me a few months ago. Cutting my hair was just an act of misery."

Aunt Margie looked first startled, then concerned. "Oh dear."

Emma shrugged. "Like I said, it'll grow."

But Aunt Margie was sweeping her arms around, gesturing at everything at once. "Well, surely it was for the best? I mean— don't you want this?" she said. "Don't you want all this?"

Emma looked around at the milling guests. She caught sight of her mother's stony face, saw Laurel's broad back bending over the buffet table. Still, she knew what Aunt Margie meant.

"Yeah, I guess." She wanted to add something else, to point out that she could have "all this" with a woman, too, but Aunt Margie looked so relieved to have straightened her out that she let it go. If Katherine were here with her, there would have been a point to it. But what was the point now?

CHAPTER 48

Jessie

For weeks after the wedding, Jessie understood that her parents were punishing her. She called and left message after message on their new voicemail, but they didn't call her back. She suspected that they had caller ID now; even when she called their land line at times they were sure to be at home, no one picked up. Each time that she heard her mother's cheerful recorded greeting, "This is the Walters' residence," Jessie felt her stomach lurch and a hollowness open up inside her. It was not an unfamiliar feeling, and that only made it worse. One minute Jessie would be a happy newlywed, eager to share some small detail with Len and Sarah, the next she would be hurtled back to adolescence, plunged into her parents' cool anger, so that even now nothing else seemed to matter but that their hearts seemed closed to her.

At fourteen, Jessie thought that she had understood it; it was easy to see how she had transgressed. When she had said she wanted to live with Laurel in Baymont, she had given voice to a dream that they would never understand. That her parents had been hurt by this was obvious at once. But it had taken Jessie years to understand the subtle distance that had come between them then.

Oh, it was such a hard thing to put her finger on. On the surface, things had proceeded as normal—her parents came to her cross country meets and signed her report cards and bid her goodnight—and yet still she had felt as if she didn't quite belong. It had been impossible to put right, impossible to know how to respond. To feel dejected, which she did, only left her dejected with no hope of comfort or compassion, for how could she lament the awful distance she felt between them, when it had been she who had first put it there? To feel angry was out of the question, since anger meant pushing away, and what did she have to push against? To answer her parents' anger with anger of her own was to risk an even wider gulf, and for this she didn't have the courage or the heart.

It was the loneliest she had ever been. Even Emma had proved little comfort, tiptoeing around her as if she were a whole new animal, unknown and not to be trusted.

It had been a raw and dismal time, a persistent ache inside her chest. And she had felt then, Jessie thought, almost exactly as she felt now. Still, Jessie found that she could not quite believe it. Would her parents truly cast her out over *this*? They were *her* eggs. A gift of compassion, not some deeper symbol of allegiance. She called home yet again, counting the five hollow rings before her mother's voice came on the line. "This is the Walters' residence. Please leave a message."

This time, she didn't. She had already left too many. She hung up the phone and sat down heavily at the kitchen table.

A moment later, Heath came in, took one look at her, and sat down across the table.

"What's wrong?" he asked.

She looked up and tried to smile. "Why do you think something's wrong?"

"You never sit down, Jessie. I have never once seen you just sit down. 'Wow,' I said to myself, 'Jessie's sitting down. Something must be wrong.' So what is it?"

Jessie laughed wryly. "You're very perceptive."

"Is it me?" Heath asked. "Did I put a paper napkin in the garbage instead of the compost? Oh no, it's worse, isn't it? I used a paper napkin in the first place."

Jessie laughed in spite of herself. "No, Heath, it doesn't have anything to do with you. It's just . . . I just called home. Again. And no one answers. I leave messages, and no one returns my calls."

Heath looked around the kitchen. "You called here? And I didn't answer? Oh baby, I'm sorry. I must not have heard the phone."

He was so deadpan, Jessie didn't realize at first that he was joking. "Not here. *Home*," she began and then stopped. "Not here," she said again. "Not *this* home. I meant my parents'."

Heath sighed. "I knew what you meant. But I was trying to make a point. *This* is home, isn't it? Wasn't that why we got married? So we'd have a home together?"

He sounded so serious that Jessie had to smile. "Yeah. But—"

"But what?"

"I think they're mad at me."

"Mad at you for what? Oh, wait, I know. Mad because there wasn't any alcohol at the wedding—"

"Can't you be serious for a second?" she snapped. "This matters to me."

Heath's eyebrows shot up, taken aback by her tone. "Okay."

He said nothing for a moment, and Jessie put her face in her hands. Now he would be mad at her, too.

"I'm sorry," she said, not looking at him. "I'm sorry I snapped."

"It's okay," he said. "I can take it. But seriously. Why are they . . . Why do you think they're mad at you?"

Jessie was silent for a moment, and then she spoke quickly, not wanting to give him time to misunderstand, to joke. "Because of the eggs I gave Laurel, Heath. Because of Liza."

Heath let out his breath in a rush. "Are you sure? I mean, maybe they're just out of town or something."

"I've called their cell phones, too, and they don't answer." Jessie shook her head sadly and met his eye. "And remember what happened at the wedding?"

Heath nodded. "I know that Emma said that your mom . . .

that Sarah had figured it out because the little girl looked so much like your sister used to. But did she . . . Did Sarah say anything to you about it?"

"No. That's the point. They aren't talking to me."

Heath said nothing for a moment; the kitchen was silent except for the drumming of his fingers on the table.

"Well," he said at last. "Maybe it's for the best. You didn't mean for it to stay a secret forever, did you?"

"No, but . . . Oh, I knew this would happen. I *knew* that as soon as they found out, I'd be on the outs again. That I'd feel like . . . Like I do now."

"But why? Why do they care what you do with your eggs? It's your decision, isn't it? I can understand them not approving . . . Hell, my parents don't approve of half of what I do. But this has nothing to do with them. Why would it make them angry?"

"They probably think it *does* have something to do with them. That little girl—she's the first grandchild, if you want to think about it that way."

Heath sighed. "I suppose."

"But I don't think that's it, really. I think it's a question of allegiances. By giving those eggs to Laurel—"

"Well, technically you gave them to Sue—"

"They wouldn't see it that way. By giving those eggs to Laurel, it's like I've aligned myself with her. Like I've chosen her over them. Again."

Jessie's throat tightened as she spoke, so by the end she was barely able to get the words out. She lowered her head into her arms on the table, heard Heath's chair scrape the floor, then the heavy clomp of his boots on the linoleum. She felt his arm come around her shoulder.

"Hey. So what? So what if they're angry? You know, I was joking before, when I said that about this being home. But I did mean it. *This* is your home. This is our family now. They don't . . . They shouldn't matter so much anymore."

Jessie nodded without raising her head from the table. "I know. But they do."

Jessie didn't believe him. After all, Heath was an only child of parents who were still happily married; there was no way he could understand what she had felt—that insidious unease of not belonging, the constant tension of torn allegiances. Still, she appreciated that he meant to comfort her, and he *was* a comfort, really. Just the solid bulk of him next to her in bed, the way his weight on the mattress created an inevitable downhill slope, so that she couldn't help but slide toward him until her side pressed tightly against his.

Jessie appreciated Heath's solidity. She knew, without needing to test it, that it would take a momentous force to rock him. Unrelentingly restless, Jessie had always thought that she needed someone who would match her unabated striving, her nonstop pace. Instead, she had stumbled upon a rock. Heath was her counterweight and her anchor, the solid shore onto which her restive soul could beat again and again and again. In those early days of their marriage, she found herself sighing with relief at random times throughout the day, grateful almost to tears that she had found him.

On Tuesday the following week, Jessie sat in her favorite armchair reading *Science*. She kept glancing up at Heath, who was disassembling his camping stove at the kitchen table. He was leaving tomorrow for an environmental impact study in eastern Washington, where they were planning to build a highway through an old burial ground. He wouldn't be home until Saturday.

Suddenly she thought of Heath's words, *"This* is home now," and, for the first time, she felt the truth in them. This was her place, her home, her little family. It felt unequivocal, final. Jessie felt something settle inside her at last.

The sense of peace lingered all week; her days had a new

tranquility. On Friday afternoon, just as she was about to turn off her work computer and bike home, she hesitated. She sat down again at her desk and opened Google, then typed "florist" and "Bakersfield" into the search field. From the heights of her new serenity, it wasn't hard to humble herself. "I know you're angry," she typed into the message box. "Please forgive me." There was an extra charge for Saturday delivery, but she clicked on the "Complete Purchase" button before she could change her mind.

The next day she was on edge. She checked her phone constantly to see if she had somehow missed their call. With Heath away, the house seemed quiet in a way it never had when she'd lived alone, and she was grateful when, close to five, she heard his pickup in the driveway at last.

"I can't believe it," she said into his chest that night in bed. "What else can I do?"

"They'll come around," Heath said, stroking her hair behind her ear. "You'll see."

The next morning her phone rang while she was clearing the breakfast dishes from the table. Her stomach lurched as she reached for it.

"Hello?"

"Hello?" her father's voice said. "Jessie?"

"Hi, Dad. It's me."

"Oh hello, Jessie," he said. There was a click on the line and for a second Jessie thought the call had been lost. Then she heard her mother's voice.

"Hi, Jessie."

There was a moment of tense silence.

"I just—" Jessie began.

"The flowers came late yesterday, just as we were leaving to meet some friends for dinner," Sarah said. "They're beautiful. Thank you."

"Oh," Jessie said. "You're welcome. I—"

"Jessie," said her father. "We appreciate the flowers. And, uh, your words. I suppose . . . I suppose you sensed some coolness from us."

Jessie nodded, forced herself to speak. "Yes."

"And do you know why?" her mother asked slowly.

"I suppose," Jessie said, borrowing her father's word. "I suppose it was because of the eggs? Because of Liza?"

Jessie tried to sound contrite, but even she could hear the note of belligerence that had crept into her voice. Because didn't her parents have something to answer for, too? You couldn't just *treat* someone like that, with not one word of explanation. You couldn't treat your *daughter* like that. As soon as the thought formed, she stumbled over it. What if Sarah and Len no longer thought of her as a daughter? What if they had already written her off, but hadn't had the courage to tell her so?

For a moment, there was silence on the line. "Well?" Jessie asked at last. "Am I right?"

"Yes," they said, in unison.

Jessie sighed. "Look, Mom. Dad. I'm sorry I didn't tell you. I should have, I know."

"It's not about you telling us or not telling us, Jessie, although you put your sister in a terrible position, you know."

"Is that what you're angry about? About Emma? Emma and I . . . We're . . . We're fine."

Jessie heard her mother sigh.

"I just can't believe that this is about Emma. What is this *really* about, Mom?" Jessie blurted out. She heard the exasperation in her voice and cringed. This was not how she spoke to her parents.

"Jessie," Sarah said, and the way she said it—cautionary, almost reprimanding—made Jessie feel twelve. But she wasn't twelve. She felt something inside her loosen, then break free. She didn't try to stop the words that came.

"Is it that Laurel and I are close? Is it that we are close enough that I would want to do something like this for her? Is *that* it? You two could never stand it, could you? You could never stand it that I might—heaven forbid—actually *love* Laurel. That I might love my mother. That I might love her and want her to be happy. I'm sorry that I didn't tell you. I'm sorry, Dad, that I put your grandchild into the world without consulting you. If that's what this is about, I can see how—"

"That child has NOTHING to do with me," Len snapped. "Nothing!"

"Then what? It was my choice, wasn't it? It's my body. My eggs. If I want to give them to God-knows-who, what difference does it make to you? You said it yourself. Their daughter—she has nothing to do with you. So . . . why should it matter to you so much? Why is it such a big deal to you that you have to . . . that you want to shut me out?"

There was a heavy clunk on the line, and with a start Jessie guessed that her father had hung up. The clunk was followed by silence, and Jessie's stomach dropped. Maybe they had both hung up. Could it really happen like this, she wondered. Could she really lose her parents over the phone?

"Mom?" she said. "Mom? Are you still there?"

"I'm here," she said. "Your father is not."

Jessie took a deep breath. "Oh."

"He's very angry, Jessie. And so am I."

"But why, Mom? *Why?* I'm trying to understand this from your perspective, I really am. But all I end up with is that you're punishing me for doing this for Laurel, and that just doesn't . . . seem *right*. I mean, it doesn't mean that I don't—"

She was going to say, "It doesn't mean that I don't love you," but she didn't get the words out in time before Sarah interrupted.

"Are you going to give me a chance to answer, Jessie? You want to know why we're angry? I'll tell you why. Your dad and I spent *so* many years trying to keep you and your sister safe. We were newlyweds, Jessie. We were in love. We were like *you*, now, overjoyed to be starting our own family. But we couldn't just be joyful, because there was always Laurel, always something to worry about. Your dad was always terrified he was going to lose you, did you know that? But worse even than that was worrying about how we could possibly keep you safe when you went up there. There was *always* Laurel, leaving you with that so-called babysitter who took you to jump off the top of dams and God knows what else . . . And that was the least of it. Do you remember the things you girls used to tell us when you'd come home? 'Mommy loves Cactus because he likes it when she sits on his face.' God, Jessie, it was enough to make me sick, imagining you girls up there by yourselves, without one responsible adult looking out for you. We could never just be happy, your dad and I, the way you are now with Heath. There was always this specter hanging over us, waiting for the letter demanding custody, waiting for June when we'd have to put you on that plane.

"But we got through it, Jessie. We held onto you and Emma. We spent what should have been the early, happy, carefree years of our marriage trying to keep you safe. So can't you see why this would upset us? Why it might make us angry? We tried *so hard* to keep you girls safe. And now? Now there is another little girl. Another little girl with Laurel for a mother and absolutely nothing we can do about it."

Sarah finally stopped. She took a deep breath. "So, technically yes, you're right: she has nothing to do with us. But maybe now you can see why it . . . why it upset us, learning what we did about how she came to be. And maybe we should have called sooner. But we were very angry, Jessie, and you just got married, remember? We thought we should let you try to enjoy this time without—"

Jessie opened her mouth to protest and found she couldn't speak. It took her breath away, to hear her time at Baymont described like that—like a gauntlet of horrors she had narrowly escaped, with Laurel as an irresponsible demon of a mother, hanging over her parents' lives like a dark shadow they couldn't shake. The picture her mother painted was so unlike her own version of her life that she could hardly believe they were talking about the same thing, the same person.

"That's not how I remember it," she managed at last.

"Of course not," Sarah said, her voice gentler than before. "You were a child."

"And Laurel. She's not like . . . She's not like the person you describe. She's different now."

Sarah laughed dryly. "Not Laurel," she said. "Laurel won't ever change."

"Mom! You don't even *know* her. You're basing this on, what? What happened over twenty years ago. People change. She's not . . . She's *different* from how you remember her. She just wants another chance to have a family."

"No, Jessie, I don't think she has changed. For Laurel, no one will ever be as important as Laurel." She paused briefly and drew a breath. "And do you want to know why I am absolutely certain that that is still true?"

"Yes!"

"I *know* that it is true because I do not think that any mother who was thinking of someone other than herself would ask her own daughter what she asked of you."

For a moment neither of them spoke. Sarah seemed to be waiting for Jessie to say something. When she didn't, Sarah went on.

"Yes, I am angry with you, Jessie. I think you were very foolish to agree to this. But I am angrier with Laurel. What kind of mother asks her own daughter to give up her eggs? To give up her child?"

"Liza's not—"

"Yes, she is. She is your biological child, whether you choose to see it that way or not. Laurel wasn't thinking of what was best for you when she asked you for your eggs, I guarantee it. She was thinking of what was best for Laurel—just like she always has and always will."

CHAPTER 49

Six Months Later

Jessie

It was still dark outside when her telephone rang. Jessie could hear it ringing but clung to her dream, surfacing only slowly into consciousness. She saw first the black beyond the windows, then checked the clock: 5:12 a.m. The ringing had stopped, the call gone to voicemail. Jessie let her head sink back onto the pillow and closed her eyes. A moment later the relentless rings began again. Heath stirred beside her; Jessie roused herself and slipped quietly from the bed. She took her phone from the dresser and glanced at the screen. It was Laurel. She stepped into the bathroom as she answered it.

"Hello?" she croaked into her phone, her throat dry from sleep.

"Oh, you picked up. Thank God!"

"Mom, it's not even—"

"I know, I know. It's too early to call. But I had to talk to you. They're gone!" Laurel's voice was hysterical.

"Who's gone? Mom, wait a second. I really have to pee."

Before her mother could protest, she set the phone on the sink and used the toilet, then washed her hands and downed half a cup of water from a toothpaste-streaked cup.

"Sorry," she said, returning the phone to her ear. "But I just woke up and I really had to go. Now—what's going on?"

"They're gone," Laurel said again, urgently. "Liza! And Sue! They're gone."

A jolt went through Jessie. "What? What do you mean *gone*? Have you called the police—?"

"The police?" Laurel sounded puzzled. "No, it's not like that. It's Sue. She's . . . she's taken her."

"Taken her? What do you mean?"

"When I woke up this morning, I didn't hear Liza. I thought it was odd, because usually she wakes me up. But at first I didn't think much of it. I just thought she must still be asleep. And then I went downstairs and there was this . . ." Laurel's voice cracked. "There was this note on the table—from Sue. She'd taken her."

Jessie's head was spinning. She went quietly into the kitchen and sat down at the table.

"Mom, slow down, please. I don't understand. What did the note say, exactly?"

"Here, I'll read it to you." There was no pause; Laurel must have had it in hand.

"Did this just happen?" Jessie asked.

"Yes, I called you right away."

"Well, what does it say?" Jessie's heart began to pound.

"Dear Jim and Laurel,

I know that you will probably think it is cowardly of me to tell you this in a letter, and perhaps it is. But I wanted to avoid a scene, for Liza's sake. I am leaving this house, and I am taking my daughter with me.

'But why?' I know you are asking, so I will tell you.

Two weeks ago, when I dropped Liza off at daycare, they asked me, 'Who will be picking her up today? You or her grandmother?' Of course they meant you, Laurel, and all at once it hit me—this is what it will be like for her for her entire childhood.

I love my daughter more than anything and I can't do this to her. I don't want her to have to explain all the time. Can you imagine how it will be for her? 'Yes, I have two mothers. No, they're not lesbians. Well, technically she's my grandmother, but actually . . .'

'I don't want that for her. Please, don't misunderstand. I want to be clear. It's not that I think it's wrong or immoral to try to do what we did. It's not that I think there's anything wrong with polyamory. Honestly, I couldn't care less what or whom or how many consenting adults choose to love.

But that's not what it's like in our case, is it? Because there's no true love between us.

'But we do love you, Sue!' I can almost hear you say as I write this, and I know what you mean when you say it. There is fondness between us, respect, companionship. But it is not the love of partners.

Maybe you two have that—I hope so, for your sakes. But I don't have it. We always knew it, didn't we? Only before, it didn't seem to matter. I always thought I was happy enough. But now, with Liza, it does matter. It won't be long before she begins to understand, and I don't want her to see her mother as some kind of perpetual third wheel, someone who never really had love of her own. I don't want to see myself that way. And I don't want Liza to have to explain, over and over, about our odd family, to always have to live with that.

If it were for true love, I would do it. But not like this, not because of convenience or to make a statement or because of my own inertia . . .

I will be in touch to work out the details. Jim, I want Liza to know her father, and I hope you'll want to know her. Laurel, I suspect that this will be hardest for you; I know you are attached to her. But I hope that you'll understand, if not immediately, then one day. Please forgive me, both of you, for I truly believe this is for the best.

Sincerely,
Sue"

Laurel stopped reading at last. Jessie, stunned beyond words, sat rigidly in the kitchen chair, her bare legs dimpled against the chill, her ear hot where she held her phone against it. Her mind whirled. She said nothing.

"Well?" Laurel said at last. "Aren't you going to react? Aren't you going to say *something*? Liza is gone. And you have nothing to—?"

"What can I *possibly* say, Laurel?" she said, cutting her mother off, her fury surging out of her. "*What?* You call here at five in the morning to tell me that my daughter is gone—"

"*Your* daughter? What do you mean '*your daughter?*' She is *my* child. She was never meant to be *your* daughter, Jessie."

"No," Jessie said, suddenly eerily calm. "She was never meant to be my daughter, that's true. But she came from my egg, didn't she? So what does that make her, exactly?"

"Ha! Before this happened, you didn't want her. She was never 'yours' before, was she?"

"Oh, just stop! It doesn't matter." Jessie's voice broke. "I gave you those eggs because I wanted you to be happy. Oh God, I never thought—"

"I called you because I thought you might comfort me, Jessie. *I'm* the one who has lost her baby. What do you have to wail about? You gave up those eggs willingly. You knew what it meant . . . She was never supposed to be yours."

"She wasn't supposed to be out there in the world with some stranger either."

"Oh, come on. Sue is hardly a stranger."

"She is to me!" Suddenly Jessie stopped, remembering something. "Wait a second. You told me . . . Didn't you tell me you were going to make it official? That you'd be the co-guardian?"

"We were, but—"

"You never did, did you? That's just great."

"We meant to. But we . . . we just never got around to it. We had a newborn to take care of, in case you forgot," Laurel said defensively. "You have no idea how all-consuming that can be."

Oh, spare me, Jessie thought, but she clamped her mouth shut against the words. There was no point in fighting with Laurel. She, herself, had made this bed. And now she would lie in it. Her chest ached and her face burned. How could she have done this? Sarah was right; she had been a fool.

When Laurel spoke again, there was a new, plaintive note in her voice.

"Oh Jessie. I never thought this would happen—not once in a million years. Sue was always . . . Oh, she was a rock. I never thought—"

"You never thought she might need love, too?" Jessie spoke dryly. All the shock of it had left her. She felt she understood why Sue had done what she did; she couldn't blame her. It was herself she blamed. As inevitable as it seemed to her now, she knew that all of this should have had nothing to do with her. It was just another stop on Laurel's train wreck of a life. She should never have climbed aboard.

"She never seemed to need it," Laurel protested.

"Need what?" Jessie asked, forgetting her own words.

"Love. That kind of love, I mean. Oh, what am I going to do? And . . . it's not just me I'm worried about. That poor little girl— she was attached to me, too, you know. What's it going to be like for her? Taken from her second mother? Her father. You can't just *do* that to a child."

"You did it, Mom. You let Dad have Emma and me. I was about her age, even. And we survived."

The silence on the line stretched so tight Jessie braced herself.

"I didn't know you blamed me for that, Jessie," Laurel said coolly. "It wasn't my fault your father left Arcata. That he took you so far away. You have no idea what that cost me."

"I don't know whose 'fault' it was, Mom, and at this point,

I really don't think it matters. But I do know you gave him custody. And I know we lost our mother early, and we survived."

"You girls had Sarah. It's not like you didn't have a mother to care for you."

"Not at first, we didn't. Sarah was our babysitter, Mom, not our—look, I don't want to talk about all that. It's over now. Anyway, Liza has Sue, doesn't she? It's not like she'll be the only kid in the world to be raised by a single, separated mom—"

"Stop making it sound so trite, Jessie. Sue's not like all the typical divorced moms out there and you know it."

"It sounds to me like that might be exactly what she *wants* to be. And, you know, maybe she's right. Maybe it's better this way. That poor girl was going to have a lot of strange explaining to do."

"Better for whom?" Laurel demanded, her voice almost a wail. "It's not better for me, for Christ's sake. There's only one thing in this world worse than being a motherless child."

"And what is that?"

"Being a childless mother."

"Oh, *come on.*" The words were out before she could stop them. "And that's you, is it? A childless mother?"

"Yes! I have just lost—"

"Did you forget who you're talking to, Laurel? I am your *daughter.* So just *how* are you a childless mother? Do you even know what you're saying? Did you even think about who you'd be talking to when you called here in the middle of the night? I AM YOUR DAUGHTER. And not only that, I am your daughter who was *stupid* enough to give you what no daughter should be asked to give her mother. Did you even pause for one second to think about how all this might feel to me? A childless mother? For Christ's sake, Laurel. If anyone's a childless mother, it's me."

"Oh, Jessie . . . I'm sorry, I didn't mean . . . I just wanted another . . . I wanted to . . . I wanted to get it right this time . . ." The words were almost inaudible between her sobs.

"I don't want to talk about this anymore," Jessie said, and she hung up the phone.

In the bedroom, Jessie's side of the bed had given up its warmth, but when she raised the blankets she could feel the heat of Heath's body rushing out, heavy with the scent of him. She pushed her chilled limbs against him, shivering.

"Jesus, Jess," he muttered, waking. "You're freezing."

He rolled over and put his arms around her. "Where have you been? Oh honey, what's wrong?"

Jessie pushed her face into the coarse hair on his chest and began, silently, to cry.

"Jessie? What's wrong?"

"Oh, God, Heath. You've married an idiot. I did such a stupid, stupid thing."

He held her while she cried, not saying anything. When, at last, she had calmed, he spoke into her hair. "Now, can you tell me the supposedly stupid thing my brilliant wife has done?"

She told him everything, murmuring the words into his chest. When she was finished, he stroked her hair and sighed.

"Well, it's a mess all right," he said. "But want to know how I see it, Jess? Yeah, maybe it *was* foolish of you. But that's not the main thing. The main thing is that you did it to be kind. You did it to be generous. And it was. The bottom line is this. You didn't really give those eggs to Laurel, even if that's what you were thinking at the time. You gave them to Sue. She wanted a child, and you made that possible for her. It was *extremely* generous of you."

Jessie groaned. "I just don't know, Heath. Now that little girl is out there in the world by herself. She has no connection to me whatsoever now—"

"She's not by herself, Jessie. She's with her mother. Hey, you must have known when you gave the eggs . . ." he went on gently. "You must have known you wouldn't be the mother?"

She sighed. "Yeah, I knew. But I thought I'd be her . . . her *something*."

"I know." He was silent for a moment, thinking.

"Well, I would hate to be accused of sounding mainstream but—"

"But what?"

"Well, maybe it *is* for the best. I always thought it was kind of a weird situation."

"You did?"

He studied her for a moment before answering. "Yeah. I mean, anyone would, wouldn't they? And wasn't that sort of the point?"

"It wasn't *my* point. I was just trying . . . I was just trying to be nice. To give Laurel what she wanted. I wanted her to be . . . I wanted her to have the chance, at least. To be happy."

"And it was very kind of you, Jessie."

"It was stupid."

He smiled grimly. "Maybe a little." Heath raised himself up on one elbow and looked down at her. "Want to know what else I think?"

"What?"

"You might have been foolish to agree to it, I'll grant you that. But Laurel never should have asked you. She never should have put you in this position. I am sure that on some level she knew you loved her and would do it because you loved her. But no mother should ask that of her kid, period."

Jessie sighed and closed her eyes. "That's almost exactly what Sarah said."

"Yeah, well, great minds and all that . . . Plus, it shouldn't be your job to make your mother happy. What about you? You deserve to be happy, too, you know."

At that, Jessie's tears began anew. Heath held her close, neither of them speaking, until at last Jessie's eyes closed and she slept.

CHAPTER 50

Jessie

When, a few days later, Jessie saw the envelope in their mailbox, unmistakable among the bills and junk mail, her stomach dove. She stuffed the other letters back into the mailbox and sat down on the overgrown grass in their small front yard. Then she tore the envelope with trembling fingers and pulled out the single sheet of folded paper inside.

Dear Jessie,

I imagine that by now you have heard from Laurel the news about my leaving, and I hope that you can understand why I decided what I did. Please know that I have only the best interests of Elizabeth at heart.

I thought that you should know that I do not intend to tell my daughter of her biological origins until she is older. The circumstances of her birth are confusing even for mature adults; I do not now believe that it is appropriate information to share with a child. If she asks, I will tell her that her egg came from an incredibly kind donor who wanted to make it possible for me to have the child that I wanted so much.

Thank you again for your generous act. Please know that I will always be grateful.

Sincerely,
Sue

Jessie read it twice, then let it fall from her fingers. She lay back in the grass and closed her eyes. There was nothing surprising in it, and yet Jessie felt as if she had just heard the news for the first time. Her mind reeled. Her stomach churned. She felt as she did during a terrible dream, when the world seemed to spiral out of her control in unimaginable ways. Jessie was a scientist at heart; she was used to looking for solutions. But here there was nothing to be done.

Jessie's whole body ached with the inescapable fact of it—that child, out there in the world, yet unknown to her. Before, she hadn't thought of Liza as hers; she hadn't, in fact, thought of her much at all. Jessie's mind was used to categories, and it had been easy to designate Liza not to herself, but to Laurel. But with that connection severed, the little girl whirled in her mind as if in a vacuum, until she came to rest, again and again, with her.

The irony of it was not lost on her. She had given those eggs to try to heal, in some small part, the damage done by her own parents' divorce. She had done it to try to ease Laurel's persistent loneliness, to fulfill her desire for a second shot at motherhood. Instead, she had cast yet another soul into the bedlam of another separation, one more family's failure to hold together.

All day, her mind would not settle, until at last she picked up her phone to call her sister.

"I understand how you must feel, Jess," Emma said gently. "But maybe . . . Maybe you could try to frame it differently? I mean, in a way Sue's just trying to protect that little girl."

"Protect her by tearing her family apart?"

"You don't have to see it that way."

"What other way is there?"

"Well, that she's giving her a chance to have a life that's a little more . . . a life that's not so complicated. It's not like she's abandoned her, Jessie. She'll have a mother who loves her, a father who may not live with her but who is in her life, at least. She's not going to have to constantly explain—never mind *understand*—why she has two moms when almost everyone else just has—"

"Emma, how can you be saying this? You of all people? You have *always* wanted kids. What if things had worked out with Katherine? I mean, what if you eventually end up with a woman? Are you saying you won't have kids because you wouldn't want your children to have two moms? That is so homophobic, Emma. I can't believe—"

"Two mothers who *love* each other is a lot different from Sue and Laurel's situation and you know it, Jessie."

"But who cares? They're grown-ups. Why should anyone care how they choose to organize their family? It's their *choice*. Everyone should have the right to—"

"But it didn't work out, Jessie, did it? Of course it was fine for Jim. Fine for Laurel, too. But what about *Sue*? It never made sense to me what was in it for her. I'm not surprised she wanted out."

"She made a commitment. She should have honored that."

"Did she? They weren't married."

"They had a child."

"Well, at least she didn't leave her child like Laurel did."

There was a moment of charged silence between them. When Jessie finally spoke, she did so calmly, but even she could hear the accusation behind her words.

"You're never going to forgive Laurel, are you? God, Emma, it was more than twenty years ago. People make mistakes. Parents make mistakes. But usually they don't lose their children because of them. Laurel shouldn't have left. But Dad shouldn't have left either. Parents can't just *leave* each other. It's not fair to the—"

"Oh, Jessie. Just stop, will you? Can you imagine what our lives would have been like if Laurel and Dad hadn't gotten divorced? Dad would have been miserable. We would have had Laurel for a mother. It would have been awful. Laurel leaving, Dad getting custody and marrying Mom—that's the best thing that could have happened. *Thank God* it did."

"Jesus, Emma. Do you hear yourself? How can you say, 'Thank God Laurel left,' and still blame her for it?"

For a moment, Emma was speechless. The silence that stretched between them was heavy and unfamiliar.

"You're right," Emma said quietly. "I shouldn't blame her for leaving us. I just wish . . ."

"What?"

"I just wish she could have left us alone. We would have been fine with Mom and Dad. I always wished for that when I was little. I had a mom. I didn't need Laurel. I didn't *want* her."

Now Jessie was silent. When she spoke at last, her voice was tight. "That's why you think this is okay, isn't it, Emma? Because Sue can do what Dad couldn't. Sue can just leave. She can take her daughter with her. She can be the mother. The one and only mother. She doesn't have to let Laurel be anything."

Emma sighed. "I don't know, Jessie. Maybe." She paused. "It will make things simpler for her. For Liza, I mean," she said softly.

Jessie let out her breath, a bitter laugh. "But what about me, Emma? There's nothing I can do."

"Jessie," Emma said gently, "your part is over. Don't you see that? When you decided to donate those eggs, you knew you were giving up whatever children came of them. It's no different now. Not really."

"But now there's no connection at all—"

"There's not supposed to be. That's why egg donation is usually anonymous. The donor gives the eggs, but it's the birth mother who's the real—"

"God, I hate that word. All my life, it's been, 'But who's your *real* mother?' Why can't it just be simple?"

"I don't know," Emma said. "But it's not."

"Emma," Jessie said, her voice breaking. "It wasn't fair. What you said about wanting Laurel to leave you alone. You loved Mom; you didn't need Laurel. But that's not what it was like for me."

"I know, Jessie."

"Emma, I should have been allowed . . ." She gasped for air, her sobs crowding out the words. "I should have been allowed to love them both."

"Oh, Jessie. I know," Emma said. "I'm sorry—"

"What do *you* have to be sorry for?" Jessie said. Against her cheek, her phone was slick with tears; she wiped her eyes fiercely with the back of one hand. "You didn't do anything wrong, Em. You're probably the only one who didn't."

"That's not true. But it doesn't matter. You said it, Jessie. People make mistakes. I'm just sorry . . . I've always been sorry . . . It was so hard on you, Jessie. More than on anyone, I think. It should never have been so hard on you."

Neither sister said anything for a moment. Jessie heard Emma blow her nose.

"Thank you, Emma," she said.

"For what? Blowing my nose in your ear?"

Jessie smiled through her tears. "No, for saying that. I think I've been waiting for a long time to hear someone say that."

"Well, it's true. Maybe it is nobody's fault. But it should never have been so hard on you."

CHAPTER 51

Emma

As soon as she arrived, Emma wished she hadn't come. Outside, the afternoon sun was bright. Bare-armed people milled on the crowded sidewalks, and Dolores Park, when she had passed it on her way, had been a patchwork of blankets and bodies. Inside the club, however, it was windowless and dark, the music blaring. Emma resisted the urge to cup her hands over her ears as they entered.

She followed Meg and Becca to the bar. Becca ordered them all shots, and Emma drank hers dutifully.

"Believe it or not," Meg had told her dryly a few days ago, "Katherine is not the only fem lesbian in the Bay Area. Just come out with us. You'll see."

Emma had thought of the last time she had gone out with Meg and Becca and hesitated.

"I don't think Dykes Get Down is really my scene," she had said.

But Meg had taken offense.

"Oh, come off it, Emma. You like women, don't you? So say you're a dyke already. It's just a word, for God's sake. And it's in the afternoon. Do you have something better to do on Saturday afternoon?"

Emma could think of a half a dozen things that she would prefer to do on Saturday afternoon, but she was tired of arguing.

"Fine," she had said. "I'll meet you there."

Now Emma moved her mouth close to Meg's ear, so that her friend might have some chance of hearing her over the din.

"Why do they do this in the afternoon, anyway?" she asked.

Meg narrowed her eyes at her.

"Why do you think?" she bellowed back. "It's not like they're going to waste prime clubbing time on a bunch of dykes. Come on, let's go dance."

Meg took Becca's hand and pulled her toward the dance floor. Becca caught her eye.

"You coming, Emma?"

Emma hesitated. She didn't feel like dancing. To tell the truth, she wanted to turn tail and go back outside, but she didn't dare tell Meg and Becca that. Emma knew that it had been Meg's little triumph, getting her here in the first place; she clearly thought Emma had been moping for too long. She saw the couple pause a few feet from the bar. Meg glanced back at her, her eyebrows arched expectantly. Emma sighed and fell in behind them.

They pushed their way into the crowd. Women shifted around them, making room; in an instant, they were swallowed by the mass of bodies. As soon as she was in the crowd, Emma felt her spirits lift. A moment before the club had seemed artificially dark and deafeningly loud. Now Emma saw the flash of limbs in the strobe lights, felt the air pulse with the heavy bass. An unexpected thrill of excitement shot through her.

All around her, bodies quivered and writhed. Emma watched the swaying limbs and undulating torsos, saw the press of back to breast, the hands that rested tenderly on grinding hips. Meg caught her watching and grinned at her. *See? I told you so*, her friend's look said.

Emma flushed and grinned back—*Yes*. She could feel the alcohol loosening her arms and legs; her body seemed to pulsate with the music of its own accord, so that she hardly felt that it belonged to her. One song ran seamlessly into the next. Sweat beaded on Emma's forehead; the bass thrummed in her pulsing veins. She felt the music lift her up, the sweep of something close to joy.

A hand grazed her hip. Emma glanced behind her and saw a woman's face, too close. The pressure of her fingers on Emma's hip grew; she was tugging her backward, pulling her close. Emma stepped quickly away.

She felt the hand on her hip acquiesce to her refusal. The pressure of the fingers eased and then was gone. Emma looked back to see that the woman who had touched her had moved toward another, a beautiful woman with luxurious black curls who did not step away. The two women moved together, torsos undulating in sync, mouths and eyes half open as if in rapture.

Emma turned away. The etherealness of the moment before flickered and was gone. Suddenly Emma was just herself again: an uptight dyke not willing to play along. Her arms felt leaden; her swaying ceased. She leaned into Meg's ear and bellowed that she was going to the bathroom.

Emma threaded herself through the crowd of dancing women, turning this way and that to avoid their undulating limbs, the little dips and dodges her body made like a solo dance of her own. Finally, she reached the edge of the dance floor. She glanced back at where she had left Meg and Becca; she had imagined that she had felt their disappointed eyes on her as she retreated. Now she couldn't even see her friends in the press of bodies on the floor.

As Emma made her way down the narrow hallway that led to the restrooms, the volume relented a little. She felt the pressure beneath her temples ease.

Women had taken over both bathrooms, but still there was a line. It didn't matter; Emma was glad to have this respite. She leaned into the wall as she waited, idly watching the women as they left the restrooms. She took in the cropped hair and the nose rings, the low-slung jeans. Meg was right, she thought. Katherine was not the only fish in the sea. But even that acknowledgment felt distant from her, as if all these women were part of a world that did not include her.

Suddenly, Emma's breath caught in her throat. Katherine had

just come out of the restroom, was walking back along the hall. Emma tried to hide her face, but it was too late. Even as her eyes darted away, she saw Katherine notice her.

"Emma? I'm . . . I'm surprised to see you here."

Reluctantly, Emma turned to face her.

"Yeah? Well, it's a small dyke world, isn't it?"

Katherine gave a little smile. "How are you?"

"Fine," Emma said coolly. "Where's Melinda?"

Katherine thrust her chin in the direction of the dance floor. "Out there."

Emma looked away again, ashamed of the spiteful hope that had flashed through her, that Katherine's greener pastures had gone sour.

"Em," Katherine said. "I . . . uh, could we talk?"

At that moment, the line moved. The woman in front of Emma was entering the restroom; she held the door so Emma could step inside, as well.

"No," Emma said, moving through the open doorway with relief. She pushed the door closed behind her. It moved sluggishly beneath her hand, and she pushed hard against it until the latch clicked into place. Emma's heart beat a little faster. She almost wanted to open the door and shut it again, just for the mean little thrill it had given her to shut Katherine out.

When Emma finished in the bathroom, she found Katherine still waiting for her in the hallway.

"Can we talk?" she said again.

Emma let out her breath. "Why?"

"Emma, I just—" Katherine sighed. "I just want to . . . to talk to you for a minute. Please?"

The thrill of the closing door had vanished. Emma nodded. She followed Katherine back down the narrow corridor and away from the dance floor to a far corner of the club, where the music was not so loud.

"Well?" she said, when Katherine stopped and turned at last.

"Look, Em," said Katherine. "I know you probably hate me. And I get that—no, wait, let me finish. I *do* get it. But I don't want . . . I *really* don't want for that to be how you remember me, Emma. I don't want that to be how you remember *us*."

Emma snorted. "Katherine, you don't get to have it both ways. You don't get to leave and still expect to feel good about it. You don't get to be a bitch and still have me think of you with little hearts and rainbows."

Katherine flinched visibly and looked away. "I know," she said. "I *don't* expect that. I'm never going to feel good about it, Em. But what choice did I have?"

Emma raised her eyebrows. "Choice? No one made you leave, Katherine."

"I know. But . . . Jesus, Emma. I wasn't in love with you anymore, okay? What was I supposed to do?"

Now Emma flinched. But she met Katherine's eye and said quietly, "I don't think that's how it works, Katherine."

"What's not?"

"Love. Love is a choice, Katherine. You didn't just fall out of love with me. You *chose* not to love me anymore."

Katherine sighed. "Is that what you think? I—"

"Yes, Kat. It is. That's the way love works. You just have to keep on choosing it." She shrugged. "Or not."

Katherine shook her head emphatically. "I guess we just see it differently then. But regardless . . . I just wanted you to know that I do feel badly about how it happened. That it was so sudden and . . . well, you know."

Emma stared at the wall beside Katherine's head; her face felt set in stone.

"I really do care about you, Emma," Katherine was saying. "I've thought about you a lot, and I have felt really, really badly about—"

Emma scoffed. "Not as bad as I have felt, I can assure you."

"I know. That's what I'm saying. Look, I know you're not going to forgive me, Em, but I just wanted to say it, okay? That I'm sorry. I really am sorry about how it all happened. I should have been more . . . self-aware. But, Jesus, Em. You had me so high up on that pedestal, I was bound to fall off—"

"Fall off? You *dove* off, Katherine. Don't put that on me. I *loved* you."

"You idealized me. I was the perfect girlfriend to you, the . . . the perfect *girl*. I'm not that perfect, Emma."

Emma let out a dry laugh. "Apparently."

"Look, Emma, this is pointless."

"You were the one who wanted to talk."

"I just—look, I *am* sorry, okay? I'm sorry that I hurt you like I did. You're a wonderful person, Emma, and I know it must have been hard on you. And you . . . Well, you didn't deserve to be hurt like that."

Katherine's words whirled in Emma's head. Just days before, hadn't she said almost the same thing to her sister? Her own words came back to her: *It should never have been so hard on you.*

Emma sighed. Nobody deserved to suffer, and yet they did, in spades. There was no avoiding it; it was the cost of human frailty. Had Katherine been wrong to leave her? Until this moment, Emma had believed that to be true. You didn't just walk out on love. But now she hesitated, and something else she had said to her sister came back to her. *Laurel's leaving . . . that was the best thing that could have happened.*

Emma believed that. She always had. If Laurel hadn't left, her father might never have married Sarah; Sarah would certainly never have become her mother. All of it—the whole mess of mistakes her parents had made—it had all been for the best, hadn't it? And yet Emma had never forgiven Laurel.

Without meaning to, Katherine had touched on Emma's own little pocket of guilt. How might Laurel's life have been different if Emma had not rejected her so absolutely? Emma had been a child, yes, but even then she had felt her own cruelty. She had not let

Laurel love her; she had not wanted her love. Her rejection of her mother had been unequivocal and absolute. Emma had felt the grim weight of it her entire life.

"Where'd you go?" Katherine said gently.

"I was just thinking about . . ." Emma shook her head as if to clear it. "It doesn't matter."

"You sure?"

"Yeah."

Katherine nodded. "Well, thanks for hearing me out, at least."

Emma nodded curtly. *It's not my job to make her feel better.* There was an icy pleasure in the thought. If Katherine was suffering with her guilt, it was no less than she deserved.

But even as Emma's mind formed the thought, she knew that she was merely taking the pulse of her own anger. She felt its feeble beat, felt it falter. She let her eyes meet Katherine's.

"Actually, I was thinking about . . ." She hesitated. "About forgiveness."

Katherine smiled wanly. "Oh."

Emma motioned at Katherine's hair that hung loose around her shoulders.

"You grew out your hair," she said. "It looks good."

Katherine shrugged. "Yours, too. You look good, Em."

For a moment, they stood there wordlessly, each studying the other's face. Emma felt a tiny bud of forgiveness begin to bloom inside her. She waited in silence as it unfurled.

"Well," Katherine said at last. "I should probably . . . Take care of yourself, Emma. And thank you again for hearing me out."

Emma nodded, her heart suddenly in her throat.

"It's okay, Kat," she managed at last. "I survived, you know. I'm . . . I'll be fine."

Katherine smiled at her. "I never doubted that, Em. But thank you."

Emma waited until Katherine had disappeared in the crowd, then she made her own way back past the bar toward the dance floor. She didn't feel like dancing, but she needed to find Meg and Becca, to tell them that she was leaving. She didn't mind doing it now. Twenty minutes earlier, she had wanted to flee, and she had been ashamed of that. But now . . . Now she wasn't running away. She just wanted to go home.

When Emma pushed open the door to the outside, she was surprised to see that it was not yet fully dark. Inside the windowless building, she had forgotten how early it still was. Now she stood for a moment, breathing in the dusk. The fog was rolling in; she could feel the chill of it on her bare shoulders. She opened her mouth and imagined she could feel the tiny droplets on her tongue. She was about to set off down the sidewalk when a voice stopped her.

"Emma? It *is* Emma, right?"

Emma looked back to see who had spoken and grinned. It was Samantha, the punk rocker from the BART train. She stood leaning against the building, one foot propped on the wall behind her. Her jeans were low on her slender hips and Emma remembered the flash of skin that she had seen there, the jewel glinting in her navel like a dew drop.

"I almost didn't recognize you without the bicycle," Samantha said. She looked Emma up and down, and Emma felt herself blush. "And the hair."

Emma put a hand to her head. "Oh, yeah. I, uh . . . I cut it," she said stupidly.

The woman cocked her head. "I'm Samantha. Do you remember?"

Emma smiled. "From the BART train. I remember."

"You're leaving already?"

"Yeah."

"By yourself? Where's your girl?"

Emma shrugged. "We broke up."

"Oh," Samantha said. "Sorry."

Emma shrugged again. "Thanks. But it's okay."

Samantha nodded but said nothing.

"What are you doing out here?" Emma asked. Her eyes went to Samantha's hands, looking for a cigarette, but found none. "You *are* here for—" Emma gestured toward the door of the club.

"Dykes Get Down? Yeah."

"What happened?" Emma asked. "Did you get tired of getting down?"

Samantha laughed. "You're funny. No, I'm just doing an experiment."

"What's that?"

"It sounds sort of stupid to say it out loud."

"Oh, come on. You brought it up," Emma said.

"It's a bit of a long story."

Emma cocked her head expectantly.

"Which maybe I'll tell you another time." Samantha smiled at her, and Emma felt something stir in her belly, as if a butterfly had unfurled its wings.

"Could I maybe have the CliffsNotes now?"

Samantha laughed. "Sure." She paused, then spoke quickly. "Basically, a couple of days ago I decided to make sure that I'm somewhere outside for both sunrise and sunset."

Emma stared. It was not what she had expected Samantha to say, and Emma saw immediately what she had done. Without even thinking about it, she had designated Samantha to a different world than her own. Samantha's world, she had assumed, was one of punk rock concerts and Dykes Get Down. Late nights in darkened clubs, not sunsets. Not sunrises. She thought suddenly of what Katherine had said, about how Emma had seen her as "the perfect girl," and a flash of shame went through her. Katherine had been right. Emma had put her in her little box; no wonder she had wanted out.

She looked at Samantha. "Can I ask why?"

Samantha shrugged. "Ever notice how the days just sort of go by?" she asked. "Sometimes it'll be totally light by the time I get outside in the morning. Or it's dark before I even notice that it's getting late. I just thought . . . Well, I wondered what it would feel like if I paid a little more attention. You know, if I just paused for a minute . . . to notice."

Emma watched her closely. "That is really *not* what I expected you to say."

"Why?"

"I don't know. I guess because I saw you as this hip punk rocker with a cool belly button ring who was probably just here to scope out the babes."

"Yeah, well, that too," Samantha said, grinning.

Emma smiled back at her. "It's nice to run into you again."

"You, too. It's a beautiful evening, isn't it?" She threw her head back to look up at the sky, and Emma's eyes were drawn to her pale throat, the hard ridges of her collar bones.

"Yes."

Emma was turning to go when Samantha called out. "Wait, Emma. I want to give you something."

Samantha reached into the bag that hung at her hip, and Emma waited, holding out her hand for the flier she knew was coming. *Who knows, maybe I'll even make it this time*, she thought. She was surprised to find herself smiling at the memory.

But Samantha was pulling out, not a paper, but a pen. She took Emma's hand and uncurled her fingers, then moved the pen lightly across her palm.

Emma stared in surprise at the neat, even digits.

"There," Samantha said, gently folding Emma's fingers closed. "Hold onto that. In case we don't run into each other again."

For a moment she kept her own hand wrapped loosely around Emma's fist. Then she winked, the lid closing perfectly over one clear blue eye.

Emma's heart skipped. Inside her, the butterfly flapped its wings.

"Okay," she stammered. "Thanks."

The next morning, Emma woke at dawn. She looked out of the window at the grey sky and smiled to herself, imagining Samantha out there somewhere, standing on a stoop in her pajamas, waiting for morning.

Emma got up and made tea, then took it to her desk. She pulled a piece of paper from the printer tray and sat staring at it, a pen poised in her hand.

Why not? Emma thought.

She was safe now. She didn't have to protect herself anymore. Maybe it wouldn't matter anyway. Maybe Laurel had given up on her long ago. But she couldn't shake the feeling that had come to her yesterday while she had talked with Katherine. Laurel had messed up; there was no denying that. But didn't everyone? Emma's whole life had been a pinball game of mistakes; she had ricocheted off one or another since before she was even born. Her father's, for conceiving children with Laurel in the first place. And Laurel's, mistake after mistake peeling off her like layers of skin she had outgrown.

And then there were Emma's own. In an instant, she could go back into that therapist's office so many years ago, with Laurel in tears before her. She could feel her own cold heart, could see her stone-set face.

What would forgiveness have cost her then? It was impossible to know. She had been hardly more than a child then; she had done the best she could.

But maybe . . . Maybe that was true for everyone. Katherine had said last night that she didn't have a choice, and maybe that was the truth of it for her. Maybe Katherine had simply done the best she could. And maybe . . . Well, couldn't the same be said of Laurel? That she had done the best she could?

Emma sighed deeply. Laurel's best—it had been far, far from enough. But Laurel's failures—if that's what they were—felt very distant from Emma now. And that distance—Emma herself had created it. She had *wanted* it. She thought of her mother's words. *To Laurel, no one is ever as important as Laurel.* There were so many things for which her mother would never forgive Laurel, Emma knew. And she, without thinking, was poised to follow that same path. No one would blame her for it if she did. By any account, Laurel had forsaken her. Emma owed her nothing. And yet, was nothing the best that Emma could do?

There was so much momentum now. It would be so easy to stay the course she had set so many years ago. Emma thought of the strange elation she had felt when she had spoken those words to Katherine last night: *It's okay. I'll be okay.* It was a strange paradox, that in speaking the words they had been made true, as if it were forgiveness that made healing possible, instead of the other way around.

And Emma *was* okay. Laurel, even with all her failures as a mother—she hadn't damaged her. Everything Emma had endured . . . No, everything they had *all* endured—she and Jessie, Mom and Dad, even Laurel—they had survived it. They were okay. They were fine. *She* was fine. What would forgiveness cost her?

She put the pen to the paper.

"Dear Laurel," she began.

EPILOGUE

One Year Later

Sarah

Heath was at work. Len had gone to the grocery store. Jessie was napping in the bedroom. Sarah sat beside the bassinet in Jessie's small living room, tracing her index finger along the soft edges of a letter folded in her lap. When she had first seen Jessie's familiar handwriting on the envelope a month ago, her heart had leapt to her throat. She had opened the letter right away, had read it standing at the mailbox outside their home in Bakersfield.

She had slipped the letter into her suitcase when she'd packed for this trip, without really knowing why. Now she was glad she had; it felt right to have it with her, somehow. She unfolded it gently and began to read.

June 12, 2003

Dear Mom,

I have this memory of you saying once that you wondered if I would see things differently when I had a child of my own. I think it was during the custody case, when I felt I had to defend Laurel with all my might, since nobody else was going to. At the time I thought you meant that when I had my own child I would see things differently because I wouldn't be able to understand how any mother could give up her children like Laurel did. And I do feel that. There is absolutely no way I could leave Mason. Not now, not ever.

But there's something else that I understand even more.

You always loved that book Horton Hatches the Egg, *do you remember? And I always understood why, even when I was little. Because of course you were Horton and Laurel was the Mayzie bird, and in the story everything was so right and clear.*

Even when it didn't feel clear for me, even when I pushed you away — and I know I did — I never doubted that I was your daughter. To me, you were always Horton, faithful one hundred percent. It was an awful double standard, I know — that I could reject you as my mother but still expect to be your daughter. But I did. I took your love for granted.

I took it for granted but I never even thought to marvel at it. I never thought how miraculous it was — until now.

Now I have Mason. The love I feel for him is unspeakable, and yet it makes perfect sense to me. He is the flesh of my flesh. When he nurses, with his sweet little body pressed against my skin, he is mine in a visceral, bodily way that I never expected. Of course I love him. I have no choice.

I'm realizing that you never had that "of course" with Emma and me. And yet you loved us anyway. You chose to love us. I don't think I ever really understood what that meant until now.

Now I think I am beginning to understand. And I needed to tell you that, to thank you for it. So, thank you. Thank you for loving us as your own. Thank you for choosing to be our mother when we needed one the most.

Love,
Jessie

P.S. I hope that you and Dad will come soon to meet Mason. Please.

Sarah refolded the letter and slid it between the pages of the book on the table beside her. She sneaked a look inside the bassinet where Mason lay sleeping, swaddled so that only his tiny face showed.

"You should nap now, too," Sarah had told Jessie forty minutes ago. "You have to sleep while your baby sleeps."

"Did you do that?" Jessie had asked, looking over at her with tired eyes.

"No, but I would have if I could. I had you two girls, remember?"

Now Sarah breathed in the quiet of the house. She settled back in the worn armchair, then picked up her book from the side table, a poetry collection that Emma had sent her for her birthday. She glanced at the baby again, gauging his sleep. Maybe she could send Emma a quick email now, just to tell her how much she was enjoying the poems. But she didn't rise. Her eyes stayed on the baby, taking in the tender, almost translucent skin of his eyelids, the perfect bow of his lips. She would see Emma soon enough, she thought. She would wait to tell her then.

Next week, when she and Len left Jessie's, they would drive west to Portland, where they would spend the night with Sarah's old friend, Kim. From there, it was only a day's drive down the coast to Arcata.

Arcata. Their lives there felt like a lifetime ago; she and Len had never gone back. Yet Sarah could remember certain things so clearly: Jessie's small, warm hand in hers as they walked home from the park in the fog; the first time she had seen Emma, lying in a bassinet just like this one; Len reaching for her hand on that beautiful day at the zoo.

They would have to go back to the zoo, she thought, smiling. The zoo, and the apple orchard. Just for old times' sake.

After Arcata, they would drive down Route 1 to the Bay Area, where they would visit Emma in Oakland. Sarah was relieved not to be so worried about Emma now. On the phone these last few months, her daughter's voice had sounded more like her old, cheerful self. She had even hinted that she'd met someone new. A friend, she had insisted, but Sarah could hear the excitement in her daughter's voice, the hope.

Sarah closed the book of poems gently in her lap. She couldn't concentrate on it now. She had promised Jessie she would listen for Mason in case he woke, but she hadn't had to listen. She couldn't take her eyes off him.

Mason would turn out just like Jessie, Sarah guessed. She smiled to herself at the thought. Here was another little alien child whom she would struggle to understand. But it didn't matter, did it? She would love him anyway, just as she had loved Jessie and Emma all those years ago. When he opened his startled eyes and cried out, she would go to him.

Jessie had said to wake her; she didn't want him to be a burden. But Sarah wouldn't, she knew that. Jessie had looked so tired. No, when Mason woke, she would pick him up and comfort him. She would hold him as long as he would let her. She would let her daughter sleep.

Acknowledgments

Without the love, help, and support of many people, this book would not have come to be.

Thank you, first, to Terri Leidich and BQB Publishing for taking a chance on *Give*, and for making the entire publishing journey such a personal and pleasant one.

A huge thank you to my editor, Michelle Booth, whose keen eye and insightful questions made this book a much better version of itself.

To Valerie White, thank you for Vermont and all its stories. Without you, I never would have had the courage to bring *Give* to the light.

To my high school English teacher, Brenda Tipps, thank you for taking my writing seriously all those years ago, for teaching me that not every noun needs an adjective, and for your patience while I learned it.

To all the early readers of this book, Lindsey Grossman, Wolf Hoelscher, Jenny Anna Linde-Rhine, Nancy Kool, Jean Smith, Margie Byington, Jennifer Myers, and Kristin Schlaefer, thank you for the thoughtful edits and wise advice, and, most of all, for helping me to believe that *Give* might grow up to be a real book one day.

I am deeply indebted to the many friends who believed in me, listened to me, and supported me during all the years that I was writing *Give*. Special thanks to Beth Coil, Renee Burwell, Holly Demuth, Stephanie Hellert, Courtney Hoelscher, Kristen Kelley, Sarah Smith, Kenna Sommer, and Ana Villanueva. You are my Asheville family.

To Kate Rademacher, thank you for planting the seed for this book so many years ago. The ways in which you helped *Give* to grow and thrive are too numerous to mention, but my gratitude for each one of them is boundless.

I am forever grateful to Jennifer Arellano, whose endless encouragement, compassionate ear, and steadfast friendship have supported me along each leg of this journey. I would never have made it to the finish line without you, Jen.

To my brother, Stefan Carpenter, thank you for your priceless sense of humor and lasting friendship, and for showing me that, with enough determination, even the most ambitious dreams can be achieved.

To my sister, Claire Carpenter, thank you for championing this book from its very first draft as if it were your own. I am endlessly grateful for all your insight, advice, encouragement, and support; it would be a lonely world without you.

To my father, William Carpenter, thank you for always believing that I would write the Great American Novel one day. Your support and enthusiasm for *Give* have meant more to me than words can say.

To my mother, Joyce Carpenter, who answered the question of what it means to be a mother before I even thought to pose it, thank you for your fierce love and unconditional support, not to mention all the years of Yorkshire puddings and countless cups of tea.

To my children, who tried so hard to leave me alone while I was writing, thank you for believing in me and in my book, and for being my inspiration each and every day. I would give the world for you.

To my husband, Donald Witsell, thank you for holding down the fort during all those hours I spent writing in the basement. You are my aid station when I falter, my drafting partner when I am weary, and the *Tour de Candler* I return to again and again, because no matter how far I go, you always feel like home.

ABOUT THE AUTHOR

Erica Witsell has a bachelor's degree from Wesleyan University and a master's from UC Berkeley. Her writing has appeared in *The Sun Magazine* and *Brain, Child's* online publication. *Give* is her debut novel.

Erica lives in western North Carolina with her family, where she teaches English as a new language and writes a blog about motherhood. She loves mountains, languages, bicycling, and dance.

Visit her online at www.ericawitsell.com